PRAISE FOR JENNY MILCHMAN

Praise for *Cover of Snow*

"A terrific debut."

—Harlan Coben, #1 *New York Times* bestselling author

"*Cover of Snow* is a luge ride of action and atmosphere, a terrifically suspenseful read. A suicide in a creepy town, clogged with snow and secrets, starts a young widow on a perilous hunt. Soon we're careening along with her as she chases clues and as the full horror of what really happened to her husband is revealed. Reading *Cover of Snow* feels like racing across a frozen lake. Heart-pounding, exhilarating, frightening."

—Louise Penny, #1 *New York Times* bestselling author of the Armand Gamache series

"Everything a great suspense novel should be—tense, emotional, mysterious, and satisfying. Let's hope this is the start of a long career."

—Lee Child, #1 *New York Times* bestselling author of the Jack Reacher series

"*Cover of Snow* is a darkly atmospheric first novel that challenges all sorts of romantic notions we might harbor about small towns and the people we think we can trust. Luckily, heroine Nora Hamilton—and writer Jenny Milchman—has the skill and fortitude to lead readers through a suspenseful story of switchbacks and surprises. A mystery that will draw in fans of darker fare as well, reminiscent of Margaret Maron's work, which is about the highest praise I can bestow."

—Laura Lippman, *New York Times* bestselling author

"In her debut outing, Jenny Milchman has succeeded in a way many veteran writers can only envy. *Cover of Snow* is a tightly plotted, wonderfully unpredictable, and immensely satisfying novel. All the elements—character, setting, pace, language—are pitch perfect. Believe me, it doesn't get any better than this."

—William Kent Krueger, *New York Times* bestselling author of the Cork O'Connor series

"*Cover of Snow* is what every reader wants—a terrific story, beautifully told. Heartbreaking, sinister, compelling, and completely original. I love this book."

—Hank Phillippi Ryan, Agatha, Anthony, and Mary Higgins Clark Award–winning author

"Absorbing from start to finish: Jenny Milchman writes a deeply felt and suspenseful story of a woman whose life is upended by a death and a dark secret. While perceptively reflecting on community and our connections to one another, *Cover of Snow* is also an insightful look at the intimacies and secrets of marriage."

—Nancy Pickard, Agatha, Anthony, Macavity, and Shamus Award–winning author

"Milchman's intricately plotted and aptly titled *Cover of Snow* is layered with suspense, sorrow, and a strong sense of place and character."

—Linwood Barclay

"Jenny Milchman's expertly crafted, dark, and smoothly suspenseful page-turner slowly reveals the layers of terrifying secrets hidden in a small Adirondack town under *Cover of Snow*. I only wish I had written this novel! Watch for this stellar debut on the Best First Novel lists."

—Julia Spencer-Fleming

"Quietly unnerving . . . Milchman reveals an intimate knowledge of the psychology of grief, along with a painterly gift for converting frozen feelings into scenes of a forbidding winter landscape."

—*The New York Times*

"The first-person account told from Nora's point of view thrusts the narrative full force into horror, sadness, and every other emotion Nora experiences as she must start over without Brendan . . . [W]hat makes *Cover of Snow* sing is Milchman's ability to make readers care for Nora as she suffers and starts anew."

—The Associated Press

"When house restorer Nora Hamilton finds that her policeman husband, Brendan, has hanged himself, her image of their idyllic life in Brendan's Adirondacks hometown of Wedeskyull, New York, is shattered in Milchman's evocative debut . . . Milchman expertly conveys Nora's grief in a way that will warm hearts even in the dead of a Wedeskyull winter."

—*Publishers Weekly* (starred review)

"[A] superlative dark, wintry debut . . . These well-defined characters take us on an emotional roller coaster ride through the darkest night, with blinding twists and occasionally fatal turns. This is a richly woven story that not only looks at the devastating effects of suicide but also examines life in a small town and explores the complexity of marriage."

—*Booklist* (starred review)

"Milchman's debut is a chillingly good mystery thriller that quickly picks up momentum and spirals into a whirling avalanche of secrets, danger, and suspense."

—*Library Journal*

"Milchman makes [readers] feel the chill right down to their bones and casts a particularly effective mood in this stylish thriller."

—*Kirkus Reviews*

"But the real triumph of Milchman's first novel is the pacing. The plot unfolds at an excellent clip, stalling in just the right moments, lingering on characters long enough for us to get to know them, ultimately rushing headlong to a series of startling revelations. I found myself completely wrapped up in the story, unwilling to put the novel down until I had reached the fascinating and unexpected conclusion."

—*San Francisco Review of Books*

"Milchman tackles small-town angst where evil can simmer under the surface with a breathless energy and a feel for realistic characters."

—*The Seattle Times*

"*Cover of Snow* is quite dark in tone and mood, which in turn contrasts with the backdrop of ever-present snow literally blanketing every scene . . . This is a memorable debut from an author who promises much and delivers."

—Bookreporter

Praise for *Ruin Falls*

"Milchman shows her chops with this sophomore effort (following *Cover of Snow*, 2013), and she carves out a new niche with this unusual mix of eco-thriller and family suspense drama."

—*Booklist* (starred review)

"Essential for psychological-thriller fanatics, Milchman's second novel trumps her acclaimed debut, *Cover of Snow*. Extreme heart-pounding action follows this determined mother as she risks everything to save her children."

—*Library Journal* (starred review)

"Milchman weaves a complex and intriguing tale, adeptly pacing the narrative as danger escalates . . . Most impressive, though, is Liz's transformation from a meek wife . . . to a strong, capable woman determined to rescue her children at any cost to herself."

—*Publishers Weekly*

Praise for *As Night Falls*

"Electric . . . Jenny Milchman mixes psychological thrills with adventure . . . to shoot her readers with an extreme jolt of adrenaline . . . Milchman's talent for building atmosphere will have readers wondering if they're shivering from the story's excitement or northern New York's winter cold."

—*Shelf Awareness* (starred review)

"Gripping . . . a fast-paced tale that should keep readers eagerly turning pages."

—*Publishers Weekly*

"The suspense starts building right from the get-go . . . The desolation set the hairs on the back of my neck to tingling, [and] there is a shocking twist. Another excellent psychological thriller that should appeal to readers who favor authors like Lisa Gardner and Lisa Unger."

—*Booklist*

Praise for *Wicked River*

"*Wicked River* is partly a who-is-my-husband-really story, partly a horror-in-the-wilderness story, and partly a Manhattan-family drama, all rolled up in elegantly propulsive prose and shot through with sinister suspense."

—Lee Child, #1 *New York Times* bestselling author of the Jack Reacher series

"Suspense oozes like blood from a wound on every page of Jenny Milchman's *Wicked River*. As scary and tense a book as I've read this year."

—John Lescroart, *New York Times* bestselling author of the Dismas Hardy series

"From time to time, I come across an action manuscript that shares my high regard for the [action] genre and the intensity it can achieve. One such book is Jenny Milchman's *Wicked River*, which I urge you to experience. It thoroughly gripped me, not only because of the excitement it creates and the inventiveness with which it does so but also because of the subtext about a honeymoon in which the various stages of a marriage are condensed in a wilderness that's both physical and psychological. *Wicked River* is a wild ride."

—David Morrell, *New York Times* bestselling author of *First Blood*

"On a honeymoon gone terribly awry, two newlyweds battle for their lives in a powerful story of survival told by one of the richest and most riveting voices in today's thriller fiction. *Wicked River* twists and tumbles and roars, carrying readers along for one hell of a thrill ride. Mark my words: this novel will jump off the shelves."

—William Kent Krueger, *New York Times* bestselling author of the Cork O'Connor series

"Jenny Milchman's characters jump off the page . . . *Wicked River* is compulsive reading—I kept holding my breath and turning the pages faster and faster. It's a book that should cement Jenny's place as a must-read thriller writer for fans hungry for domestic suspense in the style of Gillian Flynn."

—M.J. Rose, *New York Times* bestselling author

"Chock full of suspense and danger, *Wicked River* by Jenny Milchman takes you on the journey of a lifetime, canoeing fast-moving rivers and hiking through tangled forests where humans have seldom trod. This is the story of Natalie and Doug's honeymoon; they wanted natural beauty and adventure. They get both, in abundance. You'll be glad you joined them. *Wicked River* is wicked thrilling!"

—Gayle Lynds, bestselling author of *Masquerade* and *The Book of Spies*

"*Deliverance*, meet *Into the Wild.* Jenny Milchman knows how to construct a tautly wound, rawboned thriller that will keep you up like the howl of wolves outside your tent."

—Andrew Gross, international bestselling author of *The Blue Zone* and *The Dark Tide*

"A story about passion and betrayal on the high-stakes stage, *Wicked River* is intensely gripping and perfectly paced—a real standout that pushes the domestic-thriller category to its very edge. With her usual mastery of setting and character, Jenny Milchman has outdone herself."

—Carla Buckley, internationally bestselling author of *The Good Goodbye*

"Milchman has crafted a truly engrossing novel where the river is not the only thing that's wicked."

—Jeff Ayers, the Associated Press

"Riveting . . . A hybrid between John Fowles's classic *The Collector* and Erica Ferencik's *The River at Night*, this novel will appeal to fans of psychological suspense as well as those who enjoy trips to the backcountry."

—*Library Journal*

"A tense exploration of survival and psychological manipulation with a raw, sharply drawn setting sure to please fans of wilderness thrillers like those by Nevada Barr and C. J. Box."

—*Booklist*

"Milchman shakes things up with *Wicked River*; in this author's hands, a babbling brook can become a deliverer of death. The suspense ratchets up steadily, making this a highly satisfying summer read."

—*The Strand Magazine*

Praise for *The Second Mother*

"*The Second Mother* is a gothic unraveling of a novel, as moody and atmospheric as the isolated island on which it's set."

—Jodi Picoult, #1 *New York Times* bestselling author of *Small Great Things* and *A Spark of Light*

"Rich in atmosphere, expertly plotted, and populated by characters who live and breathe, *The Second Mother* is as much a portrait of survival and redemption as it is a harrowing deep dive into the secrets and troubles of an isolated island in Maine. Jenny Milchman writes with insight and compassion, creating a vivid sense of place and masterfully ratcheting up the tension page by gripping page."

—Lisa Unger, *New York Times* bestselling author of *The Stranger Inside*

"With her ever-masterful sense of place and astute psychological insight, Jenny Milchman takes us on a journey from the Adirondack Mountains to a remote island off the coast of Maine, and from the dark depths of grief into the light. This is a harrowing and heartrending story that earns its place in the sun."

—Carol Goodman, *New York Times* bestselling author of *The Lake of Dead Languages* and *The Sea of Lost Girls*

"When Julie arrives on a beautiful, rustic island off the coast of Maine—with a one-room schoolhouse, where people embrace a simple life—she is hoping for a chance to start over. Slowly and expertly, Milchman peels back the layers to reveal what lies beneath the idyllic surface. *The Second Mother* is an atmospheric thriller resonating with the weight and power of secrets. Settle in someplace comfortable, lock the doors, and turn on the lights—you're not going to want to put this one down!"

—Jennifer McMahon, author of *The Winter People* and *The Invited*

"*The Second Mother* is a tense, riveting story about a woman who flees to a remote island off the coast of Maine to escape a tragic past. Starkly beautiful, the island holds the hope of a new life and a new love, but schoolteacher Julie Weathers finds herself facing dangers she never imagined. Told with Milchman's stunning prose, *The Second Mother* is a gripping tale of obsession, secrets held close, and the dark side of island life. Harrowing and addictive, I dare you to put this book down once you've started."

—Heather Gudenkauf, *New York Times* bestselling author of *The Weight of Silence* and *This Is How I Lied*

"A do-not-miss tour de force."

—Linda Castillo, *New York Times* bestselling author

"Jenny Milchman is one of the best suspense writers at work today, and *The Second Mother* is a page-turner extraordinaire. Milchman takes the nostalgic daydream of teaching in a one-room schoolhouse and turns it ever so slowly into an urgent nightmare. That the story is set on a remote island off the coast of Maine—one of the most claustrophobic places a stranger can ever set foot—is an added bonus."

—Paul Doiron, author of the Edgar Award–nominated Mike Bowditch series

"Milchman owns a Highsmith mastery of emotional depth and psychological tension for all her rich, finely detailed settings. She is a true American regionalist artist. *The Second Mother* sweeps us away to an eerie island of complex villains . . . that will chill your blood while it breaks your heart."

—Kalisha Buckhanon, author of *Speaking of Summer* and *Solemn*

"Proving Stephen King isn't the only author who can make a scenic small town in Maine feel menacing, Jenny Milchman's *The Second Mother* is a haunting thriller."

—PopSugar

"Jenny Milchman commands the page the way the best actors command the stage. Milchman brings the suspense from a simmer to a slow boil, as *The Second Mother* becomes an agonizing exercise in escape and survival. This is the kind of book Alfred Hitchcock would have loved to adapt into a film, and for good reason."

—*The Providence Journal*

"Another gripping and satisfying story of suspense from Mary Higgins Clark Award–winning author Jenny Milchman. The author's talent for authentic description will carry readers right along with Julie on the choppy ride in the ferry to Mercy Island. They'll smell the salty air, feel the spray and mist of the ocean on their faces, walk beside her and Depot on the path to an unknown destination. They'll learn along with Julie that this lovely, close-knit community is not as welcoming and tranquil as first believed. *The Second Mother* is a beautifully written page-turner."

—*The New York Review of Books*

"Examines grief, isolation, addiction, social inequality, and legacy set against the background of an insular society desperate to prevent change and growth. Yet this is truly a story about motherhood—the connection between mother and child, and the ferocity of a mother to protect her child at all costs. On every page, Milchman raises the stakes. While grappling with dark questions, *The Second Mother* will thrill and entertain readers who desire a summer adventure."

—BookTrib

"A tension-filled, provocative, nail-biting thriller that will have your heart pounding and your hands shaking as you frantically turn page after page, thirsting for more."

—*Suspense Magazine*

THE USUAL SILENCE

OTHER TITLES BY JENNY MILCHMAN

The Second Mother

Wicked River

As Night Falls

Ruin Falls

Cover of Snow

THE USUAL SILENCE

AN ARLES SHEPHERD THRILLER

JENNY MILCHMAN

THOMAS & MERCER

This is a work of fiction. Names, characters, organizations, places, events, and incidents are either products of the author's imagination or are used fictitiously. Otherwise, any resemblance to actual persons, living or dead, is purely coincidental.

Published by Thomas & Mercer, Seattle

www.apub.com

ISBN-13: 9781662518423 (paperback)
ISBN-13: 9781662518430 (digital)

Cover design by Faceout Studio, Amanda Hudson
Cover image: © Cristina Mitchell / Arcangel; © Lisa Wiltse / Getty

Printed in the United States of America

For my father: reader, writer, teacher, justice seeker.
This is the first book I've written without you here.
I hope that it would do you proud.

Alta vendetta d'alto silenzio è figlia.

Deep vengeance is the daughter of deep silence.

—Vittorio Alfieri, 1789

THE LAST TO DISAPPEAR

It was that bleak, barren time of year when even winter is dying.

Cassius Monroe walked along the lean, curving bone of his driveway, looking out for his daughter. He had nodded off in his living room chair, surprised when he'd startled awake. Only a few minutes, fifteen at the most, but still, napping in the afternoon. Like his father used to do, like Cass was an old guy already. His boots crushed brittle leaves to dust, and he stooped to pick up branches, tossing them into the woods with the deadfall that had dropped on its own.

His days were unmarked now; he could get this half-mile drive that led to their house sparkling like a kitchen floor with all the free time he had on his hands. He hated it, hours trickling away with him hardly registering they were gone. But even though he wasn't a working man at the moment, he was still a dad who had responsibilities. In fact, with his wife the wage earner for the time being, he was the primary caretaker for their sixth-grade daughter. And he usually sensed it when Bea was due to come walking in, the school bus having let her off up at the road.

She was a little late today.

He walked into the middle of the road, turning so he could look around the curves. Salty air drifted inland as it did when the wind came in from the east, instead of being blown out to sea. His eyes stung, and he wrinkled his nose against the tang. Usually he liked being reminded of that distant shoreline, but today the smell troubled him, made him think of preservation, heaps of salt used to ward off decay. There was no hint of diesel in the air, exhaust from a school bus.

It wasn't as if Bea's bus ran like a Swiss clock, but it usually kept to its schedule pretty well. He walked over to the mailbox with an envelope in his hand—paying bills after the grace period these days—and automatically lifted the flag, thinking.

Not all the way to worried yet; a dozen things could happen to make a school bus late. Unless Bea wasn't on the bus at all? His mind was scattered lately, less focused than usual. His wife complained about it. He'd better call her at work, double-check what was on tap for today. He was responsible for Bea's afternoons, but Maggie still kept everything running, despite the second job she'd taken on to cover their expenses, all the extra hours she was working.

There were music lessons on Tuesdays and Thursdays with Mr. Hochum, but it was Monday. Bea had a new buddy this year—Maggie had told him how friend groups dissolved at this age, leaving the girls adrift. Finding someone to hang out with, share secrets with, just eat lunch with, could be hard. He couldn't stand the thought of his daughter's days marching by as toneless and unscored as his own. At least he was alone, far out to sea. Bea would have witnesses, seventy other sixth graders observing her desolation.

Would it be weird if he called the new friend's parents? But Bea wouldn't just make a playdate—or whatever big girls of twelve called them—without letting him know. He and Maggie had been prepared for all sorts of tween acting out, but even in the midst of her friendship crisis, Bea stayed close, sharing her heartache with Maggie if not with him. As if she didn't realize teenage rebellion beckoned just over the horizon. Was "a thing," as Bea would put it.

He stood by the side of the road, shifting uneasily from foot to foot while a screw tightened in his chest. Then he caught the strain of an engine making its climb up the hill, and he took a relieved step back onto the sandy shoulder. He painted a casual expression on his face for Bea, who might be embarrassed, her dad meeting the bus like she was a kindergartener. Concealing the fact that he'd been worried for a moment there. Because he spent way too much time these days floating around, no restrictions on where his mind might roam.

Then a tractor crested the hill, its driver lifting one hand in a wave as he went by. Cass stared at the vehicle as it chugged along. He didn't recognize the kid at the wheel and was unable to reconcile the sight of that little green thing when he'd been so sure it'd be a hulking yellow bus. Normally he wouldn't have any trouble telling the engines apart.

His heart thrummed, a guitar strung too tight. His father had died young of cardiac failure, and Cass had begun to register each time a birthday came around with a higher number than the last his dad had gotten to see. Like Cass was living on borrowed time, past his expiration date.

He turned and marched back to their house.

There was no way Bea could've gotten past him, but he looked for signs of her, a glass on the counter or a trail of crumbs, her viola case and backpack at the base of the stairs. Pointlessly, he walked around, opening doors. Just five rooms in their old farmhouse, and nobody breathed in a one of them except for him—short, forceful exhalations coming too close together.

He called Maggie, but it went straight to voice mail, which meant she was somewhere without signal. With their daughter, maybe, some fun plan he'd forgotten? Digging in his pocket for his keys, he remembered to text Bea.

Where are you, honey? I'm going to look. Stay put if you get back before me.

The digital version didn't feel solid enough, impermanent for how it disappeared into the ether, floating out along invisible lines. So even though he knew Bea would be on her phone the second she got inside the house and had service, he scrawled a good old-fashioned note, placing the sheet of paper on the floor where she'd have to see or stumble over it.

Then he left the door unlocked, jumped into his truck, and gunned the gas.

The radio came on, blaring the country station he kept it tuned to, but the yokel twang was so at odds with his mounting concern that he stabbed it silent.

He stopped at their neighbor's, but Don was out, so Cass drove on. It hit him as he rounded a bend that this was dumb—Bea might at this exact second be getting home, dropped off by the new friend's mom or dad, say. But by then he was most of the way to the bus yard, and he braked hard, plumes of dirt flying up around his tires.

"My daughter's route," he began as he stalked into the building. "Gus Owlbridge drives it. Did he come back yet?"

A woman sat behind a desk, a pink carton of doughnuts just one of the items on its cluttered surface. The box was empty save for a last frosted quarter, crusted over and crumbly. She twisted to check the wall clock, even though her phone sat by her elbow, screen lit up. For people their age, phones would always be appendages, afterthoughts, not parts of their bodies.

"He's been and gone. Fueled up half an hour ago." She gestured outside to the pump.

Now he saw all six buses in the fleet, parked and resting, still as animals for the night. His heart clenched like a fist in his chest. *Dad,* he thought, as he always did in these moments.

"Well, Bea didn't get off," he explained. "She isn't home yet."

She paused for a beat, then nodded with a briskness that was so comforting, his knees went weak. The motion of a woman who knew what was happening, and what to do about it.

"She's a sixth grader, right?"

He exhaled a pent-up breath. Now he'd hear something that made sense of this. A field trip he'd forgotten about. Or an assembly. The teacher kept the whole class after school.

"It's the age," she said. "I'll bet she went home with one of her friends—"

He was already swiveling, rubber soles of his boots making pained squeaks against the floor as he started to run.

He drove home, scarcely looking at the road, his feet jumping on the gas and the clutch like corn in a popper, hands slick with sweat on the wheel. The house was as empty as he'd left it. His note glowed in an afternoon sunbeam on the floor.

He crushed it beneath his feet as he ran back out and arrowed off into the woods. When homework and practice weren't eating her time, Bea liked to walk here. Never without coming inside first to call hello, dump her things, and grab a snack, but maybe today she'd chosen not to do that, lured by the first signs of spring in the air.

He was as comfortable in the Maine woods as he was in his own bedroom—more so—but now felt every one of the dangers that could've come for his daughter. A tumble down one of the pitches he himself was taking at a skid. Was Bea lying somewhere, felled by a broken ankle? He mentally recoiled at the image of his daughter, lost where he'd have trouble finding her, hurt and powerless to get help.

Fear flooded his brain, blocking any ability to come up with a plan. He was back at the house, standing outside with hands fisted, no idea where to go, what to do. Dully, after the hum of the engine should've given it away, he registered a car approaching, and spun. He heard one of its doors slam shut, his head vibrating with the thud just as Maggie swam into view. She gave the driver a cheerful wave. A coworker who'd offered rides in return for help with gas.

Overhead, a web of branches spread out, twigs forming a lace across his wife's pretty face. He walked forward, and Maggie took a quick stutter step back.

"What are you doing out here?" she called. "I'm going to be late for my shift, but I wanted to stop in and tell Bea good night."

His final hope fizzed out, like a match in water. No mother/daughter activity, then, some girlie arrangement his mind hadn't held on to. He watched Maggie catch his fear like a virus.

Then he lumbered up the porch steps and shouldered his way inside, snatching the landline from a table. No time for an ornery cell phone, his fingers fighting to light up the screen in a jittery dance he'd never been able to master.

"Bea hasn't come home," he said as he waited for the call to go through. Keeping his back turned, unable to bear the sight of the thing taking root in Maggie. Terror that would never be dug out, no matter what happened next—and that was still a place he refused to go, even in his mind. "We have to call the police."

CHAPTER ONE

Arles Shepherd sat across from her teenage patient, trays on each of their laps.

"It's taken us a long time to get here," she said. "What's your comfort level right now?"

Natalie was transforming her paper napkin into a small heap of snow. "Um, good. Like, maybe an eight?"

The napkin shredding, though. Arles inclined her head, and Natalie huffed out a sigh.

"Okay, more like a four probably. A two. I can't believe I'm doing this."

"*We're* doing this," Arles said in a mild tone. "You're not alone. Remember that."

After a moment, the girl let out another, quieter breath. "Yeah, I know. But this feels different for some reason."

"Some reason you know?" Arles asked. "Or some reason you don't?"

Natalie faced her with blue fire in her eyes, her mouth open as if words were about to brim over. Arles tended to attribute this uniquely teen brand of intensity to being on the cusp of discovering one's own world—and figuring out how little that place made sense.

"I mean, look at you," the girl said.

Arles did, making a show of glancing down at herself, twisting to try to see from behind.

Natalie gave a small laugh. The napkin abuse stopped for the moment.

"You're perfect," she told Arles. "You're like held together with invisible strings or ties or—or nonexistent glue. I don't believe you ever eat. I basically can't believe you *breathe*."

"It's an illusion," Arles said.

Natalie laughed again.

"No, really, I mean it," said Arles. "Not me putting on an illusion. Your mind creating one. Thinking that your therapist is kind of above it all, not a normal human creature, is part of why this whole thing works. How transformations occur. If you knew that I was just a poor schmo like the next guy—and I am—then why would you talk to me or listen to what I said?"

Slouched in her chair, Natalie glanced up at Arles before resituating the tray on her lap.

"Shall we get started?" said Arles.

Natalie picked up her fork, and Arles mirrored the motion. Natalie had chosen waffles with whipped cream and berries; patients got to select their favorite meal. Arles herself hadn't eaten anything yet today, and it was past three. Some role model. It was always part guesswork, doing a food session with an anorectic client. Should Arles cut a meticulous bite and nibble daintily, or saw off a chunk and cram it into her mouth? Swallow with libidinal relish, or chew as if food were nothing but fuel? The decision depended on individual factors, who the patient was, how she was behaving in treatment. Arles took a look at Natalie.

The girl sat with her utensil lifted. One bony hand, all protruding knuckles and fingers sharp as tentpoles, was clenched around the handle. Only the slightest tremor gave away her emotional state. She had the physical control of a high-wire performer.

"Nat?" Arles said.

She didn't respond. Now her chin trembled too, and light hairs, a downy mat on both her arms, quivered ever so slightly.

"I thought you'd come to this revelation that your eating disorder isn't really about food or looks or even weight. Yours, mine, the Holy Spirit's."

"That's blasphemy," Natalie responded woodenly. "But true. It's about control, my shitty father, climate stuff. You know what, though? It's still fucking terrifying when the number on the scale creeps up."

"Is it?" Arles asked.

Natalie frowned. "What do you mean?"

"I mean, who says so? What's so bad about a higher weight?"

"That's like asking what's bad about a heroin overdose. It just *is*."

"So getting heavier is a kind of death," said Arles.

A silver scrim of tears shone on the girl's lower lash line. "It's worse."

And suddenly, Arles understood. It could happen sometimes in a session, a flash of insight, the wordless transfer of revelation between client and therapist. "Is it a kind of shame?"

Natalie set her fork down. It clinked against the plate before submerging itself in a drift of whipped cream. "Total abject humiliation. Scum on the floor. Something to be flushed away."

"Yeah," Arles said quietly. "I know that feeling."

Some psychologists believed you shouldn't reveal anything about yourself to a patient, but Arles thought those practitioners were full of it. They just didn't want to own the fact that they were as vulnerable—and screwed up—as anyone paying to sit in a chair across from them.

Natalie scoffed. "Yeah, right."

"It's the worst thing in the world," Arles said. "Seeing yourself as less than. Less than everything. Less than anything."

Natalie looked at her, a quick dart of the eyes.

"You know what, though?" Arles trailed her finger through a curlicue of cream.

"You're going to say that food doesn't make me feel that way. It's something else."

"Well, sure," Arles said. "And we'll figure out what that is. But also? Yum."

Natalie's body deflated in her chair. She dipped a single solitary berry into a spot of cream and bit into it, severing the small blue globe. Half a blueberry consumed, and Arles wanted to pump her fist in the air or give the girl a hug. She couldn't—shouldn't—do either of those things. So she settled for taking her own bountiful bite of fruit.

The phone on her desk vibrated, its big body jumping.

Arles frowned, gaze instinctively flicking to her clock.

Twenty minutes before the hour, which left ten in this session. The phone squatted there, fat, toadlike. Glistening with its own obsolescence in a world gone cellular.

"You need to get that?" asked Natalie.

"Nope," Arles said, faintly disturbed. She got up and turned off the ringer before it could emit another blurp of noise. Then she aimed a smile in the young woman's direction, pleased to receive something close to one in return. "Not when I'm hungry."

As soon as Arles had wrapped up the session, she checked the voice mail she knew had been left, a button on her phone throwing off color like the light bar on a police car.

The director of outpatient mental health, Mark Rogers, had asked her to come up to the meeting room as soon as she was able, even if it meant canceling her next session. No explanation, no apology for the out-of-bounds act of having interrupted her *last* session—nothing. A sick, weighty feeling of having been here before accosted her. *Because you have,* something chittered in her brain. For a second, the universe grayed the way it did before someone passed out.

On numb feet, she mounted the stairs—**Get Your Steps In**, cheered a disembodied pair of sneakers sprouting from a sign on the wall—to the second floor. Eric Halsey, head of psychiatry, stood by the door as if granting entrance. Arles began to creep past him before straightening her spine and walking into the room with a more forceful tread.

Mark, three other fellow psychologists, and a second doc were seated around a battle-scarred table, scored from years of furious note-taking. The only positions not represented were the real underlings—BA-level counselors, interns, and Luke, Wedeskyull Community Hospital's therapy dog. Arles wished Luke had been invited to the meeting.

Behind the assemblage sat two official-looking women she didn't recognize. Automatically, hardly aware that she was doing it, Arles studied both faces, rolling back the years to try to gauge what each might've looked like as a child. It was a habit so ingrained by now that no level of stress could've made her forgo it.

"Well, well," she said when nobody spoke. "The gang's all here."

Mental health clinicians wore masks like everybody else. Hers presented an arched brow and chilled expression. Glib remarks came out of its mouth.

Mark took the first leg of the relay. "We appreciate you coming on short notice. Bonnie Parsons and Leigh Anson are both new this year in Legal. Bonnie, Leigh, this is Dr. Shepherd."

Legal, Arles heard with a thud. A poker face was as essential a tool for a therapist as a scalpel was for a surgeon, but she felt hers slip.

"Why don't you take a seat, Dr. Shepherd?" said Mark.

Despite his having procured the title of director, she and Mark had the same level of training and number of advanced degrees. They discussed cases, had at one point discussed sleeping together—well, he'd discussed it while she'd stood there, tapping one foot—and were definitely on a first-name basis.

"I think I prefer to stand," she said, ruing the *I think* the second it was out of her mouth. Wasn't she always calling attention to gendered qualifiers, verbal tics that indicated uncertainty? "Actually, I know I prefer it." *Actually* was one too.

Halsey settled himself in a chair as if to show how little her act of defiance meant. "It happened again, Dr. Shepherd. Only in this instance, someone made a complaint to the board."

She clenched the back of the seat she'd declined. The state licensing board received complaints against practitioners all the time—it wasn't as if they were some scarlet *C*—although Arles had never been the target of so much as one. But she knew that even a single dip wouldn't, couldn't, be regarded agnostically in her case.

"Who?" One word was all she could muster.

Dr. Liu replied. He was a brilliant diagnostician, and one of the rare docs who allotted precious, pricey minutes to do counseling during routine med checks. Arles liked working with him, sharing his prescription pad, getting his approval on commitments.

"A Brittany Galtry. You treat her eight-year-old daughter, Florence."

Arles shook her head. "That can't be right. I haven't seen either of them in months." Was there a statute of limitations on complaints?

Her colleagues exchanged looks around the table.

"According to outpatient scheduling, you had a session last week," said Mark.

"There *was* a gap in treatment prior," added one of the lawyers.

Arles hadn't kept track of which was which, and was too consumed with trying to make sense of this ghost session to respond. She liked Flo Galtry. She'd missed the work they had just started really getting into when the child's mother withdrew her from therapy.

Halsey's voice drifted into her consciousness.

"Luckily, nothing dire happened. This time."

This time meant *again.*

"But the hospital can't continue to risk this level of exposure," he went on.

The lawyers contributed simultaneous nods, as if they were one voiceless being.

If Arles didn't kick herself into gear, things were going to go even further south. Time enough later to check her notes, see what the hell everyone could be referring to. "I have a good relationship with Mom. Flo too, for that matter. I'll be sure to follow up right away—"

Halsey cut her off. "If this had been simply run of the mill, do you think we would've called you in here, brought all these busy people together at the last minute?"

When Arles looked at him, she saw a spark of fear in his eyes, in addition to the vindictiveness he was known for. She felt the butterfly beat of wings in her throat, her own fear alighting.

"My Spidey sense says that was a rhetorical question," she managed to get out.

Halsey was squinting at his phone. "Far from having *no* session, Mom states you kept her daughter late. Back-to-back-to-back blocks in your office."

Arles had no memory of what he was talking about. A seasick feeling caused her knees to jog, and she dropped into the seat she'd refused, trying to gather some might.

"It sounds from this description like more of an interrogation than therapy," he went on, still scanning his screen. "As if you waterboarded the poor little girl or something—"

Putting up a show of wits was the one move she had left. "Interesting metaphor for the head of a mental health facility, Eric. Therapy as torture."

Liu looked as if he were attempting to conceal a smile.

"This is the exact problem, Arles," said Halsey.

"Oh, good, we're back to first names," she said.

"And *that*," Halsey replied, red-faced.

"I assume you mean my attitude," said Arles.

"Yes. Your attitude."

"But not my outcomes."

Halsey balled his hands on the table. "That isn't enough to prevent your dismissal."

"Dismissal?" The word lodged like a stone in her throat. She'd been expecting to suffer the humiliation of supervised hours. At worst, be put on probation. Her rate of successful terminations and closed cases was the best across all of Mental Health. It was akin to having the highest solve rate as a police detective.

At last, Halsey's composure appeared to slip a fraction, and he became less overlord of the only source of comprehensive mental health services for a hundred-mile radius and more a sneering kid on a playground. "Don't have a snappy comeback to that, do you?"

Come back? She hadn't even known she was gone.

She took the stairs back down to the first floor at a sprint—sneakered sign cheering her on—and shut herself inside her office. As she sat down at her desk, she felt a prickle against her spine and stood up again to latch the bolt on the door.

She booted her laptop and ran TheraTime, WCH's scheduling software. There in a stark, serifed font was proof. Today was Monday, and on the previous Thursday, her last appointment of the day had been with Flo Galtry.

Tiny insect legs scurried up and down her back.

If she'd wanted to descend into the kind of paranoia she would've sent a client to get a med check for, she'd conjecture that Halsey had messed with the software. But trickier to explain was the note in the treatment-planning nodule, her own curt, succinct voice coming through.

After some delay pt reengages, m brought in, flu twenty-four hrs.

Back-to-back blocks, Halsey said. Did the session run long due to the delay mentioned in this entry? For what reason had she brought Flo's mother in, and what was Arles supposed to have followed up with? If she hadn't done it already, now she would never get the chance.

Lacking any ability to remember should've been most alarming of all, but it wasn't. She might not have been to this exact place before, but a sinkhole of sand in her brain wasn't new.

Her regular appointments had been scrubbed, line after empty line causing her eyes to brim. An hour ago, the idea of a suspension would've been anathema; now she couldn't even hold out hope for that. These blank hourly slots constituted proof that she'd been let go, fired, banished from the kingdom. When was the last time her week had looked like this? Not since she was a counselor in training, licensure a goal on the horizon, still working to build a caseload.

How was she going to spend her time from now on? It had been segmented into fifty-minute sessions, plus five more for notes, for so long that she didn't know any other way to count. To mark the passing of her life.

She got up from her chair. It was ugly, institutional and dull, like everything in this place, but the padding had molded itself to her body, and it was her favorite place to sit, more comfortable than a single piece of furniture she owned.

She left the hospital and hurried across the parking lot, the late-March air still chilly enough to gnaw through her coat. The lot was sparsely filled as always—acres of empty slots—and she felt as though she were walking across an apocalyptic battleground. Someplace burned out and blackened, reduced to stumps and rubble and thin spirals of smoke.

How could Halsey just cast her out like some disowned offspring? Without giving her notice, even, a succession of warnings? Vanishing from the lives of people who'd dealt with more than enough hurt, in some cases the specific pain of abandonment, would be a cruel blow coming from their therapist. That said, mental health care in a rural hospital clinic relied on disparity—systemic and systematic—plus one simple, ugly sentiment: Beggars can't be choosers. Clinicians came and went all the time.

She got into her car and checked her phone. Not a single text or DM, and no email aside from junk. Deleting it all with one furious, earth-scorching finger, she let out her breath in a cold cloud and shifted into gear. Made the drive "home"—quote marks because no place she'd lived in had ever felt deserving of the word—along steep and dented roads. She rented the top floor of a bruised Victorian, its paint flaking and driveway humped from the scouring winds and frost heaves of more than a century's worth of Adirondack winters.

The owner occupied the second floor, while the first went to short-term stays: tourists and ice climbers and summit hounds drawn to the region. Access to her unit came via three flights of exterior stairs tacked onto clapboard siding and straddling parts of the second-story roof. The metal steps broiled in the summer, clanged like a flagpole in strong winds, and had to be ruthlessly salted and deiced lest she fall to her death anytime between September and May. But, although she'd lived in Wedeskyull her whole life, she'd never wanted to take on the commitment of a mortgage.

As she started the climb, a car door slammed below. No, not a car—something bigger and heavier, the kind of vehicle that went on a rampage. But she heard no engine revving as it drove off, nor the sound of somebody getting out, and when she peered over the railing, the street was empty. Then the door on the second story opened, and the sudden intrusion caused her foot to slip. She stabilized herself, preparing for her landlord's customary wanna-hook-up *Hello*.

But when she turned to call out her equally standard no-I-do-not *Hi there*, his unit was dim and locked up tight. For a moment, she remained in place, blinking, confused. At last, she completed the ascent, exhaling in short bursts, before entering her apartment with a sense of dread trailing so close behind, she could feel its breath on her neck.

The sight of the barren fridge nearly did her in. Usually, she ate in the hospital cafeteria, and although the food there was horrid, it saved her from shopping and cooking and clearing up, chores she'd never been able to abide. As a psychologist, she understood the reasons behind this aversion, but insight didn't lessen her distaste for domesticity.

She was just covering a plate of leftover pizza-shop spaghetti with a snow of grated cheese when her phone dinged. The speed with which she leaped for it felt shameful, even though no one was there to witness her desperate lunge. She glanced at the screen, and the world beyond her rooftop dwelling—whatever had been out there and trying to get in—slipped away.

Still no message from a real human being. Not Mark checking to see how she was holding up, or any of her other colleagues, who wouldn't even have this number except on some master list of WCH staff. No booty call from either of the men she'd hooked up with this month, two being the most she'd allow herself before cutting off the flow like a bartender at last call.

This was an alert. A tiny, waving flag from a company she had hired years ago and never expected to hear from again.

She tapped it.

CHAPTER TWO

Geary sat in a cloud of sunlit dust, staring at the particles.

Louise stood outside his room, unwilling to break the spell. How she wished she could keep her son in this state forever, his sweet, upturned chin and the occasional blink—infrequent because he was so mesmerized—making him seem not just like any other ten-year-old, but like the very best version of himself. She liked her son's differences. Sometimes. At her best times.

She fished her phone from her pocket to check the time. It was muted—she was always missing texts and calls because Geary couldn't tolerate phone sounds—and she slid it back into her jeans with the same care she'd used to extract it. No matter how much she would've liked to extend this moment, they would be late to Geary's appointment if she didn't interrupt his activity. If it was an activity? Not the way she would've meant the word. But she and her son didn't do things in the same way. Most people didn't do things like Geary.

She sidled around the door and tiptoed across the carpet. Standing near that column of dust bits, interrupting their flight, would produce an effect she'd never been able to understand. None of the therapists they'd seen had figured it out, either. She paused a few steps away and crouched down at Geary's level without looking into his eyes.

"Hey, Gear, time to go see the doctor, okay?" she said softly.

He got to his feet, all ten-year-old limbs just beginning to sprawl, and she closed her eyes for a moment. Took the tiniest sip of air, her first since entering the room.

No chance he would walk out by her side, or even wait for her at the door, but that was okay. She hurried after him, registering only as she passed his tidy desk and chair setup (neat because he never used either one), that she was going too fast. Anyone close to Geary when the sun was out needed to walk at a slow pace, and be willing to change course, but today she had pushed things so late, she'd neglected to spend time on precautions.

A silent *noooo* bloomed on her lips. She stood with one foot hovering above the floor. Caught within that column of glitter, a sunlit swirl of bits from a Fourth of July sparkler.

But Geary had already made it out to the hall. Maybe he hadn't noticed, would continue down the stairs. Take his puffy coat off the hook by the door—he insisted on wearing it in all but the hottest weather—and go outside. After that, things might get tricky, depending on whether the ancient car doors opened without creaks, and if there was traffic, stops and starts on the way to the clinic. But all that would be manageable if she could just get lucky right now.

Geary stopped, his still slight and slender back to her, then turned around. She was balanced on one foot, hadn't allowed herself to move an inch since her careless, clumsy misstep. Like walking off the edge of a cliff and remaining in thin air without dropping.

The stream of dust continued to scatter around her body. Geary let out a moan while teensy nothing bits showered his neglected schoolwork area. Nothing to her—what were they to him? Not a question that mattered right now. Her son was lost in a place she couldn't get to, wrecked by something she could hardly see. He began trudging across the room as if the floor were coated with glue, shoulders slumped, head hung low.

"Look, Geary, it's already settling down. See?" She knew better than to talk loudly or reach out to touch him, but she thrust one arm forward and pointed to the dust rearranging itself.

He studied the air with an expression she called—stupidly, probably; at least all the therapists acted like this was wrong—his "math look." Louise used to like math as a kid; up till tenth grade, it'd been her best subject. Then she'd reached algebra, and it was like trying to speak a foreign language. She'd fallen further and further behind—the teachers always seemed to give all the extra help to the boys—until she'd had to go to summer school just to graduate.

Right now, Geary looked as if he'd been handed an unsolvable problem. She could remember more than one therapist nodding with polite pity upon hearing her description of this state, probably thinking something horrible, like Geary might not even *get* to high school math. Although actually he—like her at that age—was good with numbers, according to his teacher.

Then he began to shiver. It was as if the walls of the house had fallen down, letting the late-winter day inside. He shook so hard, she took her eyes off him for a second to examine her own skin for goose bumps. But it felt comfortable in the room to her. She kept the heat cranked up for Geary, skipping drive-through convenience meals and doughnut-shop coffee so she could afford the fuel bills. She pressed her hands against her thighs to force herself to stay still, knowing no blanket or coat in the world would warm Geary when he was like this, not that he would have taken one from her. She was powerless—as stumped as she used to be in math—to comfort her child, and the helplessness caused tears to spring to her eyes.

Suddenly, Geary whipped around, as if he'd just gotten the shock of a lifetime, except that nothing had changed. At least, not as far as she could tell. He ran forward—for a second, it seemed like he was running toward her—before swerving. Everything went still and cold inside her, even though a moment ago, she'd been perfectly warm.

There was no way to stop what was about to happen now.

He threw himself down on the floor, banging both knees—they'd be bruised tomorrow, twin knobs of purple—and began pulling up clumps of blue fuzz. She had experimented with budget-busting flat-weave carpet, no floor covering at all, even area rugs, but if Geary didn't have exactly the right pile, then he wouldn't be able to use it to draw his streets, or whatever they were.

He lurched to his feet and began to spin around the room, whirling in steps too fast to be called a dance. Something dark, not pleasing to see. Louise's (small-minded, judgmental, and thankfully dead) grandmother would've probably said to call the priest, especially after Geary dropped back down on the floor, all four of his limbs thrust out, electrified. His screams were a steady blast of sound, shooting into the air like rockets.

Louise clapped her palms over the sides of her face and sagged against the wall. When she lowered one hand to pull out her phone, the volume increased as if a knob had been turned. She sent an SOS to the number reserved for these situations before blocking both ears again.

Her ex arrived in coveralls and boots, taking the flight of steps two at a time, making the whole second floor shake. Geary was still screaming, but hoarsely now, his voice a low rumble. Lost, lonely sounding. Michael bent down to pick him up. He'd always been more physical as a parent, plus less receptive to the instructions they'd gotten from therapists that restricted physical contact. Geary's body remained stiff in the sling of his father's arms as they headed downstairs.

Louise ducked into the bathroom to splash water on her savaged face, reddened and sweaty and makeup smeared. With the storm subsiding, Geary in someone else's hands for the moment, literally, she lost the will to stand. Her muscles had gone tight from clenching—she'd stayed fixed in one position after disrupting the dust, then braced herself when Geary ran in her direction. She was so bereft of contact with her son, hungry for it in a way that felt shameful, that some small part of her had longed for the collision.

Water dripped down her cheeks as she sat on the lid of the toilet. She stared at the wall until the tiles merged into one seamless sheet. Finally, she forced herself to rise, taking the stairs at a dull, plodding pace before following the wails outside.

Michael had managed to bundle Geary into his puffy coat and was wrestling him across the yard. The rear door of Michael's truck had been left ajar, and he kneed the opening wider. Geary scrambled free and climbed into his booster. He'd outgrown the need for a kiddie seat a long time ago, but had stayed skinny enough that he still fit, which was lucky since he seemed to prefer its web of straps to a plain old seat belt. He squirmed out of his coat, wriggling his arms from the sleeves, while his voice sank in volume before finally giving out.

The quiet had a force all its own. It buckled Louise's knees. She collapsed into the front seat, and Michael nudged the passenger door closed for her before walking around to his side.

"Where to?" he mouthed, lowering himself into the driver's seat.

The house she lived in with Geary wasn't far from the ugly, sprawling mental health clinic on Route 22, which wound through the built-up bloat of Westchester County, then north to whatever lay beyond. She turned in Michael's direction.

Silently, he stroked the valley beneath each of her eyes, wiping the skin dry.

He hadn't touched her in ages. She hadn't been touched by anyone in so long.

"The center," she whispered. "Geary has his appointment on Mondays now. We got a new doctor again."

Michael's face went stony, and he forgot to lower his voice or tamp down the rage in it. "Let's hope he's better than the last one."

CHAPTER THREE

Night air filled her apartment like smoke as Arles continued to stare at her phone. She had no idea how long she'd been looking down at it. Minutes? Hours? Days? Time felt eel-like, slippery in a way it hadn't since she was young.

Dear Ms. Shepherd, a match for your photo has been identified.

Dr. Shepherd, she thought. *I'm a doctor now. All grown up.*

She had been searching for the girl for long enough that she wasn't a girl any longer—both she and Arles grown—and TaskMiner was the company Arles had enlisted to help. She liked the dual meaning in its name: minor online jobs tackled, tedious ones requiring minimal expertise. The TaskMiner logo—a hobbit-shaped figure with a pickax that had always appeared vaguely menacing—preceded the terse message, which was accompanied by an attachment.

Her stomach lurched, and she swallowed a trickle of something acrid, burning.

For decades, what she'd wanted to accomplish had been an impossible task. How to identify one unknown child based on an old picture? The girl could've come from just about anywhere, and even if the two of them happened to live in the same general region, they might never have crossed paths.

Which hadn't stopped Arles from looking everywhere she went, eyes peeled, engaged in boots-on-the-ground, good old-fashioned hunting. It was an eternal, exhausting, never-ending sap to her soul. She didn't meet a single unfamiliar woman—or even glance at one passing by—without trying to crank back time, envision what she might've looked like as a child. Every stranger, each acquaintance, even new clients. Always praying some random encounter would produce the person she was looking for, the happiest and most terrifying coincidence in the world.

Then the world had changed, cracked open, and all manner of things started emerging from the primordial ooze of digital life. She learned to apply reverse-image searches and age-this-child technology, hoping with a somewhat higher degree of realism to stumble upon a match in the vast internet wilderness as opposed to the geological wilds where she lived. But she'd been no more successful virtually than physically. Only TaskMiner, with its massive machines churning away in the cloud, its armies of human drones clicking, had done it.

She couldn't put off opening the attached file any longer. The double click felt like a physical feat. As the image resolved, she lost her breath, the wind knocked out of her as if she'd taken a fall. The child's face in the photograph used to be nearly as familiar as her own, but Arles hadn't examined her copy of the photo—an actual three-by-five-inch print—in so long that this screen version seemed to represent someone new. She stared until the girl's pair of summer-sky eyes wavered, her blonde pigtails went shimmery, and the whole thing blurred behind a veil of tears.

Arles had long since lost hope in her own fruitless searches, and had all but forgotten about the one she'd tasked some faceless, anonymous employee at an internet outfit with carrying out. She hardly registered the forty dollars a month that appeared on her credit card statement, as routine an expense as the contribution to her 401(k). If she did pause to think about the charge, she occasionally considered canceling—surely the endeavor must be pointless after all this time? But then she'd balk and choose to pay the bill, the service fee like a tax on her past.

Now the girl had been found.

Weak morning sunlight had just started to stain the living room its dreary March hue the next time she became alert and aware. Was this what had happened during Flo Galtry's session last week, an erasure of time more prolonged than any Arles had experienced since childhood?

The couch she sat upright on was no more or less comfortable a sleeping arrangement than her futon, purchased back in graduate school, and she frequently spent the night here instead of migrating to her spartan bedroom. But she could tell from her stiff shoulders and aching head that if she'd slept at all, it hadn't been for a very large portion of time.

A plate of spaghetti sat untouched in a gelatinous, cooling lump. At some point, she'd kicked off her shoes, though she still wore yesterday's clothes. Her laptop jumped to life when she twitched her legs against it, then abruptly died. She picked it up. No charge, which meant she must have spent an awful lot of time on it last night.

TaskMiner's email seemed to have led her online, but she had no memory of any pages or sites she had visited, nothing she'd read. And she couldn't afford to delay right now, plug in and re-create her search, not even for something as important as the girl in the photo.

The universe had a caustic sense of humor. It kicked you to the curb when you were just trying to get out of your car. Yesterday she'd experienced a dual punch of whammies.

And it was time to deal with the first.

She drove to WCH and went directly to HR, ignoring the sight of her office when she passed it, closed as tightly as a stitched-up wound. The human resources manager caught sight of Arles through the glass door and beckoned her inside.

"I'm sorry to just show up out of the blue," Arles began, "but I've had a bit of a blow—" She cut herself off upon realizing that Dusky obviously already knew.

"Why don't you have a seat, Dr. Shepherd?" they said.

Coming from Dusky as opposed to Halsey, the suggestion seemed kind. Arles sat.

"Is this . . . allowed? To just let me go?" Her throat thickened with tears, and she inwardly winced. But she couldn't help it. The way she'd phrased it—*let me go*—felt less in that moment like an employment decision and more like being abandoned.

Dusky hesitated, and Arles experienced a candle flicker of hope.

But then they nodded. "Given what happened with your teenage client last year . . ."

Arles stared down at her lap. The incident Dusky meant had been a figurative bullet dodged, and a literal midsession encounter with a knife. Maybe Halsey was right, and Arles wasn't fit to treat patients.

"I probably shouldn't be sharing this," Dusky said, "but I tried to talk Dr. Halsey out of his decision. I know you can't confirm or deny, but you treated my sibling's friend when he was in crisis, and I think you saved his life."

Arles knew the patient Dusky meant. She kept her face blank, which matched the inside of her head right now. She couldn't picture a single step to take, had no clue what to do. With herself or with her life. "I guess I'll need to schedule wrap-up sessions, then? Figure out how to spread my caseload around." Maybe by that point, Halsey would have a change of heart.

"That's already been done," Dusky said softly.

Arles frowned. "But this just happened yesterday. Late in the day, for that matter." Then it hit her. "Or I just learned about it then."

Dusky met her gaze. "Halsey organized the transfers over the weekend."

Arles let out a whistling breath. Either the guy truly had it in for her, or whatever prompted this complaint had been absolutely hair-raising. What the hell had she done to Flo Galtry?

Dusky had been talking without Arles registering it. ". . . accomplish amazing things, and there are other places to do it. Just recently, I learned about this site, sounds more like a wellness retreat than a psychiatric hospital. Why waste your talents here?"

"Am I allowed to see the complaint?" Arles asked abruptly.

Dusky hesitated. "It's meant to go through an official process—you submit a request, a hard copy is printed, but . . ." They turned their computer around. "Paper's dooming the planet."

Arles summoned a smile as she leaned closer to peer at the screen. She didn't realize she was clenching the rim of Dusky's desk until she looked down and saw her whitened fingers. As she began to read, the missing session came back to her with the force of a rock being thrown. This was what she had referred to in her notes, the thing she was supposed to follow up on.

"I'm going to need to make a call," she told Dusky. "As a mandated reporter." If therapists heard something that raised suspicions of abuse, they were required to contact Child Protective Services.

Dusky's eyebrows lifted a question, but before Arles could locate an answer in the milky fog just starting to lift, Dusky slid their telephone forward.

Arles keyed in the number and asked for the CPS worker also named in the complaint. Arles hadn't been the only treatment professional brought under fire.

"This is Liz. Is this Dr. Shepherd?"

Arles began to explain the reason for her call, but Liz interjected, picking up the case where it appeared to have been left off. Clearly, eerily, she and Arles had already spoken. Arles just didn't remember doing so, nor anything about who this person was.

"So, Florence's allegation of abuse was substantiated. Mom refused to ask Dad to leave pending our investigation, so we leaned on Grandma for a temporary placement. Will you continue to be the therapist of record? I'll let you know when outpatient treatment can resume."

"No, I won't," Arles replied quietly. "Whoever does the eval might have a referral."

She sat still, cupping her knees with her hands, so neither body part would tremble. This wasn't like that other time Dusky had referenced. Then, a patient had gotten hurt; now one had been helped. But the vacancy inside Arles that allowed both outcomes to occur was the same. Meaning Halsey was within his rights to be worried. That said, Brittany Galtry had acted out of sheer retaliation, blaming the messengers instead of confronting her child's abuser. Not a new story—in fact, an age-old tale. And consequently, this complaint would've been overturned like a bucket of dirty water if Halsey had given it a minute, the hospital's legal team charged with protecting Arles instead of denouncing her. But she was no longer sure she wanted that.

Flo Galtry had been liberated, even if Arles didn't remember her role in the rescue. Instead of the act being viewed positively—one small triumph in a sea of human suffering, the kind of thing that kept therapists afloat—she'd been fired. Perhaps all the policies and procedures, rules and regulations, the tight lane she had to swim in here at the hospital, meant it wasn't the right place for her anymore. Maybe there was a better place to do what she did.

She had spoken up for Flo. This was going to require speaking up for herself.

Against someone a lot more terrorizing and dominating than Halsey.

A shrunken, shriveled old man.

She couldn't stand to look at the person inside the little red sports car.

The car sat on the side of the road, huffing hot breaths. The vicious, twisted-up face visible through the windshield almost made her close her eyes before she told herself that would be about the dumbest thing she could do.

Don't call yourself dumb. Girls did that a lot. Once she started listening for it, in herself and other kids at school, she heard it all the time.

Ms. Mailer had brought this up in health, which was a stupid class in a lot of ways—just say no; yeah, right—but Ms. Mailer was smart, the best teacher she'd ever had.

She knew how to turn her brain on and off like a light. "Shut it down" might be a better way to put it, like a computer. She'd lose herself to the strains of classical music playing in her head, or a book she was reading. It helped in lots of situations, like when girls were being mean to her.

But it wouldn't help right now. Now she needed to do the opposite. Focus.

The woods formed walls on either side, their branch arms interlaced so tightly, it'd be hard to break through them. He wouldn't let her go that way, anyway.

Her head turned from left to right as she looked around for an escape route. Her backpack hung heavy on her shoulders, weighing her down.

Were the woods a shelter or a trap? She didn't know.

But the driver was gunning his engine. He was coming for her, so she had no choice.

She started to run.

BROKEN BOW

Suspicion had fallen initially on Hochum, Bea's music teacher. Unmarried at thirty-four and a transplant, the latter reason enough to mistrust him. As Cass and every other longtime resident of Cheleo knew, it wasn't sufficient to come from this area, or even for your parents to have been born here. All four grandparents had to call not just the state but this *part* of the state home if you expected to receive anything more than a polite *ayuh*.

As if danger didn't live in Cheleo itself, had to be imported.

Hochum had been giving Bea viola lessons since she was five. Violas produced a warmer, mellower sound than violins, which Bea said she preferred. Cass was embarrassed to admit that he could barely tell the two instruments apart. Back when Bea was small, Hochum had called her a prodigy, although that estimation seemed to have fallen, a by-product of her friend group dissolving, girls who told Bea it was weird to put so much time into playing an instrument. Recently, Hochum had been urging them not to let Bea quit. She might be scholarship material someday at UMaine in Orono, or even Bates or Colby.

Someday.

Though the cost of lessons had started causing him no end of stress, he'd never doubted Hochum about Bea's gift, and he didn't doubt what the man was saying now. Cass had been first to round him up before the police started bringing people in for questioning, and Hochum's reaction when asked if he'd seen Bea had been convincing. First, confusion licked with concern over Cass's mental state, which Hochum had probably seen cracks in lately. *Her lesson is tomorrow, Mr. Monroe, remember?* Then abject fright. Hochum had been in Bea's life for a long time. He knew what her not showing up at home after school meant.

As soon as Hochum was cleared—an airtight alibi from other students, back-to-back lessons all day—the police cast a wider net, even tracking down the kid who drove the tractor that had passed Cass on the road. Cass had pinned some hope on that lead. Young guy, also from away, who'd come to Cheleo for a really strange reason. He had moved here in order to work someone else's land, a rich-as-Croesus freckled redhead who, once he passed puberty, could've grown up to be a banker or a doctor or a lawyer, but for some reason wanted to farm.

He had put up a shed in woods that weren't his. Nailed every board by hand.

The sheriff's office tore that structure apart, two burly deputies entering with guns drawn, causing slats to separate, two-by-fours to fall, as the men turned this way and that, covering each other in the dark space. The kid's construction skills for shit.

Bea wasn't inside. The carrottop had been sleeping there with a couple of goats; you could tell by looking at the hairs. Didn't require a DNA test to prove, no need for a microscope even, although samples had been sent to a laboratory downstate.

In addition to interviewing potential suspects, the local sheriff's office conducted a massive search of the area. Deputies, volunteers, dogs from the K9 unit, even drones overhead—all examining the land between the school and their house in a radius for miles. So minutely that searchers could've reported which trees were starting to bud and how many inches the tiny tributaries of the creeks had risen with snowmelt. FBI agents from the Portland field office had flown up in helicopters. A specialist arrived from the Center for Missing and Exploited Children.

Cass couldn't think about that center without something rising in his gut. He had to put a hand to his mouth to hold back a thick, tarry eruption, even though he hadn't eaten anything.

Bea had been on the bus just like normal. It'd let her off as usual, not a thousand yards from their house, maybe while Cass had been taking his little catnap. How he loathed himself for that nap, for losing his job—for a thousand other failures.

The driver, Gus, remembered calling out goodbye, his window lowered to let in air just starting to lose its winter bite. He'd been trying to be extra nice to Bea lately, he told the police, because the other children on the bus had been giving her a hard time.

Cass loathed those children too.

Loathed everyone because he couldn't loathe the monster who had done this to Bea.

Done what to Bea?

This time, he couldn't keep parts of him from erupting: bodily fluids, bile, tissue from his guts and raw, cried-out throat.

A night passed. Somehow, it passed.

Maggie was a husk of herself, the carapace of some creature who had fled its body.

He didn't know where she had slept. Or if she had slept.

He had met her during one hopeful if ultimately pointless semester at college, a princess not just from downstate but out of state, and he still loved her, right beside Bea, two halves of his heart. Even if their decision to get married, made during the springtime of his life, was a memory he sometimes forgot, buried beneath the weight of work, then not-work, years gone by, circumstances changing, the accumulation of age. He wasn't sure the two of them were going to be able to survive this. Not if Bea didn't.

When he descended the stairs around dawn, she ran at him, both fists knotted. Hands he had once loved to hold, used to stroke and pat and just casually touch. Pretty hands with seashell nails, their own natural shade of pink; she didn't even put on polish.

"You're not doing anything!" she shrieked. "Why are you standing here doing nothing?"

He lifted his wrist, as heavy as the handle of an axe. Five a.m. The sun just starting to silver the sky through the windows.

"Get out there!" Maggie screamed. "Get out—"

She pushed him, but when he looked down, her hands weren't making contact with his body. It was the volume of her cry, the force of her feeling, that sent him stumbling backward, opening the door with one hand behind him, then reeling out into the early-morning hush.

Although Maggie didn't know it, he hadn't been doing nothing since yesterday. Even if she had been aware of what he was up to, though, it wouldn't have offset the enormous load of his ineffectuality; what he'd done barely counted even to himself. Just a way to use up the endless hours, keep every second from etching itself into his skin until his body was too scored to function. A walk right now would be a more tangible eater of time.

He chose to head into the woods, a place he and Bea in their different ways both loved. He hunted every season, one tag for a buck. A rack to mount and enough venison to last the year, after splitting it with the neighbor up the road who dressed it. Bea didn't hunt, of course, but she wandered here. Thought her thoughts, planned her plans, dreamed her dreams.

This acreage had been scraped and scoured by man and dog and drone. Boots thudding, canines sniffing, space-age devices circling. The latter getting decent shots, leaf cover minimal this time of year. He paused with the flat of one hand on a tree, catching his breath. Thinking about that drone searching from overhead had brought something to mind. Bea's cave.

When she was younger, Bea used to take her dolls there, spread out a blanket, and feed them a picnic. And as she grew up, she'd go with a book or with nothing at all. He once found her diary nestled in a cleft of rock. Could've gotten damp, so he'd carried it back carefully, flat on his palm like a precious jewel. Bea would be able to tell he hadn't fumbled with the lock, read any of her private jottings. He made sure she only went there in the summer or early fall when no bear or mountain cat would be making its den. Springtime was doubly off-limits—the cave flooded with snowmelt that came in from higher ground through openings far beneath the earth.

Water could throw a dog off a scent.

Cass reversed direction. At the lip of the cave, he ducked low, stomping through inches of watery accumulation. Blinking to let his eyes adjust, he bucked to a stop, nearly slipping on the slick surface. He had to wobble in place, pitching back and forth, so as not to disrupt what he saw. Or thought he saw, the light in here dim, his heart banging hard enough to scatter his vision.

In his mind, there was only one thing to do. Get Maggie.

"Cass, tell me, what is it?" she cried as they ran. "Slow down, you're going to give yourself a heart attack!" She clawed at his back, but he shook her off and didn't alter his pace.

"They searched these woods!" A sob hitched her shout. "They looked here, dammit!"

Her voice trembled; he could tell she was on the verge of giving up, about to come to a stop and just refuse to go on. She didn't know about this cave—probably would've stopped Bea from going near it if she had—so she didn't have any idea where they were headed. It was exhausting to keep batting back branches, to trudge up and down over rocks and roots and past obstacles as dense and unrelenting as this terrain held. Too late it hit him: They should've come down from the road. Less bushwhacking.

He would carry her if he had to.

Before returning to the house, he had stripped off his shirt and laid it on the floor of the cave in order to mark the location of the object he'd spotted. *Thought* he had spotted. His chest and arms were now bloodied by sticks, his back raked with scratches from Maggie's fingertips. Couldn't be more than forty degrees out, but he was as hot as if he stood beneath a baking sun. Sweat coated his bare skin, matted the hairs.

"Cass!" she cried from behind, her voice fainter now. She was losing ground.

He ducked beneath the overhang of rock, then thrust one arm out like a spear and pointed.

Heard her tiptoe in, little splashes through the standing water.

"That's—" Suddenly, she dived, arms outstretched, reaching.

He yanked her back so fast, her slight form swung in his grasp, and she fought him, attempting to get loose.

"Can't disturb it, Mags!" Wrestling her, their tussle, had him breathing too hard for clear speech. "Have to keep the scene intact! Get the sheriff back . . . out here. Call Brawley!"

She rounded on him. "But that looks like hair! Oh God, is that Bea's—"

He could finally speak, though he was still panting. "No! I don't think so!"

Maggie looked as baffled as he had felt trying to resolve the nature of what lay in a trickle of water across a section of rock. Long strands, like seaweed, nearly washed away.

"Not human hair, anyway," he said.

Her face clenched, angry, confused.

"Horsehair, maybe." He aimed his gaze downward. "I think that's floss from Bea's bow."

CHAPTER FOUR

Wedeskyull Community Hospital occupied space outside town, hulking on a hill just before the mountains took over. Arles thought of the hospital as a castle rampart, keeping the village within its embrace, though as she drove away for what might be the last time, she found that estimation falling. Now it was just a building, disappearing into the distance, into her past.

The residential road she came to felt shadowy and cold, despite the sun lifting itself in the sky, midmorning now, with spring finally more than a whisper. After parking, she stayed seated, balling her hands, curling her toes in her shoes. At last, she drew in a ragged breath and reached for the door handle. The mechanism felt unfamiliar in her grasp, tricky to work. She got out of the car as if bursting free from a grave, although the real burial site stood across the street.

The house wasn't large—nothing compared to the place she planned to make hers today if things went well here—but it loomed over her in an outsize way, its nose of roof and peaked tops of dormers suggesting a glare. Every step seemed to take her farther away instead of bringing her closer, like a CGI effect. She couldn't tell if the house was receding, or she was.

Becca met her at the side entrance. She and Arles had held confabs on this deck ever since Arles had finally cried mercy and hired a full-time home health aide for her stepfather. At first, these chats had been fairly formal, Becca giving reports. Med changes, symptom progression, and the like. But before long, Becca, who hoped to become an occupational therapist one day, had begun asking Arles for career advice, and over time her questions morphed into personal revelations, confidences such that by now, Arles knew her as well as she did some of her patients.

Today Becca's face looked withered; she wrung a cloth between her hands as the two of them exchanged greetings.

"Tough night?" Arles asked. "He not doing well?"

Tears swelled in Becca's eyes. "You know I love that man like my own father. And I've hoped it wouldn't come to this. But I don't think he can be managed at home much longer."

Arles turned away, facing abandoned flowerpots and dried-out beds in the garden to prevent Becca from reading her expression.

"But I want you to know . . ." Becca's tone was imploring. "I've been interviewing for jobs, and there are places your stepdad could go that don't even seem like care facilities, really. They're more like wellness spas, services you wouldn't believe . . ."

Wellness retreat, she heard Dusky say. Mirror voices, spurring Arles on.

Save for one particular situation, Arles normally avoided physical contact as if other human beings carried hemorrhagic viruses. But in that moment, something overcame her, and she reached out and touched Becca on the shoulder. "I'm very grateful for what you've done for my stepfather. I'll give him the news." And she entered the house.

Peter sat in an old sagging armchair positioned in front of a picture window. Both he and her mother had always cherished their views. The compound Arles had come here to get, or get back, was rich with expanses. Literally so—multimillion-dollar vistas. But even this second home in town, with its smallish lawn-stamped backyard, pleased Peter. He wouldn't leave gently.

"Hello," Arles said, pulling up a wooden desk chair and sinking into it beside him.

He turned his whittled head slowly. "Pam? Who is that? Janey, is that you?"

The first her mother, dead for a while now. The second his estranged daughter, whom his first wife didn't permit him to see after their divorce.

Peter looked as if he'd aged years in the months since Arles had last paid a visit. Eyes fogged, hair sparser, pounds gone from his body. But his vision seemed to clear as he peered at her.

"Nuh," she began, knowing he'd detect the tremor in her voice. She started over again, stronger. "No. It's me. Let's talk about Fir Cove." The spread of land that should've been hers.

"Not again." He took in a rattling breath. "You know I can't do a thing about it."

On this subject, he was always cut-glass clear. No matter what disease process calcified her stepfather's brain, she was pretty sure he would never grow confused about this.

"Your mother did not want you to have it, little girl," he said, his voice a gavel, confirming her assessment of his mental state. "She didn't even want you spending *time* there. Once I've made my earthly departure, Fir Cove will be left to the state in perpetuity, land forever wild, house listed on the historic registry. I will not go against my late wife's final wishes."

This last uttered with a prim properness that made the hairs on the back of her neck twitch. "You always did care so much about respecting Mom," she said, relieved to hear a bite back in her tone and hoping sarcasm wasn't beyond his cognition, which actually didn't seem too impaired right now. She wondered if he was messing with poor Becca.

He shifted in his chair. "I don't know what you're talking about, dear."

The word entered her chest like a spike. He'd never used anything besides *little girl* as a term of endearment. *Dear*. Deer. Her stepfather used to take her along on his annual hunt on the grounds of Fir Cove. One tag, one buck. He bagged only males; the kill probably made him feel like more of a man himself.

She rose on shaking legs to teeter over him in his chair. "The world has changed, you know. It's different now. You think you're safe because you're old? What you did back then matters. People care." Some people. Still nowhere near enough of them. "So you might want to rethink this noble upholding of my mother's hand-from-the-grave slap in my face."

Her stepfather craned his head up at her, creasing the loose skin on his neck. "Has the world changed enough that it will listen to one tightly wrapped woman who had to earn a degree just to try and prove she was worth something? Take your word over what a man like me says? You seem to have forgotten who I know in this town."

Arles stared at him until she felt her vision cloud over.

He wasn't done. "What would you even do with the place? It's not safe for a woman out there on her own. A hundred ways you could get hurt—or someone could hurt you."

She couldn't tell if it was a threat. A warning from this wretched old man who once posed enough danger in his home that she couldn't sleep there, couldn't eat, couldn't use the bathroom on the worst days. She braced herself against the desk, wishing she had the strength to encase his skinny chicken throat with her hands.

He looked away, apparently satisfied.

She left the security of her position, taking one steady, measured step. "Your aide is worried about your condition, Peter. She suggested I put you in a facility."

He turned back in her direction, and he did appear senile then, demented and very old.

As if on cue, Becca came running into the room. "Mr. H.! We're overdue to take your blood pressure." She unrolled the cuff with a scuffing sound.

"I'm worried it might be elevated," Arles said. "He seems to have gotten upset."

Her stepfather shifted slowly in his seat. After a moment, he lifted one arm.

Becca wrapped the sleeve around Peter's scrawny, gooseneck bicep. "You mean you told him?" she mouthed before adding, "Oh, hey, I forgot to mention something before. An update on my situation. I'll fill you in later." She sent a significant look in Peter's direction.

Arles didn't usually mind providing informal counseling, but the thought of prolonging this visit prompted a full-body quake. "Oh, don't worry about him." She hoped Becca wouldn't detect the vitriol in her voice. "Like you said, he's so addled, I'm sure he won't understand a word you tell me." Although he hadn't actually seemed all that much so during this encounter.

Becca made a sad face, then nodded. "So, my uncle? They refused his parole request."

Arles opened her mouth with an audible intake of air, as if bursting to the surface of a body of water. Because she suddenly saw a way to force Peter's hand. What would Becca do if she learned that the sweet old man she took care of was guilty of the same crime she'd put her uncle behind bars for? Loved like a father—wasn't that what Becca had said? Well, an old-age home would be a luxe resort compared to the cell where this dear old dad deserved to live out his days.

"Dr. S.? You okay?" Becca let out a laugh. "Can't have two patients on my hands."

"What good news," Arles replied, painting her voice with a trill. "Do you remember that trial, Peter?" It had made small-town headlines. She switched her focus to Becca, deliberately darkening her tone. "Probably doesn't. His mind was already starting to go when you testified against your uncle"—a barbed look at her stepfather—"and they found him guilty."

The aide nodded, equally somber.

Peter let out a pained squawk as the cuff continued to compress his upper arm.

Becca startled, her fist unclenching. "I'm so sorry, Mr. H.!" The blood pressure device released with a sigh. "I got distracted!"

The wattle at Peter's neck quivered. He sagged in his seat.

Becca was frowning over the reading. "You're right, Dr. S. It *is* high today."

Arles stared down at her stepfather. He refused to meet her gaze, appearing to focus on something long gone and very far off. But she had the sense that he remembered everything. The trial that sent Becca's uncle away, Arles's childhood, as distant as another country—all of it.

He cleared his throat wetly. "The keys you'll be wanting are on my ring, dear."

Arles turned to Becca, aping surprise.

"Left side of the desk, top drawer. I'll call the Nat Trust today. Get everything set up."

Becca removed the cuff with a Velcro rasp. "Mr. H.! Glad I didn't do any damage! You sound like a new man. So clear and firm."

"He really does," Arles agreed, hoping Becca would attribute the joy in her voice to their mutual relief over old Mr. H.'s improvement. "Completely lucid. And so sure of himself. Should we put a pin in what we were discussing earlier? Revisit the decision in a few months?"

The aide appeared to give the matter deep consideration. "I think that could work."

Arles turned, crossed to her stepfather's desk, and took out her new set of keys.

CHAPTER FIVE

Louise normally tried to sneak in errands around school, shifts at work, and Geary's various appointments, but on Tuesday, there were a ton of walk-ins at the salon, and she didn't make it to the supermarket in time. She decided to allow Geary to wait in the car while she shopped. The sun was out, and he could look at the windshield for hours, studying the specks of dirt and bug bits illuminated on the glass. At ten, he was practically old enough for this to be legal, anyway. And if he—or she—ever got caught, Louise was fully prepared to let the cop or good Samaritan find out how Geary reacted when forced to enter a store.

She left the radio on—exposure to varied forms of verbal stimulation was part of Geary's therapy—then hurried down the aisles, grabbing items. Cereal, fruit . . . They were out of peanut butter and low on ketchup; she'd do chicken tonight since it was on special. Keeping an eye out for someone running through the store in search of a missing parent—*There's a kid outside throwing a fit*—while listening for the overhead system to announce the same thing.

She got in line at the register as the person before her moved up.

Had she taken too long, been self-indulgent with a little *her* time? She was doing the weekly shopping; it wasn't as if she were at a spa. The person before her was paying now, choosing between an assortment of AmEx and Visa and Discover as if he held a pack of playing cards.

Someone came racing in through the exit doors, her head turning from side to side, and Louise's heart gave a hard, painful knock in her chest.

A supermarket employee rushed over. "I'm sorry, you can't come in this way—"

Louise took a step forward to cut the woman off. Her mouth half-open to fling out an apology—*It's okay; he does this*—while preparing to run out to Geary. She'd have to leave her groceries behind, find some other time to go shopping—

"But I forgot raisins!" the woman cried, edging past the employee, who let her go.

Louise's knees bent involuntarily; she had to lean against the side of the conveyer belt for support. Refusing to join the excited thrum of voices: *Can you believe that woman? What a Karen. Talk about entitled.* Well, for all they knew, Karen had a kid who'd raise holy hell if his mother ran out of raisins. None of these people clucking their tongues, feeling superior, had a clue. Their children sat in the seat of the cart, or walked along beside it. Maybe even went off on their own to collect a few needed items. The worst thing that might happen would be a tantrum if the kid wasn't allowed to buy a certain brand of cereal or flavor of ice cream.

These parents worried about stupid stuff because they had nothing real to fear. A child going missing, getting kidnapped? At age two, Louise's child had been stolen, in a way—parts of him at least, although really, it was more like she and he were locked away from each other. Inhabited two separate worlds, Geary's unknowable, and as distant as another planet. Sometimes she saw her son like an astronaut in outer space, exposed to conditions she wouldn't have been able to tolerate, operating complicated controls she would've had no chance of understanding. At other times, she realized she was the one adrift.

She began placing items on the belt. No credit card, but at least she could pay from a gratifyingly fat wedge of bills. Walk-ins at Glam & Go tended to tip well. She helped the clerk bag, then rolled her cart across the lot, setting everything in the trunk gently to avoid rocking the car. Then she sat down in front, turning off the blare of voices on the radio. She didn't need more bad news in her life.

She took a cautious look in the mirror, avoiding eye contact. Geary sat in his booster, blinking at a shaft of sinking sun. He must've been staring at it for some time; his eyes were watering, tears rolling down his pale, freckled cheeks.

Suddenly she aimed another look in her son's direction, less careful this time.

Geary looked like he was crying.

How she wished she could simply ask him.

Geary, did something upset you? Or were your eyes just streaming from the sun?

Come to think of it: *Why do you stare at the sun so much? What's that dust thing all about?*

It wasn't that she didn't talk to her son. In fact, she'd always been like those parents of coma patients who had conversations or read or sang to their offspring until one day the patients woke up and said they'd heard every word. Which was an offensive comparison, the kind of thing only a neurotypical would think. Geary was *more* awake than a lot of people, alert to things they didn't even pick up on. Sensory experiences, but possibly other stuff too. She'd always had the feeling—call it mother's instinct—that there was a great deal going on in Geary's mind. But she had no clue how to figure out what it was, and the puzzle nearly drove her mad.

What could've possibly disturbed him? He'd just been waiting for her in the car.

A hush fell as the sun settled in the sky, and she started to drive.

Maybe they would have one of their peaceful nights. She would fix chicken, usually a good choice. It was smooth, shredded or cut into pieces instead of breaking into bits. Anything on toast—grilled cheese, for example—was the worst. Crumbs sent Geary to an inconsolable place.

She changed lanes, a hookworm of worry still probing her insides. She gave the mirror another eyelids-partly-lowered glance to see that Geary had drifted off to sleep, silvery trails of tears glistening on his cheeks. If he didn't wake up soon, it would mess up the dinner hour, then bedtime, the strictly ordered routine that was supposed to make adapting to the pace and clock of a neurotypical world easier for Geary. Still, this was a rare treat. A peaceful drive, not late for school or work, no therapy appointment to get to, her child sleeping in the car. She took her eyes off the road, permitting herself to gaze at him.

He was still out by the time they got home. She parked on the side of the street and stared at the last thread of light until the houses on the street were all shrouded. The lamp on their stoop had blown out, but she hadn't gotten a chance to climb up on a ladder, or nag the landlord. Suddenly, shamefully, her own tears overflowed. So many tasks left to tackle tonight before she'd get a second to see to that bulb, let alone have any downtime.

Twin headlights filled the deepening dusk, and she gave a harsh swipe to her eyes while at the same time, Geary's flashed open. The vehicle behind them drew too close, its front fender crunching her rear bumper and jolting the car. She let out a startled shout before catching herself and sucking in her breath. Froze with her hands on the wheel.

As soundlessly as possible, she nudged the door open. An encounter with some oblivious driver was not what she needed. Examining damage, exchanging insurance information, arguing, even apologies—all of that took time she didn't have right now.

As she got out, Michael emerged from his truck, holding Geary's puffy coat in one hand. "He left this behind yesterday. Hope he didn't freak without it. I couldn't get away till now; it's been nuts at the plant."

"You hit me," she said.

"I assume you mean the car," he replied. He held up his phone, briefly lighting the night. "Sorry. I'll hammer out the ding. I got a text."

"Great. You were texting while driving *and* potentially causing our son to melt."

Geary got out and raced across the street. He clopped up the sagging porch steps, tripping on the uneven one, then stood at the front door, fiddling with the knob. She hurried after him.

"I don't think Geary needs me for that," said Michael, following.

A darkness overcame her, too thick to penetrate. She tensed her hands as if to claw something apart. This night, the wreck of her marriage, her life. But Geary was waiting patiently, despite his obvious desire to get inside, and she refused to upset him by fighting with Michael.

"Thanks for bringing his coat," she said at last. "Want to come in?"

She clenched her keys in her fist to keep them from swinging against each other. Forget the jingle of keys on a ring, Geary could detect the *ting* made by one key just touching another. Geary's teacher had said that the sound might be as loud as the clanging of a bell to him.

She parted the door from its jamb, entering the house in front of Michael. They stopped with their backs to the wall as Geary darted inside and arrow-shot straight up the stairs without any coaching from her or cycling through the strategies she'd learned from therapists.

She let out a long, loud exhale. "Want to stay for dinner? We're having chicken."

"I think Geary might've gotten upset earlier today," she told Michael once the meal had been eaten and she'd started to clean up. "In the car at the supermarket."

The look he gave her was as easy to read as a text.

What else is new?

"No," she said. "I mean . . . this was different."

Michael cleared the table, balancing Geary's milk cup and their soda glasses on a stack of plates. "Different how?"

"It was like something made him sad. He was . . . Well, it looked like he was crying."

Michael's face closed as tightly as a fist. "That's not possible. Geary doesn't have those kinds of emotional responses."

"I know that." She dropped a fistful of forks and knives in the sink.

"Do you?" As if to remove the sting from his words, Michael reached into the water, his hand hot and soapy as it slid against hers, feeling for the sponge.

Something equally hot climbed up her face, and she turned away before he could see. Ridiculous to blush like a schoolgirl with the man she had made a child with, the man who'd left them both behind.

Then again, why had Michael come over tonight after a long day at the job he'd gone out of his way to say was crazy at the moment? Was it really to bring Geary's coat? Their son did rely on the thing long past the season—it was what one therapist had called a favored item—but the weather was getting hot early this year. Probably true that the planet was in trouble.

Michael set the last dish in the drainer. "What do you think he does up there?"

A bold impulse took hold. She usually devoted as much planning as it took to launch a space shuttle before entering Geary's room. "Let's go see."

They climbed the stairs together, their steps slow and deliberate. Louise felt Michael's bulk behind her. The flight groaned, sinking beneath their combined weight.

Geary was leaning against his desk as she and Michael came to a stop in the doorway. The peaks of his knobby shoulders rose up and down, his stomach ballooning and deflating, although he stood as stiffly as a pole. The room was dim—Geary never turned on lights; the glare seemed to bother him—and very still, as motionless as Geary. It felt cold, as if enormous, icy breaths came from inside, something bigger than all of them chilling the hallway.

Louise looked at Michael. "Do you feel that?"

"Feel what?"

But she was unable to say. Turn the heat up, Michael would've told her if she'd tried to explain. He was always trying to fix whatever problem—never mind that the furnace was already set to seventy. Never mind that some problems couldn't be solved, couldn't even be understood.

She scrubbed her palms together in an effort to rid her skin of its chill.

What could've happened to make Geary cry earlier? Michael didn't even believe that he had, and dozens of therapists would've agreed with him. So what gave her any faith in her own judgment? She'd been told she was wrong about Geary ever since he was two years old.

"I don't feel anything." Michael's shoulders slumped. "I was hoping he was gaming."

The computer sat dead and dark on the desk.

"I don't think so," Louise said quietly. "Geary doesn't know how to use that yet." She aimed a smile toward the air above their son's head. *Which is perfectly okay.* The laptop had been a big spend, a splurge; Geary would need it if he caught up to grade level by next year.

Michael turned and began to trudge back down the hall.

"Why don't you tell him goodbye?" Louise said after his retreating back.

He stopped. "Why would I do that?"

She remained in place by the door. "Daddy's leaving, Gear. He's got to go home now."

"Cut it out, Lou."

She swiveled to face him. "Why? Because you feel guilty? About this not being home for you anymore?"

"Because he doesn't understand a fucking word you're saying!"

She took a quick step forward. "But I talk to him all the time! And I swear he gets it. Or if he doesn't right now, I act like one day he will."

"I know you do. I remember you doing it. Always drove me fucking crazy."

"But we have no idea what's going on in his head! It might be way different than you think!"

"Keep dreaming, Lou. That kind of false hope might work for you, but the only way I get up in the morning is by knowing exactly what my kid is and what he isn't—"

"Stop saying that!" she pleaded. "We don't *know* who he is! That's the hardest part!"

"I could do anything in front of Geary, and it wouldn't make a difference. Turn in a circle and sing, strip myself naked, whatever."

She closed the remaining distance between them. "That's not true."

He turned away for a moment, and when he looked back, his eyes were gleaming. "I love him too, you know."

She reached up and touched the wells beneath his eyes. Her fingers came away wet.

He grabbed her hand so suddenly, it took her a second to register what he'd done. They both looked down at their conjoined fingers.

"Christ, Lou. You've always been so beautiful."

A deep flush suffused her, heat coming up from parts of her body she'd forgotten she had. And then suddenly, they were yanking at clothes, drawing them up, pulling them off, so that they fell to the floor in a scattered trail that led to her bedroom, their bedroom, the room they used to share. But she stopped before they got there.

"Do this here. Whatever we're doing. Here in the hall, if it makes no difference to Geary."

"Christ," Michael muttered, tugging at a stubborn sock. "Let it go, can't you?"

She grabbed the sock and gave it a hard enough jerk that Michael stumbled backward.

"Tell me it matters," she breathed. "Please. Say that it matters."

He took her face between his palms, lowering his mouth to hers. "It matters." Starting to kiss her, the two of them walking as one, and sinking down onto the bed. "This matters."

He had always done incredible things with his hands, and as they slid between her legs, the skin there already slippery, she gave herself over to the one part they had never failed to get right. A sound rose up from her throat—she fought to quiet it but couldn't, and she just had to hope that Geary wouldn't hear them. And then she forgot to hope anything, so intent was she on herself, her own experience, the incoming wave.

She shuddered to a climax beneath Michael's expert, probing fingers. He kept touching her gently, with no urgency to it, until the last ripple passed, and she lay still in his arms.

She trailed her hand over the hair on his stomach.

"Lou," he said, voice gruff. "We can't do this."

"I'm not sure all of you is in agreement about that," she teased, reaching down.

Michael eased her hand away and sat up. "I have to tell you something."

She sat up too, blanket pooling around her. "Now? What is it?" A quick catch in her throat. "Is it about Geary?"

"Christ, no, it's not about Geary." Michael scrubbed at his face. "Or maybe it is. Maybe everything always being about Geary is why I have to tell you what I do. Why we're here."

"Why we're where?" She clutched the blanket to her naked chest. "Where are we?"

"I'm—I've met someone," he said. "It's getting pretty serious."

She let out a laugh that was instantly consumed by a flame of fury. "You're telling me you're in a new relationship right after finger-fucking me for the first time since our divorce?"

"Lou." He got out of bed and headed over to the doorway. "Don't."

She snatched up a towel, discarded from her shower that morning, and covered herself in case Geary's door was still open. Then she followed Michael out of the room.

The sight of him naked, wilting as he crouched on the floor to separate their clothes, unleashed a jealousy so savage, it felt alive. Michael in love. Doing to some other woman what he'd just done to her. Or, oh God, having a child with this woman, a typical, talking son—

"Get out," she said.

He pulled his shirt over his head.

"Get out!" she screamed.

"Lou, look. It's been two years. And you knew we were through even before we split—"

Her shriek boiling over, she began slapping at his back, his arms, his ass.

"All right, okay, Christ, I'm going—" Michael hobbled along the hallway, boxers twisted around his ankles as he stooped for his pants and scrambled toward the stairwell.

From his room, Geary started to hum and holler, building to a grievous howl.

CHAPTER SIX

As soon as she made it out of her stepfather's house, Arles felt her phone leap to life inside her bag, vibrating like a swarm of insects. She sat down in the front seat of her car and touched her fingertip to the screen. It was Facebook suggesting a dozen groups she might also be interested in. Parents of Neurodivergent Children, Actually Autistic, tactile sensation collectives in the greater New York City area. Only problem was, Arles wasn't a parent, she lived in the North Country, and never trawled FB. She loathed social media. A handful of dating apps was it, used out of sheer necessity, as unpleasurable and utilitarian a tool as a nailbrush.

Her exploits the night before. They must've led to this.

As urgent as she felt to get to Fir Cove now that it was hers, Arles needed to revisit whatever it was she'd been doing online, why she had spent enough time deep-sea diving that her laptop had died. And she couldn't do it from Fir Cove; its location was lost to the mountains. No connectivity, the whole spread as muffled from the outside world as a ship adrift at sea.

A hundred ways a woman could get hurt. Her stepfather's voice in her head.

Yeah, well, she retorted, here in modernity, there were a thousand. Ten thousand.

She gave her phone a rough shake, then opened the email that had felled her last night.

TaskMiner had attached a digital duplicate of the three-by-five-inch photo Arles owned, showing the face and upper torso of a young girl, and they'd also included a URL. The link took Arles to a Facebook group for parents whose kids lived with a mental health diagnosis, and the page that had gotten the attention of TaskMiner's search engine read—

> **Okay, parents! Who has a picture of themselves at the same age as their DC with their big double-digit birthday approaching?**

DC. *Dear child.*

The young girl Arles had been seeking for so long was a mother. With a child of ten, the same age she herself had been in the photograph Arles had held on to for most of her life.

And that kid utilized mental health resources, which gave Arles something of a reason to reach out, although not really, since patients were supposed to contact therapists, not the reverse. Also, mother and child lived nowhere near Wedeskyull's catchment area; according to Facebook, they were downstate. Still, the tie between her and Arles was starting to feel preordained. As were other things—TaskMiner, getting fired, as well as the glinting, fairylike possibility birthed by having secured Fir Cove. Practice elsewhere, Dusky had suggested, planting a seed.

Arles could set up the psychological equivalent of the wellness center both they and Becca in different ways had referenced. A magic mountain for the mind, a place where people would come to heal, recover from their pasts, improve their lives.

One person in particular. If TaskMiner hadn't identified the girl from the photograph, then Arles would be sitting in a puddle right now, sour and defeated. Instead, she'd been given the chance to rise. The only remaining question was, How? She had no excuse for contacting a mother hundreds of miles away, one whose child wasn't even a patient.

You're not fit to do this anyway.

Her stepfather's words a puff of foul air in her ear again.

A woman who had to earn a degree just to try and prove she was worth something.

So many men used a woman's accomplishments against her, took her strength and tried to take her down. And woe be it if she had the rare moment of weakness. That could never be allowed.

Another voice, this one courtesy of Halsey.

It happened again. Meaning: *Patients aren't safe around you.*

Florence Galtry hadn't been the first patient to cause Arles to lose time. There might even be more than two—how would she know?

You saved *Flo Galtry.*

That voice, her own.

Flo is living with her sweet old granny instead of her abusive POS father, thanks to you.

Arles scrubbed her eyes and refocused on her phone.

The things people chose to confide online seemed far too personal and intimate to forgo the shackles and protection of confidentiality, but after some scrutiny, she saw a way to make the needed connection. On the firm footing of professional grounds, with a collegial contact.

The DC's recently assigned psychotherapist, mentioned with vague resignation.

Trying a new one. Again.

Using back channels to track down someone's therapist wasn't exactly codified in the *How to Be a Good Clinician* handbook. All right, it was plain unethical behavior. Arles grappled with it as she fished around in the glove compartment and found a stale half of a granola bar. This course of action, while admittedly unorthodox, could in a way be justified, she decided as she chewed. The woman in the photograph was clearly struggling. Online, she spoke about being handed off to therapist after therapist, all unable to provide the help her son needed.

And if nothing else, Arles was a damn good clinician.

The easiest place to cyberstalk a clinician was a site called RateMyTherapist.com. Arles herself had over a hundred reviews; she'd earned a 3.9 star rating. (Halsey's was three-tenths of a point lower.) Trager was the name of the psychotherapist mentioned in the Facebook group, and he didn't have many reviews. In the ones that had been left, complaints focused less on the guy's approach to treatment than on concern over the fact that he transferred clients before therapy had a chance to progress. He seemed to change jobs almost like people changed clothes.

Which could be seen as a red flag. Therapy was a long-term kind of business.

With a little googling, she found him at a center north of New York City. Arles didn't know the suburbs downstate, but this one didn't appear to be the kind of glitzy, glamorous town where houses had six bedrooms and the garages held three cars.

She wrote up a question for a beehive-active listserv where she normally just lurked, figuring anyone who'd moved around as often as Trager would've encountered a fair number of practitioners over the years. Within a few minutes, her post had garnered responses.

> Keep any patient you have far away from the guy. And I'd even stay clear of him yourself.

> There's a reason he gets shunted around like a troop leader the BSA wants to protect.

> I'm amazed that man is still alive professionally.

> He shouldn't be sanctioned or suspended—he should be prosecuted.

Most damning of all—

> **I took over his caseload, and most of his clients met the criteria for therapeutic trauma.**

Suddenly, Arles wasn't crossing any ethical lines—in fact, *not* acting would constitute a dereliction of duty. She owed it to the woman in the photo to get her son away from this fraud.

She placed a call to the treatment center and was put on hold without a word. Anodyne music abraded her ears like a mosquito's whine.

"I'm looking for Scott Trager," she said once her hold time was finally up.

An unpleasant laugh. "That right? Well, he's in with a patient. So keep looking."

More than once in her career, Arles had dealt with admins who wielded puny power against those facing tough times in their lives. "You may want to interrupt him for this," she said. Intruding on Trager's session shouldn't cause any harm—it might even help whoever was in there. "Tell him I'm the teacher of the child he saw recently. He'll know who I mean and why I'm calling."

A shot in the dark, but one Arles thought had a chance at working. Trager treated children. And children had teachers. On hold again, she brought up the center's employee listing, hoping to identify the person who'd answered her call. A brassy-haired woman with the title of head administrator and a sly, sharp look in her eyes seemed a good bet.

After a minute or two, the admin returned and said she would put Arles through.

"Dee?" Arles got in before being transferred.

A brief pause. "Yes?"

"Be kinder to the patients you encounter. They have it rough, and you make it rougher."

"I don't know what—" A tone of outrage. "I have no idea what you mean!"

"Yes, you do," Arles said. "Now give me Trager."

The therapist answered in a high, nasally tone. Not a sound well suited to therapy.

"This is Scott Trager," he said. "With whom am I speaking?"

She kept quiet. It was a tactic that could get the most recalcitrant patients speaking.

"Hello?" he said. "Is this Oscar's teacher?"

Briefly, Arles shut her eyes. She wondered what he'd done to poor Oscar. "No. It isn't."

"I'm sorry? Who is this, then?"

Again, she kept quiet.

"I'm going to hang up. You interrupted me in the middle of session. I thought you were somebody else—"

"I know what you thought," she said. "Did you send your patient out of the room? Or are they still sitting there?"

"What do you care? Who the hell is this?"

"I'll take from your profane reply that you did the former," she said. "Smart."

Now Trager was the one not to say anything.

"My name is Dr. Arles Shepherd," she said. "I practice psychology upstate."

"And I'm supposed to care why?" he squeaked.

She wondered whether he always sounded this annoying, or if confusion had lent him the vocal cords of a boy in the throes of puberty. "Because you recently took on a case that I'd like you to refer to me."

He let out a high-pitched laugh. "Uh-huh. And why would I do that? First of all, you haven't exactly gotten things off on a high note. And second, that's a rather unethical move. If you were really a psychologist, you'd know that."

"You're not in a position to question anyone's ethics, Scott," she said. "You can check my credentials before making the referral. Google me."

He was silent for a second. "Just what is it you think you know about me?"

"More than you'd like to come out," she replied. Vague, could mean anything, but Trager would fill in the holes. "Like why you left your last position so suddenly."

"I did not hit that girl! It was a firm pat at most—and it got her behavior under control, or would have, if her hysterical mother hadn't raised such a fuss—"

Arles spoke as if he hadn't said a word, her voice so cold, she pictured it encasing the man in ice. "I can get enough former patients of yours to levy complaints that you'll spend the rest of your career under investigation, if not in prison. What you described, FYI, is assault of a child. Legally speaking."

Trager snorted. "No one has ever lodged a complaint against me."

"Oh, I'll bet they have," she said. "If not to the board, then to whichever miserable facility happens to be employing you. Which agrees to accept your resignation in lieu of passing things up the line—thereby saving themselves a world of trouble over their hiring practices and questionable staff—while telling the patient, who doesn't understand they have recourse to other options, that you've been let go, which makes them feel like their issue has been addressed." She paused. "Do I have that about right?"

Silence for a beat, and then: "I just found you online. Upstate is right. How on earth would somebody who receives treatment at this place come see you? It's not like they can travel up and down weekly for sessions. Trip takes almost five hours, according to Google."

"Tell them you've heard about a new form of treatment," she replied. "It's residential, and if they choose to take part—taking time away from work and school and other activities—the clinician believes they'll stand a good chance of returning to their regular lives with significantly greater self-understanding and improvements in functioning."

"I have to say, you sound like a nutjob to me."

"Given that I suspect your diagnostic skills leave something to be desired, I'll try not to be too shaken by that assessment."

Trager took in a strangled breath. "Let's say I do make this referral. You'll leave me alone? No more calls to this facility or anonymous reports to anybody? I have your word on that as a fellow clinician?"

"You have my word," she said solemnly. "Absolutely." Pinkie swear.

Trager's voice grew more solid, like someone recovering from a bad bout of flu. "You accept managed care and Medicaid, I assume? Our population doesn't exactly go private pay."

"Of course," she said, although it took months to get on insurance panels, and the type of treatment she intended to practice might never get approved. Fir Cove was going to have to be fee-for-service for those who could afford it, with a sliding scale for everybody else. From this particular patient, however, Arles would never expect payment. She had a 401(k) she could cash in. It'd allow her to get going, past all the start-up humps.

"Give me some time," Trager said. "I'm booked solid the next several days, but after that, I'll move a few people around, schedule an emergency session. What's the patient's name?"

"You've got till EOD tomorrow," she told him. "I'll expect to hear from your patient's mother by evening at the latest." That was the most she would allow before she contacted the state licensing board, and Joint Commission, the organization responsible for accrediting Trager's current therapeutic treatment facility, plus any others she could identify that had in the past offered him employment, not to mention Child Protective Services. They wouldn't hire this man to hand out discount flyers on Broadway by the time she was through.

Trager heaved a resentful-sounding sigh. "The name, Dr. Shepherd?"

She crushed the granola-bar wrapper into a pellet in her hand, staring out through the windshield. So many children in this world. And so many of them hurt by it. Fir Cove had been a site for the same when Arles was young. Now it could make amends, be pressed into a new kind of service. She adjusted the rearview mirror, catching a look of bleak satisfaction on her face.

"It's Geary," she said. "Mom is Louise Drake."

The man wanted to feed her. Offer her treats.

That was the first thing she figured out after he'd locked the doors and she'd stopped screaming. Both things happened scary quick, even though they seemed to take forever. She quit making noise faster than the girls in movies did. She'd always been quiet; on report cards, teachers said she needed to talk more in class. She didn't keep still in a pipe-down kind of way, the type where children should be seen and not heard, especially girls. More like she stood back, taking everything in, so if she had to, she could deal with it.

This wasn't something she could deal with. Seeing it in movies didn't help. There was no jump cut in real life. She liked movies best after music, and jump cuts were when film directors skipped over some of the steps. No missed beats here, though. She experienced them all, felt every last sensation. Like her feet hurting through the thin soles of her sneakers. Fashionable ones so the girls at school would think she was the same as them, instead of shoes built for action like the boys wore. Her legs were tired from having run; her chest ached from that final spurt of speed.

She had her backpack. That might be helpful, though she couldn't think why.

She let her gaze slide down to the rubber floor mat where the backpack sat. What did it contain besides books and her pencil case and assorted junk? Something tugged at her brain, like homework you knew had been assigned but couldn't for your life remember.

She was sitting in the front passenger seat of a van—no windows in back, just white panels, and the glass up here was tinted—with her seat belt on like a good girl.

Time to stop being a good girl. Good girls didn't save themselves.

Then the man leaned over, reaching across her lap, and she flinched, even though she knew it would make her look scared. She shrank back as he unhinged the glove box.

That's when she saw he had a gun.

MURDER MOMS

In the wake of his daughter's disappearance, Cass turned to true-crime podcasts, consuming countless episodes with his headset plugged in. He used to watch YouTube tutorials while tackling tricky household jobs; now he lost himself in a different kind of media. To prove he wasn't alone, the one person on earth that crime had come for. And for an orientation to this vile new world he was forced to inhabit. Following his discovery in the cave, he found himself leaning harder than ever on this dogged, dedicated group. These folks were smart. Knew things he didn't, were able to speak a language and make sense of a universe he couldn't.

The bowstrings had led to a highly trained team out of Boston being sent to the cave and the surrounding section of woods. They'd located Bea's bow in a pile of look-alike sticks. Waterlogged, so its scent had been erased, camouflaged in appearance, but neither done deliberately, according to the experts. The setup appeared accidental; *inadvertent* was the word they'd used. Bea's viola was discovered toward the back of the cave where the rock roof rose to standing height, and that turned out to be an even trickier piece of the puzzle because while the instrument's body was intact, its neck had been shattered. Split into long, sharp shards.

That whole area of forest had been cordoned off. It bristled with stubs—little prongs stuck into the ground to mark the places where a piece of evidence had been found. Hundreds of pictures taken to allow investigators to try and re-create what might've happened, speculate as to various scenarios. Each individual splinter of wood bagged and tagged and sent to a laboratory downstate for analysis. And still, Bea stayed gone.

Cass was not one of those Mainers who dreaded winter, couldn't wait for it to end. Joshing around with folks waiting in line, bantering with people pumping gas, all huddled up in coats. *Cold enough fa yuh?* And, *We got four seasons, and they're all winta.* He worked inside, or he used to, and when he spent time outdoors, it was for enjoyment and sport: hunting, snowmobiling, ice fishing. But this year, he hated the season's relentless hold. How the temperature sliced at a man, sank into his soul. He kept picturing Bea out there somewhere. Cold.

He'd wound up in the kitchen, an emptiness in his gut he knew wouldn't be filled by food. Still, he opened the fridge, reaching for a platter a neighbor had brought by. Chewed mindlessly, his jaw moving up and down, unable to say what type of sandwich he'd selected.

"How can you eat?"

Maggie stood in the pass-through between the kitchen and dining room. They wandered by each other now without making contact, let alone conversation. Moved through the house like ghosts, detached from their bodies. He set the unfinished sandwich on the counter.

She crossed to the cupboard and took out a plate. Put the sandwich on it and held it out. "I'm sorry. We have to eat. Keep up our strength."

"For what?" He didn't take the plate.

She stared at him mutely for a moment. "I don't know."

He leaned over the sink, bracing his elbows on the rim of the counter.

"Cass," she said. Silence, as if this might stop there. Then, "You're crying."

Tears made bigger blobs of drops of water in the sink. He couldn't think of a way to reply, how to claw out what was inside him. She grasped his heaving shoulders from behind, worked to spin him around. But she had no luck turning his body, and so she gave up and just stood there, breathing hard, he guessed from the effort she'd expended to try and move him.

"I took a nap," he said, so low he didn't think she would hear.

"What? When?" But dully, as if she already knew.

"That day." That day that wasn't really a day. Not a twenty-four-hour block, no delineation to it. That day still hadn't ended. "When Bea was supposed to be getting home from school." Putting a shape to the words he'd held inside should've done him in, left him bent over, sobbing again. But he seemed to be all cried out.

"Bea comes in by herself," Maggie said. "She has since she was nine. So what difference does it make if you were asleep or not?"

He turned in time to see her put it together, her eyes slowly widening, fuzzed with fear.

"We know where Bea went." He jabbed a hand in the direction of the cave. He did it so roughly that if there'd been something solid in the way, any substance besides air, he would've smashed every bone in his fingers. "That monster must've been close by. And I was asleep."

His wife had begun shaking her head, her hair flying like corn silk with the motion. In refusal and denial and condemnation. From this point forward, she wouldn't be able to stand him. Which was all right. He'd long since stopped being able to stand himself.

"Asleep for it," he repeated, tormenting both of them, like sticking a thumb in a wound and mashing the flesh. "Asleep—"

"Oh, my love," she said, cutting him off. "You didn't know. No one could've known what was going to happen. No one expects something like this."

He clamped his lips together.

"Besides, if we're getting around to blame," she said, her tone taking a sudden, sharp swerve, "don't you think I deserve my fair share? Wouldn't you like to send some of that good stuff my way? I've been working so many hours I hardly even see Bea anymore. I wasn't there to take care of her." She opened and closed her mouth silently, before starting up again, like she was a machine that had needed a cranking. "Do you hear me? I wasn't even here—"

He'd had no idea she was doing this to herself. "Because I got let go! You're working like that because I lost my fucking job—"

She was so light that when she threw herself at him, he barely felt the impact. He gathered her into his arms, her face slick and wet against his damp shirt, and they swayed together, back and forth, back and forth, in a kind of coming together, a ghastly sort of dance.

That night they shared a bed for the first time since Bea had disappeared, but once he made sure Maggie had really good and fallen to sleep, Cass went downstairs with his phone and charger and headset.

Two Girls & A Criminal was the podcast he was listening to right now, Jan and Tracy the names of the hosts. This pair spoke to him; he liked how smart and quick and thoughtful they were. They made him think about what Bea was going to be like when she grew up. The show he couldn't stand, even though it covered crimes that bore relevance to theirs, female victims snatched from rural areas, was *Murder Moms*. A group of four women who made his skin crawl like a whole swarm of bees had landed on him. They laughed at their sick obsession with killing and killers. They tittered, they chortled, they giggled, getting all the way to hysterical over the horrors they unearthed. There were probably a lot of smart layers Bea would point out in his reaction to this batch of women. It was problematic when men called women silly, the patriarchy at work.

But that didn't stop Cass from hitting "Pause" almost hard enough to crack his screen in order to shut them up before they could get to cackling over the worst pain anybody was ever going to have to live through without even bothering to learn the family's last name.

An alert blinked on his phone, and he looked down.

It was an email from *Two Girls & A Criminal.* He'd written in to ask a question, and one of the hosts had gotten back to him. He felt his heart clutch in his chest, a brief flicker that usually frightened him, but right now, he welcomed. Because it meant his adrenaline was spiking, hope and anxiety surging. It meant something was happening.

Don't let me die now, Dad. A prayer to the force Cass used to fear more than any deity. He was about to click or tap or whatever you called it when you opened email on a phone.

But then he heard a voice.

"Cass."

Ghostlike again; he hadn't even felt her appear.

"Come back to bed."

Slowly, creakily, joints moving like rusted tin, he got to his feet.

Maggie crossed to help him, placing a palm beneath his elbow. Her touch like a songbird alighting. "Someone at work suggested we get therapy," she murmured as they walked together, slowly, barely covering ground. "For help coping. Not . . . They didn't mean grief counseling."

Her face folded. Even though he wasn't sure what was causing that pain, at this moment at least, he had only one need in the world besides finding Bea. To make his wife's face smooth out, get her not to look like that anymore. Crumpled. Reduced beyond any hope of repair.

"Okay," he said. "Maybe that's a good idea."

They had arrived at the bottom of the stairs, standing and looking up as if considering a long trip before setting out. Maggie put her foot on the first step.

"They found us a person who's supposed to be good. Can't be at the place where I work; that's a conflict of interest or something, and whoever this is just opened a new office. It's a bit far away, but I figured . . ." Her voice trailed off, a faint wisp of smoke.

He looked away. "We have the time."

CHAPTER SEVEN

Louise stopped at the front desk, looking sideways to make sure Geary had entered the building along with her. Aside from the brief episode during Michael's thundering run out of the house the other night, their son hadn't had any meltdowns since the day of his last appointment. He was engaged at school and occupied with his usual focus and involvement in his room at home. But Louise had dreamed about those twin trails of tears on his cheeks. She was glad this new doctor had asked them to come in a second time this week, almost as if he sensed the same heightened need she did.

Dee looked up, and Louise braced herself. This woman had a way of making a person feel stupid for saying hello. But then Dee's mouth shaped itself into a weird sort of smile.

"You can go right in." She spoke around the smile thing. "Have a good session."

In the office, Geary took a seat, and Louise dropped into a chair beside him so as not to block his view out the window. She turned to the doctor, trying to look pleasant and easygoing, like a good little patient. Make him want to help them.

"I was glad you called us in." Maybe he scheduled two sessions per week with all his new patients? "Something happened with Geary the other day that I don't understand."

A flash of what looked like annoyance crossed his face, but then she second-guessed herself. Doctors didn't get annoyed with patients. Or if they did, they weren't supposed to show it.

"It was at the supermarket," she went on when he didn't respond. Getting the words out felt like trudging through mud. Where was the open-ended question designed to help her share, or at least an encouraging nod?

"Geary was sitting in the back of the car, and when I looked at his face—" She realized she was talking about her son like he wasn't there, just like all those people who assumed they understood what he was and wasn't capable of. "You seemed upset that day, Gear. I'm still not sure if I got that right, or what it was all about?"

The doctor heaved a sigh. He actually huffed out a breath, like a sulky teenager, the kind of behavior Geary would probably never display. An upside to his diagnosis.

"Upset how, Mrs. Drake?"

"Ms.," she said. "I'm divorced." What on earth made her choose to tell him anything about herself? Not least because this doctor was starting to seem even less inclined to trust her perceptions than the ex she'd just referred to. "I think Geary might've been crying. It seemed like something happened while I was in the store." Hopefully, he wouldn't report her for leaving her son alone in the car. "Is that right, Gear?" She looked at her son as directly as she dared.

The sun was clouding over, and he'd twisted himself into a pretzel in his seat, facing the glass with a look on his face as gray as the day.

"Your son doesn't get upset like normal people," said the doctor. "He has Autism. Is Autistic, we're supposed to say now." He made an ugly sound in his throat.

"Yes, I know that," she said. Like this dickhead doctor had to school her. "But I swear he was crying."

"Have you ever seen behaviors in your son before that didn't turn out to really be there?"

"What?" she demanded, making an effort to lower her voice. "How do you mean?" Was he gaslighting her? Except that she had. The answer to his question was yes.

He wheeled his chair over, leaning down like a king from his throne. "I brought you in today because I have a referral for your son. A clinician who will be able to help sort out these impressions of yours while improving Geary's behavior. I've written down the information and also texted it to your phone." He held out a folded sheet of paper.

Louise was used to getting passed between therapists, but this took it to a whole other level. "But we only just started seeing you. Don't you think you can help us?"

Dammit, despite everything, she actually felt rejected. She took the piece of paper.

The doctor sat back in his chair with a smile. "Of course I could help you. I've had luck with even the most disturbed children. However, from what I've heard about this practitioner and read in her published papers, she is second to none with cases like Geary's."

Disturbed kicked the ass of *normal.* She should take this referral and run with it.

Louise took in a steadying breath. "How exactly will she be able to help Geary?"

"Look, no one is ever really going to help your son. Not in the he-gets-better sense."

She gathered another breath. "Right. I know that. The goal isn't to change who Geary is; it's to help him live with his differences in the fullest way possible—"

The doctor held up a hand. "But the woman in question practices in a residential setting. And that kind of immersion tends to hasten whatever improvement you're likely to see."

The word snagged her attention. "Residential? How does that work?"

"This treatment will take place twenty-four seven as opposed to in fifty-minute blocks."

She frowned. "But what about school?"

"He leaves school for the duration. I assume tutoring is provided for children his age, although, let's face it, Geary can miss some instruction and not come to any harm. How much do you think he really absorbs?"

His question punctured her lungs; she had to fight for air. "I'm sorry, but Geary can't leave school. He'll lose his spot. There's a waiting list for Elward, and it took us years to find it. We wasted whole grades with him in the wrong type of learning environment."

She got up, and Geary slid off his seat as well. As if they were partners, in something together for once. Maybe he had already picked up on what this guy was all about, and Louise had missed it at their first appointment.

The doctor stood too, facing them in an unsettling manner. "You're making a mistake, Mrs. Drake. A serious error in judgment. What I'm suggesting has the power to alter the future course of your son's treatment for the better."

Coming to a stop with her back to the door, she experienced a tremor of doubt. He was the professional, after all, the one with education and training, and she was just a nail tech.

"Do you hear me? Not just Geary's treatment. His whole life! This could save him!"

The high, hysterical note his voice hit clinched it. She and Geary had gone to see an awful lot of doctors and therapists over the years without encountering one like this. It was as if Dr. Trager had some ulterior motive, although that was obviously crazy. When she turned around, his eyes blazed with a desperate, fiery look that made adrenaline sizzle in her veins. If she had met this man on the street, she would've crossed to the other side.

"Thanks for the extra session, Dr. Trager. I agree that Geary would be better off with another therapist." She opened the door. "But I think I'll find someone myself."

CHAPTER EIGHT

Up in the high peaks, where Fir Cove was situated, a late-season snowfall had stuck, the heavy coating of white forcing Arles to abandon her car inside the gates and complete the rest of the journey on foot. She would have to contact a plowing service, get things set up in time for autumn. The road she was slogging along, snow packing her shoes and sticking in clumps to her pants, hadn't been cleared in the years since her mother died. Arles thought about all the snow amassed through every single one of those winters, tons of it, falling and melting, washing the place clean.

Her mother's great-grandparents had built this place, or had it built for them, the sweat and toil of the laborers long and egregiously forgotten. The largest of its structures sprawled across a knoll, over six thousand square feet of stone and beams, lording itself over the rest of the property. The sun cast down rays like beams from an alien ship, encircling the residence.

She took a last look over her shoulder at a far-off dimple of lake. Then, eighteen-inch iron hinges protesting as she shoved at the immense slab of door, she entered the house.

Cloudy columns of sunlight slanted down through a hall. Flat stones, polished by generations of walking, formed a surface for her feet. Walls made of wood gave off the earthen smell of lumber while ghostly sheets draped hulking, hidden furnishings.

Handyman work needed, she noted as she walked along. A crack in a window, a place where a sill had rotted. Parts of the ancient ceiling were crumbling, leaving pitted holes; she could see through to the bones. *It has good bones,* she heard someone say. A positive, usually, but amid these signs of quiet decrepitude, the phrase caused a shudder.

Suddenly, she sank into a squat, arms wrapped around her shins, and closed her eyes. Very bad things had happened in this place, and the rooms held on to their residue like creosote in the twelve-foot-wide chimney. Poisonous events within these walls, on the sweeping front porch, and in a hunting blind high in a tree in the woods in pursuit of a stag.

She of all people knew such experiences never evaporated or left. The idea that she could transform Fir Cove suddenly struck her as ludicrous, absurd, the kind of unrealistic thinking she would work with a client to address. She couldn't even function here, stand on her own two feet. Her breath was sucked away like a wave on a beach, air reaching her lungs in a trickle.

Someone hurried by, moving so swiftly they seemed to take flight, floating a few inches above the flat stones. Arles felt their presence as no more than a breeze. A ghost, a mirage.

She lifted her head, heavy as a medicine ball. "Mom? Is that you?"

The person was gone by the time Arles forced herself to open her eyes.

Memories began swarming her like wasps, so that crouching was no longer sufficient and she had to lie down. Tucking her knees against her chest, she brought her nose to her legs and curled into a potato-bug ball, small enough not to be found. Shivers took hold, racking her body along with an unhealthy dose of self-hatred.

She wasn't a child anymore; in fact, she was an adult with a valuable property to her name. She had the knowledge and finally the means to help a great many people. What was she doing, lying on a freezing stone floor in need of a good mopping?

She got up and strode over to the hearth, able to step inside the fireplace at full height, no ducking required to open the flue. She would gather logs from the woodshed and light a blaze to dry her pants, which had gotten soaked, thanks to the spring snow. In addition to the repairs, there was cleaning to do, and decorating too. A little sprucing up was definitely in order.

Would people come to a site so cut off from the world, without Wi-Fi or cell signal? She thought that they would. The therapy she intended to provide might even make that a feature as opposed to a bug, a selling point versus an impediment. Facilitate intense treatment minus smartphone-era interference.

She'd given Trager a deadline, which meant she had to be out of here by nightfall. That was a necessity, anyway. Fir Cove was off the grid, so once the sun set, she'd be kicking it circa the nineteenth century with candles. Unless the fuel delivery she'd arranged happened to arrive earlier than expected? In any case, she decided to start with window washing. As soon as the soaring panes of glass were clear, sun would flood this place like stadium lights.

By late afternoon, she was coated with the dirt and detritus of years. Her yellow gloved hands had stayed protected, but her arms were fuzzed with gray up to the straps of her tank top. Grime delineated the creases in her neck, and she caught peripheral shadows of smudges on her face every time her vision switched focus. She had stripped off her button-down shirt once it soaked through, sweat slicking her body despite the lack of heat in the house. But the work had a satisfying dimension to it, even though the tips of her rubber-coated fingers had gone numb and her feet rang out high, painful notes from standing for so long, as did her muscles from squatting and her kneecaps from crawling around, poking broom bristles beneath furniture and radiators.

Ages of accumulated grunge swept up, scoured off, scrubbed away.

Ridding the house of everything unclean: memories and acts and filth.

Doing the work herself made the place hers, sealed with sweat equity her stepfather's transfer. It should've belonged to her, anyway; by threatening Peter, she had simply restored a rightful balance. Six generations of Shepherds, each mother bearing a firstborn daughter who inherited the estate. A female-forward structure of bequest unheard of to this day.

If there were siblings, they divided other assets, all spent or squandered by the time Arles's mother arrived on the scene. Only Arles would put a cap on centuries' worth of epigenetic entitlement. She had long ago made a vow not to have children.

Her mother had withheld Fir Cove as an act of retribution. She blamed Arles for what Peter had done, enabling her to deny her own share of responsibility. Arles had worked this through during postdoc therapy, but understanding didn't make the taste of blame and betrayal any less bitter in the back of her throat.

She trudged over to her supplies for a fresh sponge; she'd reduced three to shreds already. When she reached the hall, someone was pounding on the front door, a muffled but insistent beat. She stopped as suddenly as if a pool of cement had solidified around her feet.

She pictured Trager, coming to track her down—but no, he couldn't have found this location, surely—instead of complying with her demand. Intuiting how weak she really was, her display of strength just that, mere show. Or else this would be Peter—old, shriveled, barely mobile, yet here to take back what he'd stolen. Unless it was her mother, extending a skeletal finger, as dirt-clotted as the floors Arles had just been scrubbing. Reaching up from underneath the ground, beckoning Arles over to a rift in the soil.

The banging was ongoing, deliberate, even though the door didn't budge in its frame. The materials from which this house had been constructed were so thick and solid, she wouldn't have known someone was at the door if she hadn't walked within a few feet of it.

"Anyone home?" The call muted by boards. "I'm from MacKinnon! I've got your fuel!"

Arles forced her feet to move.

She swung open the heavy door, her overworked arm feeling the strain. A cylindrical truck was parked by the side of the house. She couldn't believe she hadn't heard it pull up the long road, its huffing engine bestial and intruding. A thick grooved hose lay spooled out on the ground like the trunk of some prehistoric mastodon.

The guy who stood on the porch in coveralls and boots, holding a clipboard in one hand, tipped her a charming half grin. Most men didn't smile like that, so open and unprotected. He was youngish—though not so young as to explain the guileless smile—and, quite bluntly, hot.

Arles was constantly on guard against automatic apologies—women had a tendency to say they were sorry far too often—but she figured a *My bad* was in order in this case. How long had the guy been there before she registered his presence? But instead of a *Sorry about that*, what came out of her mouth was a brisk "Intake's over there."

That smile again. "Yup. I saw it."

For a second, she considered how she must look. Probably didn't smell very good, either. Once the fuel was replenished, she'd get the pump working, go take a shower. It was a pleasing enough prospect that she muttered a terse "Thanks" before heading back to her tasks.

With the muck gone, she embarked on a polishing pass, all gentle microfiber cloths and fir-scented cleanser that made her nose tingle. As she watched the wood take on its remembered gleam and honed the stones to a fine luster, a feeling of homecoming suffused her.

But it wasn't she who was coming home.

The other patients who would soon start to pass through Fir Cove's halls were all secondary. She'd never let them sense such a thing, of course, but in her deepest, innermost core, like the rod in a reactor, she was aware. She wouldn't have forced her stepfather's hand if TaskMiner's alert hadn't appeared. Louise was like the child Arles was never going to have.

It was an illusion, because the two of them weren't far apart in age, just a couple of years. But since the only image Arles had of the woman was from when they were both young—and a photographic one at that, not even a live memory—Louise was forever stuck in her head as a kid, perpetually ten years old, like a character in *Tuck Everlasting*.

"Hello?" came a shout.

The fuel guy appeared in the archway of the room Arles had all but stopped cleaning, her hand an unattached appendage, moving cloth around in slow circles like a record winding down.

"Sorry that took so long," he said.

She hadn't been aware of much time passing at all.

Had Trager tried her phone, letting her know his deed was done? Could Louise have already called?

"Someone didn't dump one of your tanks. Not us—we took over from the company you were using then. Anyway, what's left is completely rotten. Don't worry; the second tank will be enough to get you up and running. And I'll send someone back tomorrow to do the clean."

She winced. "Sounds expensive."

He took a look around. "You getting the place ready for sale? Or to short-term rent it?"

Arles straightened her spine. "I'm moving in myself."

He let out a low whistle, then offered the apology she hadn't given for her belated response to his arrival. "Hey, I'm sorry; that's great. So many people are Airbnb-ing these days, everything from a shack to a new build. I figure you could make a killing off a place like this."

"I'm not interested in making a killing."

She'd killed his smile at last, though. Took some doing.

He held out a sheet of paper. "Here's your receipt. I only charged you for what was put in today. And I'll see about the cost of that remediation. Maybe spread it out over a few payments."

"You can do that?"

"Hey, I'm a MacKinnon, one of them, anyway. I should be able to do what I want."

"I'd appreciate it," she said.

He gave a nod. "Number's on that sheet. Call if anything doesn't power up like it should. I mean, really, that'd be your electric or water company. But give a holler if it's oil related, and my guy who does the cleans will be out here tomorrow."

"I appreciate it," she said again, and led him to the door.

She didn't take time for further pleasantries; she had a lot left to do. The entryway hall split into two branches after the kitchen, and she took the fork that skirted a utility room before dead-ending at a flight of stairs. The steps led to the basement, which ran the length and width of the entire house, comprised of a warren of largely unused rooms.

Slowly, taking care, she descended the series of steps like entering a cave. Sunken wells had been worn from footfalls over the years, making passage uneven, throwing her off-balance.

The first thing she saw when she got to the bottom was a thin line of impossible light.

There was a paradox concerning trauma.

Memories could cut sharper than knives. Arles had been reduced to a blob on the floor, quivering like a snail's antenna, by nothing more tangible than returning to the house where in the past bad things had happened. But when there was physical potential for danger, a real reason for fear, everything inside her shut down, quieted, and she entered commando mode. Became a warrior. In this state, she could fight; she could destroy; she could maybe even kill and not be frightened. She might not even remember.

The light was coming from beneath the door of a small, sealed room.

She turned around stealthily, her back to a stone wall. Out of sight if someone opened that door. No power in the house, so the source of the beam had to be a phone or a flashlight. Her first thought was that the fuel guy had come downstairs for some reason, but he'd probably been glad to take his leave of the rude, dirty homeowner who in his eyes was just another gentrifier.

Silently, she lowered herself into a crouch, attempting to peer beneath the door. She flattened herself out on the cold floor, breathing in dankness and forest and burial—the smell of old things—while wrinkling her nose against a sneeze, but the slit was too narrow to see anything. She stood up. No sound except for her own irregular breaths, the thrum of her pulse in her ears. But somebody had to be in that room, or just recently left. Batteries didn't last forever. If she called out "Hello," demanded to know who was there, she'd relinquish the element of surprise. Better to fling the door open, then jump back and wait to see if anyone emerged.

She heard a muffled whisper, then a word or two hissed in return, and nearly screamed. Enough. She wasn't going to be intimidated in her own house. She strode forward with a series of forceful steps, placed one hand on the doorknob, and gave a yank.

Inside the room huddled a woman with her arms around a child.

"I told you, Lissa!" the woman said, rising to loom over the small form beside her. "I told you not to be scared of the dark! Now look what's happened!"

"We can't stay here anymore?" came the response, timid and uncertain.

The question presented no diversion. "The dark isn't anything! It's nothing! The things to be scared of, they're all out here!"

Pieces slid together, forming a whole.

"No, no," Arles said, hop-stepping over the threshold. She leaned down to talk to the child. "Lissa, is that your name? It's okay. You're not in any trouble." She straightened up and faced the woman. "It's okay. Really."

The woman's face looked haggard and careworn. She wore jeans two sizes too big along with a heavy sweater that Arles recognized. It had belonged to her mother, who'd stored it here because this house was draftier, held on to heat less well than the one in town.

Those quick, running footsteps Arles had heard. They hadn't belonged to a ghost.

"You've been squatting here?" she asked. "This is your daughter?"

"Just in this room, I swear!" the woman burst out. "And only for a day or two. My landlord decided to divide up our rental, and we got evicted."

Camping lanterns turned out to be the source of the illumination. It looked like the pair might've been here longer than a day or two. A pallet of bottled water took up space on the floor. Two toothbrushes and a tube of toothpaste leaned against each other in a bowl. There was one carton of neatly folded clothes and another of laundry; a sealed plastic bag ballooned with trash. Blankets and pillows made twin nests on the floor, and a circle of stuffed animals appeared to be in the midst of some game. A shelving unit that once held tools was filled with books, nonperishables, and sundry household items. It seemed as if they had settled in.

"It's okay," Arles said again, as if by rote, her mind numbed by how hard life was, for parents in particular, and especially, *especially*, for mothers. This woman and her daughter had made do without electricity or heat or plumbing. They didn't appear to have a car; just the trips to town would've posed a burden. Who had carried that bottled water?

The woman was tracking her gaze. Arles didn't want to make her any more self-conscious than she obviously already was. Distract her by asking about her child. It was a never-fail tactic.

"Do you homeschool Lissa?" she asked.

The woman gave a quick nod. "Even before we got thrown out of our rental." The color on her face bespoke pride. "Lissa learned long division in kindergarten. She can memorize anything. Lists of vocabulary words, strings of equations. The school can't keep up with her."

"That can be a problem," Arles agreed. She actually liked Wedeskyull Consolidated, worked frequently alongside its teachers and staff. But it could fall down with kids at the extremes of the normal curve, those at the very top and very bottom. "What's your name?"

"Stephanie. Stephanie Fletcher."

The power dynamic at work here, Arles thought, suddenly stricken. This woman answering so promptly, anything Arles asked—she had a feeling she could get quite personal, and still the woman would comply with questioning, because what else could she do?

Arles needed to restore the woman's dignity. Let Stephanie give her something instead of the reverse. "So, I was just about to turn the power on. Then I was thinking we could go upstairs and see if there's any coffee or tea to be had. But honestly"—Arles gestured with a thumb to the woman's stockpile—"it looks like you're better set up to host than I am."

Stephanie squinted at her, appearing uncertain.

"That came out wrong," Arles said easily. "I just meant that I could use a Snickers, if you wouldn't mind." She displayed her raw, reddened arms. "Been scrubbing all day."

"Oh, please, yes, of course!" Stephanie said. "Lissa, could you get this woman a—"

The girl was already making her way over to the stand of shelves. She returned with a candy bar, shyly held out in one hand.

Arles asked Stephanie and Lissa to stay till the next day. She couldn't turn them out at such short notice, and she herself needed to get back to town to stock up on supplies, and more importantly, check her phone. She would sleep in her apartment tonight, pack and terminate her lease, without having to leave Fir Cove unoccupied. She went outside and climbed into her car.

Her phone came alive with a musical note as soon as she got within range. Four calls from the 914 area code. Trager's turf. She had stayed too long at Fir Cove, missed her earliest opportunity to hear the news she'd been waiting for. But why had he called so many times?

"Dr. Shepherd!" he said, answering on the first ring.

He sounded happy, although she had the perilous feeling that whatever might make a man like him happy wouldn't produce the same emotion in her. She pulled over to the side of the road and kept quiet, always the power move. Her hazard lights twitched, as nervous as she.

"I'm afraid little Louise did not take me up on your offer," he said.

Something broke apart inside Arles, windows shattering, floorboards coming loose.

"I don't think there's any cause for concern, though," he went on, while Arles listened listlessly. "At least, not for me."

She needed to end this call but couldn't summon the will. The red phone icon seemed a taunt, too far off for her finger to reach.

"You see, I did as you recommended and googled you. Then I made a call to a little Podunk rural hospital. Took a page from your book and pretended to be someone else, asked to make an appointment with you."

A long enough pause that Arles had to bite her lip to keep from speaking.

"I don't think you're in a position of strength here, Dr. Shepherd." Upon getting no response, he went on. "Let me be clearer. You rat me out, and you'll have an infestation on your hands. I'll track down the electronic file of the call you made to me and send it not just to the shit place that probably fired you, but as high up as the APA."

A pickup swerved onto the shoulder, nearly slamming into her car. She shifted into gear with a hard jam of the mechanism and pressed down on the gas. Trager's voice faded out when the Bluetooth failed to connect, and she finally stabbed the red circle. She doubted he'd had the foresight to record their first call and was equally skeptical that his provider would give up its digital content. Besides, Trager would soon be so embroiled in fallout from the reports she had filed, he wouldn't have time to carry out his threat.

Not that it mattered, she acknowledged, making the turn into her driveway. Trager's failure with Louise lessened the stakes of his trashing her professionally, obliterated them, really. He might have the power to end her career based on what she had done—blackmailing a clinician to get him to manipulate his client. And given that it hadn't worked, would she care if he did?

Just a day or so ago, Louise had been like the pulsing beacon on a lighthouse, glimpsed only through the distant fog of memory. But TaskMiner had brought her within sight, conjuring up a possibility that Arles had long since given up on. Now, she couldn't imagine how to go on if she never met Louise. Getting this close had made encountering the woman necessary, essential.

There was only one thing to do at this point. The act that served as comfort and distraction and succor whenever she got this low. Usually, she turned to Tinder or Bumble or the unsubtly named HookUp. But today, she had a better option.

She'd brought along the bill of sale from the oil delivery, and the fuel guy had jotted down his name—Dan—beside ten digits on the sheet of paper. The number had to be his own; it didn't match the one above the company's slogan: *We Keep You Up and Running!*

She called, and he picked up.

"You were at my place earlier," she said for a greeting. "Told me to reach out if I needed anything oil related."

"Do you?"

"No. I'm at my apartment in town. It uses propane."

"At your apartment? That right?"

"I assume so. There're those canister thingies. Like for a grill but bigger."

She could almost feel that smile of this. The phone had gone hot in her hand.

"What I meant was, you're at your apartment right now?"

"I am."

"Want to text me the address?"

A flush climbed up her body, tingling beneath the hair on her scalp. "I already did."

"Yeah?" A pause while he must've checked. "Great."

"Great?" she echoed. "Because you'd like to try and switch my landlord to diesel?"

"Nope," he said. "That's not what I was thinking at all."

She ended the call, feeling the familiar swell in her mood. She needed to get ready.

Afterward, she would figure out a different way to lure Louise.

CHAPTER NINE

Louise got the call Thursday morning at work while she was in the middle of a complicated luster mani. She had to beg Sue in the next chair to take over. Her breath came in short spurts as she raced down the hall of the Elward School. When she passed what the students who weren't nonspeaking called the take-a-chill room, she skidded to a stop and doubled back.

What she hadn't told Dr. Trager was that Geary was on shave-thin ice at his awesome school, the best in a hundred-mile radius for kids with disabilities. Her guts knotting, Louise took a step forward and peeked through the one-way glass. Inside stood Geary, with an aide keeping a respectful space between them.

The room had pale-blue rubber mats for flooring, a color chosen for its calming effect, and beanbag chairs with various covers—faux fur and soft fleece and cool vinyl—to address a range of sensory needs. A screen, which came out from the wall at a safe height, played a loop of nature scenes soundlessly, visible only if students chose to position themselves to look. One corner had a shelf that held fidget devices and toys requiring manual operation, including a few tricky puzzles, but aside from that, everything was intended to be low-stim and soothing.

All four walls, and even the door, were covered with gymnastics mats, and Geary was launching himself at them face-first in a rhythmic sequence. Bouncing off safely, but Louise could see that the tip of his nose had reddened, and she flinched. Due to the distress he must be experiencing to do this to himself, and also because if his nose started to bleed, intervention would be required: staff to apply the hug hold or possibly even restraints, meds from the nurse, a ghastly spiral she couldn't bear to see her son go down.

She placed one hand flat against the glass, even though—or because—Geary couldn't see it. Comforting him, giving him a pat in the only way she could.

Then she turned and walked the rest of the way to the office, no reason to hurry now.

The director's face looked kind when Louise took a seat in front of his desk. No bizarre fiery blaze in this guy's eyes—everyone from students to staff to parents loved him.

"So, unfortunately, Geary's had to make five departures from class to the breather room so far this week," he said.

"Five times *this* week?" she echoed. "That can't be right."

He tilted the screen of his computer to read. "There has been an uptick, it's true—"

Louise interrupted him with a nod, the motion feeling frantic, as if her head had come unhinged from her neck. "Something's been troubling Geary! But I don't know what it is."

The director gazed at her, and the look in his eyes was the worst one she could've seen. Because it wasn't that he didn't believe her—it was that it didn't matter if he did. It wasn't going to make any difference.

"The fact remains," he said gently, "that Geary requires more individualized and intensive support than we are able to accommodate in our behavior plans. Though it saddens me to say so, we are not the best facility to meet his needs."

When Louise got to feeling sorry for herself, she thought about everybody who looked down on the parents of children with disabilities. As if the different ways these kids perceived things or exhibited challenging behaviors or required accommodations added up to there being something wrong. And also that, if something were wrong, then Louise must've caused it. Screwed up somehow: ate crap when she was pregnant, contributed lousy genes, parented badly. She was too indulgent or too strict. Spent too much time on her phone or gave her son too much access to devices. Could be anything, so long as the other person felt safe and assured, content that things like this didn't just happen; someone, usually the mom, had to be at fault.

She felt tears bud in her eyes. "Does Geary have to leave Elward?"

The director hesitated briefly. "I'm afraid so, Ms. Drake."

"He's had so many placements already," she mumbled. A mom she chatted with online said it felt like rehoming a dog each time a school pushed her kid out. Louise had thought it a disgusting comparison, but she felt the truth of it now. "This was supposed to be our last."

"I'm terribly sorry," said the director. "We all like your son. We see his potential. But this clearly isn't the right setting for him."

"What is, then? Where does Geary go from here?"

This time his pause lasted longer. "I'll be straight with you, Ms. Drake. There isn't a great answer. You can turn back to your public school system. They have a legal responsibility to educate. But in a situation like Geary's, with options as far along as Elward exhausted, what that will mean is not something you're going to like."

An icy fear filled her belly. She had thought he would comfort her with different choices, plenty of possibilities left to try.

"The places on offer will be rigidly structured," he went on. "Every minute accounted for, days divided into very short blocks. All privileges are earned, even yard time and unattended use of the bathroom. There will be a containment room that provides more safeguards than ours."

"But . . ." She could hardly shape the words. "What you're describing doesn't sound like a school. It sounds more like a mental hospital. Or a prison."

The director pressed his lips together. "Parents do tend to find it difficult to deal day-to-day with their child in such a setting. That's why most of them are residential."

"Something happened to upset him," she said again helplessly.

"And what do you think that might've been?"

She grabbed at the question like a rope. "We were at the store. I left him in the car."

The director looked appropriately unfazed, a person who knew what was important to worry about when it came to kids, and what amounted to just making it through.

"When I got back out, it looked like he was crying."

The director studied his computer again. "That would be somewhat unexpected given Geary's psychosocial profile."

She nodded, so grateful he was taking her seriously that it felt pathetic.

"Could he have seen some sort of commotion outside the car?"

"I have no idea! It could've been anything. And he wouldn't be able to tell me."

The director held up both palms, equally at a loss. "Or just heard something out there."

The statement, even though the director obviously had no more of a clue than she did, sounded an alert, a ringtone through the white noise blizzarding her, the fact that she had no idea what to do next for Geary.

"Or maybe not outside the car," she said, rising suddenly. "Maybe inside it."

The radio had been on. She let her mind gnaw at the relevance of this as she drove home with Geary buckled into his booster seat. She'd turned the station off when she sat down in the car, its blare bothering her. What had been playing? Music? An ad? Something else?

Once Geary had gotten himself settled in his bedroom, she went into her own room and lay down on the bed with her phone. But she quickly saw the pointlessness of her task. She wasn't even sure which station she'd left on—some death-metal song might've played, a shock jock could've raged, and never mind if it'd been tuned to talk. Fifty stories in the news right now, all competing to out-gruesome each other. Would any of those things have made Geary cry? It seemed at least as likely a weather report had warned that the sun wouldn't be out for days.

Something else the director had said was cycling through her mind now, anyway. The schools left to try were residential. Same as the referral Dr. Trager had tried to make.

She checked her texts for the one he had told her he'd sent, her vision fuzzy by the time she finally stopped scrolling. Reading messages from last Christmas, from back when she and Michael had still been together, from the age of the damn dinosaurs. She hoped Dee was still in a good mood, wouldn't make Louise feel like an idiot for calling. She would fix lunch for Geary while getting the other doctor's contact info from Dr. Trager. Maybe she'd brave up and ask why he thought this clinician was so amazing. He was a real superfan of hers, clearly.

Louise found the treatment center in her contacts and placed the call.

She had never seen a pistol before, not for real. In movies. On TV.

Her skin went puckery, and she squeezed both hands into balls. Imagined swinging her arm like a club, breaking his face with her fist.

He looked at her. "Oh, don't be scared of that. You're not scared, are you?"

She shook her head, which was sort of true. She'd been around guns her whole life—rifles, shotguns, though. This thing looked puny by comparison, like a toy. But it wasn't a toy.

"I drive for a living," he explained, as if that wasn't obvious.

A) Men like this tended to have jobs like that. Made committing their sick crimes easier.

B) This stupid van filled with boxes in back and no windows. Watch TV for one hour, and you knew what it was good for.

"Figure I need protection out on the road," he added, massaging the gun with his hand.

You *need protection, she thought. She almost said it out loud, sarcastic-like. But she knew he wasn't letting her in on details about his sick life because he thought the two of them should get to know each other. He wanted her to see he had a weapon. He was warning her.*

He closed the glove box and eased himself back over to his seat. A gust of cooling air replaced the heat of his body, and she shivered with relief.

"Want a blanket?" he asked. "I've got one in the back."

He'd kidnapped her, and now he wanted to cover her, like a mom or dad did a baby.

"Don't look like that," he said, voice suddenly growly. "Don't you look at me that way."

She wondered what her face had just done and worked to smooth it out. She had always been more comfortable talking to grown-ups than other kids. And this might be the most important conversation she would ever have. "How do you want me to look?"

He turned to her, eagerness in his eyes, like a dog finding a piece of food on the street.

SILK-WRAPPED BLADES

Tracy from *Two Girls & A Criminal* asked in her email if Cass wanted to Zoom, suggesting Thursday morning for a meet. It took a few seconds for his slow, creaky internet to make the tiny circle on his screen quit spinning, for some behind-the-scenes magic to take place, and then the two girls were in his living room.

That came out creepy, Dad, he heard Bea say. Also—

Dad! They're grown-ups!

Two women, he corrected himself, in response to his daughter's finger wag.

The pair introduced themselves, although he knew he would have trouble remembering which one was which. They looked about the same age, whatever that age might be—*grown-up*—but otherwise nothing alike, one white and blonde with a sleeve of tattoos, the other Black with blue and silver braids and a pierced nose.

Cool, the two of them. Was that the current terminology? He himself had always felt decidedly *un*cool, out of sync with the times, including his own. His father's life had been a foreshortened one, and Cass found that somehow aged him. He didn't relate to men his own age. His neighbor up the road was the closest thing he had to a friend, and Don was a generation older. After dropping out of college, Cass stopped spending any time hanging out with the guys, making excuses to skip beers and pool after work. He went hunting each fall alone. He had his girls, Maggie and Bea, and they were all he could ask for in the way of companionship.

He wondered what two girls as hip—maybe that was the right word—as these would make of him. *Okay, Boomer,* Bea sometimes kidded, a joke she was too young to understand. It wasn't even apt—he was a good eleven years younger. Gen X.

The girls—*women*; he'd done it again—were talking, must've been at it the whole time his mind was ambling to things like age and coolness, looks and hair color. When he should've been hanging on their every word. Recording them, assuming they wouldn't have minded, and he could figure out how to do it. These days his brain was like mud. He kept getting stuck in it.

"Listen to us, Mr. Monroe," said the one with braids, "because we know your daughter."

"What did you say?" It had sounded vaguely threatening, although probably the thick sludge in his brain was just changing things around. *We know your daughter. We have your daughter.* Someone at one of the alphabet agencies was monitoring each call, text, and email that came in on any of Cass's or Maggie's devices—their landline too—in case whoever took Bea made contact. He never would've believed he'd pray for a ransom demand. *We want money in exchange for your daughter.*

"Not like that, Mr. Monroe," said the blonde one.

Jan, he was pretty sure.

"We mean that we *know* your daughter." The other took over. "Based on what you've said in your comments on our show. And that email you sent us. The kind of girl she is."

He felt bewildered. He would've said he'd barely described Bea. How perceptive this pair must be to do what they did, analyzing crimes and their perpetrators, men more monsters than human beings. "What do you mean? Who is she?"

They spoke at the exact same time. "She's a silk-wrapped blade."

He went so far as to mouth the words. They left a taste on his tongue, sharp and sweet.

"They're a group, a breed," the one with braids told him. "These females, these fighters. Your daughter belongs to it. You've got to hold on to that."

Unexpected tears flooded his eyes. He felt ashamed, helpless to hold them back, no box of tissues, even. But over who knew how many miles, across the infinite distance of cyberspace, both girls held his gaze, all the kindness in the world in their own.

At last, one of them said, "We have a theory, Mr. Monroe. If you want to hear it."

Tracy and Jan had been following the activity around Bea's case from the start.

Lord, how he hated his daughter having a case.

They'd learned about the discovery Cass had made, and the rest of the evidence that law enforcement officers—Tracy referred to them as *LEO*—had collected. Tracy's father was police commissioner in a Midwestern city. She seemed to know this world.

"What's the name of the chief or the sheriff or whoever caught the case?" she asked.

He mopped his face with the sleeve of his shirt. "You're talking about Abe Brawley?"

"Right. Him. He seems good."

Cass felt a flicker of hope. Tracy thought Brawley was good.

"How near the road is that cave?" Jan asked.

He considered. "That depends on how you're measuring. As the crow flies, not too far. But no one would know the cave was there if they were driving or walking on the road." The woods formed a giant's castle of wall, so thick and dense that it swallowed any signs of anything, closing over landmarks as a pond did a stone.

"Bea would know," said Tracy.

"It was her hideaway," added Jan. "Right?"

He went silent for a second. "Why don't you tell me what you girls are thinking?"

The two believed that Bea's bow might've fallen out and gotten accidentally trampled when she opened her viola case. He was trying to come up with some reason that Bea would've needed her instrument—unable to keep from hearing in his head the beautiful butterfly notes she played—when Tracy elaborated.

"We think she might've been running away from someone. Heading toward her hideout, and when she got there, she tried to use her instrument as a weapon."

Jan nodded. "What's that part of the violin called? Its handle?"

"The neck," said Tracy.

"It's a viola," Cass added pointlessly. His head felt scrambled, trying to keep up.

"Right, well, so, the neck must be pretty strong, huh? While the what-do-you-call-it, the body—"

"The part with the pretty cutouts," Jan put in.

"Is kind of light. Because it's hollow."

"I guess that'd be right," he said slowly.

"Now, she cradles her instrument most of the time, right? That's how she holds it."

"Sure," he said, seeing a picture of Bea playing, and finding that it hurt.

"Whereas someone like me," Tracy went on, "would pick it up by the neck, swing it like a bat. But that'd be stupid because that hollow wood wouldn't do as much damage if it hit someone. Not compared to the neck, which is pretty substantial if you really bring it down."

"That's what we think Bea might've done," Jan said.

"Because the neck was shattered when they found it. Split like a log."

"Which it kinda is, Trace. A skinny one."

"True," Tracy replied.

"Also, there are those sharp sticky-out parts on the neck. They could really mess someone up, say, if you hooked their face with one."

"It's definitely the better weapon, aside from I guess you get torque if you swing."

"Much better," said Jan.

"I mean, this is how we're seeing it," Tracy said. "None of this is for sure."

"I get that," said Cass.

Jan took over. "So, what we're thinking is that Bea, being a musician, knew to pick up her violin—"

"Viola—"

"Viola by its *body*, so she could smash the *handle*—"

"Neck—"

"Yes, right, the solid part—"

"Against her attacker when she had the chance. Got close enough and all. Or maybe she used her viola's neck more like a sword, to keep him at a distance. That could be it too."

"Either way, she's a fighter."

Tracy let out a low breath. "That bastard might be walking around with some seriously vicious wound right now."

Cass had whiplash. He wasn't sure if anything these two were saying could be right. It might not even be worth sharing with the police, although he couldn't see any harm in passing it along. But he himself was struck by a couple of things.

One, the amount of time these girls voluntarily devoted to thinking about events so grisly, so horrible, he had never spent a second of his life considering them until he'd been forced to. And two, the hope they had given him to grasp on to, like falling off a cliff and grabbing its edge.

"I want to thank you girls," he said, wiping his face violently again with his sleeve.

"Sure," Jan said. "Email us anytime."

"We're in this with you now," added Tracy. "We want to hear the second Bea is found."

"Cass?"

Maggie had come into the room. They were both home all the time now, by turns as separate as two spinning spheres, and involved in micro-minutes of each other's day. Coworkers at Maggie's jobs had pooled their vacation and sick time to donate to her, while for him it was harder than ever to be out of work, and also the only way things could be. He wouldn't have been able to cope with being at the warehouse; the once-soothing rhythm of operating the lift, loading and unloading miles of shelves, would've flayed him, rubbed him raw.

"Are you talking to somebody?" she asked.

He rose from his chair.

"I just got us an appointment with that therapist," she told him. "She had a cancellation. But we have to leave right now. We have to hurry."

CHAPTER TEN

Gauzy yellow light caused Arles to stir.

Her body held on to a familiar looseness, a psychic and muscular wringing out. It was a feeling of satiation so complete that in this state, it always seemed she might never again have to do what she'd done last night.

She wasn't on the futon in her apartment; instead, she lay beneath the musty sheets of a bed that had been made up long ago and not slept in since. That was why the sunshine looked hazy—it shone through windows still in desperate need of a washing. She hadn't made it up to the second floor during yesterday's cleaning frenzy. Light saturated the sky, producing a warm glow all over her skin. She couldn't recall ever waking with the sun this high.

But the other strange thing, even more bizarre actually, was that someone lay beside her.

Her body went still, even the air in her lungs staying put. She'd never had to confront what she did in the stark reality of day because her hookups always took the little she had to offer and didn't ask for further engagement—seeming, in fact, quite content with their end of the bargain. Which included leaving immediately afterward.

Repetition compulsion was the psychodynamic interpretation of what she did; modern sensibilities thought of it as taking ownership. *You can't hurt me if I do it to myself first.* Arles didn't tend to favor jargon, though. Maybe she just enjoyed this. Sex positive over here.

But why had she come to Fir Cove? Time lost again. That was happening a lot lately. Although it didn't explain the guy staying. Even dissociative Arles wouldn't have allowed that.

Dan, she recalled, shifting carefully to look at him. His name was Dan.

She hadn't known people slept like this, so freely, innocently, as if sleep were a state they slipped into instead of a war zone where anything might happen.

She sat up on the bed, assuming her motion would disturb him. It didn't.

"Wake up," she said.

He didn't move.

She said it again louder.

When he still didn't stir, she reached out and shook his shoulder. Okay, maybe she hit him on the shoulder. His muscled—although not too much so—not gym ripped, just strong from life, shoulder. A quick recollection of how the arms beneath those shoulders had felt wrapped around her last night lit up her nerve endings, but she shunted it away. Gave him another shove.

Finally, he blinked a few times, rousing. His gaze roved around the room for a second before settling on her face.

"Hey, you," he said softly.

She stared at him. He really was a tremendously good-looking guy, long-limbed and angular with dark hair and Irish blue eyes. Skin so clear it shone, except for where it was covered by a fine mist of freckles and a morning scruff of beard. But she wouldn't let any of that distract her. "Why are we here?"

"Is that a philosophical question?"

She didn't answer.

"Um . . ." He signaled her to wait, then climbed out of bed and walked naked across the floor to the adjoining bathroom. She heard him open a few drawers, then the sound of water running, before a rumble of gargling. "Hope you don't mind my using your toothpaste," he said, climbing back into bed beside her.

She scooted sideways. "That's not mine. I don't know whose it is. It's probably a million years old. This is the guest suite."

"I don't think toothpaste expires," he replied. "But I'm getting the feeling you don't want me giving you a morning kiss, minty fresh or not."

She looked at him again, then repeated her question.

"Um, because we had sex last night, Arles. That's why we're here."

"What was wrong with my apartment?"

"Nothing," he said. "But you seemed to feel strongly that we come out here." Something appeared to hit him then. "You don't remember? You didn't seem that drunk."

"I wasn't drunk at all," she replied. "I don't drink." A pause. "Are you saying we drank together? You asshole—you would've had to give me Rohypnol to make that happen—"

"Hell, no, I didn't *roofie* you!" He jumped out of bed, still naked, though he didn't seem aware of it. "I thought maybe you were drinking before I got there. Since you don't remember what happened. After we met up, we didn't drink, or eat, or anything. We just—"

"Fucked," she said.

"I would've put it a little differently. But right. Once at your apartment. Twice here."

"Why?"

"Why did we do it so many times?"

"No. Why would you have put it differently?"

He began looking around for his clothes, sitting on the edge of the bed to pull up his boxers and jeans, then standing to put on a T-shirt and flannel button-down. "Uh, because it was pretty goddamn great is why. At least for me. I'm sorry it wasn't more memorable for you. It's always a bad sign when a woman gets amnesia after sleeping with you."

"Happens to you a lot?"

"Not that I know of. But maybe they wouldn't remember to tell me." He tipped her one of his smiles, although it was a somewhat deflated one.

"Well, don't take it personally," she said, a little miserably.

He gave her a look, then sat back down on the bed. "Hey, look. It sounds like things were really messed up, and I missed it. I'm sorry. It seemed . . . You seemed like you were into it."

"You mean I faked it well?"

"No, actually. I knew you didn't finish. At least, I was pretty sure you didn't."

Arles looked at him. She was a psychologist, treated couples, occasionally even did sex therapy, but she had no idea how to have a conversation like this. "Finish? Is that a euphemism?"

"Sure," he muttered, going red-faced. "I guess."

She decided to give him a break. "I didn't come, no."

He glanced away, his face taking on an even darker hue.

She gave him another break. "Don't worry. I never do."

He looked back quickly. "You mean with a new person, you don't usually—"

She held his gaze. "I mean that I never have."

He turned away, but not before she caught a recognizable expression on his face. Men wore this look when they got more of a woman than they could handle, waded into something deeper than they felt like dealing with. She'd never spent enough time with any one guy to have been the recipient of the Look. But she saw it when she counseled couples, especially straight ones.

This was not an interaction that belonged in her bedroom. She didn't give men too much of herself—she gave them nothing. Not one iota of Arles was handed over once she had finished with a guy. Used him for her purposes, then tossed the rest aside. And yes, she understood whom she was really screwing with this deal. Her stepfather. Herself. It didn't matter.

Arles giveth and Arles taketh away was her means of getting revenge.

She climbed out of bed. She was undressed too, but didn't go for her clothes. It was the power move. "You can leave now."

He stood up and took a few steps toward her.

"Go!" she screamed before he could get any closer. "Get out of my house!"

He did.

She got into the shower. Washed him off her, then washed herself off her to the extent that she could. She would've liked to be rid of herself completely. She started downstairs, her steps ponderous, her mind slow and oozy, as if she were in fact hungover. She had to find a way to get Louise to Fir Cove. That was the only thing that would save her now.

She reached back to touch her phone in her pocket. Dead and cold, useless here. Even if she could think of some excuse to get in touch with the woman—you've been randomly selected to receive a free month of therapy!—she wouldn't be able to do it until she'd driven miles away.

At the bottom of the stairs, a hum of activity told her that leaving Fir Cove might not happen anytime soon. A carton sat next to the wide-open door, along with a garbage bag stuffed so full that its plastic had gone translucent. A small figure darted out onto the porch with a backpack slung across one shoulder. Arles had completely forgotten her overnight guests.

Oh God, she hoped the woman—Stephanie, was that her name?—had been telling the truth when she said she and her daughter only inhabited the room in the basement. If they spent time on the other floors, and came up last night, then they might've overheard Arles and Dan—

His truck was still parked outside. He hadn't left, as she'd asked. Well, demanded. Ordered at top volume, really. She'd been a witch, a shrew, hysterical, all the terms bestowed upon women to get them to be less angry. Internalized misogyny. She loathed the echo of her own scream in her ears, the muscle memory of her body in its state of fury, rigid and clenched.

He came back inside and hoisted a case of water onto one shoulder while she went weak with self-loathing. For yelling at a total stranger. For sleeping with a total stranger.

Stephanie returned and picked up a box.

"Okay, I think this is it," Dan said to her. "Ready to go?"

Somehow the sight of this man entering her house—which presented a greater violation than his entering her—compelled Arles to call out a ringing, "No!"

They both turned and looked at her.

"Sorry, Arles," Dan said, sounding more pissed off than apologetic. "This woman needed some help, and I said I could give her and her daughter a ride into town."

Stephanie turned to Arles. "Thank you so much. For not doing anything." She gave the box she held a jog. "And again, I'm really sorry."

Did the statement work on two levels? She might've been thanking Arles for not calling the police or pressing charges, but there was a way in which not doing anything didn't warrant appreciation. Arles wasn't lifting one finger to help out a pair of people who clearly needed it.

Lissa came in from the porch, a stuffed bunny dangling from one hand, her feet dragging. "Mommy?" She spoke with a tired whine in her voice. "*Now* are we going?"

"No," Arles said again. After all this time, Louise was going to have to wait. "I mean, would you mind not leaving yet, Stephanie? I had—I have an idea you might be interested in."

"Um . . ." The woman reached for her daughter's hand. "Okay. I guess so."

"Great," Arles said. "I can run you into town afterward. Collect your things from Dan if he doesn't mind keeping them in his truck for a few hours." She forced herself to look at him. "Is that okay? I'm sorry if I'm messing things up." She could play the double-meaning game too.

The skin around his eyes crinkled, the expression in them softening. "Sure. Text me."

Stephanie had been true to her word. Not one item in the kitchen looked out of place or as if it'd even been touched, the room a museum of the last time Arles's mother had cooked here. Pots, pans, and mixing bowls neatly nested. Plates evenly stacked. Glasses and cups lined up in rows as orderly as soldiers on a field. Utensils lying in a drawer side by side like orphans in their beds, cans and cartons of foodstuff displayed label-side out. So brutally neat that Arles was surprised to see a thin coating of gray, the dust of disuse, had dared to accumulate.

"Sit down, please, both of you," she said, pulling out chairs from around a table that bridged the width of the room.

She crossed to a cupboard and began rooting around for coffee. She was pretty sure this was where her mother had kept it but couldn't get her hands on the container. There'd be sugar in a deep drawer to her left. No, to her right. She located the bin full of white crystals—her mother had been a baker—and lifted it out with two shaking hands. No milk or cream, of course, the refrigerator bare, and she wasn't sure what to serve a child. But the coffee maker was plugged in; she just needed to locate a filter. Suddenly, she yanked her hand out of the drawer as if something had bitten her. Brought a finger to her mouth and sucked it. Maybe she had mice?

"Can I help?" Stephanie asked. "I mean, would you mind?"

Arles lifted her chin a notch. But she took a step back and sank into a chair.

Ten minutes later, Stephanie set two steaming mugs of coffee on the table. She located a packet of hot chocolate and held it up to Arles, who nodded an *Of course.*

Arles felt relatively comfortable, despite the strangeness of the situation. Many was the time she'd sat before a new-to-her parent and child and got them off on the right foot.

"So, first, I should introduce myself," she said, looking at Stephanie. "Is Lissa allowed to call grown-ups by their first name?"

Stephanie frowned. "I don't know. Back when she was in school, the teachers were Miss Ellen, Mr. Peter, like that. And to be honest, we haven't met too many new people since then."

"Mr. Garvey at the library," Lissa piped up. "And Brittany at the market." She looked down at her drink. "Are there any marshmallows?"

"Lissa!" said Stephanie. "This is very nice for you to have cocoa."

"Marshmallows go stale," Arles told the girl. "So we didn't keep them. Because no one has cooked anything in this kitchen for a very long time."

"Why not?" asked Lissa.

"Well, that's what I wanted to talk to you and your mom about. But first, let's settle the what-to-call-me issue, okay?"

Lissa nodded while Stephanie watched Arles.

"I'm a doctor," Arles said. "The kind people talk to about their problems."

"A talking doctor sounds way better than the real kind," Lissa said.

Arles bit back a smile. "Yes, well, I happen to agree with you."

"She means she's a therapist, Lis," said Stephanie. "Remember, you went to go see one when Daddy and I were deciding not to all live together anymore?"

Lissa looked away without responding, which Arles mentally noted.

"So, anyway, I thought maybe Lissa could call me Dr. Arles. And just Arles is great, of course," she added to Stephanie.

"Why are we calling you anything?" asked Stephanie.

"Mommy! Your voice sounds very rude!"

Stephanie swallowed visibly. "You're right, Lis. I'm sorry." A pause. "I just wonder—"

"You wonder if the fact that your circumstances got desperate and I wasn't a total ass—I'm sorry, Lissa—a jerk and did something really execrable means you're now obliged to sit here with me and call me by name and even fix me coffee?"

"Well, something like that," Stephanie mumbled.

"The answer is you don't, of course," Arles said. "But I have an idea I think could help both of us out. If you'd like to hear it."

"I would!" chirped Lissa.

"Okay," Stephanie said slowly.

So Arles told them about Fir Cove.

"You're saying that I'd work here while patients come all this way to get their therapy?" Stephanie said once Arles had finished. She took a look around. "It *is* a pretty amazing place."

Arles nodded. "And since I treat families, there will be children at times." She paused to smile at Lissa, who smiled back. "Out of school for the length of their treatment. So your ability to teach would be a huge asset to this place."

"When you were first talking . . . I thought you meant for me to cook and clean."

Arles frowned. "That seems like it wouldn't hit your skill set. I know homeschooling parents. What you do isn't easy."

"What she does is easier than what she makes me do," Lissa stated.

Arles laughed. "Now on that, I bet you are right."

"Will there be kids my age?" she asked. "At this school my mom's going to teach?"

Arles considered. "Well, now, there could be. How old are you, Lissa—eight?"

The girl nodded. "Practically nine."

"Nine in five months," Stephanie amended.

"That *is* practically, Mommy! Because it's more than half the year."

"I can tell your mom's good at teaching math," said Arles.

"Math's my favorite," Lissa responded.

"Excellent. Hope that stays true. Nine is the age—"

"When girls start to lose it," Stephanie put in. "I'm going to fight like hell."

Arles smiled. "I know one ten-year-old who I think is going to be here." She held up crossed fingers. "And ten isn't very far away from a month more than eight and a half."

"Yay," Lissa said. "So does this mean we get to still live here?"

Arles looked at Stephanie.

"I can't shake the feeling that this is charity," she said. "If we hadn't happened to invade your home, it's not like you wouldn't have come up with some other teaching solution."

"First of all, you did not invade my home; you squatted in it. Which is a thing people do. And second, until very recently, like the other day, Fir Cove wasn't mine, either. I rent an apartment in town, and if my landlord hadn't already subdivided it within an inch of its life, I could easily have gotten kicked out too. Way things are going up here."

Stephanie gave a slow nod. Everyone in Wedeskyull knew what that meant.

"Point being, I'm about to grow this place into something it's never been before. It will take a lot of work, and if it would help you and your daughter to be part of that process, then to my mind, good on all of us. But if it isn't the right option, that's completely understandable."

"I think it's the right option, Dr. Arles!" said Lissa.

"I'm happy to hear that," Arles said. "Although sometimes what feels good to one person doesn't to another." Truer words seldom spoken.

"No, she's right," Stephanie put in. "You both are. This is a pretty damn great option."

"Oh," Arles replied. "Well, then, I'm very glad. We'll have to discuss a fair salary."

"Minus rent," Stephanie stated.

"Of course," Arles said, distracted now. She'd given this as much time as she could. No point in enlisting Stephanie—in taking possession of Fir Cove at all—if she couldn't figure out a way to summon Louise.

"This kitchen is awesome," Stephanie said. "Did I mention that Lissa and I love to cook? Losing our kitchen was the second worst part of being evicted."

"What was the first?" Arles asked. Her mind roaming away from the conversation, seizing on one possibility after another, each increasingly far-fetched, before discarding them all.

Stephanie shook her head. "Story for another day."

"I have five recipe books," announced Lissa. "And I also read blogs."

"You do?" said Arles, refocusing. "Well, you two can do as much cooking as you want. I'd love that. I barely even know how to open a jar of spaghetti sauce."

"Why is spaghetti sauce in a jar?" asked Lissa.

"If you're serious, I say we have pasta for dinner," said Arles, then suddenly jumped up.

Because she'd figured it out. Something that at least posed a better chance of working than any of the other ideas circling her mind like runners on a track.

She'd forged this arrangement with Stephanie because kids went to school, including, obviously, Geary. And in that Facebook group, Louise had spoken glowingly about the educational facility her son attended, as well as how his enrollment was in jeopardy. It was a long shot, tenuous at best, but perhaps the director would consider Arles's new treatment facility a referral for students not thriving in his own place of tutelage and instruction.

CHAPTER ELEVEN

The day before, Louise had decided to end her call before Dee could answer.

She wouldn't have been able to deal with the receptionist's scolding voice, or cope with telling Dr. Trager the news about Geary getting dismissed from Elward, with an entire school-free afternoon still ahead. This morning she let Geary sleep in, no reason for him to get up at the usual time, which gave her some space to try and put the next part of their lives together.

As she went downstairs to cook breakfast, fresh morning sunlight made her notice something. A piece of paper lay on the table by the front door on top of a jumble of envelopes. She walked over and unfolded the sheet, smoothing out the crease. A name and phone number were scrawled beneath treatment-center letterhead in messy handwriting. Dr. Trager's, obviously—the man's total lack of caring embodied by letters and digits. She couldn't remember bringing this into the house, let alone putting it where she dumped the mail and assorted clutter.

She had never been a big believer in religion, or even God. Her mother was a mostly lapsed Catholic, Louise's late grandmother so fervid in her devoutness that she apparently hadn't made rosaries and Lent and ashes, going to Mass and confession and taking Communion, all the conventions of the church, very appealing. Louise's father was a pretty strict something—Methodist, maybe—but he acted like religion was an act more private than bathing. "Just between me and my God," he used to say.

When Louise had met Michael, he'd barely noticed her lack of affiliation, being an atheist himself. (He said he'd been raised with reality, not religion.) They had a friend get ordained online so he could marry them. So all in all, she hadn't had much exposure to faith.

But now, she wondered. It felt like some divine hand had put this piece of paper here. A being who knew they'd lost Elward and come up with a solution. This thing was lying in a freaking sunbeam, for God's—ha—sake. Like a spotlight was shining on it, making the wooden table glow. Even how pushy Dr. Trager had been about his idea. It'd been presented a bit early—maybe this god's timing was off—but the road it opened up seemed heaven sent right now.

The phone rang and rang. No secretary picked up, or even an answering service. Finally, Louise got voicemail. It sounded like a personal number, which was weird. Who called doctors on their private phones? But the name delivered in a calm, low tone was correct. Arles Shepherd.

Does anyone leave messages anymore? Well, if you want to, go ahead.

Louise stared at the screen for so long she got the command: *If you are not satisfied with this message, press three to rerecord.* She told the doctor who she was and asked to be called back.

Ending the call, she went upstairs to see if she could tell whether Geary was awake, placing one ear against his door. No noise coming from inside the room, although there often wasn't when Geary was keeping himself occupied, intent on whatever consumed him. Disturbing this peace would be like forcing herself to jump into an ice-cold lake, so after trying the phone number again, she decided to scramble some eggs for Geary, then google the doctor.

Her search led her to a classy-looking website. Arles Shepherd, PhD, licensed psychologist and specialist in child and family counseling. Plus, she was something, or had something, called a diplomate. Her picture on the home page, along with candid shots elsewhere on the site, was beautiful. The doctor had long auburn hair, eyes a bright enough green that their color stood out behind a pair of cool glasses, and a complexion Louise knew cost a lot to maintain. She noted her nails; she always did. A subtle rose color.

Another page named a clinic that was part of a hospital in some town with an unpronounceable name. No way did this doctor work there—it was like four hundred miles away, in a part of the state Louise hardly knew existed. Lots of mountains. Dr. Trager couldn't possibly have thought she could get there with Geary. She called and was relieved to find that indeed Dr. Shepherd wasn't employed at that hospital.

She tried the private number once more. The doctor was going to see some random woman blowing up her phone. Had Dr. Trager told her to expect a call from Louise?

Louise's grandmother had been full of it. Michael was right; this was reality. What kind of god would play with somebody like this, not to mention a ten-year-old boy? It was cruel. And this doctor was cruel, purposely ignoring her phone; mental health professionals usually at least had someone to screen for emergencies or left a number to call. Maybe she and Dr. Trager had spoken, and Dr. Shepherd concluded that Geary wasn't a good fit for her program.

Louise shuffled in the direction of his room again. The whole world could turn its back on her son, but she would not. She opened the door just a crack to see Geary stirring on his bare mattress, sheets and covers folded neatly at the foot of the bed, and at that moment, her phone lit up. Muted, as always, but the screen glowed like a star. *Unknown caller.*

She took a few steps back down the hall, already swiping. "Hello?"

"I'm *so* sorry I missed your calls. I was somewhere without signal."

The low, resonant voice from the voicemail. Comforting, reassuring; Louise's sense of distress flowed out of her like water. But what did she mean, without signal? Like, in 1999?

"Um, that's okay."

"Louise. You're Louise. Louise Drake."

"Uh, yes, that's right."

A soft laugh. "I was just—making sure. It's hard to believe. I mean, it's a pleasure to talk with you after all this time."

"Yeah, thanks." Another statement that was hard to make sense of. "All what time?"

Silence for a second. "Well, you left a couple of messages. That's what I meant. There was an unfortunate delay before we connected."

"Oh, right. Of course." *Duh,* Louise thought. "I'm looking for a new therapist for my son." Losing both Geary's school and his therapist put a frantic note in her voice, made the announcement more of an appeal. "And Dr. Trager—did he tell you I'd be calling? We're not seeing him anymore, that's a long story, but anyway, he said you're really good."

"Kind of him."

Her tone had a bite to it that Louise liked. "Can you take my son on? As a patient?"

"Oh, I should think so," she said. "I'd like to see you both. Let me tell you about what I do. How I practice. Then you'll see why your former therapist thought we'd be well matched."

—

Although it was true that Dr. Shepherd was no longer at the hospital with the funny name, the new place where she worked was in that same distant land upstate. At first, the whole idea seemed impossible, and everything cascaded down inside Louise. They were no better off than when the doctor hadn't been taking her calls. But then she stopped to think.

Why couldn't she go wherever? If it meant getting Geary the best treatment, who cared how far away it was? They no longer had Elward. Michael was starting a new life for himself. What held them here? Not extended family—she and Michael were only children, and his parents were deceased while Louise saw hers only on occasion. They had trouble dealing with Geary's diagnosis, especially her mother. If Louise left her job at Glam & Go, she could probably get it back, and if she couldn't, there were other salons. She and Geary lived in a minimally kept-up rental in an overcrowded suburb. She hated it. Hated every part of her life, except for Geary.

"And you take my insurance?" she asked. "It's Childcare through New York State."

"I do," Dr. Shepherd said. "You don't have to worry about any of those details, Louise. You don't have to worry about anything."

Louise let out a laugh whose ugliness she hoped Dr. Shepherd wouldn't notice. Then again, she was starting to get the feeling that this doctor noticed everything. "I haven't not been worried in eight years."

"I understand that," said the doctor, and it really sounded like she did.

Louise felt her body assume a strange sort of ease. Even her eyes fell shut.

"Why don't you tell me about your son?"

Louise went and peeked inside Geary's room again. He'd gotten dressed and was sitting on his carpet, making tracks in the blue fuzz with one finger. Even though countless therapists had told her this was probably some form of sensory stimulation, the tracks always looked like a complex network of roads to Louise, parallel lines and corners at perfect right angles.

She whispered good morning and told him breakfast was ready downstairs just as he climbed to his feet and came to close his door. Louise backed away before the wood panel could hit her in the face, then placed the phone against her ear. "Okay, well, Geary stopped talking just after he turned two. Twenty-five months to be exact." And one week and a day and six hours.

"Stopped talking," Dr. Shepherd repeated. "So he was verbal before that?"

"Well . . ." She felt her face heat even though the doctor was hundreds of miles away and couldn't see her flailing. "I would've said so. More babbling—Geary was late at everything—but I could understand him."

"He was hitting speech milestones; they were just hard to interpret."

Louise hung her head. "I mean, my husband—ex-husband now—wouldn't have agreed. Other people, like my parents, were concerned. The pedi referred us to early intervention. But if you'd asked me, I would've said he was on his way to talking."

"You're the mother," Dr. Shepherd said. "So that means a great deal."

Louise felt unexpected tears well in her eyes as she was hurtled back to that time, that desperate time, when she was always trying to convince Michael of something, plead with him to take her seriously, not give up on their son. "Geary would be screeching or crying or shrieking . . . He screamed so much that year, I was worried he'd blow out his vocal cords. But every once in a while, in that big garbled jumble, I caught something that sounded like a word."

"That must've been very frustrating. Frightening, even. To be the only person who understood something so vital and important, and have no one believe you or see or hear what you did. Like Cassandra."

Louise didn't know who the doctor meant, but tears threatened again, and she had to pause to regroup. "So then we started to go see a whole bunch of doctors—more than you could imagine—psychologists like you and OT and PT people and also the kind that does medicine."

"Psychiatrists."

"Uh-huh. But none of the medications helped Geary. They tried ones to get him to focus and others to calm him down, and some they said were mood stabilizers, but nothing worked; and now he's just on the lowest dose of Sersezodine, but I don't think it's really doing anything."

"Heard."

Louise smiled. Dr. Trager had been right. She liked this doctor.

"Louise, can you Facetime or Zoom or one of those? I'd like to meet Geary."

They switched to video, and the doctor turned out to be as stunning in the fuzzy screen image as she was in her photos. They smiled *hellos*, then Louise indicated *one sec*, which she hoped the doctor understood might wind up being more like one minute, or one hour, or feel that long, anyway. Then she placed her hand on Geary's doorknob and rotated it. When she heard the snick of the catch, she eased the door open, inch by careful inch, and took a step inside.

He sat on the floor in front of his desk, chair shoved all the way across the room. No tracks in the carpet pile; he must've smoothed them out. The warm bath of sunshine and Geary's peaceful pose made Louise momentarily relax. She felt proud of her son, all uncombed brown curls, suddenly long limbs, and bright, sparkling eyes. How soon he would grow to be handsome, not just cute. She felt adulthood coming for him like a truck on a collision course.

"Hey, Gear," she said. "There's a new doctor I'd like you to meet. On the phone; we don't have to go out today." She put on an exaggerated *whew* face. One therapist had called this "cueing," a way to try and build a body of receptive responses in Geary. They'd stopped seeing that therapist when he slipped and called such responses *normal*. She crouched down, angling the phone. "Dr. Shepherd, this is my son. Geary, meet Dr. Shepherd."

"Should I say something?" Dr. Shepherd mouthed.

Louise felt herself smile again. The doctor was handling it perfectly. "Yes, I think so."

"Geary, it's nice to get to talk with you," she said in that low, balanced tone of hers.

Louise positioned the phone so the two of them could see each other better.

"I'm Dr. Arles. I'm going to meet you in person soon at this pretty cool place where you're coming to stay. At least, you might think it's cool. There's a lake for swimming. Just has to get a little warmer up here, unless you don't mind cold water."

The doctor gave a mock shiver; maybe she was also a fan of cueing.

Geary loved to swim—it was as if Dr. Shepherd somehow knew an optimal form of reward—and actually never seemed bothered by getting cold. Despite his sensory issues, he'd stay in the water till his lips grew blue and ghoulish.

"Isn't that awesome?" she said to him, then spoke into the phone. "Geary's a great swimmer. Here, there's even a picture of him at the Jersey shore on his wall—" She tilted the phone so Dr. Shepherd could see. When she turned back to the screen, the doctor was squinting as if to get a better look. Louise brought the phone closer to the photograph of the beach.

"Actually, Louise, do you mind waking up Geary's computer?"

"What?" she said, switching focus to the desk. "Oh, he doesn't use that. We have it because they said fifth graders will need them." *If we find a place for fifth grade,* she thought, concealing her face from Geary in case the thought showed.

"Humor me," Dr. Shepherd said. "Just give the mouse a jiggle."

Louise frowned, although her feet were already in motion. Moving in order to accommodate this request from their new doctor, without bothering to check and see where she was going, just crossing in front of the window like it didn't even matter. As if taking an easy couple of steps in her son's room could ever be easy. She forgot to crouch down, waddle-walk to avoid disrupting the light, the air, the invisible texture of the universe.

Geary dived forward. Headfirst, like he'd once done in a wave on a long-ago day when everything had gone about as perfectly as it ever did; she'd been in a good enough headspace to snap the picture that now hung on the wall. The rough, dry sand had presented a problem at first, but then Geary had simply waited to kick off his slipper-shoes, the only pair he would wear back then, until he reached the part where the sea stained the shore, groaning in delight as he marched back and forth for hours, water nipping at his toes.

Louise leaped out of the line of light, quick as a gymnast, but it was too late.

Geary started humming so loudly that it caused a vibration while he tore fistfuls of fuzz out of the carpet. Louise almost began wailing herself. Dr. Shepherd would never take them now. How could she let a kid who did this come to her out-of-the-way treatment center? It'd be a risk, a—what was the word?—liability. What if Geary got hurt when they were far away from medical care? Just then, the hum he'd been making burst like a balloon, transforming into a shriek.

Desperate, she cried, "He doesn't usually do this, I swear—" A lie.

He threw his body in a loop-de-loop, landing so hard that his skull jounced against the carpet with a sickening thud. Geary didn't treat heads or faces with the same care neurotypicals did, and for Louise, it had always been one of the most upsetting aspects of his disability.

She was so overwhelmed that she'd forgotten to change the position of her phone, just kept it aimed at Geary. She lunged over to one side—as clumsy a motion as he was making—while continuing to babble.

"Something happened recently that made his behaviors change—" Not a lie. Maybe.

"Well, then, we'll have to figure out what that is," Dr. Shepherd said as calmly as if all virtual hell weren't breaking loose in the room.

Her quiet acceptance blew a bubble around Louise.

Then the doctor said, "But for now, I want you to walk out into the hall."

Maybe she had her volume turned down? Louise couldn't allow Geary to be alone right now. She never left him during meltdowns; he might get hurt. And it wasn't as if this advice would shorten the length or anything. These episodes contained clocks of their own, therapists had told her, needed to run themselves out. Dr. Shepherd may as well have suggested saying, "Abracadabra" or waving a magic wand.

"You can do it," she said, as if reading Louise's thoughts.

Geary began prodding at the bald patch of carpet for anything left to pull up, and Louise took a step backward, then one more. Reached behind her for the doorknob before letting herself out. She nudged the door most of the way shut, just a slit to allow her to keep an eye on Geary. When she came to a stop in the hall, unmoving, breath held, it was as if a fuse had blown.

Screams sucked into a vortex, a vacuum. Nothing rattled, shook, or knocked.

Silence settled, the quiet of a land left in ashes, disintegrated to soot after a fire.

Geary's meltdowns never cut off abruptly. They wound down, losing force and heat slowly—a cyclist coasting to a stop, a driver running out of gas. But something had changed ever since that day at the supermarket, and the success of Dr. Shepherd's intervention only made that clearer. The end of this episode was like a faucet shutting off, the source of Geary's dysregulation there and then gone. What could it have been? There were a couple of possibilities Louise might've anticipated—a new doctor, the virtual introduction. Firsts were hard for Geary.

But his distress had evaporated the instant she'd left the room. Just the thought provoked pain, a sharp scissoring inside her. Could she be the reason her son had been overtaken in there, been taken down? Was it something about *her*? What the hell had she done?

CHAPTER TWELVE

The second Arles ended the call, sweat broke out all over her body, a dewy shine she could feel, while everything inside her drained out. She slid off the futon in her apartment, limbs as limp as boiled noodles. Back to jargon: a blend of countertransference and projective identification, wherein the therapist took on the emotional tenor of her patient, had her in its teeth right now. She was Geary after his meltdown.

To someone unfamiliar with neurodivergence, meltdowns could be seen as temper tantrums, or worse, fits. A spiraling hysteria, the sufferer overcome, just as men used to describe all those women dropping onto chaises, salts shoved at their nostrils to bring them around.

Instead of a state of sheer overload—sensory and otherwise. Involuntary, not behavioral, especially in the *badly behaved* sense. The neurodivergent brain became overtaxed and erupted like a volcano. There was a reason the preferred term was *melting down*. As in a nuclear reactor.

Witnessing Geary's torment and unrest would've been rationale enough for any reasonably empathic clinician to wind up in the condition Arles now found herself. But there was an added cause in her case. Meeting Louise had made time wobble, sending Arles back to the sherbet swirl of girlhood when that photograph wound up in her possession. She'd turned her attention to Geary because she was supposed to focus on her new patient, but Louise was all she could see, the one who knocked the wind out of her, buckled her spine.

After the intake came to its crashing halt, she'd spoken with Louise while Geary calmed down in his room, causing Arles to slip even further from the here and now. Not visibly, she hoped. She was fairly certain she'd switched automatically into therapist mode, treating Louise like the mother of any patient. Made suggestions, talked things through, clarified. But the whole time another part of Arles had been living, thrumming, pushing up through the earth. That photo had been with her for the majority of her life, an appendage that showed up around her twelfth birthday, at a point when so much else about her had been in the act of bursting into being.

Somehow, although Arles couldn't say in what way, the picture was conjoined with all that new life. So, in a sense, Louise was too.

The fact that Louise had gotten in touch before Trager could pull his plug was a break Arles had chosen not to question. There'd been too much else demanding her attention, such as the fear that she would give herself away. It was too soon for Louise to suspect that she and Arles had any deeper a link than a mother seeking treatment for her son. But before being able to catch herself, Arles had acted out of knowledge she had no right to possess.

Asking Louise to introduce her to her son could've easily provoked suspicion. From the director of Geary's school, Arles had learned the boy was no longer attending Elward, but Louise might easily have been alerted by a child psychologist proposing a face-to-face with a fourth grader on a weekday morning. Louise had been distracted. Arles had gotten lucky.

Also, the swimming. There'd been chat online about how Geary's sensory issues didn't apply to water, so Arles had used the boy's love of the activity to establish rapport. But she hadn't paused to consider that her mention might sound an alarm, and indeed had perceived a fleeting suspicion in Louise's eyes before the woman mentally readjusted—all kids liked to swim, some rationale like that. Then, with a blush of pride, she'd displayed a shot of her son by the sea.

Beaming at both the real life and photographic versions of her child, her smile as bright as the sun Geary focused on so fiercely. Her love for him tangible, apparent, even though things must get terribly tough, as a single mom, especially. From Facebook, Arles knew about Louise's divorce, but hearing that Michael had discounted his ex's belief in their son's early speech added a dimension, not least because Arles's gut told her Louise was the accurate reporter in this case.

Something happened at around age two, some sort of big disruption—that seemed clear. It was the age when Autism tended to become apparent to parents and professionals.

Arles had tried to be an ally ever since her internship days when she'd worked with people with a range of neurodivergent profiles, many of whom would sooner have given up their hands, or their mobility, than their differently wired brains.

But Geary's presentation was not one she had seen before.

The psychologist in her yearned to help this child with his challenges, assist in finding a setting where he would thrive and be supported, independent of the bond she intended to forge with his mother. Which was what had prompted her to ask Louise to display Geary's computer.

Just before the hurricane flew and the boy became utterly overwhelmed.

The machine had been booted when Louise went into the bedroom; Arles was sure of it. Louise had been laser focused on her son, and the computer had gone to sleep within seconds. But the phone was tilted in the right direction, and Arles thought she had seen flickers coming from the desk area. Had Geary been doing something on his computer, struck a key to make it go dark, then sent his chair rolling across the room while he dropped down on the floor? When the doorknob had turned and he'd realized his mother was coming in? Louise had entered cautiously enough that it would've allowed Geary sufficient time to conceal his actions.

Was this the correct read of a sequence that had gone on behind a closed door?

If so, Arles didn't have any kind of hypothesis for what might be on that computer.

Or why, in the midst of his distraught frenzy, Geary had looked right at Arles in the camera and mouthed a single clearly shaped word.

Hurry.

"Just be nice," he'd said after she'd asked him how she should behave.

Well, what a surprise, she thought, still sarcastic. A man wants me to act nice.

Ms. Mailer's voice again. The two of them sometimes talked after health ended. It was the period before lunch, so there was no rush, and the classroom was so colorful and welcoming.

Ms. Mailer had a poster on her wall that read: WELL-BEHAVED WOMEN RARELY MAKE HISTORY, *with a wild-furred cat waving a banner.*

She had suggested that it should read "her-story" instead, but then Ms. Mailer told her that the word "history" wasn't actually composed of "his" and "story" but derived from the Latin root "histor-" meaning "wise" or "learned." Ms. Mailer was always teaching, not just in class.

The man turned the key to start the engine. "We've got a long drive ahead," he said, easing the van off the shoulder and onto the road. "You never want to sit around in one place too long. Attracts the wrong kind of attention."

You *might not want to. Concealing the thought from her face. But how about* me?

She twisted, seat belt digging into her skin. Because she could use some attention right about now. Somebody she could signal for help. But there wasn't one other car around. This road was long and lonely. He could drive on it forever—and that was what it seemed he intended to do.

Why did he want to, though? Not just to feed her treats. To make her act nice?

Her mind worked, trying to figure it out, like a hard problem in math. Maybe she could learn something that would help her. Finally a reason for being so good at talking to grown-ups. And even better at getting them to talk back. Most adults, especially men, loved to hear the sound of their own voices and didn't have many people who'd listen.

But she would. She would listen to every single word this man had to say.

A SIGHTING

"I do a lot of this kind of work," the therapist said to Cass and Maggie once introductions had been made. The woman spoke in a gentle, level tone, the kind of voice that probably never got upset. "I'm asked to step in during crisis situations—that's my primary area of specialization."

Cass sat down awkwardly, too far forward on a couch. Maggie took a chair.

"So I understand that instead of being set to silent, phones have their volume turned all the way up in here," the therapist continued. "My clients keep one eye on the door, plan for a quick exit. That's the opposite of how therapy usually works, but necessary with my cases."

He didn't know what to say, how this was supposed to go.

"A child in the hospital, a jury about to return a verdict, the arrest of a teacher at school. Those are all real situations during which I've treated one or more of the involved parties."

"When Leo gave me your name, I thought you were too far away," Maggie told her. "Even though this is only fifteen minutes down the road."

The therapist nodded. "Because what if Bea chose right now to come home?"

The hypothetical hit him like a slug to his chest.

But Maggie gave a grateful nod, as if saying it straight out like that had comforted her. "I've barely set foot from our house since it happened. This felt like going to another planet."

"And how are you tolerating it so far?" the therapist asked. She turned to Cass, one hand extended in his direction. "Cassius, what is this like for you?"

"Cass," he said. "Um . . ."

"We asked a neighbor to come stay until we get home," Maggie said as he faltered. "He lives up the road; he's like a grandfather to Bea. He's known her since the day she was born."

"How wonderful you have such support," the therapist said.

"Actually . . . ," he said. "Dr. Reynolds?"

She nodded encouragingly. "Ms. is fine. I'm a masters-level clinician."

"I was a little worried about leaving Don in charge. He's like family to us, like Maggie says, never had kids of his own. But he's getting on in years. What if Bea—" He took a breath that felt thick, solidifying in his lungs. "What if she does get home and needs help? I don't know if Don would be physically able—"

"There's police presence too, Cass," Maggie said quietly. "They're constantly patrolling. And Don's been retired less than a year." She aimed her next words at the therapist. "I know from my job how therapy helps people stay upright. For the first day or so, Cass and I walked around like zombies. No food or sleep, not even talking. But we have to be functional right now. For Bea."

Ms. Reynolds watched them both, her eyes bright, glistening, like a bird's.

Finally, he nodded, and Maggie's shoulders dropped a little. He hadn't been aware of how rigidly she was holding herself till then. She got up and took a seat beside him on the couch.

He laid his hand on top of his wife's. "So how does this work? What do we do now?"

"In crisis situations, we don't normally talk about the crisis itself," the therapist replied. "Things are too uncertain, too unresolved, and also, it's kind of obvious, isn't it? If I asked how this was making you feel, a standard therapeutic catchphrase, there'd only be one answer, right? Bad. Lousy. Terrible."

That's three answers, he thought.

Maggie shifted her hand, digging her fingers into his.

"So what we do instead," Ms. Reynolds went on, "is discuss things in your life that may make it hard to *deal* with the crisis. To function optimally, as you said, Maggie."

She nodded, and he figured he might as well copy her. But then he realized he had no idea what the therapist meant. He felt like he was playing a game without knowing the rules. Or a game that had no rules. "Like how?"

"Why don't we start by you telling me what things were working in your life and what things gave you trouble before this happened." She held up a finger as if she'd caught herself at something. "Sorry. Euphemism. Before Bea went missing."

"Everything was working." He said it fast, to keep from hearing the echo of the therapist's last four words. Her calm, even tone had started to grate on him. "Things were fine."

Maggie shifted on the little couch. "That's not really true."

He didn't say anything.

"Can you say more, Maggie?" asked Ms. Reynolds.

"Well . . . the warehouse where Cass worked had recently been shut down. All the work was sent to a facility overseas."

"So he was out of a job."

Maggie gave him a quick glance, then said, "Which meant I had to take a second one." She switched her focus to Ms. Reynolds. "That's how I met Leo. He hired me on as an admin. I changed to evenings at Walmart down in Porter's Grove."

The therapist nodded. "Sounds like a stressful time."

They were talking like he wasn't even there. He felt a boil of rage. "I'm a failure. Why don't you just come out and say so, Mags?"

"That's not what I'm saying at all! You couldn't help what happened at the warehouse! Now you're responsible for the rise of a global economy?" Her tone, if not the therapist's, bit.

He turned on her, and she shot back, as far as she could get on the couch. He saw Ms. Reynolds register it, and worked to smooth out his expression, borrow a little of the therapist's calm-and-even, no matter how much of an act it was on his part.

"I haven't been worthy of you since the day we met."

"What—" Maggie broke off. "I honestly have no idea what you mean."

"Don't you, though?"

"Cass." She closed part of the distance between them. "I really don't."

"Perhaps you can tell her, Cass?" suggested the therapist.

He averted his face from his wife's, finding it easier to put what he had to say to a stranger, even one he didn't like. "Maggie comes from a town in Massachusetts. Sudbury. Doesn't that say it all?"

"I'm not sure what it says," the therapist replied, still mildly.

Only now her tone suited him, allowed him to flood the blank, open space with words. "Look, I was a boy from Maine, still wet behind the ears. I'd never even left the state. And Maggie—well, just listen to her talk. Just look at her. She's smart and beautiful, and she dazzled me from the second she said hello. We were standing in line to register for classes. She was looking at environmental science and wasn't sure if it fulfilled the math/science requirement. I had just signed up for eco studies, so she asked if I knew."

"Sounds like you both had things to teach each other," Ms. Reynolds said.

"We didn't, though," he said. "That's the thing. I dropped out of college after one semester." The shame of it still filled him. He was supposed to have been the first in his family to earn a degree. "Maggie taught me everything about everything. I wasn't even right in my guess about environmental science. I thought it'd have to be bio or chem or physics, one of those; turned out earth science was just fine." A pause to collect himself. "Maggie took me to experience life, but I had no place to take her. Nothing to see. She showed me the world, and I showed her—"

"Love," Maggie broke in. "That's what you showed me. And as you know better than anyone else on earth, no one ever had before."

He shifted in her direction on the couch.

She made him lift his gaze to hers with the sheer force of her eyes. She nodded.

Their phones rang.

They had them in their hands at the same second, standing and turning their backs on each other to avoid one talking over the other, to keep from missing a word. They ended the calls at the same time too. Twisted their bodies around, now face to face.

"Sheriff Brawley," Maggie told him.

"Lucinda," was his contribution. "In dispatch."

Then they both spoke at once.

"There's been a possible sighting."

Neither was sure what that meant. They had both been given the same instructions.

"Lucinda said Brawley doesn't want either of us driving at this time," said Cass.

"He's coming right now in a car," Maggie responded.

He nodded. He knew.

"What does it mean?" she asked.

He lifted his shoulders helplessly.

They spun in the therapist's direction.

"Why—I think that sounds like someone saw Bea," said Ms. Reynolds.

"No." Maggie advanced on her. "Don't you say that. Don't you do that. Unless you're sure. Unless something in your training—or your professional experience—"

Her voice so thin and ragged, it split. He had never heard his wife talk to anyone like that, talk like that in any capacity ever. It didn't sound like human speech.

"You're right," the therapist answered. Still so smooth, unruffled. As if this didn't carry the slightest bit of weight for her. They might as well have been discussing the price of eggs at the market. "I apologize. The police will have to inform you."

Outside, the shriek of sirens and a hoarse thrum of engine.

CHAPTER THIRTEEN

As Arles drove past the gates, back at Fir Cove for good, the conundrum posed by Geary continued to occupy space in her mind, causing a delay in her realization that something was wrong. Invisible currents in the air, like a heat mirage on the otherwise cool day. She refused to doubt this feeling when it came over her. It had enabled her to survive her childhood.

She shut off the engine, letting the car roll back, out of sight of whoever might be around. Something or someone lay ahead that was making the hairs on her arms stand up like tiny antennae. She pushed on the door handle till the catch released, then climbed out and eased the door shut, avoiding a bang. An image of Louise gaining entrance to Geary's room in a similar manner played across the backs of her eyes.

She stood with her hands squared on her hips, Geary's plea or request or command an earworm, a tune stuck in her head. *Hurry, hurry, hurry.*

Her ears picked out distinct sounds: the ticking engine, a faint rustle of leaves, a mix of calling, squawking, and singing from faraway birds. But nothing looked out of place along this strand of road bisecting the woods. She needed to get within sight of the house.

She took a few steps to one side and was soon swallowed by trees. Arles both loved and loathed these woods. They had been the scene of some of her worst horrors; they'd also hidden and harbored her. Her stepfather had brought her to these woods; she'd run from him through them.

Now she made short work of her trip, flinging back branches with barely audible snaps, covering ground fast. She wove around a scatter of outbuildings, then the row of tiny cabins that were going to house the patients. These had been built behind a berm of soil, where she halted, breathing hard as she concealed herself amid a sweep of fir boughs.

Stephanie had just exited the house, one hand visored over her eyes. She stopped at the lip of the sweeping porch, where a man stood looking up from the base of the wide stone steps.

Silently, Arles pinched a branch with her fingers and moved it to one side.

"Steph. Took a minute to find you." He placed one foot on the first step.

"How did you—" Stephanie began.

"Tate," he interrupted her. "Guy I go fishing with, remember? He saw our stuff in Danny MacKinnon's truck."

"My stuff," she said. "That's all my—"

"Danny wouldn't tell me nothing," the guy went on as if Stephanie weren't speaking. "So I had to follow him around for a while. He made a trip out here a few hours ago."

He did? thought Arles.

"I parked a ways back and saw Lissie running around," the guy concluded, sounding pleased with his own cleverness. His left foot followed his right onto the step, and he looked down as if contemplating his next move.

Stephanie went running down the rest of the flight. "Listen to me, Nicky. I don't want you messing this up for us. Please. Lissa and I—we've got something good going. She'll be happy here, I can tell."

"I'm not gonna mess anything up," he said, looking hurt. "So long as you don't give me any trouble when it comes to seeing Lissie, you got nothing to fear." His voice dropped, the low caress of a steel claw. "No trouble about seeing you, either. You hear?"

Arles took a few steps backward in the direction of the cabins while keeping an eye on Stephanie. The woman's shoulders appeared to deflate, although her voice hardened, a change in tone detectable even from a distance as Arles made her retreat.

"Cut it out, Nicky," she said. "You know we're through."

Arles arrived at the fifth cabin, opened its door at a run—these structures didn't have locks—and darted inside. She didn't have to go any farther than the entrance. What she wanted was propped against a small side table. She grabbed it.

Nick rasped out a laugh whose sound carried. "I know you *told* me we're through."

Arles ducked back out of the cabin, retracing the route she'd just taken but being judicious with her steps. Taking care just in case. Her stepfather had always counseled precautions. She kept the road to her left to ensure she'd exit in the right place. Spied tire marks different from those made by her SUV. Ruts in the road, not metaphysics or clairvoyance, had signaled the alien presence.

"I just don't remember agreeing," he was saying.

"It's not about whether you agree or not," Stephanie replied.

Nick laughed. "I love it when you get feisty, Steph—"

Arles stepped out of the woods. "I'd say you agree."

They both turned.

Stephanie's face went a sick, heated red. "Arles. I'm so sorry about this—"

"You have nothing to apologize for," Arles said.

"Damn right," Nick said. "Don't apologize for me. I'm not a fucking *this*."

"Whatever you are is between you and Stephanie. She can obviously handle herself in addition to handling you." Sometimes saying something made it so. Instilled confidence. "The extent of my participation will be to make sure you never come onto my property again."

He faced her with a languid, drawn-out swivel. "I don't think there's any way you're gonna stop me, lady."

Arles brought her arm out from behind her back and lifted the Winchester.

"Whoa." Nick took a step backward. "What the fuck? You're gonna threaten me with a gun for coming here and talking to my girl?"

"Oh, I'm not threatening," Arles said mildly. "And it doesn't sound like Stephanie is your anything to me. But that's none of my business."

"You're damn right it's none of—"

"There's only one thing that is my concern," Arles said, casually sighting the rifle. It had to be unloaded for her stepfather to have left it the way he had, and even that a sign of his ailing mind. She wouldn't have known what to do if it contained ammunition, anyway; Peter hadn't been interested in teaching her to shoot on those trips. But she'd watched him enough to make this look natural. "And that's protecting my land. Which includes shooting you if you show up again without an invitation from me or Stephanie."

An ugly grin split his face. "Whatever. Congrats, Steph, you've found someone as psycho as you are. I hope you two bitches enjoy each other."

She started to reply, her mouth a furious open *o*, then looked at Arles and shut it.

Arles kept the gun trained on Nick as he climbed into his truck, until the menace of its engine faded out, and the last contrail of dust had dissipated.

Once the ghost of the pickup was gone from the air, a small figure emerged, squiggling out from underneath a chaise in a corner of the porch. Lissa got to her feet, wearing a princess costume. "Mommy? Is Daddy gone? I put on my mask and hid."

Stephanie squatted, and the young girl ran to her. "Good job, Lis."

Arles looked down at the two of them, her mind filling in blank spaces.

Stephanie cast her head upward, then gave her daughter a squeeze. "I have an idea."

"What is it?" The girl's voice was muffled; she spoke into her mom's shoulder.

"You know the groceries you unpacked? I bet we got enough for you to fix a snack for us all. Dr. Arles and me and you."

Lissa lifted her head. "Really?"

Stephanie nodded. "Don't use the sharp knife without me. Or the stove."

"A cold spread!"

"Yes. A cold spread would be perfect."

Lissa whirled around, the hem of her dress parachuting. She ran off, leaning back with all her weight to open the heavy front door before disappearing inside the house.

Stephanie faced Arles, her lips set in a line as thin as a blade. "Remember how I told you losing our kitchen was the second worst thing about being evicted?"

"Was Nick the first?" Arles asked.

Their landlord had needed some justification for eviction; it couldn't just be that he wanted to chop his house into units and make a fortune. He chose Nick and Stephanie's fighting—which had included a few calls by neighbors to police—as grounds. The couple had been together since high school, but after Lissa was born, Nick began displaying his true self: possessive, demanding, overbearing. Arles had seen this more than once—men who revealed their monstrous sides only once "their" women became mothers. It could go in reverse too, brutal edges scoured away by fatherhood. But somehow that seemed to happen less often.

"He tried to control everything," Stephanie said. "Especially me. I wasn't going to let my daughter think that was how we were supposed to be treated. We women or the two of us."

Arles gave her a small smile. "Math and strength. Two things hard to nurture in a girl."

Stephanie locked a fierce gaze on hers. "You're a therapist, so you'll understand this. My father beat the crap out of my mother. There wasn't a day I saw her without makeup and long sleeves. But Nick never laid a hand on me, and I fell hard for him. I thought he was gentle." Her mouth collapsed around the final word, her lips losing their shape, all ability to vocalize further.

In her office, Arles would've had tissues; out here, the best she could do was a cleaning cloth. She held it out. "Unused, at least. I haven't gotten to the porch yet."

Stephanie worked up a smile. She took the rag and blew her nose. "Let me do the porch."

Arles gestured to two wicker chairs. "So Nick will be coming here then? For visitation?"

Stephanie let out a half rasp, half laugh. "That was bullshit; he doesn't care about Lissa. She's just another thing he can use to dominate me."

Arles gave a nod. "May I ask you something?" She paused. "I realize you might not think you can say no. But please feel free."

"I'd kind of like to hear what you find worth asking about this age-old story."

"Is that why you had Lissa hide? Because Nick uses her against you?"

Stephanie turned bleak eyes in her direction. "Okay, so this one time, it was after I'd kicked him out, Nick came over while I was in the shower. He still had a key. He got Lissa to go with him; I came down, and she was gone." She went on, speaking as if set to automatic, as if this story had been told and retold, at least in her mind. "I called him—I assumed it had to be Nick—but he totally played me. Acted worried, said he had no idea where she was. I panicked. Beyond panic. I thought she'd been kidnapped. I called the police; I've never been that scared in my life. Nick let this go on for an hour. The cop who came was a friend of his; he went along. I'm pretty sure that's illegal, but I never filed a complaint. The cop took down all the details, told me there'd be an

Amber Alert. He even asked for a photograph. Then Nick showed up with Lissa. 'Hey, look, I found her!' he goes, and burst out laughing."

"That's the cruelest thing I've ever heard." Arles felt her face set like cement. "And I have experience with cruel."

All the ways women were just props in men's lives. Used by them, for real and for fun. There in movies, thrillers, crime stories, true and fictional. Bodies to be gored, chiseled, played with, then thrown away or buried. Flo Galtry at the mercy of her mother's refusal to see. Lissa hiding from her father, even after Stephanie found the strength to throw him out. Arles herself.

And how many more? Forever and ever, amen.

"I can't do this to you," Stephanie said, rising from her seat. "You don't deserve my mess. Lissa and I can pack up and go tonight."

"I hope you won't, though," Arles said quietly.

Stephanie looked at her.

"You said it yourself—I heard you. Lissa will be happy here. And I frankly don't know how I'll do everything that needs doing without an extra pair of hands, never mind the teaching." Arles paused. "Besides, I can handle Nick."

Stephanie hovered over her chair. "How? It's not like you're really going to kill him."

"Of course not," Arles said. "I'm not the best shot."

"What, then?" Stephanie asked.

"It tends to just come to me," she replied. That had been true long before she became a psychologist. Maybe it was *why* she'd become one. "In the moment, like. When I need it."

Stephanie sank back down. "That sounds amazing. I wish something would come to me when I needed it."

"It isn't magic," Arles said, though sometimes it felt as if it were. "Let's start with my asking you a few questions about Nick. Tell me a little about his life. What he used to be like."

—

They headed inside when Lissa called them, her voice high and excited.

Arles wasn't sure what the words *cold spread* had led her to expect, maybe some fruit—peeled oranges, since Lissa wasn't allowed to use the knife on her own—and chips from a bag. But when the girl led her and Stephanie into the kitchen, half the long table was covered with plates that held an array of small sandwiches.

"I made us tea!" Lissa crowed. "I mean, not tea 'cause you said not to use the stove, but tea sandwiches. And cookies."

Arles hadn't caught sight of the cookies till then, lopsided and chunky.

"I didn't use the oven; don't worry. Even though you only said the stove, so I could've gotten away with it—"

"No, you couldn't," Stephanie said, shielding a smile.

"I mean *technically*, Mommy, but it's okay. They're refrigerator cookies."

"I've never seen anyone cook like this in my life." It was a lie, and Arles rarely lied, especially not to children. But she didn't want to import one iota of her mother to this meal.

The three of them spent the rest of the day readying Fir Cove, Lissa as able and willing as any adult. Arles noted her competence, compliance, and capability, all at outsize levels, and all flagship behaviors of a child raised by a terrorizing parent.

Stephanie's ex showing up had alerted Arles to a slew of chores that needed doing. Big tasks like securing every gun on the property, smaller ones such as checking that the NO HUNTING/FISHING/TRESPASSING signs tacked to trees were still intact, posting the fifteen-mile-per-hour speed limit along the road, and placing ropes by the beach at the dock along with warnings about swimming at one's own risk. The hazardous ravine she left for another occasion. It was deep enough in the woods that nobody would have reason to make the trek out there.

She and Stephanie moved on to the cabins, Arles using the mental downtime to continue to process her intake with Geary. That single mouthed word meant he had access to productive speech, which would be mind-blowing to Louise, who doubted herself when it came to his verbal development. Arles's own angle on the issue was a bit different, however.

What required a rush, and why would Geary think that Arles might be able to help? Unless he was just expressing a child's wish for any adult to step in, make things better. But why not his own mother, who seemed to want nothing more than to support him? Then again, Arles needed to guard against projecting her image of Louise, based on that long-ago photograph, onto the adult woman. Maybe Geary had good reason not to trust her.

Louise possessed a parent's right to be made aware of this turn of events, but Arles had an equal obligation to present it in a logical light, get some handle on the situation before revealing it. And to be sure she was correct. Imagine the hope she would ignite, only to cruelly douse it, if she had misread the shape Geary's lips formed in his fervor. She wished she had recorded the video feed on the call, could go back and freeze the boy's face in that second.

With the cottages scrubbed and gleaming, Stephanie sent Lissa up to the house for a last load of towels. Before the girl could leave, however, Arles spoke up casually. She was a big believer in mining the expertise of children. They tended to prioritize the intuition most adults discounted.

"Hey, Lissa, can you think of any reason a kid would tell a grown-up to hurry? Just out of the blue. Someone the kid didn't know very well. Barely knew at all," she concluded.

Lissa took the question as seriously as Arles had expected, and her reply set the field of tiny hairs rippling all over Arles's skin again.

"They would if they knew something bad was going to happen," she said, then ran out.

Arles was so lost in thought over the reply that it took her a beat to recall Stephanie's presence. "Just something from a therapeutic exchange

I had earlier," she explained, forcing a light tone. "It's okay for Lissa to go up to the house on her own?"

Stephanie smiled, smoothing a plaid blanket with the flat of one hand. "Don't worry, I understand confidentiality. And yes, Lissa can handle whatever. Better than me in most cases."

Arles worried about the weight of so much trust and expectation on a child but chose only to say, "She seems like an incredible kid."

Stephanie's smile grew bigger. "Best thing I ever did or will ever do."

"That's enviable, isn't it? To have something you're so rightfully proud of."

Stephanie crossed to the nightstand and flicked a few specks off a lamp. She turned it on, bending to inspect the glow. "Yeah, well, you have this place. Pretty goddamn great."

Arles laughed. "You don't have to compare intergenerational familial wealth with your amazing child to try and make me feel good."

They left the cabin together, standing on the path and looking around.

"Lissa!" called Stephanie.

Arles parted a scrim of twigs, peering toward the house.

"She must still be inside," Stephanie said.

"She's taking too long," Arles told Stephanie.

They began pushing past trees, elbowing back branches as they ran for the house.

Lissa was struggling through an opening in the doorway, clutching a laundry basket bigger than she was. "At first the dryer didn't dry it all the way!" she called. "So I had to wait."

Arles halted abruptly, smoothing fear from her face. "I don't know how you do this."

Stephanie looked at her with serious eyes. "Thank you for going there with me."

—

Arles left Stephanie behind to put Lissa to bed while she drove into town with a Santa's-length list of groceries. As soon as she got within range, her phone buzzed. She pulled over.

> hey this is dan mackinnon sorry to ping you out of the blue but this guy was asking about that woman who stayed at your house i dont have the best feeling about him so i wanted to make sure alls well no need to respond if it is or if this is overstepping just wanted to check

She placed a finger above the screen. Paused. Hovered. Touched.

It didn't even get a chance to ring. "Arles?"

She kept quiet.

"Hey, Arles, is that you?"

She didn't know how to have this conversation. "I don't know what to say."

A pause. "You don't know what to say to a greeting?"

She bit back the first response that came to mind. "No."

"Okay, well, let's start with me asking if everything's okay."

A gap she didn't fill.

"Is it? All right? Because that guy Nick seems like trouble to me."

"He is trouble," she said after a pause. *Hey, look, I found her!* "But I dealt with it."

"That's good. He could use some dealing with."

She hesitated. "So what now? In this whole make-pleasant-chitchat realm?"

"Not so sure talking about somebody's stalker ex constitutes pleasant chitchat, but . . ."

Arles bore down on a smile. "I'm a psychologist. This counts."

"Hey, now *that's* pleasant chitchat. You tell me what you do. I say, 'That sounds really interesting. Please tell me more.'"

"Okay," she said softly. "And what happens after that?"

"Then I ask if I can take you to dinner sometime."

"Ah. And the next part is where I say yes."

"I think you've got it."

Arles purchased every item on her list, then drove home, *home*, car laden. Feeling a tether grow taut, like a rubber band tightening. In just two days, Louise and Geary would be here.

And Arles could figure out what she was supposed to do.

CHAPTER FOURTEEN

The night after Geary melted down with Dr. Shepherd, Louise slept on the floor beside his bed, something she hadn't done since he was a baby and spiked a fever. Her bedroom, which she'd shared with Michael then, wasn't big enough to add a crib. And by the time Geary was a toddler, he could no longer tolerate Louise staying in his room, even when he was sick.

She worried her nighttime presence might still be too overwhelming for him, especially given how the FaceTime had wound up, but Geary didn't appear to notice her, just passed out as if he'd been slugged, still as a log in his bed, no blanket or covering atop him.

Some of the parents she chatted with online described their Autistic children as being locked away, locked inside themselves, but Louise had never seen Geary like that. It was more as if *she* were the one locked out, blocked from a universe too complicated for her son to convey. And sometimes frustration over her or other people's failure to understand triggered a meltdown.

But the recent episodes, the ones that had occurred starting the day of the first appointment with Dr. Trager, felt as if they went beyond overwhelm and frustration. It was like Geary was erupting, a state more terrifying than anything Louise could imagine her own brain or body experiencing. Something was trying to get out of her son. And whatever it was, she didn't want to leave Geary alone with it.

First thing the following morning, she let the owner of Glam & Go know she'd be glam and gone, then drove over to Michael's house.

He met her at the door with a look of concern. "Hey, everything okay? Geary?"

She felt a bloom of warmth. "He's fine. But you got my text, right? About Elward?"

"Yeah," he said. "Sucks. What are we going to do?"

Another bloom at the *we*. "Well, I found a new doctor. But she works really far away."

"Huh. That's something, I guess. How far?"

"New York State most of the way to Canada. It's what they call a residential facility, though, so Geary can live there for a while. And I can too."

"You guys are going to get therapy in *Canada*?"

"Practically, I said. No passports." She took a breath. "Anyway, this doctor believes the whole family is important. You can't just give therapy to one person, even if it's a child."

He was nodding. "Tell you the truth, that makes more sense than what any other therapist has told us. We all have to help each other out, right? And we set each other off too."

Louise took in a relieved breath. "So you'll come then? When it's your turn?"

"To *Canada*?"

"I don't know for sure if you'll have to, but Geary does spend a good amount of time with you, so I wanted to make sure you had warning—"

The screen door opened. "Hey, Mike, you're gonna be late to work. Oh, hi!"

Mike? Michael had never let Louise call him that. Mike was his dead father, a real dick.

The woman standing in the doorway was small and slight, almost girlish in proportion. Her face was the opposite, though. Older than her years, fine-lined and mature around the eyes.

"Hi," Louise said, a chill in her tone that Michael must've picked up on.

"Terra, hon, this is Louise. Louise, meet Terra."

"Of course, I figured!" Terra responded, still friendly. "Geary's mom. Nice to meet you."

Louise nodded.

"He's such a neat kid," Terra added. "Quiet. But you can tell there's a lot going on."

Louise felt herself soften, her tensed posture ease. *Sucker,* she inwardly accused herself.

"Lou, I'm sure I can make it work if I have to. Take a day off, drive all night."

Louise started to tell him she'd text the info, but Michael was already turning around, guiding Terra back into the house, getting started on another day in this other life he had made.

The next visit was going to be worse.

Her parents' house appeared as tidy and well kept as always, shutters displaying a glossy coat of paint, neither her mother's new sedan nor her father's Ford Transit parked in the driveway. Perfectly nice vehicles concealed in the garage. Her parents were big on curb appeal. Her father must've recently shorn the lawn, the blades as even as a buzz cut. He was currently on the three-days-off part of his schedule, with an outfit that stocked and serviced vending machines.

Louise shut off the engine, then got out and waited for Geary. Sweat prickled her body, and her heart clanged inside her chest, breaths descending no deeper than her throat. Though her knock felt feeble, her mother opened the door right away. She and Louise's dad almost never got callers or neighborly visits. The house was dim, curtains drawn against the sun. This place had always been a poor candidate for Geary's dust pursuit, thanks to her mother's ruthless and relentless housecleaning. Without a word of greeting, she led the way into the kitchen.

"Where's Dad?" Louise asked, dropping into the chair that had been hers as a child.

"You know he makes up for sleep on his off days."

Louise nodded, steeling herself against the disappointment of getting just her mom.

"Sales keep getting harder. His company is expanding its region but laying off drivers," her mother said bitterly. "How's that for topsy-turvy? And what if they give him more routes?"

It wasn't like her mom to share her worries. "You'd miss him."

Her mother gave a short, hard jerk of her chin.

"So, Geary's doing pretty well," she said. Her mother was acting like he hadn't arrived right alongside her. Louise knew she should go find him, but she couldn't bear to draw him into the unwelcoming space of this kitchen. "Hey, mind if I have something to drink?"

Her mother gave the refrigerator door a vicious tug. She got out a Coke and set it before Louise. Then she removed a carton of juice and poured some into a glass.

"He still like orange? It's all we've got."

"It's his favorite," Louise said gratefully. As long as there weren't bits of pulp; she always strained it. But her mother would see that as pickiness, scoff at the very idea. Louise popped the tab on her soda can and took a gulp. Carbonation sizzled on her parched throat.

"Doctor put your father on a low-carb diet so I'm the only one drinking much besides water these days. Oh, how he misses his beer," her mother added with a doting smile.

"That must be rough." Her father was pretty mellow—he'd have to be in order to stand her mother—but got more so with a beer or two in him.

A frown hardened her mother's face. "Why don't you tell me the reason for this visit?"

Louise took a last swig of soda. "So, Geary has a new therapist who thinks she might be able to really help him."

Her mother looked up quickly, a spark of something in her eyes. "Get him talking?"

Could that spark be hope? Deep down, did she care about Geary, want his life to be easier? "No," Louise said in a small voice. "He'll likely never talk. I've had to accept that."

Her mother pressed her lips together. "That's not normal. Boy his age should be talking."

"Of course it's not *normal*, Mom. Most ten-year-olds talk." No one else put her on the defensive like this. "But 'should' statements," she said, quoting a past therapist, "*should* be avoided."

Her mother ignored that. "Your grandmother would've said he's of the devil."

"Mom!" Louise gasped. "That's a disgusting thing to say."

Her mother crossed herself in a swift spasm, like a tic.

"One day people will come to realize that what we don't understand about Geary says a lot more about our limitations than his." Tears blurred Louise's eyes, the glass of juice, traffic-cone bright, swimming in her vision. Geary didn't need a serving of OJ; the sugar would only rile him up. He needed a grandmother who saw him for who he was, not what he wasn't.

Louise swallowed a salty slick of tears. "Anyway, his therapy is going to include family members. It's in this special kind of clinic, pretty far away. I'll be going there with Geary first. Then maybe Michael. And she—the doctor—might want to see you and Dad too."

Her mother's hand fell away from her chest. "We're not getting therapy."

"No, I know that. Of course not. This would be for Geary."

"We're not doing that, either," her mother said.

Like the door of a vault coming down. Louise would've had to walk through a wall of steel in order to get what she'd come here for. She stood up and went to look for Geary, picking up the glass. On second thought, he deserved some juice.

He wasn't standing in the hallway, and when she peeked into the living and dining rooms, they were both empty. She pulled back a curtain and spotted Geary walking along the driveway toward the backyard. She had no idea when he'd left the house, but he wasn't a kid who played outside, and a terrible thought pierced her.

"He heard you!" she cried. "Oh God, I think he must've been listening to us talk!"

She started to run. The juice sloshed, spattering the floor, and she set the glass down on a table before pulling at the front door.

Geary moved as if sleepwalking, like he was caught in a dream. Hearing his grandmother's hate speech must've sent him into some kind of stupor. Louise had to get him into their car, away from this place before something even worse happened.

So many sources of dust out here, visible glints and particles, she realized as she began heading in Geary's direction, step by guarded step. A glowy grove of trees shot through with sunshine; the garden shed with cloudy windows alive with shafts of light; empty planters with traces of dirt scattered across their terra-cotta bottoms. Her mother was an on-again, off-again gardener; judging by the bare flower beds, this was one of her neglectful periods.

Louise forced herself to keep to a slow pace as she drew near. She needed to avoid knocking Geary out of this state of eerie quiet into full-on meltdown mode, where a blizzard of bits could fell him. Model calmness, but don't try to impose it, Dr. Shepherd had said.

Just then, her mother came running up from behind, passing at such a fast clip that Louise couldn't grab hold of her. She reached out a hand, but it slid off her mother's arm.

"Mom, please, I know what to do—"

Her mother swiveled the top half of her body around like the lash of a whip. "You *don't* know what to do, Louise. You have never known what to do in your life. And your father's asleep. With the window open for some nice fresh air. You think he needs a commotion on an off day?"

"Geary won't wake Dad up if you just let me—"

But her mother launched into a bullet-straight path, reaching out from behind to lower Geary down to the lawn. They went as one, Geary starting to strain and protest on the way.

Louise stood with her hands balled into helpless fists.

"He's the most out-of-control child I've ever seen. Throws fits like a toddler. Thinks he can do whatever he wants"—gasping as Geary squirmed beneath her—"anything he pleases . . . at someone else's house, even—"

Louise was staggered. Geary didn't act this way because he was doing what he wanted, like he was *spoiled*. He had a *diagnosis* that made his behaviors hard to predict or understand. But how could she ever explain that to her mother?

"Just walks into our yard like a damn prince, like he's king of the hill—"

Grandmother and grandson formed a log Louise had no chance of separating. They might as well have been glued together, as tangled as a skein of yarn on the ground. Both their voices now filling the air like smoke, only her mother's had the additional factor of poisonous words.

"Just look at him," she said, a hissing breath. "Look at what this child has become."

"He's my son," Louise whispered, even though neither of them was about to answer.

"I know he is, Lulu," said a voice from behind, and Louise tripped, spinning around.

Her father stood there, his form tall enough to block out a section of sun. Kind-faced, weary, a little out of it from sleep. He'd pushed his eye mask up on his forehead; Louise's mother preferred curtains to blackout shades. When Louise was a baby, she'd been scared of the sleep mask, or so the story went. Always trying to tug it off. Louise felt a deep and lasting love for her father. She missed him when the months piled up between visits.

"Hello, my girl," he said, then looked down at his wife. "Tina."

Her mother cut off mid-rant, keeping a wrestler's hold on Geary.

"Leave that boy alone."

Her mother's arms stilled while Geary's shrieks split the air into fragments.

Her dad turned to Louise, raising his voice to be heard. "Can you get him into your car?"

She nodded. "I think so."

"Try," he said, the sound muted by screeches, but the word clear on his lips. He spoke up, giving her a tired smile. "Before the neighbors start wondering what's going on over here."

"Hey, Gear," Louise said without approaching. "Stand up, okay? Time to leave now."

Her dad leaned over to take her mother's hand. It disappeared, small in his grip. She got to her feet and stood by his side. He bent down, tenderly brushing blades of grass off her legs.

Geary made it onto his hands and knees and scrambled madly away, spittle flying and strings of snot swinging. One of his feet hooked a rock, and he went over face-first, smacking the close-cropped lawn so hard that his forehead and nose came up smeared with green. But he didn't cry out or complain, and Louise nearly wept at this display of tolerance and strength. There was a scrape on his chin, blood already beading. Tiny things like dust or crumbs might send Geary into a spiral, but something that would make another child whine and whimper, he put up with like a warrior. He kept on going, charging forward with shoulders squared, gaze intent, and she was jolted back in time to when he was a baby. On all fours again now, zigzagging frantically toward the driveway.

"We can do this," her dad said suddenly. "Can't we, Tina? Take a trip to see that doctor?"

In mid-pursuit, going after her son, Louise twisted around. Her father had heard.

"Go on, Lulu," he said as their eyes met. "Go get your boy, then let's get him some help."

CHAPTER FIFTEEN

Before Arles could greet Louise and Geary, other patients were due to arrive at Fir Cove. After all, mother and son couldn't be the only family to attend her brand-new treatment facility. What kind of *Down a Dark Hall*–style odd note would that strike? It'd be creepy. Louise would probably turn right around and leave, picturing the gates behind her swinging shut for good.

Anticipating the arrival of the woman Arles knew only from a photograph would not deter her from delivering care to her initial crop of clients. None of whom needed to know that Louise was the Scarecrow to Arles's Dorothy: *I'm waiting for you most of all.*

"I can't fucking believe this place," Natalie called, lowering the window of a speckless black Land Rover now rolling up to the half-moon drive in front of Fir Cove.

Stephanie had spent the morning raking gravel while Lissa planted a border of pansies. The blooms would probably be killed by frost but looked awfully nice at the moment, perky and purple. Stephanie had decided to make the first weeks at Fir Cove into an integrative unit: econ and business, the history of great camps, living science, and a very basic intro to psych. Clearly, things were going to need to be tailored based on different students' aptitudes and abilities.

"Nat, please, your language," her mother said, climbing out. "We just got here."

Natalie ignored her. "And look, Dr. S., it's the shitty dad. He actually showed."

"Nat, I'm asking you to watch—"

The man behind the wheel emerged from the vehicle with a low whistle. "Some place you've got here. When Natalie told me about it, I said it sounded like a facility where billionaires would go. Tucked away; no one really knows about it."

Natalie mimed a gag behind her dad's back while Arles painted on a neutral expression.

She had been trying to get Natalie's father to participate in a session ever since the teen was referred for treatment after an inpatient stint on an EDU. Natalie had entered the eating disorders unit at seventy-nine pounds and was discharged when she reached a weight that meant her life was no longer in peril.

"Welcome," Arles said. "I'm so glad you all could come." She made sure to send Natalie an affirming glance. "Even if it took some doing."

"Losing that hospital office probably didn't hurt," Natalie's sister noted. "As you can tell, my father prefers upscale."

"It suits him," the mother said quickly. "He's worked hard to achieve our lifestyle."

"Which brings me back to . . . I can't believe this place," said Natalie.

No curse this time; she'd gotten the desired response.

Lissa appeared on the porch as planned. "Hi! Do you want a tour?"

"Would you like to start with a tour?" Stephanie murmured from behind.

While applying finishing touches the night before—stalky arrangements of the earliest spring growth in vases; snack baskets and Keurig machines for each of the cabins; a tier of logs at every fireplace—Arles had oriented Stephanie to best practices in a psychotherapeutic setting. HIPAA compliance, emergency procedures, and a daily schedule, subject to change.

Clearly, Stephanie had prepped her daughter.

"I know when the house was built—1882—and who built it," Lissa said. "I can tell you other stuff too, and also, I won't give away any secrets because I'm really good with secrets."

Natalie and her sister gave the younger girl identical smiles.

"Gretch, let's take a tour with secret-keeper over here."

"I don't think I have any secrets," her sister replied.

"You've never been in therapy before," Natalie said. "Trust me, we have tons."

"Meanwhile, Stephanie"—Arles waved a hand in introduction—"and I will bring your things to your cabin. If you could leave everything in front of the porch, that'd be great."

Natalie's father lined up four suitcases that matched the car's condition—gleaming—and were equally top-of-the-line. They could obviously afford Fir Cove, but Arles had a real equity-and-access issue on her hands if she didn't want this place to turn into what Natalie's dad had called it out as: a therapy resort for the rich. He and his wife strolled off to join their daughters.

Arles turned to Stephanie. "Well, this just got real."

Stephanie gave a nod. "You're definitely off and running. How does it feel?"

Arles smiled, sharp and sudden. "That's usually my line."

"You didn't answer the question," Stephanie noted.

"That's usually my other line," Arles replied. "Come on. Let's collect their stuff."

Stephanie had asked to be put in charge of meals until the number of kiddie patients reached a volume too sizable for her to manage both duties. She told Arles she found it healing to cook, and indeed Arles watched her take what looked like genuine joy in stirring a giant pot of soup on the eight-burner range and tearing ragged croutons off a loaf of homemade bread.

Just before lunch, two more patients arrived: a young couple exiting a cultish church.

Group sessions were to take place in the parlor. Arles had polished every inch of woodwork till it glowed, used a steamer to restore richness to the rugs, and arranged cushioned chairs in a circle. She started with intros, noting the way Natalie's dad volunteered to go first. He spoke in a booming voice, hands linked just south of his crotch, legs widely splayed.

"I'm Jim Merritt," he said. "Like to say I *am* a Merritt, and I've *got* merit."

Both daughters snorted, and their mother fixed them with a glare.

"I'm a finance guy—futures, mainly. Used to work on Wall Street during the week and come up here to be with my girls on the weekends. But now I divide my time: a few days in the city, a few in these parts. I've discovered the joys of some peace and quiet." He settled back in his seat, which creaked beneath his heft.

Natalie's mother gave him a smile. "I'm Fleur, Jim's wife. And Gretchen and Natalie's mother." She lifted her hands, palms up. "I don't have anything else to say."

"That's enough, hon," said Jim. "That was very nice."

Arles had a tendency to give men who took up space like this a pass, absorbing the way their voices drowned out others. That was just the usual silence; nobody noticed when women failed to speak, often objecting only when they did. It was a blind spot she'd dealt with in supervision, the way she forgave even catcalls and whispers, her barometer having been set to the truly gruesome and ghastly, flagrant abuses to body and psyche. But here at Fir Cove, she was going to have to confront the way a softer sort of violence could erode a woman's soul.

Natalie huffed a breath. "You run a whole Etsy business and display at the gallery in town, Mom. How about sharing that?"

"Oh." Fleur still seemed at a loss. "Well, sure, my art. I work with mixed metals. Collages, mostly, but I make small household items. Just silly things like toothbrush holders."

"Toothbrush holders that go for—what was the price of the one you sold last night? Three hundred ninety-five dollars. And that was a special. Just because Dad makes a stupid amount of money assigning value to things that have none doesn't mean your work isn't totally admirable."

"Your turn, Gretchen, honey," said Fleur quickly.

Her eldest responded with matching alacrity. "Oh, me. Right, sure. Let's see. I'm about to finish my second year at Bryn Mawr. It's spring break, so I'm going to therapy instead of Florida." She let out a giggle. "I chose an HWC intentionally, not because I couldn't get into Swarthmore or Haverford or anything."

"Historically Women's College," Natalie muttered in explanation. "I may apply to one too, but only after taking a gap year. Which I'm definitely doing." She paused to glower at her father. "Maybe Barnard in the city. If I can get in."

"You'll get in," Jim said, his voice loud in the cavernous room. "I'll hire you a consultant if necessary. And in case I haven't made this clear, ladies, I think girls' schools are just as real as Harvard or Yale."

"Thank you, Merritts," Arles said. "You're clearly a very accomplished family."

She looked to the other two clients.

"I'm Patience," said the woman. "I was raised in a very religious family. Ben and I met at church. I guess that's my *about me*."

"The church was more like a cult," Ben said. "Can that be my fun fact?"

Arles looked around the ring of faces. "I'll wrap things up. Has everyone gotten a chance to look over the welcome package that was left in your cabins?"

Nods all around.

"Great. So then it won't come as a surprise—if the zero bars on your phones haven't already given it away—that there's no Wi-Fi or cell signal at Fir Cove. At some point, depending on how things go, I may have satellite internet installed. But for now, a digital detox strikes me as potentially therapeutic." She paused for mutiny, relieved when there wasn't one. "Aside from that, it's pretty much the current decade here, if a little isolated and remote."

"The current decade has its downside," Patience said primly.

Gretchen snorted. "Say that again. Been to a sorority bash lately?"

"Thank goodness, no."

Arles gave them both a smile. "Now a brief overview of what kind of treatment you all will be taking part in. It's called FIT, which stands for Family Immersion Therapy, and is what I would describe as the most powerful form of clinical healing I've ever practiced."

"Only the best for a Merritt," Natalie's father interjected with a hearty haw-haw.

Arles had started calling him *Big Jim* in her mind. "The theory is that the family is the essential core inside every individual. We grow in relation to those who grew us."

Expectant faces met her gaze.

"All right," Arles said, bringing her hands together. "Stephanie, whose talents you were introduced to with that soup, has dinner planned for us at six. That leaves two hours to get to know Fir Cove. Feel free to stroll the grounds, take a hike on one of our marked trails, or relax in your cabin. In days to come, there will be activities planned. And I'll see you all this evening."

That night two meals were served, on two distinct planes of being. One hummed with the excitement of novel connections forming and new pursuits being tried. Gretchen and Patience appeared to be chums already, sitting side by side at the table and disrupting the Merritt family's quad. Ben had gone off alone to fish, and Stephanie fried his catch for a first course, while Natalie had embarked on a hike with her father. Big Jim described the final leg in his raucous tone, upping the difficulty of its scramble, his own version of a fish story, as his daughter fought to contribute an opposing account, excessively humble, self-deprecating.

Night fell in a series of layered losses. Dark, darker, darkest.

The patients couldn't have known who else ate there that night, the reason Arles moved food around on her plate in a manner to which Natalie could surely relate. In this other realm, Arles's mother had cooked, not Stephanie. Peter tended to consume even fewer calories than his stepdaughter, a man of different appetites. He used to pass dishes without taking a serving, touching Arles's hand when she was forced to accept his offering. No one sitting around the present-day table appeared to detect the pair of monsters among them, felt the disturbance of their breath in the air. When dinner was over, the patients ambled off with plates of dessert in hand, and Arles heard a voice call out. She got up and strode into the front hall, trying to shake off the tattered stitching of her past.

Dan stood on the sill of the doorway, poking his head inside. "Oh, hey, sorry. I knocked, but no one came. The door was unlocked, so I opened it."

He didn't talk like a typical guy, as generous with apologies and responsibility-taking as someone of a different gender. She wondered how he'd come by the traits.

His expression changed. "Oh, shit, are you having a party that I just crashed?"

She turned back toward the buzz and thrum behind her, then stepped out onto the porch. Stood with fists folded on her hips. "Nope. No party."

He mimed a *whew*, wiping a palm across his forehead. "You don't have phones out here, and I wasn't sure how to reach—" He broke off. "Was this creepy of me? This was creepy."

His presence here didn't feel problematic, actually. But she didn't know how to say so.

"Damn, and you just had to deal with that asshole Nick Rudd. Not that I'm like him."

She chose to go for her usual type of rejoinder. Less risky than voicing what she was really feeling. "Not that your saying you're not like him makes me think you're not like him."

He lifted a touché finger. "I came to ask if I could take you to that dinner tonight. Actually, how you'd feel about having dinner at my place? My sister is a food blogger, and what she calls fails taste better than what you get in most restaurants."

Arles hesitated. She felt stuffed despite not having eaten much of Stephanie's meal.

"Creepy again?" His voice seemed to wilt.

Arles reached for his hand. "If you don't mind going around this way—so as to avoid the throng inside—"

"Which isn't a party—"

"That definitely is not a party—I can offer you something here."

Dan let her lead him toward the side of the house, where they took the back stairs to her bedroom, kicking off shoes, peeling off clothes. And this time, whenever she started to float, felt herself leave her body, she gave her skin a brutal, bruising pinch, bringing her back again.

Afterward, Dan spoke first.

"Did you—you know?"

Arles squinted one eye, not quite a wink.

"Oh, wait, I forgot you don't like euphemisms. I can do better."

She squinted the other eye too.

He propped himself up on his forearms, holding himself above her. "Did you reach the apex of womanly pleasure? Did your flower unfold?" He lowered his face to hers. "Did the fruit of your loins bud? Did your whisk spin? Did your tunnel of love—"

"I feel like you're making some of these up," Arles said against his lips.

He kissed her, and she forced herself not to lose time.

The sheer focus it took caused her to break out in a sweat.

"Dan," she said when they paused for breath, "don't take this on, okay? Seriously. It isn't yours to carry. This is my thing. I don't go there.

And yes, I'm using a euphemism. But I haven't in the past, and I won't in the future. And that's okay."

He flipped over on his back, reaching for her hand. "No, it's not," he said softly.

"Hey." She spoke sharply, though she allowed their fingers to be threaded. "That really isn't your call. Or your place to say. My sexual encounter isn't there for your ego gratification."

For a second, he kept quiet. Then he said, "You're right."

She stretched and rolled over, winding up in his arms. It took her a while to realize she should say something, then even longer to think what it could be. How did people put a cap on the day? At last, she murmured, "I'm going to meet someone tomorrow for the first time."

He stroked her collarbone with one finger. "This therapy business make you a psychic?"

She settled herself in his hold. "Not really. Well, sometimes. But in this case, no."

His tone turned serious. "What do you mean, then? Who are you going to meet?"

She felt herself start to drift. Impossible, incomprehensible that she could fall asleep in the presence of another person. Especially here.

"Good night, Arles," he whispered after a pause. "Sleep well."

Her jaw cracked with a yawn. "A woman whose photo I've looked at for twenty-five years."

The weird thing was, the man turned out to be pretty easy to talk to.

For a while, anyway. Easier than most of the people in her life. Correction—as of today—all of the people in her life except for Ms. Mailer.

"Why did you do this?" she asked boldly. "Why did you take me?"

Go big or go home.

God, how she wanted to go home. Wouldn't have believed it, but she did.

"It gets lonely out here," he said, gesturing at the windshield. "All this space and long distances. Empty roads."

"Yeah," she said. She knew what lonely was like.

Maybe he heard something in her voice. That she understood him, yucky as that was.

The steering wheel began to shake, kind of twitch in his hands. The van crossed the line between lanes, which didn't matter because no one else was there. Then he swerved back.

"You can't imagine what it's like to grow up. When I was your age, man, my mom used to listen to every single thing I said. Like it was made of pure gold. She hung on every word."

It sounded like both the most wonderful and disgusting thing in the world.

She chose to go with the wonderful. "Your mom must've been nice."

She thought she had said the right thing. She was just praising herself for how smart she was, Ms. Mailer would be proud—

He swung the van over so suddenly, two of its tires went down lopsided in a ditch. Unlatching his seat belt with a clank, he held himself over her, his face folding up, changing, becoming something else altogether, until she shrieked, helpless as a little kid, like some kind of scared squawky bird.

"Now it's time for you to be quiet," he said. "Now I have to make you be quiet."

DESPAIR ISN'T MEASURED IN POUNDS

Cass and Maggie didn't return to therapy. He couldn't stop seeing the therapist's bird-bright stare, how her interest seemed aroused by their calamity, while Maggie refused to get past the slip Ms. Reynolds had made at the end, the fleeting hope she'd blown air into, like a balloon.

The days following that appointment were so leaden with despair, their bodies weights they couldn't hold up, that they were barely able to leave their bedroom, anyway, let alone get to an office outside of town. Maggie, always slight, had lost every ounce of padding that ever adorned her. She appeared as stooped and bent as a ninety-year-old woman, and he didn't look much better, although ironically, the weight loss was probably helping his heart.

They kept going over and over what had happened after they'd left Ms. Reynolds's office in Brawley's police vehicle. Chewing on it like tasteless gum. Grinding till their teeth were chalk.

"He did warn us," Maggie said as they lay side by side on sour sheets, then again as they staggered into the bathroom to scoop up water from the faucet, wetting their parched mouths but not coming close to quenching their thirsts. "The sheriff wasn't deceptive."

As they'd driven off, tires squealing, Brawley had cautioned them not to get their hopes up. Cass had found it absurd. He and Maggie were sitting as far apart from each other as the bench seat allowed, each occupying their own distinct bubble, a place that couldn't be shared. They were as alone and distant as if they'd been sent to different planets. And they were nothing but hope. Pure, yearning need. Take it away, and they'd shrivel and wither like flattened balloons.

"I want to say right up front that we don't know if this is Bea," Brawley said as he drove. "My deputy—Jack Gantz, you met him that first—" He cut himself off. "You've met him before. Anyways, he cautioned against bringing you in till we can call a counselor to talk to the girl, get her to open up some." He ended on a note of disgust. "And cleaned up."

"What girl?" Maggie had asked in the same inhuman voice she'd used when Ms. Reynolds offered her definition of the word *sighting*. Kind of an airless gasp. She sat as far forward as she could get on the seat, all ten fingers gripping the grid that separated her from the front of the car. "Who are you talking about?"

Cass watched her hands clench, then unclench, white and skeletal.

Brawley gave the wheel a spin, entering a highway. "A woman spotted a girl in the back of a van at a gas station. She's the right ethnicity and age, at a rough guess. The woman had seen the story on the news, so she phoned in her sighting. She was able to get a partial plate; we put out an all points and managed to pull the guy over fairly fast. No chase; he stopped right away."

Maggie whimpered. She sounded like a wounded animal.

Cass placed one hand on her back, patting robotically.

Brawley accelerated, veering left, as if their despair had a force, propelling him onto speeds in excess of eighty miles per hour, ninety, faster. Drivers grew aware of the patrol car behind them, began switching over, so that the lane cleared out, a gray river before them.

"Thing is, this fella claims to be her dad," Brawley said. "They're living the van life, he says. They sleep in there, eat at rest stops, whole coast is her classroom. Now, the girl looks to be in pretty rough shape, so even if his story shakes out, this won't be the end of things. But there doesn't seem to be a whole lotta reason to believe that it's Bea. Excepting as we've got no identification from either of them, and our Samaritan put the two together."

"So it could be," Maggie had rasped.

Brawley lifted his eyes to the rearview. "Fella claiming to be her father refused permission to snap a photo of the girl, let me send it to you folks for a look-see. And she's hiding herself away pretty good anyhow, anytime someone goes in there. That's why we're driving all this way." A weighty pause. "But I don't want you folks getting your hopes up."

They were nothing but hope.

The car ate up miles. Untold numbers of countless miles.

—

The sheriff led Cass and Maggie across a parking lot and into a police barracks. Looked a lot like the one in Cheleo, except Cass had a feeling they were very far from home. *I don't think we're in Kansas anymore*. Bea repeated that line from the old movie all the time: on the first day of school, when he and Maggie left her off at strings camp, or even just let her go see Don and Beth up the road, where Bea didn't have rules to follow or healthy food to eat or bedtime if it was a sleepover. The Parkers liked to indulge her in something of a free-for-all.

He and Maggie passed a desk with a dispatcher sitting behind it, speaking nonsense into a radio—Cass couldn't make sense of one word—and walked on toward a row of chairs. A man occupied the last one. He wore dirt-scuffed boots and a pair of filthy denims with an even filthier plaid shirt, and sat with his forearms resting on his thighs, back rounded like a shell. Light hair that swung, overgrown, concealed both sides of his face.

Maggie rushed him. *"What did you do to my daughter!"*

Her fingers formed hooks she dug into his arm. He reared back, and a strip of his shirt wound up in her fist, ripping with a harsh rasp.

Brawley made himself into a cage around the man, getting him onto his feet and pushing him backward down the hall, while the dispatcher and a deputy in uniform, plus a few other men—maybe police, maybe not—all hurried in the direction of the commotion.

Cass wrapped his arms around his wife from behind; she twisted and fought.

"It's okay," he panted to everyone pitching forward, ready to step in. "She's okay."

The uniformed deputy broke off and strode down the hall, calling back to the two of them. "Here's where we've got the girl." He placed his hand on a doorknob.

Everything stilled as if cast in cement. Cass felt unable to move, and Maggie went rigid in his hold. The pause seemed to last forever, like nothing would ever bring it to a close. At last his wife shoved free of him so violently, it felt like she had broken his arms.

The deputy opened the door.

The room held a table with wooden seats placed around it. A cushioned chair that had clearly been dragged in for the purpose was wedged into a corner, and a young girl sat slumped in it, her head lolled back with one arm across her face.

He knew instantly that it wasn't Bea. No matter what might've happened to her out there, what changes she'd undergone, there was no way this was their daughter.

"Mags—" he said, his voice soundless in his ears. "It isn't . . . This isn't her. It's not Bea."

Maggie walked forward like she was stoned, or asleep. No, like she was possessed. By the devil known as hope, a dybbuk that caused her to extend her hands toward the girl, who bucked awake as if sensing someone coming, revealing flashing eyes that weren't Bea's.

"Leave me alone! He's my dad! We're fine! We're happy! We live like this all the time!"

Her hoarse, raw voice nothing like his sweet daughter's.

No crime, no matter how brutal, circumstances he couldn't bring himself to picture, specters raised on the podcasts and better left there, could've brought about such a change.

Still, Maggie kept plodding forward with her arms out, zombified, so that the girl had to scooch backward, using enough force to make the chair strike the wall.

"You sure about that, Mr. Monroe?" Brawley asked.

Cass turned around. He couldn't grab hold of his wife again; he had the feeling it wouldn't work this time, anyway. She was reaching, patting, feeling; she needed to descend from this pinnacle on her own, come to the right conclusion herself.

"Yeah," he said. He left the room and entered the hall. Stood facing the wall, his forehead resting on the cold cinder blocks. "I'm sure."

—

When the doorbell rang the day after their trip with Brawley—or was it the day after that? The next one? The next one? The next?—Cass and Maggie leaped out of bed at the same time. The unlaundered sheets tangled around his bare legs, and he went down, palms flat on the floor.

The bell ringing out of the blue meant something terrible.

Unless it meant the most wonderful thing of all.

"Go!" he commanded. "I have to get dressed—find some clothes—"

Maggie was hardly more clad than he, but at least she wore a nightgown. There was a pair of jeans badly in need of a washing on the floor, and he yanked them up over his boxers, not bothering to locate a shirt before stumbling into the hall, the hem of one pants leg caught underneath his heel. Hopping on one foot while he freed the other, he made it down the stairs.

Maggie had just pulled open the front door. "Oh." The word a trickle of air expiring.

Cass felt himself still as he reached the bottom of the flight.

Don stood there, shifting from foot to foot on their porch. "Just wanted to check in on you folks. I know how rough that was the other day." He cleared his throat, a *haw* that sounded unwell. "Beth were still alive, she would've made a casserole."

Don thrust forward a sack of groceries; Cass saw a jug of milk peeking out from the top, some stalks of green, a box of doughnuts. "Maggie," he said. "Ask him in."

They sat at the kitchen table. Don brewed a pot of coffee, serving it to them with the doughnuts he'd brought, though he was the only person to take one. "How long has it been?" he asked, wiping crumbs off his lips with the back of a hand. "Five days? And they still got nothing?"

It felt like five years to Cass. Or five seconds.

Maggie turned her head away, facing the wall.

Cass took a sip from the mug Don had filled for him. "Lead they thought they had was a dead end. I followed up with Brawley. State has the girl in care, hoping for a relative to take her in. Her dad did three tours in Afghanistan, came back with about what you'd expect. Paranoid, thinks the government's out to get him—hell, he's got a point, what he's been through—so he rid himself of paperwork, stays offline, lives in his van. His wife left him and didn't want the girl."

"Stop," Maggie said, a hiss of air escaping from between her lips. She placed a hand on top of his, though the gesture felt the opposite of loving. Lethal, her skin hot as a brand.

Cass heard the echo of his words—*didn't want the girl*—and lowered his head.

Don set his doughnut aside unfinished. "I just can't believe it. This day and age."

"Right," Cass said, not sure what he was agreeing to.

Don went on speaking in stops and starts; Cass felt each partial sentence like a stone hitting his chest. "The police, all their tests and technology. Computers, you know. Search of the whole country. But they can't find anything. Not a single trace of her?"

Maggie stood up. Cass saw then how sheer her nightie was: breasts clearly visible, the vee of her panties. He didn't know how to tell her, if he should usher her upstairs. Why bother, really? What did it matter? Civilized conventions had all fallen away. She was beyond modesty.

Don averted his eyes.

"Thanks for the groceries," she said. "We'll let you know as soon as there's news."

"Or if I can help out again, come over, anything. All you have to do is call. I keep my phone on that vibrate mode now, so I feel it ringing." He patted the pocket of his work pants. "My hearing's going, Beth musta told you before she passed, drove her crazy. *You never listened to me before, but it's gotten even worse.*" His mouth formed a fond smile as he rose to his feet.

Cass fought to smile back, but the most he could manage was a nod.

"So I don't always catch the doorbell or someone knocking. Might not hear if you just stop by. Best to call so I feel the buzz. If for some reason I'm not home, I mostly stay within range. Anytime, you hear?" He picked up his mug, drank down the dregs. "I'll see myself out."

By the time Cass turned around, Maggie was gone.

Had disappeared from view like the ghosts they'd both become.

When the doorbell rang for the second time that day, they were sluggish about it.

They had settled on the couch with plates on their laps, some dish Cass couldn't identify, even though he'd already taken a bite. Once, food had distinctions; there'd been different kinds. Now what this plate held could've been lasagna or oatmeal, mealy and flavorless in his mouth.

"It's Don," Maggie said heavily. "Let him think we've gone to sleep."

"Mags. He'll see the light on."

She heaved herself sideways, plate tilting perilously, and flicked the switch on the lamp so that the room was instantly covered in shadow. Every piece of furniture, their food, and even themselves grayed out.

"There, that should do it. As we know, he can't hear too good." Her tone mocking, mean. "So we'll just keep quiet. Not a big ask these days."

"Don didn't mean what he said like it came out. He's just worried. He loves Bea too."

"Not like we do."

"No. Of course not like we do."

"He's a lonely old man who's nothing without his wife, and he's got our trouble mixed up with his tragedy, looking for some way to feel useful or needed—"

The bell rang again.

He set his mostly full plate on the coffee table and got to his feet.

When he opened the door, a woman stood on the porch, tall, all made up, hair bundled on top of her head in a way that looked messy but also nice. Not from here, almost certainly. He twisted to look over his shoulder at Maggie, who had begun rising from the couch, clearly forgetting her own plate so that it tipped, contents landing with a wet *plop* on the floor. Maggie grabbed hold of the dish before it could fall and smash into pieces. She dropped it behind her onto a seat cushion. Her hand came away streaked with red.

Lasagna, then.

She crossed to join him at the door. They both looked at the woman.

"I'm sorry to just show up like this. I'm the one who saw the little girl in the van."

This time, no coffee or doughnuts. They didn't venture as far as the kitchen, instead returning to the living room, where Cass removed the plate and took that part of the couch, feeling sauce seep through the fabric of his jeans. Maggie dropped down beside him—not in her nightie anymore; at some point she'd gotten dressed—while the woman occupied an armchair.

"I am so, so sorry about what you're going through," she began. "I have children myself, and I can't even begin to imagine, and I don't know if my saying that makes it better or worse."

She should've been the crisis therapist. Had Ms. Reynolds beat by a fair shake already.

"That girl in the van wasn't Bea," Maggie said, short and hard.

"I know she wasn't," the woman replied. She took in a breath whose ruffle he could hear, see air inflating her chest. "I don't think the police pulled over the right van."

They turned to her as one; he watched his wife do it while feeling his own body move.

"What?" Maggie whispered.

"Who are you?" He needed to know.

The woman went red. "I forgot to tell you my name. It's Brit Warren. I live in a small town called Gardnerville. About three hundred miles away from here in Vermont."

What's Bea doing in Vermont? He almost said it aloud. He felt his eyes swell with tears. This woman had come all this way—traveled so far—why?

Maggie reached for his hand, bearing down when he grasped hers.

"But . . . you saw the plate. You gave them a license number," his wife said, her words choppy, coming out in pieces. "That's how they tracked down that man. The veteran. And his daughter. His poor daughter."

"I gave them a *partial* plate," Brit corrected. "It's all I was able to get." She paused, flexing and fisting her hands. "Let me back up. So, my three-year-old is potty training, right?"

She stopped again, maybe sensing what the mention of her child might do, a movie reel of memories spooling backward in his mind. Bea, a tween, a schoolkid, a toddler having accidents, a baby in diapers. Raising children condensed the years and drew them out. Made time something meaningless, irrelevant.

"We had a pee emergency, couldn't wait to get to the restrooms. There might've been a line," Brit went on at last. "I took him around to the back, where there were dumpsters and some privacy. The van was parked with its rear doors open. The driver slammed them shut and drove off as soon as he saw me and my son come running over. I didn't think to look at the plate until he was pulling away." Her face flushed; she appeared angry. "I feel terrible about that."

"Not your fault," he forced himself to say. "Sounds like you acted pretty quick."

Brit shook her head. "Not quickly enough," she said, her tone matching the expression on her face. "At any rate, I gave them what I could remember. And they pulled over a van. And that van did have a little girl in it."

"You're saying it was a coincidence?" he asked skeptically. "Two different vans, shared part of their plates, and two separate girls?"

Brit nodded. "It's not all that unlikely, statistically speaking. Lots of vans on the road, lots of drivers and young girls." Momentarily, her mouth twisted. "That alert went out all over New England."

He guessed she was probably right.

"Anyway, here's why I think it was the wrong one." She ticked a finger, her nails polished red. "The girl was in the passenger seat when police pulled the van over. But the one I saw was in the van's cavity, you know, its cargo area. The cop said she must've moved up, simple enough, but the girl I saw wasn't in any condition to move. Lying back there, passed out cold."

Better that way. The voice spoke inside his head. Better for whichever child this woman had spotted, if she were unconscious, so out of it she wouldn't remember a thing.

Another finger. "The van I saw had something on its side, a sign or a logo, I'm not sure. Whereas the one they stopped—according to the cop who questioned me—might've *once* had something on it, but it'd been removed, probably some time ago. The paint was faded in two areas. Maybe the veteran guy bought a vehicle aftermarket or one that'd been decommissioned."

"I don't know," he said. "That's a lot to hang on what you yourself said happened pretty fast. This guy peels away; you couldn't have gotten a very good look. I'm sure the police were careful. They wouldn't just swap out one vehicle for another."

"I'm sorry to tell you this, but the police make mistakes *all* the time," said Brit.

Maggie squeezed his hand so hard, her nails dug ditches in the skin. "So many people are telling us things. And at the same time not saying anything. We don't know what to listen to."

"Did you see the man they brought in?" Brit asked.

"The father?" said Maggie. "Yes. We saw him."

Brit nodded. "So did I. And though I didn't get a good look at the driver of the van I'm talking about—couldn't recall with any accuracy his eyes or hair color or what he was wearing or even how tall he was—I did notice one thing about him."

"What?" Maggie asked.

"The man I saw had a gash on his forehead, kinda just below his hairline. Really deep and nasty-looking. It stood out, even as he was making his getaway."

Maggie couldn't have known why Cass dropped her hand as fast as if it had burned him.

The reason he was on his feet, fists balled.

She craned her head to peer up at him, looking confused.

In his worst and darkest moments, he had come back to this. All of his moments were dark now, the inside of his mind matching the outside of his life, a cave fathoms deep without an ounce of light. But there were gradations even in lightlessness, and one of them was this place, these words, where he could mentally wander simply to have the relief of blinking.

Either way, she's a fighter.

That had been no wild conjecture. Tracy and Jan were onto something.

That bastard might be walking around with some seriously vicious wound right now.

"It was Bea in the back of the van," he said. "That man has Bea."

CHAPTER SIXTEEN

If their suitcases hadn't been back at home, Louise would've turned north instead of south after fleeing her parents, driven straight to Dr. Shepherd with Geary thrashing and wailing in his booster seat. How could her mother have grabbed him like that? Geary had hated being touched since he was two. Changing his diapers at that age took the planning and strategizing of a war. Giving him a bath was impossible; luckily, Geary took to water on his own early. No hugs, no kisses, no holding his hand when they crossed the street. Other moms complained about what a workout it was to lift their growing toddlers; she'd had to quit carrying Geary when he still felt light in her arms. And his grandmother had gone and tackled him like a linebacker.

He wasn't quieting down. Louise went to turn up the volume of the music to try and drown out the noise, then remembered the incident at the supermarket—whatever its nature had been—and slammed the radio silent with the flat of her hand. She might be making things worse.

In addition to not having any of their stuff, she'd also been studying maps and couldn't imagine navigating the sword-thin roads to Dr. Shepherd's treatment center in the dark. It was already past noon. Plus, there was a lack of cell coverage in the area—like that was a thing—and the idea of being on the road with the sun fading, her phone as disconnected from the rest of the world as a ball of wax, a useless rope tied to nothing, made her insides quiver. The image of that last bar disappearing felt like a fall from the top of a flight of stairs.

She and Geary were just going to have to tough out another night before leaving.

She woke when a glow of light penetrated her eyelids. It took a moment for awareness to return, her memory of the day before; then she shot to her feet, blanket dropping to the floor. She had fallen asleep in the hall outside Geary's room. After the ghastly encounter with her mother, she hadn't been surprised when he closed his door, shutting her out. But she couldn't stand to be too far away from him—even her room down the hall didn't feel close enough.

At first, she assumed the light that had disturbed her must've come from the moon, but when she swiveled to face a window, there was just the normal haze of orange-tinged pollution in an otherwise blank, black sky. She had a vague sense of it having been blue light, anyway. Maybe her phone had glitched, some reminder firing up the screen, although it was as dark as a stone now, a reminder of its uselessness to come tomorrow.

What had awakened her?

She cracked open the door to Geary's room and tiptoed over the threshold to get a reassuring peek at him. He wasn't in his bed. The usually neatly folded coverings lay wrinkled at the bottom, as if they'd been kicked. She couldn't make out Geary anywhere in the room, and her heart gonged, her head jerking sideways. Then she spotted him.

He was kneeling on the floor underneath his desk. As her eyes adjusted, she squinted, able to see what he must've been doing in here ever since they got home. The lines he normally traced in the material of his carpet, crushing the threads until they were tamped down and stayed that way, had been expanded. Greatly, hugely extended. A giant, intersecting grid that ran all the way to the spot where he knelt beneath a roof of desk, crossed the room to his closet before disappearing underneath its door, then led up to the sill where she was standing. She took a sudden step away, a backward leap, so her tread wouldn't mess up his perfectly laid track.

They had never looked more like a system of byways, streets, and roads to her.

Where on earth did Geary mean them to go?

—

As the real roads heading away from home crisscrossed and changed, Louise registered with new clarity the packed-in crowding of suburbia. The eye clutter of signs and billboards and a sky blocked with buildings. The constant insect buzz of people who could afford it getting their lawns and gardens tended to by people who couldn't. While the place where she and Geary were going looked empty on the map. Lakes and forests. Blue amoeba shapes to break up all the green.

They had both slept in, tired out by their predawn exertions, and she exited the thruway at a rest stop when her stomach grew fangs, even though a break would push them later.

"Come with me or stay in the car?" she asked, lifting herself to peer over the seat. "Hey, you remembered your puffy coat," she said, jutting her chin toward where it lay crushed up beside his booster. "Good job." Her oversight—forgetting a favored item—must've been borne of exhaustion. "It might still be cold where we're going."

She glanced through the windshield at the parking lot. Packed with rows of big expensive-looking SUVs, and even bigger pickup trucks, plus minivans, U-Hauls, and cargo vans. Semis and tractor trailers corralled off to one side. This place was massive. Probably not safe to let Geary wait alone. She was about to say so when he opened the door and climbed out.

Her steps slowed as they approached a run of glass walls. Places with loud noise, lots of people, and lights were hard for Geary, plus all the glass would make for a visible snowfall of dust. A meltdown now might make her just lie down and let the hordes of travelers trample her.

His eyes appeared to be focused on the acres of vehicles. A pair of doors slid open, and with a relieved breath, she registered him trailing her on the march toward the food court. She stopped when she saw the length of the line. There had to be fifty people waiting for burgers.

Geary was doing okay, though, so she made a bubble around the two of them, keeping a few feet back from the family in front. She gazed at the menu board as the line moved forward, her cheeks cramping at the thought of food. "I'm getting fries *and* a shake," she announced.

"Did you say something, dear?"

A grandpa-aged man had gotten in line behind them. He was crowding in close; she didn't know why Geary hadn't yet made clear his objection. She took a look around. "Did you see my son? He was just"—she broke off, frowning—"standing where you are."

The old man shook his head. "Line's moving." He gestured. "Are you going to go?"

Her breath sped up. "But he was right here. Ten years old? Brown curls?"

The old man pushed ahead of her, revealing a crush of people impatient to get past the obstacle she was presenting. A jammed-together procession so long, snaking back to the restrooms, that she couldn't pick out distinct faces or bodies. To her suddenly terrified eyes, it looked like one of those CGI shots in a movie, a mass of thousands.

She'd never developed the skills other parents had, like gluing a hand to her child's shoulder to keep him close in a crowd. Or letting one eye do one thing—read the menu, count the cash in her purse—while the other stayed on Geary. Which warnings to utter to make sure he didn't wander off. She'd never had to do any of those things; on the relatively rare occasions when they were out and about, Geary was good at staying put. She also lacked that sixth parental sense of instinctively sizing up the people around her, deciding who might pose a threat. So many people posed a threat to Geary.

Her blood pressure mounted, a buzzing hive in her ears. "Geary!"

The hum of the crowd so loud that at first, no one heard her cry.

"Geary!" she shouted.

At last, people started to notice the shrieking woman. Some instantly tugged children close—*their* sixth sense on fire—while others shoved forward, nothing and no one better interfere with their lunch. A few looked to companions, faces painted with obvious dilemmas.

"Mrs. Lady?"

A little kid—younger than Geary—had come up and was tugging Louise's arm.

"I see a boy where he not supposed to be."

And then she was grabbing this child's hand and running—too late it struck her, taking someone else's kid away; oh, but she'd keep him safe; she just had to find her son—toward the bank of windows where he was pointing. She caught a glimpse of Geary outside just as a woman jogged over, glowering as she hoisted up the boy who'd helped Louise.

"What the actual fuck?"

Louise didn't take a second to answer, just raced toward the exit, praying Geary wouldn't move before she could reach him. As she got outside, she spotted him for a second in a gap between cars, but almost every parking space was taken, blocked by pickups, SUVs, and vans all towering over her son. He was soon swallowed up, invisible in a sea of vehicles.

She ducked between rows, darting, dashing, relying on a splintered memory of where she'd last seen him, but he was moving and so were the cars—

There. A single empty space with Geary coming to a stop smack in its center.

His head turning this way and that, twisting side to side so fast that his curls swung.

Looking in every direction except the one that held a truck about to turn into the slot where he stood, its driver clearly not seeing the boy who wasn't yet tall enough to rise over the grille—

Louise let out a shriek and ran. Passing cars—a bruising clop from a side mirror, the rust-flecked flank of an old hatchback abrading her skin—until she was nearly close enough, almost there, could thrust both arms out and grab a clump of his curls, one wrist, without even thinking about what she was doing. She gave a hard enough yank that both her shoulders wrenched in their sockets, snatching Geary out of the way just before the truck turned in, and only then slammed on its brakes, jolting to a stop on the blacktop where a moment ago her son had been.

The woman from the rest stop came flying up, clutching her child's hand. "Is he okay?"

Louise held on to Geary, this child she hadn't had physical contact with in eight years and now was barely able to feel, her fingers numb and senseless.

The driver of the truck jumped out, sputtering and rageful. "He was in my way!"

"Boys and their cars, right?" the woman murmured. "Mine spends hours looking at 'em."

Geary wasn't fighting to free himself. Louise had never felt anything so still; a metal rod would've had more life to it. She was panting, trying to force air into her lungs, while he didn't even seem to be breathing. A knot of people had gathered around them but were now backing off, their thrum of excited murmurings dying away. Phones back in pockets, video moment over.

As Louise's fingers finally began to unclench, to loosen their hold, it struck her that not even a therapist as good as Dr. Shepherd seemed to be would have the skills to bring a child back from this state. Louise crouched on the ground with engines growling and gusting around them, vehicles blasting their fiery breaths, until reality bent, a portal to another world opened, and she had never gotten Geary away from that truck. He stood beside her, tolerating her touch, because he was dead.

They both stayed like that for minutes, hours—the thought of getting going again a mountain too tall for Louise to climb. Her son had never shown the slightest interest in cars.

What the hell had he come out here to do?

CHAPTER SEVENTEEN

That morning—*A Day*, as she'd come to think of it, *A* for *Arrival*, for *Arles*, for *At Long Last*—she woke in a state of total brain-body excitement, and took the steps to the first floor at a jog. If she hadn't feared being seen, she would've sprinted.

Dan followed her downstairs and she let him out through the side door, remembering belatedly to call a goodbye. Then she headed over to the dining room, where Stephanie had set out homemade muffins, deviled eggs, fruit, and juice. *A cold spread.* Arles had eaten in the morning only once in her life, on a day when she was twelve, and sworn never to do that again. In her family, breakfast had been a war zone. Affectionate overtures from her stepfather all studiously ignored by her mother as she dished out food, inquiries from him as to how Arles had slept when he'd been right there to witness her unrest.

From upstairs came the chime of a childish voice along with the faint vibrato of skipping steps through the heavy plaster ceiling, the school day already begun.

Arles entered the parlor to start group.

"Things are conducted a little differently in FIT," she began. "Instead of the usual confidentiality between patient and therapist, we all share our diagnoses or primary issue with each other. The openness required to be able to do that is in itself liberating. Mental health problems are nothing to be ashamed of. Would you hesitate to tell a friend you had a cold?"

Big Jim took the floor. "I don't get colds. And if I had one, I'd pretend that I didn't."

Well, he was honest, at least. "Broken leg, then," she said. "Diabetes."

"But . . ." Fleur sounded genuinely at a loss. "What if we don't have a diagnosis? My husband and I and our older daughter are all perfectly fine. We're just here to support Nat."

Uh-huh, Arles thought. *Sure you are.* "Thank you, Fleur. You raise an excellent point. Remember how I used the term *primary issue* as well as *diagnosis*?"

A mix of hesitant nods, faint frowns, dropped gazes from the assembled group.

"Well, we all have those," Arles went on. "In this room and on this planet. They say of life, no one gets out alive, and the same can be said of psychological issues. No one plays this game without having at least one." She smiled. "And in case you doubt me, I'm going to begin."

Everyone looked up, their expressions sharpening.

"I will be sharing what I'm about to not only in the guise of walking the walk, but as a demonstration that I've experienced my own psychic pain, come through much of it, continue to struggle with some of it, yet am able to live a happy, productive life." *Sort of. Not always.*

The room possessed the hush of a theater before the curtains were drawn.

"The issue I contend with is a history of childhood trauma," she said simply. "Thank you for letting me share. We'll go around the room now, okay? Would somebody like to go first?"

A few people leaned forward in their chairs before settling back again.

At last, Natalie lazily lifted one hand, waggling her fingers. "Might as well be me. As Mommie Dearest over there pointed out, I'm the sick one."

There was an immediate pile-on.

From Fleur: "Nat, that's not what I said at all!"

Big Jim: "Show your mother some respect."

Gretchen, quietly: "Well, kinda."

Arles sat forward in her seat. "These are all important responses you're having, Merritt family. But during Personal Share . . ." The official FIT-designated term. Arles always thought of it more like a game show: *Now it's time for Share! Your! Issue!* "We don't cross talk. Each person has the floor until they finish. We signal that by saying something like *Done* or *Next* or *Someone else can go now*. Natalie? Back to you."

"I have bulimia nervosa, anorexia, and a compulsive exercise disorder," she said, fast, the words smashing into each other. "There. I'm done."

"Thank you," Arles said. "I know that took a lot of guts, going first."

"You used a stomach metaphor for me intentionally, right?" Natalie said.

Arles grinned. She truly liked this girl. "Who would like, or be willing, to go next?"

Patience lifted a timid hand. "I struggle with depression and anxiety, but only occasionally. Dr. Shepherd, you've said they're—what's that word? Subclinical. My real issue is, like, fallout from religious indoctrination." She gave a nod. "Done."

"I guess that goes for me too," said Ben. "And now I'm done in more ways than one."

The three remaining didn't say anything. Arles offered encouraging nods, then sat back in her seat to let silence dispense its potent elixir.

Natalie fixed her parents with a challenging stare until enough time elapsed that she gave up and sent her sister an imploring raised eyebrow.

Ben tapped his foot on the floor with increasing velocity, while Patience twisted all ten of her fingers, her knuckles popping like tiny firecrackers.

Finally, Big Jim let out a guffaw. "Think this might be the first time in my life I'm at a loss for words. I've always got something to say."

Arles judiciously allotted time, then spoke deliberately if disingenuously. "If you're finished, and you can let us know, that would be great, Jim."

His heavy eyebrows knit. "What? Oh, hah. Nah, that wasn't my issue. I was just saying."

"Oh," Arles said, laying on disappointment thick in her tone. "That's too bad."

Natalie watched her intently.

"Because growing aware of when it might be better not to speak, how to give others in your family and in the wider world the microphone, strikes me as an excellent goal," Arles said.

He aimed a challenging stare in her direction and she returned it.

Gretchen spoke up suddenly and fiercely. "I started cutting this year."

Arles's gaze dropped instantly to the young woman's forearms. Cuffs pulled low, over her hands. Arles had missed the tell. She was more preoccupied than she'd realized, off her game.

Fleur looked searchingly at her husband, as if waiting for him to weigh in.

Gretchen tugged her sleeves up, exposing a few pale-pink streaks of mostly healed skin. "Not deep. Online, I'm what they call a scratcher."

Big Jim spoke up. "Why would you want to hurt your pretty—"

Arles fixed him with another look, and he cut himself off mid-sentence.

Natalie reached out and took her sister's hand.

"Oh, sorry. I'm finished," Gretchen said quietly.

Fleur glanced at both her daughters. "I don't have an issue."

"Jesus, Mom . . . ," said Natalie, then fell silent.

Gretchen let go of her sister's hand and began to rub her own ribbed wrist.

Big Jim gave his wife a nod. "You're too busy taking care of me to worry about anything else." He laughed as if he'd said something amusing.

Fleur held up a finger. "Wait. I didn't say *finished* yet." She stared down at the floor. "That *is* my issue. That I don't have one. I don't have anything that's mine. I've been thinking, as everybody spoke, and everything I kept coming up with—well, it had to do with you, Nat. Or you, Gretchen, or Jim, yes, you too. Nothing just for me. Of me." A pause. "And now I'm done."

Arles let out a breath. "This has been very good work for one morning."

"It wasn't as bad as I thought," Fleur said, sounding surprised.

The patients dispersed, the Merritts walking off in pairs—Natalie and Gretchen with their parents behind them—while Patience and Ben left the room arm in arm.

Arles glanced at her wrist; at Fir Cove, she relied on a watch for the time since phones were useless for so much. How many hours until she got to meet Louise? Allowing for travel glitches, the inevitable hiccups of somebody making their way to this land for the very first time.

After lunch, the assemblage walked the grounds, Arles pointing out sites of historic interest, like the ruins of what had once been a still, and the family graveyard. Stephanie and Lissa joined in at the end, leading a lap through the woods—Arles making sure they gave the ravine a wide berth—then down to the lake to point out flora and fauna unique to big, relatively untouched parcels in the Adirondacks.

The final session of the day found Arles mentally pacing back and forth with expectation, physically all but bouncing on her seat. She let the patients know a new family would be arriving in the same way a schoolgirl finds excuses to bring up her crush.

She checked and rechecked the cabin Louise and Geary were going to share, laying in extra blankets, both fleece and wool, plus a stockpile of towels in plush and flat weaves to accommodate Geary's sensory issues. She added kid-friendly snacks to the basket, then looked at her wrist for the hundredth time. It was earlier than she'd thought, minutes oozing by.

What if Louise had engine trouble, broke down somewhere? Something seemed to have caused a delay, and the lack of signal in the area was bring-you-to-your-knees astounding for people who weren't used to it, basically anyone other than locals. The thought of Louise standing by the side of the road made Arles's heart clench like a fist inside her.

She set off walking along the long dirt drive.

By the time she reached the gates, the temperature was dropping, and light had leached from the sky, staining the clouds a lurid rose. *Red sky at night.* It wouldn't do to hit the paved road on foot; if she went looking outside Fir Cove, she needed to get her car.

She was back at the house without having been aware of getting there. She ran in for a jacket and flashlight—bestowing quick hellos and a "How was dinner?" or two on the patients all milling around—then went outside again, dismayed as she took the porch steps to find no new vehicle in the gravel drive.

A sudden spill of headlights penetrated the dusk, causing her to stop so abruptly that puffs of dust rose up around her shoes. She lifted one trembling hand in a wave, and the car pulled over. An old Toyota, not a four-wheel drive; it was lucky Louise hadn't gotten stuck in some mud-season patch of muck.

Arles had always been a good actress; therapists had to be. Neutral expressions no matter what was revealed, empathy summoned for clients who'd committed atrocious acts. But facing Louise was going to require an Oscar-worthy performance. How to conceal the fact that she knew this woman, at least in a way? Felt closer to her than she did any of her own family, alive or dead?

Louise rolled down her window. "Dr. Shepherd?"

Arles gave what she hoped looked like a nod, though it felt more as if her head had come loose on her neck. "Yes, hello! I'm glad you made it."

"Thanks for coming to meet us. I wasn't sure this was the right way."

"You're good." Arles let out a breath of exhaled emotion. "Park up there and I'll be right over." She set off after the car, so fleet on her feet, she could've matched its speed.

But as she got close, all feeling of fleetness vanished, and her steps began to drag. This moment was twenty-five years in the making, and yet she felt completely unprepared. What was going to happen when she finally met Louise in person? A sense of completeness such as Arles had never known? Pieces of her life assembling, shards in a stained-glass tableau?

Louise shut off the engine, then got out of her car, and the living, breathing sight of her felt to Arles like gripping a live wire. She shoved one hand into her pocket, talisman-touching the photo. Its card stock smooth, edges soft and curled with wear. She couldn't muster a word.

Louise began scuffing the dirt with a worn sneaker. The silence built, a force collecting.

There was no sense of completeness. No splinters of glass reassembled into anything.

And yet if Arles had passed this woman on a city street, she would've known her to be the girl in the picture. The straw-blonde hair was the same, if amped up with highlights. The fragile frame hadn't changed. Really, though, it came down to the eyes. The same ones Arles had looked into for two and a half decades.

Someone needed to speak; the quiet had grown as powerful as a wave held back.

But Arles couldn't bring herself to say one word, her tongue thick and useless.

At last, Louise remarked, "This place is amazing."

Arles bore down on the photo till it threatened to tear. Soon, Louise would start to question her rash decision, turn around and drive away from this place. And for the sheerest of seconds, it seemed as if that would be the right outcome. There'd been no reason to bring this woman all the way out here—with her child, no less. Arles had no clue what to do with either of them. Then, with her hand still concealed, she gave the flesh beneath her jeans a vicious twist, and pain kicked her into gear. She felt her lips form words that her mind hadn't seemed to produce.

"You'll learn all about it tomorrow from our excellent tour guide, Lissa," she said. "Lissa is eight, and I hope will be a good friend to Geary."

Louise's face lit like a match in the gathering dark. "Did you hear that, Gear? Come on out."

The sight of the gangly boy climbing out of the car posed a relief from Arles's study of Louise, which was burning her vision, hurting her eyes. "Since it's late and I'm sure you're tired after your trip—"

Louise interjected an emphatic nod that Arles couldn't respond to.

"Let me bring you to your cabin. Dinner's been left in a hamper; I thought it might be best to meet everyone after you've had a good night's sleep. Less overwhelming for Geary."

Another vigorous nod that Arles had no choice but to ignore.

She scarcely parsed Louise's exclamations of delight upon seeing their quarters, nor the upbeat remarks she kept making to her son. Whose entreaty—*hurry*—Arles had to make sense of, but how was that supposed to happen now? Determine the meaning behind a nonspeaking child's enigmatic utterance? Arles couldn't imagine ever speaking again herself, let alone conducting therapy. Meeting Louise had puddled her, dissolved her into a slick on the ground.

She backed out of the cabin and veered off into the woods, branches clacking like bones as she surged forward between them. Senseless, dangerous to hike at night, not wearing the right clothing, or packing any gear, without an ounce of water. Peter had taught Arles better; what she was doing constituted a naive, flat-footer mistake.

Flicking on her flashlight, she began mounting a slope. It was muddy, as slippery as a fish in water, and she had to claw for purchase with her hands. The first leg took her past a creek roiling with snowmelt and across a bridge made of rotting wood. *Repair job,* she noted dully.

Her clothes had soaked through with sweat—cotton, another potentially lethal rookie error—and her chest was heaving by the time she reached the boulder field and scrambled out onto a ledge. She sat with her legs dangling in the air, jeans encapsulated with mud and shoes ruined beyond repair.

She didn't dare touch the photograph with her hands this filthy, which was all right since she no longer wanted any part of the thing. Her brain set a dreary reminder to find a hiding spot for it. This part of her life had to be dead and buried now, decayed to chalky dust. No matter what, Louise must never get an inkling that the photograph existed.

Full dark had fallen, the sky a moonless, starless brew. The bulb on her flashlight was dimming, probably hadn't had its batteries replaced in years. Making the downhill version of this trek with a failing light would be past stupid and all the way to suicidal.

Suddenly, that dark pitch threatened. How easy such an act was to commit, so simple to slip off this ledge. Her legs hung over the edge, heavy and dragging, laden with mud. She could fall two thousand feet through soft, supple air, land on a canopy of trees. It almost sounded nice.

From the moment Arles had first caught sight of this photo when she was twelve years old, it seemed to exist with a halo around it. A heavenly circle of pearlescent light, as if the girl it captured were an angel. Arles had sensed its import and essentialness to her life in that initial glimpse, and during every day going forward. But now, such awareness resided in a pit muddier than her hands, a swamp of unanswerable questions that hinted at a bleak, grave darkness.

Until Louise arrived, Arles hadn't been sure. Or rather, she *had* been sure—that things would click, slide into place, as soon as she saw the woman in person. She couldn't fathom what to do now that they hadn't. How to resolve the single greatest mystery of her life.

In what way did Arles come by this picture, this all-important, lifesaving—like a rescue breath when you were drowning—object she'd held on to for so long? Why had the photograph wound up in her possession?

She had no memory, and no idea.

CHAPTER EIGHTEEN

Geary walked through the cabin, one arm extended, patting some surfaces while avoiding others. Shiny log walls, a painted coffee table, and clever chairs formed from something Louise thought she might've seen in an old movie once—they looked like overturned metal milking jugs—all were apparently tolerable to touch. Unvarnished wood windowsills with a few splinters visible were not. He placed one finger against a couch whose material looked rough, then pulled it back as if the upholstery had burned him. His shoulder grazed checked curtains, and their worn fabric swished around his cheek without causing any disturbance.

Louise peeked into a covered basket. "OMG. You are not going to believe this, Gear."

He came and examined a strange, new-to-him stool, studying the food she was arranging before he took a seat. She set aside a packet of crackers—crumbs—instead handing Geary a skewer of meat. Red but not beef, with a green leaf—she had never smelled mint outside of toothpaste or gum—and a dab of what looked like ranch but tasted different. Geary took a bite while using a spoon to make a whirlpool in a container of cold pink soup. She sniffed it. Berry.

But the whole time the two of them ate the most unusual meal they'd ever had, without any of the newness causing its usual threatening, incoming-tsunami feeling, an uneasy thought prodded her, like the stroking of a finger. Because Dr. Shepherd seemed different in person.

Cool, maybe even all the way to chilly, Louise conceded with a sinking feeling. This person who was supposed to start giving Geary therapy tomorrow hadn't said one word to him, not even *hello*. She'd actually barely seemed to notice he was there.

Of course, Dr. Shepherd was obviously rich; she lived in a castle. And rich people acted superior. Just look at the guests—*at Glam & Go, you're not a customer, you're our guest!*—whose nails Louise would meticulously shape, only to be told to make them rounder, or more square, or *longer*, for God's sake, like she had the power to make nails grow, even as the women refused tips or wraps. Mold issues, blech—as if she wanted to hear about past fungal infections.

She stood up, hugging her arms around herself. The air in the cabin was cold, which would not work for Geary; she should figure out how to light the fireplace. It would add a cozy note to a place that suddenly felt not just new but alien, unfriendly.

She went to unpack, laying out Geary's pajamas on a twin bed in one of the bedrooms. She put their toothbrushes in a tin cup in the bathroom, and the simple acts began to restore a sense of warmth. This reminded her of summer camp. Her father used to bring her as part of his route. The drives to and from had been as much fun as camp itself, her mother at home so that she and her dad had been able to talk, laugh, even sing. To breathe. Those trips smelled of pine and smoke and fresh air in her memory. Awash with love and a feeling of jittery excitement.

She stood in the doorway while Geary finished in the bathroom, his hands scrubbed clean, lips rimmed with toothpaste like they always were at night. He went to lie down.

"Good night, Gear," she whispered, also as always. "Sleep well. I love you."

In the morning, Louise tugged on jeans, thick socks, and a heavy sweater—in April!—then went to see if Geary was awake. He wasn't in his bed, and the rest of the cabin was small enough that a quick dash through the rooms told her it was empty. She went outside.

If there had been a word to describe living in the country, Louise might've guessed *gentleness*. No traffic noise: horns blurting, sirens wailing, brakes squealing. Or battling crowds, everyone in a rush to do too much in too short a time. No Grand Canyon between those who had more than enough and those who had nowhere near enough.

But *gentle* was not what came to mind as she spotted an opening in the trees and ran toward it. There was a jagged roughness, a violence to the peaks that thrust themselves into the sky, spiking the clouds. This forest was fairy-tale thick, branches woven as tightly as yarn, tree trunks as tall as a giant's legs. She pictured animals whose roars would shake the earth, this land big enough to swallow anything that got too close to its mouth.

Somehow all of that didn't feel threatening, though, less whistling wind through an empty chasm and more of a blown bubble, or a warm embrace. Some force greater than any she had ever known was at work, protecting her, and most of all, Geary.

She heard faint chatter and saw the shadow of the house that was really a castle through the trees. Breaking through a patch of brush, she came to a group of people standing above her on an enormous stone porch, columns as tall as trees to hold it up.

A woman caught sight of her. Youngish, with a long braid, and freckles scattered across her face. She looked like somebody's kid sister. "Hi, I'm Stephanie. Geary's with my daughter."

The statement sounded so natural, so lighthearted, that it stole Louise's breath with a quick, sharp stab to the chest. This was the way things could be, how life was supposed to go. She and Geary had been compromising on a lesser version.

To one side of the house, a gap in the brown, spent grass of winter revealed a puddle crusted with ice. Geary squatted, drawing lines in the surface with a stick while a girl with the same dark hair as her mother—except two braids instead of one—spoke at a high, sweet pitch.

"It isn't deep enough for ducks or fish, but I think I saw a tadpole yesterday."

Tears began coursing down Louise's cheeks.

Stephanie slipped a hand into her jacket pocket. "Mom fail," she said, coming up empty. "I don't have a tissue."

Louise brought her sweater-clad arm up to mop her face. "I'm sorry to be weird. I just never saw Geary do this before." She pressed her arm to her eyes, the woolly fabric damp. "She seems really sweet, your daughter. And smart."

"Lissa's a nice girl. Not a Mom brag—that's all her. She doesn't like everybody, though."

Louise looked up quickly, her vision not yet fully cleared. "Really?"

"Yeah," she said. "Really. I homeschool her, and one of the reasons why was she didn't get along with other children, never really found friends. She said a lot of them were assholes."

Louise laughed. "They are."

Stephanie grinned. "Should we give them some breakfast?" She turned toward the house. "I know the clients have been wondering when Arles—the doctor—will be coming down today."

As they approached the porch, Louise had the sense that something was off. Voices spoke loudly, clamoring to be heard, and everyone faced each other with tense expressions.

Stephanie led Geary and Lissa into the house while Louise stayed outside to try and figure out what was going on. Someone noticed her standing there: a large, bulky man, red-faced but polished, with nicely buffed nails. Louise always noticed that, especially on a guy.

"You must be the new patient," he announced, thrusting out a thick hand.

Hesitantly, she took it. He gave a shake that squashed her fingers, actually hurt.

"Jim Merritt," he said. "This is my wife, Fleur, and our daughters, Gretchen and Natalie."

"Welcome to our nightmare," the skinny one said.

Natalie, Louise was pretty sure. She wasn't the nice-in-a-bathing-suit kind of thin. More just hungry-looking.

"Louise Drake," she said. "I'm here with my son, Geary. Nightmare?"

"That's a bit extreme," the mother said.

She sent her daughter a horrible look, face twisted, eyebrows drawn into sharp angles. Louise instantly felt sorry for Natalie, experienced a completely weird urge to hug the girl.

"Dr. Shepherd's late today," her sister explained.

Greta? Gretel? Something pretty like that.

"We were trying to decide whether someone should go up to her room," said a guy Louise hadn't noticed till now. Bland-looking, his clothes a little big on him and the opposite of country casual. Button-down shirt, pants with creases, laced shoes.

"Which I think would be weird," the woman who was with him said. She wore a long dress and had her hair in a bun. No makeup, nails unpolished. Kind of Instagrammable pioneer. "Let the doctor sleep, Ben. She works hard enough."

"She works for *us*, Patience," Ben replied. The entitlement in his voice got Louise's back up. "Which she isn't right now. So we knock on her door."

Natalie turned to Louise. "I know you just got here, but do you have any opinion?"

"Well . . ." It was stupid, but Louise felt flattered to have been asked. She wanted her reply to contribute something. "What time does she usually come down in the mornings?"

"There is no usually," Ben replied. "We're all almost as new as you are."

"This whole facility is new," Patience added.

Louise hadn't realized the place she'd come to was new. For sure, the buildings weren't.

"Look, we need to stop screwing around," Ben said.

"Ben!" gasped Patience.

Louise had no idea what had gotten her so upset.

"Sorry," Ben muttered, looking for some reason skyward. "But what if she's dead in her bed, and we don't find out till too late? We could administer CPR or something."

"You sound like you want to give her CPR," Patience said darkly. "In her bed."

The Merritt daughters snorted. "Go, Pat," the one who wasn't Natalie said to Patience. Then she took a look around. "Hey, where did Dad go?"

Fleur immediately darted to the front door. "Honey?" she called in a worried tone. "Jim?"

It reminded Louise to go check on Geary. Handing off her duties to such clearly capable hands had been an embarrassingly welcome break.

A thud of heavy footsteps came from inside, and Mr. Merritt stomped onto the porch. "The doctor isn't in her room or anywhere else in the house, and her bed hasn't been slept in," he stated. "Anyone know her plans, whether she was going to be on premises last night?"

"She's our therapist!" said Patience. "We're not supposed to know things like that!"

Mr. Merritt held up both hands. "Didn't realize that. Never had therapy before."

"Yeah, Dad," said Natalie. "You've mentioned that a few times."

"Natalie," her mother said, her voice caught between a plea and a warning.

Natalie let out a huffy breath. "She said something about having a meal session first thing this morning. But if it was supposed to happen, she missed it."

"Is that normal for Dr. Shepherd?" her father asked.

Another huffed breath. "No, *Dad*. I told you, I really like Dr. S. It's literally never happened before."

Her parents exchanged looks.

The sister spoke up. "I saw her with a guy. Sorry, Pat, but I did. Going up to the second floor the night before last. Maybe she's with him?"

"That could be," the mother said.

"Having some dude in her life shouldn't make her miss work," Ben said sulkily.

"I'm going to leave here, drive to where there's signal," Mr. Merritt said after a few seconds. "You should all begin checking the grounds. But be smart about it; don't cause a second problem. Lotta empty land out here. Ben, I'm putting you in charge of the search."

The whole group looked to him, falling in line.

Louise felt something bite deep in her belly. This couldn't be happening. Not when things were starting out so well for Geary.

Mr. Merritt brought his hands together in a ringing clap. "Let me see what's out there, try to get a hold of Dr. Shepherd. If I can't, then I'll make a few calls."

He didn't say who he'd be calling, and that seemed more worrisome than anything else. Who did you call when you wanted to find a missing doctor? Mr. Merritt gave his wife a peck on her cheek, squeezed both daughters' shoulders with his big, meaty hands, then took the porch stairs down to the driveway, where he climbed into a huge SUV and drove off, gunning the gas.

The man wanted to give her something to drink.

But she knew the rules. Every girl on the planet knew them.

She'd heard the older girls talking about it in the bathroom at school, or out on the little kids' playground, and on the bus. At parties, especially, not that she had gone to many parties.

She could not take one sip from the drink the man was mixing in a paper cup, hunched over in the back of his van, fiddling like a mad scientist with a potion.

She'd made him angry before, and he still had a glower on his face, fury in his hands as he shook the contents of a tiny envelope out over the cup.

"All my girls need to be quiet when I say so," he muttered. "Have to just stop talking and shut the fuck up."

Icy liquid filled her belly, everything inside her going loose and runny. She felt panic come at her like a shark, turning her head into mush, a roar of waves through her brain. She dug the nails on one hand into the thin skin on her other wrist, drawing blood, and it snapped her to.

It had hit her when she felt her bladder start to give way. Something she could do. Worth a try, at least. "I can't take a drink right now." Her voice weak and gasping; she forced herself to raise it. "Not yet."

He kept stirring his mixture. Ignoring her. Like she hadn't said anything at all.

"I mean, I want to. I'm very thirsty." Her tongue useless and floppy with fear; it was hard to form words. "But first I have to pee. Is that okay?"

If he let her, then she'd be saved. No way could he contain her once she was outside the van. Didn't matter how way far out in the country they were, she knew this land or land like it, had never lived anywhere else. A chase through the woods? Might as well be on a racetrack.

Still stooped over, he held the cup steady, walking back with it in her direction.

LIKE A GOOD NEIGHBOR

After Brit Warren left, Cass didn't sleep, and he was pretty sure Maggie stayed awake the whole night too. Even when they weren't talking, he could sense her alert beside him. Feel warmth coming off her skin, smell her breath—which managed to stay sweet as the hours wore on—hear the gentle sounds of her stirring. By contrast, he was all heat and sour odors and rough rolling around, dragging the blankets with him, then heaving them off.

"He had that long hair." Maggie spoke in a whisper, as if in deference to the darkness and ghoulishly late hour. "Really needed a haircut. Did you even see his face? Close enough to tell if he had a cut on his forehead or not?"

"I saw it," he said, right out loud into the night. "He looked up when you—you know, kind of came at him." He didn't want to embarrass her; he just wished she would remember so she could join him in his certainty. "No wound; not a scratch. And his forehead wasn't dirty like the rest of him. It was probably the cleanest part he had that wasn't covered by clothing."

The silence went on for long enough that only her having fallen into a deep, motionless slumber would explain it. Except he knew that she hadn't.

"Mags?" he said, still speaking loudly, his voice lashing the night.

"Not now," she said, nearly moaning the reply. "Whatever it is, not now. Give me some time. I need to think. Put a few things together."

He didn't know what that meant or how to explain the desperation in her voice. Helplessness—the sheer impossibility of doing anything—besieged him. "I'm gonna head to Vermont at first light."

"Didn't Sheriff Brawley tell you he'd get in touch with the local police?"

"Doesn't mean I shouldn't be there too," he replied. "I can drive around, keep an eye out for that van. Maybe I'll see something. Knock on doors if I have to."

"Cass," she said, back to moaning, her voice hoarse and broken. "Please give me a little time. Come morning, I'll have gathered my thoughts."

She spoke as if a force greater than any he possessed were opposing her, as if she were engaged in some mighty celestial battle.

He lay wide awake by her side. Not talking. Giving her time.

If what he hoped more than anything was true, if the outcome he now clung to with all his might had a chance of being real, then Bea had put a powerful hurt on the monster who'd taken her. Thinking back to that dread, dark day when the world had flipped, life went from light to shadow, Cass realized he had underestimated his daughter from the start.

Looking for her in the woods, he had feared she'd gotten hurt and was just lying there, waiting for aid to arrive like a cartoon princess in a fairy tale. In addition to the fact that he now wished like hell Bea had broken her leg that day—could no longer imagine such a minor mishap provoking concern—he also knew good and well that if anything like that had happened, Bea never would've just stayed there, helpless.

No body matching Bea's description has been found, Tracy had written in a recent email. Bloodless, blunt, the way these two girls, who voluntarily submersed themselves in violence, had of being. Their own kind of survival mechanism, maybe. We're checking every report we can get our hands on, believe me. My dad helps. He wants your daughter home safe too.

Jan followed that up with a note of her own, saying obviously bodies weren't always found—even more blunt than Tracy, just laying out the end of his life—and some of them stayed hidden for years, for forever, or got destroyed. Still, she wrote, it was something.

What was it? he had messaged in a comment on their site late one night when the three of them were all awake and online. What does it mean, what you're saying?

If she's alive? Jan had responded.

And we're thinking she is, Tracy had chimed in.

Yes. From Cass. That was it. One word. But he meant so much more by it.

Who are the ones who survive? How do they do it? What are they doing to do it? What is happening to my daughter right now?

Tracy seemed to understand, judging by what she said when she messaged him back. She's fighting like hell on multiple levels. The wound is one. But I'll bet it goes further than that. I'll bet she's working this sociopath for all she's worth. Manipulating him. Using her brains to give him a reason to keep her around. Putting her smarts to work. Till she can get the hell out.

We followed this one case, Jan had jumped back into the thread. Where she cooked and cleaned for the sicko. Remember that, Trace? That's all he wanted. The victim figured it out. He didn't take her so he could hurt her, or have sex with her, anything like

Cass had to shut off his computer then, didn't even finish reading the sentence. He darkened his screen to blot out the sight of those words, got to his feet, walked away from his desk.

But he came back.

that. He just wanted a girl servant to mommy him and make him feel good. And this vic did it till she got the chance to go to the grocery store and buy ingredients for his favorite meal, and he was so lulled by then, he trusted her so much, that he let her go in alone. She walked right up to customer service, asked them to call the cops, and the psycho got arrested in his car. While he was waiting for her to come back with his food.

That was a good one, Tracy had typed.

When the first gray of dawn charcoaled the windows, Maggie started to speak as if she had never gone silent. "I have to tell you something," she said, lying flat on her back, arms by her sides, not moving except for the faint flutter of words on her lips. "And you're not going to believe me. You're going to think that I'm crazy, but I want you to listen anyway."

"I would never think you're crazy," he said, wishing he could make himself go as still as she was. Every nerve ending tingled inside him. He could feel his cells dividing and dying. "And I would never not take you seriously. You're the smartest person I know."

"This isn't about being smart, Cass." She took a quiet breath, just a sip of air. "I'm going to say something awful. It's going to sound really ghastly. Okay?"

He felt suddenly scared. Jolted from his now-constant level of all-the-time fear to a state of axe-sharp terror.

"It will mean we've been wrong about something horribly important. Something we missed. And you're going to want to deny it." Another breath, louder this time, like air sucked in over rocks. "But I've been thinking all night, and I've turned it over and around in my mind, and I really think that I'm right. I think this is true, and if it is, then that means—" She lost her breath then, sobbing and gasping in a way that made her body buck on the mattress.

"Maggie!" he cried, gathering her into his arms, pressing his forehead to her soaked cheeks. "What can it be, sweetheart? Of course I'll believe you. Just tell me, Mags, please. Nothing can be this bad!" Only one thing. And they were already facing that.

She shoved herself free of him. Pressed her hands to her face with such force, they left imprints when she took them away. But her eyes had gone dry, her expression hard and flat.

"It is that bad," she said. "It's our fault. This is all our fault."

He began shaking his head but aborted the motion—*you're going to want to deny it*—wrenching his head to a stop.

Maggie wrested herself into a sitting position. "I know who has Bea."

"No," he said when she told him.

Briefly, she hung her head.

You're not going to believe me.

But when she lifted it, her eyes were blazing. She moved closer to him on the bed, her hands curled into small fists.

He held up one palm. "I'm sorry," he said quietly. "Go on. Tell me why you think this."

She began counting on fingers, the darkest of lists. "He had access. Bea would've gone with him, no problem, no question at all. She wouldn't have thought to call us or even check."

"Just because he could do it doesn't mean he would," he said helplessly.

She sat forward, touching her forehead to his so that he felt her breath on his skin.

"If you switch the lens," she said, "just for a second assume that what I'm saying is true, then it all makes sense. A lot of things fall into place. He always had what I see now—working at the psychotherapy practice and picking things up—an unhealthy focus on Bea. How he wanted to spend so much time with her. What adult enjoys spending that much time with a kid?"

"Grandparents do, right?" he said. "They never had any children of their own."

She gave a firm shake of her head. "But they *weren't* her grandparents. Not really. And that makes it strange."

"A nice woman like Beth would never be married to a—"

"Think about Beth," she interrupted. "She was distant. Sharp, even. You know that. She kept other people at arm's length, all the neighbors besides us, most everyone in town."

Cass frowned because it was true. He and Beth had traded many a warm word—she was kinder to him than his own mother had been—but even he had wondered why he was the only person to earn that type of attention. Beth had never been able to find a local doctor willing to take her on as a patient, which might've been why she died so suddenly and unexpectedly. She hadn't known she was sick. She'd alienated so many of the clerks at the local Grocer Green that she had to drive out of town to do her shopping. She stopped attending church when the pastor got too many complaints about her unchristian behavior from congregants.

"Beth seemed to like Bea so much, and Don always acted like such a sweetie"—a twitch of her throat as if she'd burped, burning and sharp—"so I wasn't going to put up any barriers to Bea spending time over there." A second convulsion. "I figured everyone else might be wrong about Beth, or perhaps she was unpleasant with them but really liked us. I think I was flattered, Cass! I think I thought we were special!"

He shook his head brokenly. "We liked that she loved our child, Mags. That's all. Any parent would be swayed by that."

"*Seemed* to love our child," she said, as brokenly as he. "Because what if Beth held everybody at bay to keep them from discovering the truth about her husband? What if she behaved badly as a distraction, so nobody realized *Don* was the messed-up one? There goes old Beth Parker; no one likes her; husband must be a saint to put up with the hag." She licked her lips, and he saw how dry they were, the lower one cleaved by a crack.

He got up to get her a drink of water from the bathroom; they'd brought up cups. Settling in to their constricted and foreshortened new lives.

She drank it down in one gulp. "One of the therapists at work was talking to me a few months ago. About a kind of psychology called family systems theory. It's where every member of the family has a role to play in holding up, supporting, and maintaining a very sick dynamic."

"A sick dynamic," he repeated.

She nodded. "So what if Beth's role in *her* system was to be unpleasant in order to turn attention away from her husband who was the real monster? She acted just bad enough to make you believe she was the worst their family could get. And no one gave Don a second thought."

He shrugged helplessly. "I gotta say, Mags, what you're saying sounds like Greek to me."

"There's also something called overcompensation."

More therapy-speak. He lifted his eyebrows.

"It's when you do a lot for someone, too much, really, because deep down what you actually want to do is hurt them. But you can't allow yourself to, so you overcompensate in the opposite direction. Something like that; I don't fully understand it myself."

"So why are you bringing it up now?"

She stared down at the bed, and he saw that her eyes were brimming.

"Because what if the reason the Parkers were always so overindulgent of Bea, plying her with treats and games and no limits on anything, was because Beth knew Don had some sick interest in her? Bea, I mean. And she, Beth, kept Don from acting on it; that was her role in the system. But now she's dead, and so he finally did!" She ended on a high crow's caw.

"Bea would've told us if anything like that ever happened," he said, his own voice choked. "She had all those assemblies at school—and you taught her—not just about stranger danger but to stay away from anyone who raised her hackles. You called it trusting her gift—"

"Of fear." She was nodding, a little calmer now. "I agree. I don't think Bea was ever molested by Don. I think she feels safe with us and would've confided if something bad had happened. But I also think that Beth dying unhinged something in Don. Took off the restraints."

He stared at her bleakly.

She softened her tone. "Cass, why do you think Don asked us all those questions? About the investigation. Whether the police had any leads."

"Because he's concerned?" he said, a plea. "And loves Bea?"

"Or because he's trying to stay close to the case. Apparently, perpetrators do that," she countered darkly. "It might also just be practical. He wants to know if the police are closing in on a suspect. Whether he's safe."

Cass didn't answer. He was all out of words.

"He didn't want us just stopping by," Maggie said. "Remember that? He said to call because he might not hear a knock or someone ringing the doorbell. The whole phone-on-vibrate thing. What does that tell you?"

He stared at her blankly.

"It means he wants advance notice," she said, dull and sure. "He wants us to call so he has time to prepare, knows somebody will be coming over. Don't you see? So he can make Bea be quiet or hide her away in his basement or woodshed or wherever the *fuck* he's got her!"

In addition to the almost unheard-of swear word from his wife, he heard one thing.

The shed. The word struck his brain like a sledgehammer. And then he knew.

The deputies had ransacked the wrong shed. Bea's abductor wasn't the young carrottop who came to town to farm somebody else's land. It was their neighbor and his good buddy up the road. Ole act-like-he's-your-grampa Don.

Cass jumped to his feet and bolted for the bedroom door.

Maggie ran after him, placing a hand on his arm. Light as a falling leaf, her body seemed to have lost all substance, but still her touch made him halt mid-step.

"We have to do this right," she said. "Not fast. Right."

He looked at her, the pressed thin line of her mouth, her desert-dry eyes, bleached of all color. She swiveled to return to their bed.

"Right," she repeated, sinking down on the mattress as if her legs had given out. "Otherwise, if what I'm saying is true, we're going to lose Bea for good." She took in a breath that seemed to rip her lungs. "That man will do whatever is needed to cover his tracks, and if that means he has to take our daughter—take Bea and—"

"Stop it!" he cried. "Stop! Yes, I heard you. I get it—"

She clamped her lips together. Curled her spine, hunching over her lap as if enshelled.

"You're saying we don't just go storming in there," he said.

She nodded.

"Call Brawley, then?"

"Oh no," she bit out. "That isn't what I meant. Don *knows* Abe Brawley. They're chums. Don's like a brother or daddy figure to half the people in this town."

He nodded slowly, catching on. Hard to believe such a thing of your friend. He was having trouble wrapping his head around it himself. But he had no idea what to do instead.

"Which is another thing that got me thinking," she said. "They say these predators are always the nicest men you could hope to meet. The last person you'd suspect. They're your priest, your coach, your Scout troop leader." She paused leadenly. "Your next-door neighbor."

"So who can stop a devil like that besides the police?" he asked. "I say we go in, visit Brawley in person. Lay everything out. Just like you did with me. So it all makes sense."

She shook her head back and forth. "Didn't you hear Brit? The police mess things up all the time!" Another wild, furious head shake. "The sheriff probably already asked Don where he was that afternoon.

I'm sure he had a story to tell them. If they show up now, it's all over. At this point, Don trusts us. He doesn't think we suspect him. And we can use that."

"How?" he asked, his voice tearing, harsh in his ears.

His wife was the thinking half of their pair, the one who always stayed a few steps ahead, repeated the saying about an ounce of prevention. While he tended to shoot things off, move and act fast, unthinkingly. He made errors that way. And in this case, they had no room for mistakes.

She got up creakily, rising from the bed as if something were trying to hold her down, placing giant hands on her shoulders. She made her way down the stairs into the kitchen, and he followed, his steps quicker than they'd been in days. She opened the refrigerator and began removing casseroles, covered dishes, tinfoil-topped pie plates and platters of cake, stripping the fridge of its neighborly leavings and thank-God-it-isn't-us offerings.

"Let's start by finding something to bring over. So we can thank Don for everything he's done. With the perfect dish, all ready to eat."

He kept quiet, waiting to see where she was going.

"He'll welcome a meal. He's a widower now, and as we know, doesn't cook." She sneered in the direction of the bag of groceries they'd never unpacked; for a moment, his wife almost looked ugly.

"Why?" he asked. "What's the point of that?"

"If I'm right about this, then the last thing Don's going to want is us coming into his house," she replied, her words gathering steam. "Where he has Bea, or keeps the key to his shed, or whatever it is we're going to find that will let us figure out where he's got her."

He gave a quick nod. "So, when he tries to keep us out, or makes some excuse to send us away, that'll be like proof. And *then* we go to Brawley."

She seemed someplace very far away, didn't even pause to contradict him.

"I'm going to spill the dish," she said. "The one I'm carrying as a thank-you. I'll trip accidentally at the door." Like a side note to herself: "Have to make sure it spatters me." Then back to Cass: "Wrap it loosely."

Something sparked in his heart. Not painful or worrisome. Possibility. A chance.

"What we choose to bring is important; throw those pies and cakes in the trash. It has to be something that gets heated. You'll rush me to the sink so you can get cool water on the burn."

Desserts in garbage, check. Since Bea disappeared, any sort of food prompted nausea, with sweets being the worst. And once they had their baby girl back, they would never want to see anything brought over by a well-meaning neighbor ever again. Fake burn, double check. Cold cloth, a salve or solution, something to keep Don busy and distracted.

Maggie set her shoulders, two sharp peaks. "And then we'll be inside."

CHAPTER NINETEEN

Usually when Arles lost time, parts of her continued to function. Drove, had sex, conducted therapy. Last year, in a session with a teenager who'd made a disclosure of sexual abuse, the therapist part had vanished for a blip of time. Vacated the building, psychically speaking. Which ultimately led to Arles getting fired, and to a large extent, being on this mountaintop right now. In her office mere minutes had passed, according to the clock on her desk, before she'd come to with her patient sitting on the floor, holding a razor blade to a red river on her wrist. The cut had been horizontal, not vertical, and the patient wound up physically fine. Arles counted herself extremely lucky, most importantly because the patient had been admitted to an acute partial program and was now doing quite well, and next because there had been no lawsuit or revocation of her license.

Meeting Louise for the first time had triggered an even longer plummet, although some small sliver of Arles must've remained in contact with this realm of reality, if for no other reason than that she was alive. Huddled beneath an overhang of rock where she had obviously taken shelter, as out of the way of the elements as it was possible to get once her flashlight had died. Silver dawn lit the sky; she shoved the useless flashlight deep into her jacket pocket.

If she hadn't been prepped and primed as a child, she would never have survived this night. She owed her stepfather a debt. Thanks to him, she'd learned to tune out physical pain and distress. Peter had taught her how to let her mind float untethered, free of its body.

He'd also schooled her extensively in wilderness survival, which meant that she knew the danger she was in. Last night's temperature had dropped into the forties, and she was hypothermic. No longer shivering, though her muscles were achy and sore, which told her she had spent hours shaking, her body's attempt to warm itself before giving up in defeat.

She hadn't had anything to drink in twelve hours or so—unprepared before she set out—but thirst could wait; she had a clock of eight hours or longer before dehydration would set in. Any notion of food didn't bear consideration; you could go days, weeks, in a pinch. What she needed now was to get dry so she could coax her core temperature up safely.

She took a fall during her descent, muscles cramped and slow to react to the terrain. Caught herself on an exposed clump of roots, twisting her wrist at so sharp an angle that it started to swell. She scraped her face against the trunk of the tree that had lent its root bed to save her from sliding the rest of the way down.

Although she'd made an attempt to follow the trail, she lost her way toward the base of the mountain and had to navigate based on the rising sun and a rudimentary knowledge of compass points, which stretched her exhausted and depleted mind to the point of tearing.

By the time a glimpse of peaked roof finally penetrated her consciousness, her wrist had swollen as thick as her bicep, blood trickled in a series of drops toward her chin, and she couldn't feel her feet or fingers. Heat was being shunted away from her extremities in a last-ditch attempt to keep her organs pumping. She staggered onward. It was that or collapse.

She collapsed. Cold ground rose up to greet her, but it felt surprisingly warm. Welcoming, like a bed—or a grave. Her eyes drifted slowly shut. She felt the fans of her lashes when they struck the wells above her cheeks. Every sensation singularly strong.

Her skin becoming one with the soil. A few final fluttery breaths.

When an angel stalked forth out of the border of trees, she let him scoop her up.

"Arles—what the hell—where've you been—what happened?"

No response came to mind. And she couldn't make her lips move, anyway.

Dan headed toward the house, cradling her in his arms. "Side entrance, I know . . ."

She clamped his forearm in the claw of one hand. Felt as if she were squeezing with sufficient force that he should've cried out, but he didn't even seem to register her touch, just kept weaving between trees, the house growing larger, looming like a thing with wings, a cape.

She had to stop him. If any of the patients saw her like this, she'd at best conjure up transference issues that would impede treatment, and at worst, sacrifice their trust forever. She parted her lips, and the parched skin tore, depositing a metallic tasting liquid that enabled her mouth to move. Sustenance maybe, the blood. "No . . ."

That caught his attention. "No, don't worry about it? I don't need to use the back stairs?"

She fought to turn her head from side to side, her eyes wild, and he got it.

"Oh—not the house, you mean? Arles, Christ, I've got to get you indoors somewhere—"

"Cabin . . ."

She forced out the two syllables, and he swerved into the woods.

The cabin he chose—the first they came to not occupied by a patient—had been her stepfather's favorite. His man cave, his lair. But by that point, Arles was so far gone that she passed out before she had to relive the experience of being carried over the threshold just like Peter used to do—*my bride*, he would joke—so many years ago.

Dan fetched an emergency blanket from a bin of supplies and sat her outside in the sun swathed in crinkly silver. She sipped tepid water from a spoon until she was able to down a mug of tea bolstered with salt and sugar. Eventually, she got into a bath. He taped her wrist, fed her the correct combination of acetaminophen and ibuprofen. Disinfected the cut on her face—*this might need a stitch*—while she scoffed, applying a butterfly bandage herself instead.

At last, he dropped down beside her on the love seat. She'd traded the emergency blanket for a wool one by then, sitting with her hands and feet tucked to encourage them to heat up.

"Thanks for saving my life." Conversant again. Amazing. "How'd you know to come?"

He studied her as if assessing her condition, a look Arles usually gave others.

"So this guy comes stomping his way up and down Water Street, right?" Dan said. "Looking like he'd be more comfortable in a board-room, acting like the whole town worked for him. I realized I had no better way to reach you than he did. But I do know the lay of the land."

Big Jim. Damn.

Dan placed a hand on her thigh. The heat from it penetrated even through the wool.

"Will you promise to figure out a phone solution for this place?" he said. "And, um, not do anything like this again?"

"Why?" she asked.

"Why what?"

"Why shouldn't I do it again?" She hugged herself within the blanket.

"Jesus, Arles. Because you could've died, all right? As you yourself just noted."

She was silent, eyes fixed on his beautiful blue ones, her vision back to clear.

"And because I've never felt this way before in my goddamn life," he mumbled when she didn't say anything. "I haven't stopped thinking about you since the day that we met."

"Sorry," she said. Breezy. Not close to the brink any longer, where each word had been a death-defying act. "I don't do feelings. I barely even do meetings."

"You're a therapist who doesn't do feelings?"

"Well, not my own."

He pushed himself off the love seat, standing before her. "Yeah, right, I get it. You don't do feelings, and you don't orgasm, and you don't die when your core body temp plummets. Has it ever occurred to you that you might not be human?"

She looked up at him through a film of sudden tears. "Only every single day."

He dropped down, kneeling on the floor and rubbing her arms with his palms. "What happened to you, Arles? Not out there last night. I mean, was there anything else?"

Maybe it was because she really had almost died. Or because the level of fluid in her system had still barely crossed the threshold of pushing her blood around, getting her circulation going. Because her body had consumed all its calories and was entirely emptied. Or due to some nameless, unnamable factor. Nothing she had the power to name at any rate.

Whatever the reason, she told him.

The case her stepfather's home health aide had testified in was a unicorn. Men who went to prison for doing what the uncle had done to Becca, along with a host of other young girls, were such a rarity that the whole town had been abuzz with the trial. Front-page news, back-porch gossip. Peter's wealth and privilege, the men he was connected to in Wedeskyull, meant he would never have had to undergo a similar fate. So Arles had kept his secret—and her own.

She'd disclosed Peter's crimes to just one person in her life. Not her mother, for obvious reasons. Her mother hadn't been in denial about her husband's violations; she'd implicitly sanctioned them, paved a road for access. Arles hadn't told her supervisor in graduate school, or any of her fellow students, or her training psychologist. She hadn't brought it up during the in-depth certification for FIT. The only person who knew that her stepfather availed himself of her over a period of years was her childhood best friend.

Arles revealed it during a sleepover when they were twelve. It was morning; they were both existing on too much sugar and too little sleep. Rory had been giggling blithely about a crush. When was it okay to go all the way? Sixteen? Eighteen? Her sister, older by two years, had already done it. Maybe it was hearing about a fourteen-year-old girl who'd voluntarily chosen to engage in the act Arles was being forced to commit that enabled her to share her own situation. (Although as an adult, she'd revamped that estimation, wondering what the real story between Rory's barely-a-teenager sister and her so-called boyfriend had been.) Or perhaps Arles's confession was due simply to the preponderance of sugar and lack of sleep.

Snug within the confines of the sleeping bag Rory's mom always laid out, not lifting herself up on her elbow to look at her friend, Arles had disclosed. She could still remember the exact words she'd used; to this day, they caused a toxic, burning flush to suffuse her skin.

My stepfather makes me do what you said. What we've been talking about.

Rory hadn't said a word. She pretended to have finally gone to sleep, rolling over in her bed, a few feet above where Arles lay on the floor. But Arles could tell by Rory's tense, rigid position, the way she clutched the edge of her blanket in both fists, that she was awake. People's hands uncurled when they fell asleep. And they didn't hold their breath.

Arles had stood up, the sleeping bag falling off her like snakeskin. She'd gotten dressed, yanking clothes out of her backpack, kicking her heels on the floor to get her shoes on, taking no pains to be quiet, in the hopes that Rory would say something.

At last, she had given up and walked down to the first floor, her feet heavy on the stairs.

Rory's mother was in the kitchen, fixing breakfast.

"You up first, Arles?" she'd said. "Must've been a late one last night. I pooped out while you girls were still giggling. Here." She slid over a plate of waffles. "Eat."

Arles did. She went and committed the extraordinary act of eating breakfast while waiting for Rory to come down and admit that she'd heard what Arles had said. Or even just behave as if nothing had happened. Anything besides hiding herself away in her nice, normal bedroom where nothing bad ever took place, because she had a nice, normal mother who made waffles. Not so the mom could stick her head in the sand and her ladle in the batter while ghastly acts went on all around her, but for the simple reason that she wanted her child to be nourished.

The secret Arles shared was so shameful that Rory had to put a whole floor between them. By that Monday, she would put a whole friend group between them, and by the following autumn, several hundred miles, transferring to enroll in a private school downstate.

But that day, Arles ate. She asked for seconds, consuming them slowly enough that Rory's mother got impatient. She had things she needed to do, and Rory did too, but she didn't want to wake her daughter. Rory must really be tired, right?

She wanted to let her child sleep late. Catch up on her rest.

At last, she'd offered to run Arles home.

Arles had thanked Rory's mother for the sleepover and breakfast but refused the ride.

Instead, she walked.

And the following day, though she didn't know how, who or where it came from, the photograph of Louise had turned up in her backpack.

—

It was a sign of something, though she wasn't sure what, that she'd revealed the sick secret of her childhood to Dan, but bit down, wrenched her story to a screeching halt, once it came to Louise. Her connection to the woman—along with her failure to understand the nature of that connection—sat like a smoldering coal inside her. Allow oxygen to touch it, give breath to the words, and Arles would burst into flame.

At some point during her telling, Dan had eased himself into a sitting position on the floor in front of the love seat. Giving her space. She wondered how he knew to do that.

"Can I"—he gestured—"sit beside you?"

And how he knew to ask. She nodded.

He settled himself on the little sofa. "There's nothing to say. Is there? Maybe I just don't know what to say."

"There's not much to say," she agreed. "I've repressed a lot of it. It's a defense mechanism—obviously, I realize that—but we have those for a reason. So there're parts I don't remember and probably never will."

"Saying *I'm sorry* sounds stupid. It's too small. And not mine to apologize for. *I'd like to kill that bastard* is too . . . something."

"Macho," she said. "My hero."

"Okay. That."

They sat silently side by side.

"Arles?"

He spoke her name with a muted ferocity, and she looked at him.

"I wish I could kill that bastard. And I'm fucking sorry you had to live through that."

She swallowed down a thick mass of tears. "That was a pretty good thing to say."

Dan had enlisted one of his brothers to take his morning jobs, but was risking rebellion if he didn't get out there. After touching her cheek to determine its warmth, filling a water bottle at the sink, and bringing it to her along with a slapped-together sandwich, then extracting a promise that she would text him to check in by tonight, he headed off.

Arles gave herself a once-over in the bathroom mirror. The dressing she'd applied was modest enough not to be startling. Nothing to do about her taped wrist, but the sleeve of her sweater would cover the bulk of it. Her clothes were fresh—Dan had gathered a change when he went up to the house to let the patients know she was okay.

She swallowed a last fragment of sandwich, then left the cabin forsaken, littered with the detritus of her resurrection. Walked up the path at a determined clip.

As she approached the house, she saw gingham cloths spread out with picnic baskets crowning them, the patients gathered for a feast on the lawn. Stephanie was filling glasses from a pitcher while Lissa darted around, doing cartwheels and asking Geary if he'd seen the last one.

"Hello!" Arles called.

The chatter ceased as if a cord had been yanked.

"I don't mean to interrupt the festivities, though I do want to thank you all for sounding the alarm earlier today. And apologize for worrying you!"

Stephanie caught her gaze, and Arles mouthed a second, private "Thanks."

The patients responded with *Are you all right* and *What happened to your face* until Arles held up one hand. "I didn't mean to be an object lesson," she told the group. "But I'm going to lean into it. Now you know that your therapist can fu—" A swift course-correction in deference to Lissa and Geary. "Mess up like anybody else. And also, that Fir Cove is a strange and wonderful place, but it encompasses a lot of wild land, and it's possible to get into trouble."

Big Jim nodded. "Like I told you all this morning."

"So beginning tomorrow, Wilderness 101 will be mandated for all FIT participants."

Murmurs of *That's a good idea* and *I'm in.*

There was really only one part of the grounds where patients could encounter serious danger, providing they didn't do something as foolhardy as Arles just had. She set a mental reminder to warn them about the ravine that scored the interior.

Ben remarked, "It'll be like at Bible camp."

"But for now," Arles went on, bringing her hands together in a clap, and noting that she hardly felt the twinge in her wrist, "finish up that gorgeous lunch Stephanie prepared. And then get ready to meet in the parlor. It's time—way past time—for group."

She set out first, preceding everyone to set up the room.

She needed to find out who Louise was to her, and fortunately, FIT would provide ample opportunity for investigation. Arles would do her best to attend to the other patients, and to her fledgling connection with Dan. But she had to learn what she and Louise meant to each other.

It was all she cared about now, filling in the gaping hole in her consciousness that last night had almost taken her down.

CHAPTER TWENTY

"Apologies again for our late start," Dr. Shepherd said after everybody took seats in the fanciest room Louise had ever been in. It looked like something behind ropes in a museum.

"I'd like to focus this session on the Merritts, but first, we have a new addition to welcome into the fold in our FIT way," Dr. Shepherd went on. "Louise, please share a quick intro with the group. Why you've come and who you're here with."

Louise felt like a kid about to read a book report aloud. "My name is Louise Drake. I'm here with my ten-year-old son, Geary. He's Autistic. Nonspeaking with sensory issues. And—I'm sorry, what do I say now, Dr. Shepherd?"

The doctor gave her an encouraging smile. "What difficulty do you deal with personally, Louise? It could be a mental health diagnosis—there's often more than one per family—or it might be less formal, a struggle or issue of some sort. FIT protocol dictates that clinicians speak to this along with clients, so I've let the group know I have a history of childhood trauma."

Louise never would've guessed. Dr. Shepherd seemed to have everything together, so much so that she could do the same for others, reassemble all the Humpty-Dumpties. Even her lateness today, and the cut on her face, didn't detract from that impression. If anything, they added to it—this doctor could handle whatever, turn it into a new outdoors program for patients.

"Hmm, well, I've never been given a diagnosis, though it wouldn't surprise me to learn that I have one." Everyone in the group, except for the big red-faced man, nodded. "But I definitely struggle. Every day. I struggle to be patient with Geary. To learn from him—because I know he has a lot to teach me about different ways of being—and to enjoy him because he sometimes makes life pretty damn hard. To understand myself better, so I can understand him, but also to accept there are some things that can't be understood. And a hundred other things too, probably, but maybe that's enough to start," she concluded.

"Thank you for that very honest introduction," Dr. Shepherd said.

Louise felt embarrassingly happy. Praise from Dr. Shepherd was like being showered with flower petals.

"All right, Merritt family," the doctor went on. "I will now ask somebody to kick things off. Anyone who wishes to. First person to say something."

The less-skinny sister spoke up instantly. Her cheeks flushed pink, and her voice trembled. "I'm going to go. Dad, why did you put Ben in charge of the search this morning?"

The mother matched her speed, jumping in. "Gretchen, let's keep the focus on your sister, all right? She's the one we're here for."

For a second, Gretchen sagged in her plush chair. But then she shot forward. "No, she isn't, Mom. Weren't you listening yesterday? We're here for all of us. We all . . . participate. Have a role to play in what's going on in our family. Isn't that right, Dr. Shepherd?"

"Maybe you'll study psych in college," the doctor said.

Gretchen looked pleased. Then she prodded: "Dad?"

"What's that, honey?" asked the red-faced guy, beefy arms folded across a chest that strained his collared shirt.

"Ben. Search. In charge of," she intoned. "Why not Mom, as the other member of your gen? Or Pat or me or Nat? It's because Ben's a man, isn't it?"

"Sweetheart, if that's what they teach at that girls' school of yours, then absolutely," answered her dad. "Guilty. Driller and Tate has hosted a dozen in-services alerting us partners to how the gals don't take charge of as many accounts or get assigned the high-dollar clients. Next time, I'll come up with a different way to pick who's in charge."

"Historically Women's College," Gretchen said through gritted teeth. "And that would still be you deciding—"

Her father talked over her. "Hell, I'll even put the little boy—what's his name, Geary?"

Caught off guard, Louise gave a nod that she abruptly cut off.

"In the ring along with the cook's kid. We'll draw straws. Didn't you girls tell me the way we used to pick a winner is now off-limits for some reason? See, I *do* listen." Grin.

Gretchen slumped back and this time didn't straighten.

Her sister took over. "That's great, Dad. I think you managed to put Gretch down while also throwing a little racism, ableism, and classism into the mix."

Her mother turned on Natalie with the same terrible expression she'd worn out on the porch earlier that morning. Fairly snarling. Instinctively, Louise winced, looking down at her lap.

"Louise, you look like you're having some sort of reaction," Dr. Shepherd said.

"What?" she asked. "Oh, I'm sorry. I didn't mean to. I know this is their family's time."

"It is their family's time," Dr. Shepherd agreed. "But we as participants in the expanding constellation invoked by FIT have a role to play. Is there something in the interaction that you're responding to?"

Louise was about to make some excuse, then considered what she would want another patient to do if *her* mother ever looked at her like that. "Um, I think I saw the mom—"

"Do you mind talking louder?" said Patience, the pioneer-looking one. "I can't hear you."

Louise spoke directly to Dr. Shepherd, finding that easier. "Well, it's just that I saw Mrs. Merritt give her daughter kind of an unpleasant look. Really nasty, actually. It was upsetting."

"Thank you very much for contributing," said the doctor.

Louise ducked her head. Gold star on the book report.

"Does anybody in the family have a response to what Louise perceived?"

"My mom does that to Nat all the time," the sister said. "It's true. I see it."

"How does that make you feel, Gretchen?" asked the doctor. "To see it?"

"Sucky," she replied. "I'm sure this is easy to say, but I think I'd rather my mom hated me than my sister. I'm older. I should be the one to take it."

"I do not hate Natalie!" Mrs. Merritt cried.

"Of course you don't, hon," said Mr. Merritt. "You're too sweet to hate anybody."

"Well, Mom, you look at her like you do," Gretchen muttered.

The silence began to add up, long enough that the other patients started fidgeting, and Louise shifted around in her seat, wondering if the mother was lying to herself—or her family.

Then Dr. Shepherd spoke. "Has anyone noticed that the only family member we haven't heard from is Natalie herself?"

Louise turned instantly toward the skinny sister. She needed to know what was going to happen next with the same urgency as if she'd been bingeing some can't-turn-it-off show.

Natalie sat rigidly upright, twin tracks of tears on her face.

"I can see how upsetting this is for you," the doctor said, nudging over a box of tissues.

Natalie pulled out a clump but didn't blot her eyes.

"Is what your sister said making you feel this way?" asked the doctor. "Or your mother or father's response? Or is it something else altogether?"

Natalie gave a sharp jerk of her bony shoulders. "I've always known my mother can't stand me. Especially since I stopped eating. We've talked about this, Dr. S. How me getting sick called out an issue in my family instead of letting us keep representing the healthy, wealthy all-American dream. Sic. Like the American dream was ever a thing."

Louise wasn't sure she understood everything that Natalie meant, but one thing stabbed her like a knife. The part about Natalie's mother not being able to stand her daughter. Louise turned away, hiding her face so Dr. Shepherd wouldn't have to deal with two crying patients.

"That makes so much sense," Gretchen said with a sharp intake of breath. "You stopped eating to shine a light on the rot—"

"There is no rot!" Mr. and Mrs. Merritt said at the same time.

"Please let Gretchen finish," Dr. Shepherd instructed.

"And also, to punish yourself for being the whistleblower? At the same time?"

"I used to think that was it," Natalie told her sister.

Gretchen frowned. "Not anymore?"

Natalie shook her head. "Not as of this session. What you said made me realize."

"What did I say?"

"About Dad choosing Ben. He went instantly on the defensive. Put you down because you had the gall to question him. *Girls' school* when we've both told him about a bajillion times not to say that. Even *sweetheart* when usually he calls you *honey*. *Sweetheart* is condescending. It's every asshole on the street's term of endearment."

Gretchen nodded slowly while Mr. and Mrs. Merritt watched their younger daughter warily, like people crossing the road to avoid a menacing dog. But Louise didn't see Natalie as any kind of threat. She thought the girl must be incredibly brave.

"Dad puts people down so he can put himself up. The stockbroker whatevers who work for him, a waiter at a restaurant, some driver who cuts him off. Always with a grin. You might not notice it what with all the jollity and big, brash I'm-such-a-dude crap." Natalie took a visible breath, her sunken chest inflating. "You and me too. Starting with Mom. Her most of all."

"He most certainly does not put me down," Mrs. Merritt stated. "If anything, I put myself down, or off to one side, anyway—"

Mr. Merritt held a palm in front of his wife's face, then seemed to catch himself doing so. He folded his thick hand, lowering it to his lap. "Let her finish, Fleur."

"He makes everyone feel small," Natalie said quietly. "You diminish me, Dad."

Silence fell over the group like a length of drapery.

"So you began to diminish yourself," Dr. Shepherd said at last. "Literally."

Mr. Merritt stared down at the floor, then lifted his head, aiming a frown in Dr. Shepherd's direction. He looked like he meant to tell her something, but instead cleared his throat and turned toward Natalie. "To beat me to the punch. So you could get there first."

Louise's eyes were now dry; she'd found the dad stuff less relatable than the part about Natalie's mom. After group ended, she sat still, watching as the gorgeous room emptied out. The chair swaddled her, cushy and comfortable, but it was what she'd just witnessed that kept her pinned. She yearned for some of Dr. Shepherd's magic to bedazzle her own life. She wanted it for herself in the same way someone with a terminal diagnosis collected stories from people who had managed to beat the disease. *Please, let it go like that for me.*

"Ms. Drake?"

She glanced up, caught off guard. She hadn't been in another world; she'd been in an alternative universe, a version of her life that had gone some other way.

Stephanie's daughter stood a ways off in the doorway. Maybe she'd been told coming into this room was off-limits. "Yes, sweetie? What's up?"

"Is it okay if Geary has a sleepover with me at the big house tonight?"

For a second, Louise couldn't respond. What were you supposed to say in a situation like this? "Yes, that's okay. Of course." Then a fast, belated: "If he wants to."

"He does," Lissa said. Just as quick.

Louise almost laughed out loud. *How would you know?* But maybe Lissa did. Kids had a way of communicating that didn't always depend on words.

"My mom says he can stay after we finish school for the day and play till it's dinner and bedtime." The little girl paused as if trying to recall something. "If he doesn't have therapy."

"Nope," said Louise. "Not till tomorrow."

"Yay!" Lissa replied, then turned and ran off.

Louise finally possessed the will to stand. She paused at the table in the dining room, which held drinks and fruit and snacks. Selecting a brownie, she took the broad stone steps down from the porch and set off jogging along the path, her mood light, somehow made shimmery.

She went into the cabin and flipped open their suitcase—she hadn't gotten a chance to finish unpacking yet—to fill an overnight tote for Geary. As she removed a jacket and change of clothes, her hands swept across an object tucked in at the bottom.

Flat. Hard. Heavy when she got her fingers underneath it. Geary's computer.

It was dead when she tried to turn it on, and Geary hadn't taken the charger. She removed every item in the suitcase, sliding her hands into pockets, including the zippered one on the outside. He must've added the computer after she'd packed for him. He might not even realize it needed to be plugged in. Had its placement beneath everything else been a coincidence, the spot Geary just happened to choose? The laptop almost seemed hidden away.

She had no idea why he had brought it, but she took it as a hopeful sign. Maybe he understood they were coming here for help. He might see himself starting to learn like the big kids. Or maybe he just wanted something from home, like a neurotypical child might bring along a teddy bear or blankie. Despite this being out of step with the times, and the current recognition of how many varied ways of functioning there were, she owed it to herself to ask if deep down she yearned for her son to have selected a so-called normal, more relatable (to her) object. From past therapies, she knew if she didn't acknowledge that wish, then she'd never be able to let it go.

She studied the stack of still-small clothes she was assembling, sizes she knew wouldn't stay juvenile for long. The computer with its lid shut like a mouth. If only Geary had brought it because he actually used the thing without her knowledge. Gaming, like Michael had wished for. That would pave the way for so much else in his life.

She feared for her son's ability to manage adulthood with its constant juggle, its never-ending never enough, when he had trouble walking through a sprinkle of nothing in the air.

Having to live among neurotypicals must feel in some ways like being a traveler to a strange land to Geary. While his own world was one from which Louise was largely banished.

What if Dr. Shepherd were able to provide them each a road map?

It seemed possible they would find a way to each other that had never existed before. But it might be equally likely that they'd both get lost forever.

CHAPTER TWENTY-ONE

Arles had lost nearly a whole day between leaving Rory's house and discovering the picture of Louise in her backpack. Twenty-two hours gone, as if there'd been a snip in the space-time continuum; she'd crossed from Saturday to Sunday morning as easily as stepping over a rock in a creek. What took place during that period went missing, unrecorded. Unless it had never happened at all, one full whirl of the earth on its axis blotted out with a giant, planetary stamp.

While every agonizing second of the sleepover was imprinted on her brain. Telling Rory the truth, Rory's faked slumber, the sickening consumption of waffles with Rory's mom. Picking up her backpack from the kitchen floor, walking out the front door with a second demurral in response to an offer of a ride. *No, it's not too far.* Wedeskyull kids were used to being outdoors. They took shortcuts across fields, hung out in the woods, swam in depthless lakes. All she had to do was walk a mile or so down a country lane, then turn onto rural Route 40 for a spell.

She'd covered the distance in a state of numbed disbelief. She and Rory had been best friends since kindergarten. Arles didn't know who she was without Rory. She half suspected she wasn't anyone. Plus, what if Rory told somebody? Her mother? A teacher? Another kid in their class? Just because she'd stayed silent so far didn't mean she would forever. Arles wasn't sure whether the betrayal of her secret constituted an outcome to dread or wish for.

She'd made the turn onto the paved road without having any idea what she was doing until her feet registered asphalt, soft with a give like wax beneath the sun instead of the crumbly dirt and summery meadow grasses on the lane.

Not much farther to her house. She needed to stay to one side in case any vehicles came along. This was a forty-five-mile-per-hour zone with sudden, sharp crooks that caused drivers to overcorrect onto the shoulder. Though at this time of day, early on a weekend morning, the road was fairly empty. Mostly free of traffic noise, just birds trilling in the woods, small animals skittering, and leaves rustling restlessly in a warm wind.

She stepped all the way over to get out of the way of a snort of exhaust. A van passed by, and with its bulk out of sight, Arles caught a sudden glimpse of Rory in the passenger seat of her father's shiny brand-new car. He was going fast for the road, really speeding. To this day, Arles could see his taillights flash red, like flares, and hear the little car stop with a squeal of tires.

After group ended, Arles went to set up for tomorrow's lesson on navigating without GPS. They would start at the dock where the cleared expanse of lake, open to the sun and sky, would allow for a demonstration of compass points. Heading away from the house, Arles crossed paths with Louise, who was headed toward it, a tote bag hanging from her arm by one strap.

"Louise," she greeted her, "how did you find group this afternoon? And how are your accommodations? I hope you and Geary are settling in okay."

"Group was absolutely amazing," she said. "And Geary seems to be adjusting great."

"That's wonderful," Arles said. "I'll hear more details during our session tomorrow."

Louise gave a quick nod, but then her eager expression faded. "Some weird stuff happened with Geary *before* we got here, though."

Arles waited, head tilted. Opening a space. "Weird?"

"Well, the really scary thing was in a parking lot on our way up. At a rest stop with tons of cars." A pause. "Actually, now that I think about it, the other thing happened in a parking lot too. Something's going on with him—different than the usual—but I have no idea what."

Now was the time for Arles to tell her about that mouthed word. *Hurry.*

But she couldn't bring herself to do it. Despite knowing what the revelation would mean to Louise, she still had so little handle on Geary, the most mystifying patient she'd ever taken on. A nonspeaking Autistic child with a highly sensitized sensory system who may have been developing speech until age two, and if so, had retained or progressed enough to try to communicate with words. One word, anyway. Did Geary have a different or additional disability, then? Had he been misdiagnosed or only partially diagnosed? Selective mutism was a possibility, although any therapist worth their salt should've ruled it out. Then again, plenty of therapists didn't possess enough salt to season an egg.

FIT taught that the thornier the tangle, the more the resolution was likely to lie within the broader family base. "Your ex-husband will be arriving tomorrow?"

Louise nodded.

"And your parents after that," she went on.

Louise gave another nod. "The next day."

"Good. By the time we've all had a chance to work together, I bet we'll get a handle on this parking lot thing." She had no idea why the words planted an ice pick in her brain, merely felt when it poked and probed the soft matter. "And some other things too."

"Thank you, Dr. Shepherd. That sounds great." Louise raised her arm, displaying the tote bag. "I'd better get this up to the house. Big sleepover tonight!"

She headed off with a little wave. And it didn't take clairvoyance, or even any special therapeutic insight, for Arles to surmise that Louise ran with a lightness and joy she hadn't felt in a very long time.

As if the girl in the photograph lived once more.

At dinner that night, the Merritt family occupied seats as far apart from one another as the long table allowed, and ate—or in Natalie's case, nibbled—with Tin Man–stiff jaws, not speaking to the dining companion each had selected. It was common behavior after a breakthrough. What happened in group had sent a shock wave through their family, and it took time to recover from an earthquake. After everyone finished and Stephanie came in to clear, the children were sent off to tackle small jobs in the kitchen while Arles circled the room, spending time with each patient.

Then she left Fir Cove to send Dan the promised text.

But before she could do so, a notification popped up on her phone.

> Therapist shot by father claiming son was assaulted during treatment

Arles had set up a Google alert to keep tabs on Trager. She did a little research to confirm that the guy was going to live—if never practice again—before finally texting Dan.

He responded as swiftly as if he'd been sitting around with his phone in his hand, which people did a lot less in Wedeskyull than in other parts of the world with ubiquitous connectivity.

> hey, glad to hear from u

And—

u want company tonight?

Arles hadn't expected Dan to text back. She'd checked in. It was nice of him to have asked her to do that, and now he knew she was alive. What more was called for?

She certainly didn't expect to send anything in the way of an answer herself.

And still less what she wound up replying.

yes

Once the two of them were in her room at Fir Cove, Arles got undressed, then walked around the bed naked. She started to help Dan off with his clothes, unbuckling his belt, undoing shirt buttons.

He caught her wrist gently in his fist. "Hey, don't, okay?"

She looked up at him, threading the fingers of her free hand through his hair. He wore it long; the dark, silky strands somehow mysterious, like some substance of the night. He took the hand she was stroking his hair with in his other hand, kissed both of hers. Then he stepped to one side, shucking off his jeans before climbing beneath the covers in his boxers and T-shirt.

"What are you doing?" she asked.

He yawned a touch exaggeratedly. "Long day. I'm beat. You must be too, after what you went through last night."

Arles didn't say anything. She stood there, unclad, arms crossed over the taut tension in her belly. She registered the cooling night air against her nipples and between her thighs, but did nothing to conceal herself. Understanding like a bitter wind swept over her.

"Why did you come over tonight?"

He propped himself up on one elbow. "What do you mean, why'd I come over?"

"Was it for a pity party?"

"Am I here to throw myself a pity party?" He looked genuinely confused.

"Me. To throw one for me." When his expression didn't change, she went on. "I'll spell it out for you, Dan. In no way do I believe you're here just to sleep."

"You're right, I'm not here just to sleep . . ."

Arles hoped that the patients had all headed down to their cabins for the night by now, that Lissa and her overnight guest had already fallen asleep, and that Stephanie had the discretion to put on headphones or take a shower or something. Then again, the stout walls of Fir Cove, real horsehair plaster and lathing, muffled most sounds.

"I'm also here to see you—"

She spoke loudly over him. "But since you're not engaging in any other act, I'm left to conclude that my revelation earlier today prompted you to feel sorry for me. Or disgusted."

Dan sat up in bed, the covers falling off. "God damn it, Arles! If I were—what did you say—holy shit, *disgusted* by you? You're the most beautiful woman I've ever seen. And why would I have suggested we get together? *I* solicited *you*, remember?"

"I don't know," she said coolly. "You're asex? Or to satisfy some sick kink now that you know what happened to me as a child?"

"Well, the first you know isn't true. If you don't remember, you can take my word for it. And the second—ick. No. Not that, either."

It was the way he so seamlessly raised the possibility that she might not remember the times they'd had sex—which for the most part, she didn't. No details, anyway, just her own internal straining to get away, the longing to be anyplace besides up against the limbs and length of a man. Not to mention the way he'd behaved in the cabin today after she had disclosed.

"Oh my God. You're a survivor too. No." Her mind corrected, picking up on some all-but-undetectable rearrangement of his features. "Someone else in your life. Your sister?"

His eyes met hers in the dimness of the bedside lamp. "It isn't mine to tell, but she's pretty open about it, talks a lot online. So, yes. Her high school boyfriend raped her." A pause. "Maybe you really are psychic."

Arles sighed heavily. "Is there room for a self-absorbed psychologist in there?" She didn't know how to convey—even to herself—the gratitude she felt that he hadn't used the excoriable term *date rape*. As if there were levels or gradations, one abuse and misuse of a body worse than another. Some people thought child predators deserved a lower rung on hell's ladder, and maybe they were right. But she herself would never presume to make such a determination.

Dan held back a corner of blanket. "That's funny. My sister's site is called The Self-Absorbed Cook."

"Comes with the territory," she muttered, getting into bed.

"What do you mean?" he asked as she settled herself in the crook of his arm.

"Side effect. Collateral damage. They want to act like we don't exist? Like we're just there for their taking, no substance or feelings or will of our own? Well, at least we don't have to exclude ourselves. From anything. We become like Godzilla stomping through a city. Or what's her name in *Monsters vs. Aliens*. Bigger than anyone or anything else."

"Ginormica," he murmured. "I used to watch that movie with my nephew."

It sounded like he was falling asleep.

"People like me don't do stuff like this, Dan."

"Like what?" he mumbled, rolling over so that she slipped free of his hold.

"Anything," she said softly. "We don't do anything. Except hold on for dear life." A hard, short pause. "And don't tell me I need to let go."

"I wasn't going to." In a flash, he came awake. "But maybe we can hold on together?"

She squinted at him in the low light. "You're even crazier than I am."

"That your professional opinion?"

"It doesn't require a professional to see it. Just look at me."

"I am," he said. "Light's weak, but still."

"Still what?"

"I still like what I see," he said, repositioning himself so she lay once again in his arms. "You are the most interesting . . ."

The pause went on long enough that she interrupted it. "Something about interesting?"

"Powerful . . ."

She spoke into the silence again. "Uh-huh?"

"Bold and unique person I've ever . . ."

This time, try as she might, she couldn't jump-start him. He was asleep.

She must've fallen to sleep as well, because when the shaking of the heavy oak door in its frame got her attention, it was being pounded on in a sustained way, as if someone had been standing outside her room for quite some time.

She lay utterly still. Alert and waiting. Picking up on signs as the banging continued so she could figure out what to do, which play might be called for here.

Dan startled awake beside her. "Huh! What's going on?"

The thunder booms paused, door going still in its jamb.

She lifted herself, looming over him. Placed one finger to her lips. Then stood up and tugged a blanket loose from the bed, wrapping it around her body toga-style as she crossed to the door, which she opened a crack.

"Arles, I'm so sorry!" Stephanie said. Her hair had come unbraided and fell in a wild craze down her back; the expression on her face looked equally frantic. "Can you come? Please? Something's the matter with Lissa!"

The man drove for so long after she made her pee request, she thought he was refusing.

Like teachers who wouldn't give out the pass even when you were about to wet your pants. But at least he'd set his little drink of death in the cup holder for now. At last, he took a turn down a twisting road and pulled over in a turnout, the van blocking access back to the road.

"All right," he said, unlocking the passenger door from his side. "Go."

Her legs felt wobbly and weak, two pieces of string. She couldn't climb out of the van, let alone run anywhere. He leaned over to shove her door open, and the fresh air got her moving.

As soon as she climbed down, she saw the problem. This slice of gravel dropped off into open space. They were on the edge of a cliff. Impossible to walk down, or even slide on her butt—one step and she'd be somersaulting to her death. Her stupid plan had no chance of working.

Don't describe anything you do as stupid, Ms. Mailer said in her head.

She called out. "I can't go here. There aren't any trees. There's no privacy."

"Promise not to look," he said, his voice all singsong. Then he picked up the cup like he was toasting.

She began walking so fast, she tripped and had to jump up, brushing dirt off her knees, plucking pebbles out of her skin. She edged closer to the drop-off.

"Careful," he called. "It's steep. Wouldn't want you to fall. You might get hurt."

She crouched down. No way would she be able to pee with him so close by; she would have to just pretend. As she looked over the side, a flash of color caught her eye.

On a ledge maybe twenty feet below, someone had stretched a blue tarp between two trees. Like a homemade tent. She went instantly still, her bent legs trembling. Her instinct was to shout, to call out, but the tent was still fall-to-her-death far away. And it might be empty.

She shuffled back and forth in her squat, sending a rain of rocks over the rim.

Far below, someone pushed up a flap of blue plastic.

INSIDE JOB

The burn didn't wind up being fake.

Second degree, Cass thought, after he rapped on the front door, and Maggie, a step behind him, deliberately tripped over the sill of the porch, splashing sauce in seeming slow motion. Red liquid rose in a plume from the casserole dish to scald her smooth forearm.

That's going to blister. Better get the cool cloth they'd talked about back when they were still coming up with this plan. Then, his mind speeding up: *Shit, we need to treat that for real.*

"Don, out of the way," he said. "Let us get to the sink!"

"Ayuh, go on. You hurry now," the old man said, clumsy on his feet as he shuffled to one side in the narrow entry hall. "Kitchen's thataway. More space in there." He bent down stiffly, twitching the lock on the door to a powder room beneath the stairs.

Unsuspecting, just like Maggie had planned. His wife the investigative mastermind, right now not bothering to stifle a very real whimper of pain.

He scanned the house as he hurried Maggie to the kitchen. Could their daughter be right nearby without them knowing it? Not ten feet away? Don had seemed awfully intent on making sure they didn't enter the powder room. Saying where the kitchen was when they perfectly well knew. Out of some need to steer them clear of the half bath?

He nearly lunged for the door beneath the stairs right then. Only the echo of Maggie's voice—*we have to do this right; not fast, right*—along with the tiny white bubbles rising beneath splatters of sauce on her arm held him back.

They reached the kitchen, its counter laden with the remains of frozen dinners, countless trays that hadn't been rinsed out or tossed in the recycling bin. Maggie had been right about Don not being much of a cook. Or a housekeeper either, apparently. Cass had to heave a stack of dirty dishes out of the sink to clear enough space to wrench on the tap. Maggie thrust her wrist under the flow, washing away runnels of tomatoey liquid that mixed with clumps of food in the drain.

They stood with their backs to the room, looking through a window that faced the yard and the woodshed. Breathing hard, getting ready.

Before making the trip up the road to Don's house, heating the casserole, or even getting dressed—the feel of clean clothes foreign and strange, a sign of the depths to which their self-care had plunged—they'd forced themselves to wait until a decent hour.

"Old men sleep in," Maggie had said bitingly. "Even ones with twelve-year-old girls locked up." Her tone so venomous, he was surprised it didn't poison her. "He'll be on guard if we arrive too early."

Which led to a related point, she'd continued. She and Cass had to cast themselves out of the grievous reality they inhabited and onto a whole other plane.

"We're going to act this like Hollywood movie stars," she'd said, facing him from the oven she'd turned on to preheat. Going method, she called it. "Because I've been reading online, Cass, disgusting stuff, things you wouldn't believe—"

Oh, but he thought that he would.

"And some of these monsters—if they think they're going to be caught, then they do things they otherwise wouldn't." There'd been a thick pulse in her throat, a spasm that didn't look right on his delicate wife. "Criminal after criminal all said the same thing. They felt cornered, so they panicked. 'I didn't want to kill her,' they kept saying during their trials." She had walked across the room toward him, and at first, he thought she was going to lean in for a hug, or else just talk real intently, get close to his face. Instead, she gathered the front of his shirt in a twist in her fist and spoke so ferociously that flecks of her saliva hit him. "We need to make sure Don has no idea that we know. Until we have Bea in our arms."

Cass loosened her grip, enfolding her hand in both of his. "They're gonna award us gold statues at that goddamned ceremony. You hear me? One for each of us. I promise."

"Don, you got any, you know, salve of some kind?" Cass said from the sink. He didn't turn around to see where the old man stood in the room. "And a first aid kit?"

"Aloe's supposed to be good," Maggie said.

She spoke faintly; Cass hoped it would be attributed to pain.

Don's voice rumbled behind them. "Let me go check."

All of a sudden, Maggie screamed, "No!"

Cass read her meaning as clearly as if she'd still been instructing the two of them, guiding this charade. If they gave him free rein of his house, Don might decide to shuttle Bea off to a different location. Subdue her with drugs. Or commit the act Maggie had warned about and Cass wouldn't allow himself to think of, especially not now when they were so close.

"I think it'll hurt to put anything on such raw skin," she said swiftly, covering. "Let me leave it exposed to the air." She swung around, talking gaily. "Sorry for the fuss and commotion, Don! We brought you a casserole."

"A casserole," he repeated.

Maggie nodded; Cass hoped the motion didn't look as frantic to Don as it did to him.

"To say thank you! For all the help you've been giving us. It's chicken," she added.

"Chicken," he said. Still repeating.

She bobbled her head again. "With mushrooms, I think. Cass, does this have mushrooms?" High-pitched, her voice. Squeaky. "In it? Does this dish contain any mushrooms?"

"I think so," he said, having no idea. "Mind putting some coffee on, Don? Maybe add a shot of whiskey to hers?" He jutted his chin in Maggie's direction.

She sent him a wild glance, admiring and desperate at once.

Bea would've accused him of using the hysterical-female scenario. Just two men, figuring out how to manage the little woman. *You know what, sweetheart?* he said fiercely to his daughter. *You're right. If it gets you back, I'll do anything. And apologize to both of you later.*

"Sure thing," Don said.

He hobbled toward a kettle on the stove; Cass noticed how slowly he moved. He really did look elderly, only a few short steps from joining his wife in the grave. Was it guilt over what he had done that aged him? Beth dying unhinged something, Cass remembered Maggie saying.

The smell of coffee filled the room. Don stirred granules around in three mugs that didn't look the cleanest, though Cass didn't imagine even his fastidious wife would care about that right now. Don added generous slugs of whiskey to each of them.

"Figure none of us can't use some," he said with a sheepish smile.

He padded over to a round kitchen table. Still wearing his slippers, Cass saw, even though it was gone half past ten in the morning. Going down, down, down, just like they were to a place where attending to the necessities of life, never mind the niceties, no longer mattered.

They sat in flimsy chairs, metal framed with cracked vinyl padding. Cass took a gulp of coffee, singeing his throat, his flesh burned along with his wife's. She lowered her nose to her drink, and he watched her breathe in steam. Don sipped with gusto, appearing to enjoy his nip.

"Because of Beth, right? That's why you can use a tipple in your midmorning cuppa?" Maggie's tone as sharp as the blade of a hatchet.

Watch it, he thought. *Careful.*

Don's eyes grew rheumy. He nodded.

"You miss her," she said.

Softer now, wheedling, though Cass detected the steel coated by her vocal caress.

Don scrubbed his eyes with one forearm. "More than I know how to say."

"Be nice to have a little company," Maggie remarked. "Wouldn't it?"

Don jerked his head up. "You mean one of those sites they got now? Nah. Not me. I had one woman. She was all I ever needed or wanted, and if the good Lord chose to take her first and leave me behind, well, I gotta contend with that. Do the best I can here with my remaining time."

Maybe they were wrong about this. Fools driven by desperation to heights of hysteria that had no male or female to them, just the same burning need. Not gendered, Bea would say. No, she wouldn't say that. She'd tell him that everything was gendered. He turned his head in his wife's direction, the heat of their folly in his gaze as he tried to signal her. There was no way this man had launched a missile directly into their lives. He was almost as broken as they were.

Then Don said, "You know what I get to wondering about? What's killing me in addition to Beth being gone?"

Cass shook his head while Maggie frowned.

Don's eyes began spilling over, and he didn't bother to wipe the tears—this from a man who hadn't cried at his wife's funeral. "What if Bea was walking up the road that day? Coming over to pay me a visit? And that's how come somebody was able to snatch her?"

And Cass heard it the same as he knew Maggie did.

Don was taunting them, just daring them to figure things out.

Maggie lifted herself out of her chair; Cass caught the popping of her knees. The burn on her arm red and angry. Must've hurt like hell, but his wife's face was smooth.

"Mind if I use your bathroom, Don?"

"Uh—" He broke off.

"I really need to go," she said. "Coffee always goes right through me."

Don was still hesitating. Why would he be hesitating?

"Straight to the ole bladder," she went on, practically singing.

Good as any actor Cass had ever watched on TV, though Don didn't budge or blink.

Getting nothing, she added: "Also, it's my time of the month."

She was past that now, had hit menopause early, which was why they only had the one child, but Don wouldn't know that. Or notice, Cass prayed, that Maggie didn't have her purse on her, no place to keep supplies if she really had been on her cycle.

At last, Don stood up creakily. "Uh," he said again. "Okay. Lemme show you."

"I know where it is," she said. "You relax. Drink your coffee."

Don leaned on the table as if he required support. "Powder room under the stairs ain't in use. You'll have to go up to the second floor."

Cass got to his feet and fetched the whiskey bottle from the crowded counter. He topped off Don's mug, hoping to prompt the old man to take a seat again. But Don didn't move.

Cass heard clops on the steps, the old flight resisting weight upon it, even the slight amount presented by his wife. Her trip back down was made more quietly, stealthily. She'd figured it out same as he had: Don had to be barring access to the powder room for some reason. With any luck, the old man's ears were failing badly enough that he missed Maggie's too-quick return. Her opening up, if Cass were hearing correctly, the half bath. He thought he caught the click of the knob being turned, then a pop. An exterior lock on a bathroom door. Who needed that?

Maggie shrieked.

An ungodly smell wafted through the first floor, a smog so nauseating that Cass retched, helpless for a second he didn't have to spare. In that time, Don whirled, unsteady on his feet but moving more purposefully than he had since they'd arrived. He went to stand behind Maggie in the entrance to the powder room, the narrow space too cramped for two people to fit.

"Why'd you go in there?" Don asked. "I said not to. I told you."

A flamethrower sent a ball of fire through Cass, and he met them in the hallway, shoving Don aside. The old man stumbled, throwing one arm against the wall to keep from falling. With the other hand, he reached for Cass. "Don't look—"

Cass threw him off; it took no effort at all. Don felt like a sapling, Cass a strong wind.

Don sagged against the wall. "No. Please." He began crying again, tears wetting his shirt in droplets. "I'm so ashamed."

Cass wedged himself beside Maggie so he could see.

An image of his daughter floated before his eyes. Like an apparition or an angel. Bea as she'd been the last time he had seen her. Running up their drive to catch the school bus, viola case banging one hip, backpack snug against her spine, overloaded, so heavy; the kids had to carry too much weight, all the parents complained. They'd hurt themselves, ruin their posture.

Bye, Dad! Her voice floating on a current of soon-to-be-spring air. *See you later!*

Have a good day, sweetheart. No day of his own to go to. Already awaiting her return.

His eyes blurred, filled, overflowed.

Maggie squeezed his hand so hard, it hurt. He hadn't realized she'd reached for him. A blister popped, releasing slimy fluid, but she didn't appear to register him touching her burn, her ravaged skin. When he tried to extricate his hand from hers, she bore down.

The bathroom was a horror show, the toilet a stinking cesspool of spatters and stains. Its bowl full to nearly overflowing, and the floor below it unclean. A filthy towel hung from the bar, so twisted, it appeared knotted. The sink was streaked with grime.

Don wheezed behind them. "Beth always kept things so nice. I have to call Robby, but how can I ask a plumber to see to my mess? I've known that boy since he was knee-high." A sputtered sob. "The one upstairs will be just as bad soon. Then what'll I do?"

Maggie let out another shriek and began racing from room to room, up the steps to the second floor, banging open doors, closets included from the sound of how many she got to. She came running back down so fast, she went sprawling.

Both Cass and Don leaned over. Maggie grabbed Don, not clutching the old man for support, using him to stand up, but pulling him down beside her on the floor. Gripping his narrow shoulders, kneeing him in his bony back to hold him in place.

"Cass!" she screamed. "The shed! Go! Look!"

Her certainty had the thrust of a jet engine, sent him barreling toward the rear of the house where he hauled the back door open and crossed the yard in a zombielike stagger.

The shed was padlocked. A rusty chain looped around a hasp.

With his daughter missing, the world was fanged, frightening in a way Cass hadn't experienced since he'd been a boy at the hands of his father. He felt fear now like he had then.

He didn't want to open this shed.

But he had no choice. Now he was the dad. The one who had to take care of things.

Get a crowbar. Pry apart the chain. Don wouldn't give him the combination, obviously. Was now the time to call Brawley? It took Cass a second to realize. For his vision to clear.

The lock hung there, useless, flaccid. Its inverted U-bolt not secured.

Cass tore it off and yanked at the shed doors. They opened with the high, grating squeal of a pig. In addition to not attending to housecleaning, Don had been neglecting WD-40 as well.

The interior of the shed was hazy with dust. It smelled pleasantly pungent. Wood, grease, metal. As neatly as Beth had kept the house, so Don kept this shed. Stacks of split logs nested like bunkmates. Tools categorized by task. A chest of tiny drawers for bits and nails and screws. Mower, snowblower, wheelbarrow all draped with tarps.

Cass threw off plastic sheeting, inhaling punishing clouds of grit. Unsure of the point, who or what he thought might be hidden alongside these pieces of equipment. The silence in the shed was complete, even the sounds of chittering birds damped by the walls.

His heart couldn't bear much more. What was Maggie doing to contain Don, and how would Cass manage to look their innocent neighbor, the family friend they'd suspected of inhuman acts, in the eye again?

He plodded back toward the house, his attention drawn to things he hadn't registered on his trip out, when he'd been propelled by Maggie's conviction. The fence around Don's property needed work; many of the split rails were rotten. Cass should take care of that; the old man was clearly in no shape to tackle the job, and it'd serve as an apology. The gazebo Beth had decorated with a pretty little table and chair set, bunting draped from its rafters, wasn't faring a lot better. Winters in Cheleo were long and brutal; anything outdoors tended to decay.

Anything outdoors tended to decay.

When had that shed been unlocked? Was it when Don saw them coming up the road?

Cass swerved sideways.

A piece of screen hung from one wall of the gazebo, as if it'd been torn. And something lay across part of the bench that encircled the interior.

He swallowed past a clot in his throat.

His girls both made fun of how he was about clothes. He would deliver the laundry, his main household task other than outdoor work, with the items all mixed up.

"This is Mom's!" Bea would howl, sliding a tank top into one of Maggie's dresser drawers or tossing a pair of jeans onto her mother's side of the bed.

It happened in reverse too. He wasn't good about judging sizes, or telling the difference between which styles his wife and daughter favored. But despite that limitation on his part—women's fashion; who could make sense of it?—he was sure of what he now saw on this bench.

Bea's favorite sweater.

CHAPTER TWENTY-TWO

Arles hurried alongside Stephanie down the darkened upstairs hall. Low yellow light from sconces provided the only illumination, throwing shadows across the thick runner of carpet beneath their feet and onto photographs in frames on the walls. The pictures were from days gone by. Fir Cove being built; the cabins under construction; the lake minus its dock; a hunting blind high in a tree. Arles averted her head from that last one. Stephanie and Lissa occupied adjoining rooms at the back of the house, and right now the distance felt endless.

She heard snuffling before they reached the end of the hallway. Stephanie grabbed her arm to tug her forward, but Arles had already sped up on her own. Stephanie unlatched the thick wooden door, and the sounds grew louder, sobs and sucked-in breaths.

Lissa sat on her mother's bed, a quilt bundled around her. Head hanging, slight shoulders shaking. Her braids had come undone, and she was twisting a hank of hair around one finger so tightly that the skin beneath it looked purple.

Stephanie turned to meet Arles's raised eyebrows, shaking her head and mouthing, "I have no idea." Then she said, "Lis? Honey? Look who's here. I brought Dr. Arles."

Lissa didn't look up. She didn't seem to register their presence.

Arles gave Stephanie a smile intended to reassure. This was her territory, after all, even if she didn't officially inhabit such a role in Lissa's life. And even if right now, the relatively ordinary sight of a distraught child clawed a long, hooked fingernail against Arles's spine.

She crossed to the side of the bed. "Jeez, Lissa, this isn't how I usually see you. You're always running around, doing cool stuff." Steer right into the weirdness of Arles being here in the middle of the night, then make the child feel known. "Something's really gotten you upset."

Lissa took in a shuddering breath. After a second, she nodded.

Stephanie let out a quieter exhalation, while peripherally, Arles saw her shoulders drop a notch. Her child had gone from near catatonic to minimally communicative.

"Is it the kind of upset you can talk about?" Arles asked. "Where it'd help to share?"

Lissa clutched the quilt around her waist. Tears dropped in silent plinks, making tiny wet circles that spread outward on the fabric. She shook her head.

"I understand," Arles said. "I have things that don't help if I share them."

Lissa looked up, her face blotchy. "Li—like what?" she asked on a hitched breath.

"Is it all right if I sit down?" Arles asked.

Lissa wriggled over, making room.

Arles dropped onto the bed, bending over folded arms. "I don't know, Lis. Really upsetting stuff. Things I would be scared to have a child know about, even one as smart and mature as you. And that your mom almost definitely would be."

Out of the corner of her eye, she saw Stephanie open her mouth, but Arles shook her head minutely and Stephanie went still.

"I know bad stuff too," Lissa said.

Arles looked at her.

"Like about my dad."

"Yeah," Arles said, allowing heaviness to seep into her voice. "Your dad."

Lissa began twisting the hair around her finger again.

"You can talk to Dr. Arles about Daddy—" Stephanie started.

Arles held up a cautioning hand. "But that isn't what's made you upset now, is it? Your father?"

Lissa shook her head miserably. A tear wobbled on the bottom of her nose. "How'd you know that?"

Arles wasn't sure. "Well, he isn't here. Although I guess you could've just been thinking about him. Or had a bad dream."

"That happens sometimes," Lissa agreed.

"But not tonight?"

Lissa shook her head again.

"Sometimes I figure things out," Arles said. "And I can't say how exactly. I just know them."

Lissa looked up at her. "Like a superpower!"

Arles gave a little laugh. "Uh, *no*," she said. "'Cause if I could have a superpower, it'd be flying. Obviously."

"Mermaid tail," Lissa said instantly.

"Oh, that's a good one. That'd be a lot of fun." Pause. "But is it a *superpower*?"

"Okay," Lissa said. "Stretchy arms. So I could reach anything."

"Excellent choice." And a meaningful one, probably. "What would you reach for?"

Lissa let out a ragged sigh. She unwound the loop of hair from her finger; even in the dim light of the room, Arles could see the indented flesh throbbing. The girl sat on the edge of the bed, legs dangling. Then she slid to the floor, landing with a thud. She walked over to the closet and, using her weight to pull the door open, slanted one arm upward like a sword.

"I would get Geary's—" she said, then broke off.

Arles couldn't believe it hadn't hit her. She'd been thrown by the sleep-disturbing upheaval, the lateness of the hour, and Lissa's distress. She spun around. "Where is Geary?"

"Asleep," Stephanie said swiftly, gesturing. "In the next room. I just double-checked."

Arles took a second to let her worry recede, then turned back to Lissa. "Okay. All right. So something Geary has? That you need stretchy arms to reach."

Lissa took a deep breath and closed her eyes, as if about to take a plunge into cold water. "Geary showed me his—" And she stopped again.

Arles's heart heaved. Geary was just a boy, but he was older and bigger than Lissa, and Arles, along with every other woman on the planet, knew how this story went. Was the closet the place where an incident took place? *Incident.* Loathsome euphemism. She forced herself to speak in a neutral tone, designed not to lead. "Showed you his what?"

Stephanie had clearly also gone to a place of concern. She pushed past her daughter, stopping at the threshold to the closet. Went up on tiptoes and patted her hands around on a high shelf. After a second, she dropped down, holding a laptop in her hands.

Lissa took a step back as if the laptop radiated heat, like she was standing in front of a roaring fire. "That won't turn on," she said. "You need a plug. Geary keeps it in his winter coat."

The rooms were separated by a bath. Arles told Lissa and Stephanie that she would be the one to go in and retrieve the power cord. The bathroom ceiling fixture provided scant light for the search; Arles didn't want to turn on a lamp in the bedroom and risk waking Geary. If he had a meltdown prompted by her intrusion, then not only wouldn't she get the chance to figure out what had gotten Lissa so worked up, but she'd lose Louise's faith as well. What kind of clinician would disturb an Autistic child sleeping peacefully in a novel location?

Arles stood on the doorsill, letting her eyes adjust. Shadows shifted as objects and furnishings took shape. A dresser hulked against the back wall. Two windows were draped in gauzy white muslin, the curtains stirring like ghosts in an invisible current of air. A bookcase heavy with volumes tilted threateningly, like a drunken man losing his balance. *Needs to be secured to the wall,* Arles thought numbly. *Could be dangerous. He might pitch over.*

It might pitch over.

She gave a nub of skin on her thigh a tweak, and tears jumped to her eyes.

Lissa's twin bed was rumpled, and Geary lay below it, mummified in a sleeping bag. Louise had mentioned that Geary refused bedclothes even on the coldest nights; Arles made a mental note to tell her a sleeping bag might be worth trying, its slick skin tolerable to him. Same material as the coat Arles was looking for. She couldn't see it. Her gaze was fastened on Geary.

He looked just like she had, lying on the floor below Rory's bed. The past was squirming and writhing, alive in her head in ways it hadn't been in years. As a psychologist, she understood the reasons for the resurgence of long-ago events. TaskMiner, the photo, Fir Cove. All stirring the dark depths of her mind like a stick did a cauldron.

"Arles?" someone said from behind.

She jumped what felt like feet in the air, wrenching an ankle on the way down.

"I'm sorry," Stephanie whispered. "You were taking a long time, and I—"

She was?

"Wanted to make sure you were okay. Also, I see the coat." She pointed.

Arles tiptoed across the room, giving Geary as wide a berth as the space allowed. She hooked the coat by its collar, lofting it high so the fabric wouldn't shush across the floorboards. Soundlessly, she turned.

Geary's eyes opened.

Arles froze as abruptly as a child in a game of tag, teetering on her toes.

She clutched the coat to her chest, feeling a snake of cord within its folds. It would wrap itself around her. Sink fangs into her flesh and bite her through the puffs.

Geary's gaze met hers. In the faint light reflected from the bathroom, she detected glitter, a jittery look of fear in his eyes. "Geary?" she mouthed. Then a whisper: "Are you all right?"

His eyelids drooped, blinked, before falling shut. As Arles crept out of the room, she watched him succumb to slumber, face slackening, the sleeping bag deflating. His mouth took on the unmistakable shape of a crescent moon, something in his sleep causing him to smile.

Back in Stephanie's bedroom, Arles set the laptop on a sideboard and plugged it in. She flipped open the lid and watched the machine boot up. The password box appeared, and she entered a series of possibilities. Geary's name: first, no, last, no. Then she tried both. After that, *1234*. The word *password*. Finally, she frowned. She'd underestimated Geary, proceeded as if he weren't a member of a generation far more savvy about tech than her own.

She turned to Stephanie, who stood beside her. "I'll ask his mother in the morning, but I get the feeling she might not know, either—"

Lissa spoke up from the bed, her voice wobbly. She'd made a tent of the quilt, leaving a narrow sliver for her face to poke out. "I watched Geary enter his password."

And now Arles had gone and underestimated this child too. "Can you remember it?"

Lissa nodded, though she didn't emerge from her blanket fortress.

"Do you want to tell it to Dr. Arles?" asked Stephanie. "Or type it in yourself?"

Lissa shook her head, her eyes wide and frightened.

Children, far more than grown-ups, understood that secrets lived like coals inside. By adulthood, that fire lay beneath so many banked layers, it was all but impossible to exhume an ember. But at Lissa's age, the only thing Arles had to do was open up a space and let in a little air, allow the heat to disperse before it burned the holder of the secret alive.

"Geary showed you something on his computer tonight, right?" she asked.

Lissa fixed her gaze on Arles.

"Something scary," she continued.

Lissa delivered two rapid jerks of her chin.

Stephanie frowned.

"So scary you're afraid to see it again?"

Another nod, even quicker.

"How about if you just write the password down on a piece of paper?" she suggested.

Slowly, Lissa lowered the blanket covering from her head.

"I won't enter it until you leave. You can let your mom tuck you in," Arles went on. "It's super late, and you must be tired. Let the grown-ups handle whatever is on this machine. Till tomorrow or when you decide to talk about it." Choice was a huge aspect of recovery.

Lissa knee-walked out of her nest and across the bed. She scrambled down and ran over to the sideboard. Arles gave her a scrap of paper and pen, and Lissa scribbled a combo of letters and digits. Her mouth forming a circle of yawn, she started to head over to her mother, before stopping and doubling back. Stephanie stood waiting by the door while Arles remained in place. Lissa rose up on tiptoes, smoothed back a loop of Arles's hair, and gave her a kiss on the cheek.

Geary had closed his tabs but hadn't cleared his search history, so Arles was able to recover it. A dozen or so sites came up. Just the Facts, Ma'am. Holmes & Watson. Two Girls & A Criminal. Murder We Wrote.

Geary appeared to be a fan of true crime, and as Arles scanned the screen, taking in the measure of what Lissa had been exposed to tonight, her heart hammered. Gruesome stories of criminals and victims. Failed escapes, near misses, bad outcomes. Gory details; shadowy, pixelated shots; bloodied crime-scene photos. No wonder the girl had gone into retreat.

Though Arles was well aware that no one could tell what went on in an Autistic person's mind based on how they presented on the outside, it was still a sock to the gut to consider what this indicated about Geary's capabilities. Technical ones, like setting a secure password and keeping his computer running at a low enough level of charge that it wouldn't power on without being plugged in. Search techniques and a precocious level of reading comp, depending on how much of this material he grasped. Then there was the social aspect. Perspective taking—the understanding of what others did or didn't know and which things might upset them, such that he'd taken precautions to conceal his hobby from his mother.

Arles propped her elbows on the sideboard and began reading in earnest. One breaking story kept coming up, delved into particularly by a pair of bloggers/podcasters named Jan and Tracy, although the crime was receiving coverage all over the web. Arles was surprised she hadn't caught wind of it herself, showcased as it'd been in mainstream news. Then again, she'd never been a big consumer of the news. She preferred stories where she could make a difference.

A twelve-year-old girl had gone missing in Maine.

Vanished with nary a trace, every lead a dead end.

Jan and Tracy had connected the crime to a string of young girls, ten, eleven, twelve years old, who had disappeared, plucked out of seemingly thin air. Some of their bodies had been found, having been kept alive for a certain period of time judging by the degree of decay; others lacked even that ghastly closure. The duo speculated that the same person might be responsible for dozens of unsolved cases; whoever it was at it for decades, his territory expanding over the years.

Something membranous and putrid, toadlike, climbed up Arles's throat.

Silently, she lowered the lid of the laptop, muffling its snick with her hand.

She removed the cord from the outlet accompanied by a crackle of sparks—the ancient wiring not up to twenty-first-century demands—and replaced it in Geary's coat pocket. She could hardly bear to touch the computer—she understood why Lissa had behaved as if the thing breathed fire—but forced herself to carry it over to the closet and place it on the high shelf.

Geary might look for it in the morning.

She met Stephanie returning to her bedroom, hair neatly braided, face damp from washing, mouth giving off a toothpaste aroma. Arles handed her Geary's coat. She caught a glimmer of a question, Stephanie starting to ask something, but Arles shook her head just once. A warning—at least, it must've looked like one—because Stephanie took a startled step back.

Arles stalked off down the hall without feeling her legs move or her feet touch the floor. She was no longer tethered to this planet; gravity had lost its connection to her, ceased holding her down. And the worst part was, she had no idea why. She entered her room—she must have—because suddenly, she was standing by her bed, towering over a mound beneath the coverlet.

"Arles! Jesus!"

"What?" At first she wasn't sure who was shouting. "What's the matter?"

"What do you mean, what's the matter?" Dan said. "Nothing with me! But you—"

"What?" Leaning down, staring into his wavering face. Nothing would stay still right now. She needed to make him go still, so she clutched him by the arms, his skin shredding underneath her nails. "I what?"

"You look—I don't know—like you're being chased. You look scared to death—"

Arles didn't answer. Her mouth was so dry, no words would form.

"What happened?" he asked. "With the little girl?"

She had to swallow but couldn't. She was going to choke. On nothing. No, on something.

"Did you see anything just now?" A pause. "Or—remember it?"

Blood oozed, warm and viscous between her fingertips, but Dan didn't pull away.

"About your stepfather?" he asked. "Arles, please, tell me what's going on!"

She dug her fingers into his flesh until he finally flinched. The words, when she forced them out, were worse than any answer she could've given. *"I don't know."*

CHAPTER TWENTY-THREE

In the morning, Arles woke with a vague, heavy sense, a nonspecific feeling of disturbance, as if sometime in the wee hours, a gate had swung shut in her mind. As she lay in bed next to Dan, that gate grew taller, and its slats filled in, forming a wall.

Whatever lurked on the other side was unseen, unknown, unreachable.

The photograph appeared muzzily in her head. Arles was overcome by a nearly unfightable urge to go retrieve the picture from the place where she'd concealed it, stare at its glossy surface, stroke it, and swim through the blue orbs of Louise's eyes. At the same time, she couldn't have compelled herself to touch the thing if she'd tried with all her might. With the remnants of last night still clinging to her, pulling her down, the thought of reaching into the hiding spot she'd chosen felt tantamount to forcing her hand between the jaws of a shark.

From beside her came a guttural grunting; then Dan reached up and scrubbed his face. "Sorry if I conked out on you," he muttered, shielding his mouth with one hand. "Took a while to fall asleep after you got back. You get any rest at all?"

Arles slid out of bed. "Yeah, a good amount. Thanks."

He lifted himself on one elbow, a frown taking hold of his features, which despite the sleep-rumpling—or perhaps accentuated by it—still assumed a perfect constellation on his face. "Really? You were able to sleep?"

She frowned right back at him. "Sure. That's what people do at night, isn't it?"

His frown deepened. "Um, yeah. I guess so. But—"

She cut him off. "So, I've got a beyond busy day today. Two clients left me a note asking about transfer; new family members are arriving, oh, God, it's going to be nuts." She paused, one hand to her chest. "Sorry, bad therapist. Shouldn't say *nuts*! But it's going to be really busy."

Dan sat up in bed. "Arles, can you hold on just a second—"

She spun around en route to her dresser.

"You were really upset about something last night, and now you seem positively—"

She began yanking out clothes, speaking gaily with her back turned. "Oh yes, right, but do you know what *also* happened last night?"

"No," he said from the bed. "No, I definitely don't know what happened—"

She walked a few steps toward him while still keeping her distance. "Well, last night I learned that one of my patients is doing all these things that nobody suspected! I mean it, you would not believe the directions this kid could go in, depending on the type of therapy he gets."

"Wow," he said. "That's great—"

"I can't say too much, confidentiality and all, but I am pretty psyched, as you can tell."

"Yeah, I can tell," he muttered, climbing out of bed. "You're something, all right."

Momentarily, her eyes took in tiny divots that had been dug in his forearms, miniature sickles of red. But her gaze swung away, and the dots disappeared from sight, and awareness as well. "What's that supposed to mean?"

He yanked on a pair of jeans, then faced her, shirtless and shoeless. "What it means is that I don't know what to make of this. Okay? I'm sorry. I don't."

"Make of what?" she asked, still merry. Not sure why he was being so heavy and unwilling to dig, look around too much in there. She twisted her hair into a knot and secured it.

He stood beside the bed.

She crossed to him, rising on tiptoes to deposit a kiss on his lips. "So, it's going to be intense around here today—the next couple of days, actually—but I'll text as soon as I get a breather." She smiled. "And I won't climb any mountains between now and then, 'kay? Promise."

"Okay, Arles," he said, bending down to the floor for his shirt. "Whatever you say."

She watched a veil shift over his eyes and allowed it to descend.

The patients were gathered around the long table for breakfast when Arles got downstairs to the foyer. Stephanie walked into the dining room from the kitchen, carrying a bread board with a freshly baked loaf on it. When she spotted Arles, she set the board down abruptly and hurried into the entryway.

"Wait! Arles!"

She hissed it urgently enough that Arles looked around to see if anybody in the other room had overheard. "Good morning! That bread looks fantastic," she told Stephanie.

"Thanks," Stephanie replied, giving Arles a searching look. "Listen, Lissa seems a lot better—thank you so much for last night—but I still need to know what—"

Stephanie was resting one hand on her arm; Arles hadn't even felt her make contact. She slipped smoothly free and began walking toward the group room. "I'm sure you must have a ton to discuss," she said over her shoulder. "There's just a lot I have to do today, and everybody's going to be itching to get started. We'll talk later, all right?"

The patients looked up when Arles entered.

"Morning, all. Restful night, I hope?" Crossing mental fingers. There'd been no tangible disruption, at least not as far as she recalled, though the events of the nighttime were so muddied and unclear, soup in her head, that she couldn't be certain. With any luck, it was only her insides that felt upended, overturned.

The nods and smiles seemed to confirm it.

Big Jim stood over the table, cutting the bread and passing out slices.

"Why, thank you, honey. How perfectly lovely," Fleur said, as if he'd gifted her a diamond tennis bracelet, or maybe baked the bread himself. It was like when a dad was seen giving his child a shoulder ride, and all the moms swooned as if he'd just birthed the kid right out of his head, Zeus-like, and was already up to running around.

"Thanks, Dad," Gretchen said, offering a wan smile.

Arles noticed she was wearing a long-sleeved hoodie again, despite the warmer weather today.

"Hey, don't mind me, I'm just the shitty dad. Trying to be a little less shitty."

Natalie grinned. "So, not-as-shitty Dad, too much to ask you to pass me that crock?"

The occupants around the table seemed to hold a collective breath as Natalie painted a thin sheen of butter on her bread.

Fleur said, "Nat, really, the cursing—" She broke off, her gaze skittering around the circle of her family. Then she said, "My husband cursed first, but I put the blame on Natalie."

Arles felt her eyebrows lift into arches. "Fleur, if you keep picking up on things like that, then I have a feeling Natalie might start cursing a little less." She studied the array of Merritt members at the table. "For that matter, all of you seem to be making great progress." She glanced in Gretchen's direction, but the older sister didn't meet her gaze.

Big Jim bloomed visibly beneath the compliment. "Look, I'm not gonna claim that what the girls—sorry, women. That's what you want to be called, right?" He didn't wait for a response. "My *daughters* told me yesterday is something I haven't heard before. My latest eval at Driller and Tate resulted in a PIP." His face flushed a garish shade.

Fleur gasped exaggeratedly. "That's outrageous, Jim! Your performance doesn't need any plan for improvement. You've *made* that firm."

"Aw, hell, I probably deserve it. My confidence got me to the top, but it's causing problems, way things are now. I guess the way they've always been. I just never had to think about it."

"Go, Dad," Gretchen murmured. She lifted one hand in a cheer, then winced.

Arles noticed a bright-red strand on her skin as the cuff of her hoodie fell away, and experienced a flashback to the incident at WCH, although Gretchen's wound was clearly superficial. Still, it was not an issue suited to treatment in a family setting, and it called for swift action.

"Well, if Dad can see that, I guess I can try this fucking amazing-looking bread. Sorry, Mom," Natalie said, and took a dainty bite.

Arles came to a decision. Patience and Ben had asked to be discharged after breakfast; they were going to give pastoral counseling a try. And something vague and shadowy, a foggy leftover from last night, told Arles that they should not be the only patients to leave.

"Okay, Merritts, I have a proposal. A challenge." Phrased to pique Big Jim's interest, compel him to support an intervention for his older daughter at this acute stage.

The quartet paused their repasts, Natalie swallowing a last morsel.

"You've surfaced some very important issues, and I can see your family functioning in more positive ways. However, other matters deserve attention, and those are best addressed on an individual basis. I can make referrals to outside practitioners for now, and we'll all circle back a few months down the line."

The Merritts looked to each other, trading slow nods, then at Arles, who nodded in return.

Fir Cove was clearing itself out.

Soon only Arles and Louise would remain, the way things were always meant to be.

Arles met with Louise in the study, a more intimate space than the parlor where group was held. Geary sat in front of a floor-to-ceiling window, absorbed and giving no indication that he recalled any middle-of-the-night intrusion.

"His dust thing, right?" Arles said, gesturing to the slant of particle-filled sunlight.

Louise looked over at her son with an expression that provoked a flare of envy in Arles. To feel that much love for someone. To be that connected to another human being, an astronaut to their ship, protected from the infinite maw of outer space.

"Let's dive right in, shall we?" Arles suggested, flexing her hands so as not to form fists. Every muscle in her body felt like a coil of wire. "I'm not convinced Geary has been properly diagnosed."

Even through her layers of mental muffling and padding, Arles couldn't fail to register the quick bolt that shot across Louise's face.

"What do you mean?" she asked. "A million doctors have told us. The way he doesn't make eye contact. Or allow anyone to touch him. His dust thing—that's classic behavior."

"It's called monotropic mindset, and you're right, and so are those doctors. I suspect Geary is in fact Autistic, but his support needs and abilities may be far different from what you've been led to believe. And neurodivergence might not be the only thing at work, which has made his disability tricky to address. There may be a second diagnosis."

"Like which one?"

"Right. So, unfortunately, it's extremely hard to say, given Geary's inability to self-report," said Arles. "But there are therapies that I hope might work for him. Letter boards, iPads, interventions to aid communication. None of this will happen overnight, of course."

Louise indicated understanding with a drop of her chin, but her position on her chair, seated far forward, perched on its rim, conveyed something else entirely. Sheer, urgent desire. A vicious need to know.

Arles felt her mind strain for something more immediate and tangible. "At roughly age two, you noticed things change precipitously, right? Geary's heretofore delayed speech was totally arrested. The screaming and meltdowns began. You've told me he was never cuddly as a baby, but he got even less so, unable to tolerate any form of physical contact."

Louise nodded again, faster now.

"The lateness fooled everyone," Arles went on, feeling her way. "If there'd been zero speech development—and you've said it was really only you who felt sure there was any—"

More nodding.

"That would've painted one picture. But the verbalizations you picked up on muddle things a bit. A lot. Exactly how his neurodivergence operates and what else might be at work."

Louise shifted to face her son with an expression so heated and hungry, Arles worried about its impact on Geary, especially if he were able to parse all that she now believed he could. Being in the presence of such wild longing made Arles realize one thing. If she were mistaken, if whatever burgeoning theory she applied was incorrect, then she had just committed an act of blatant cruelty. She might as well have administered Louise a lethal dose of poison.

And in that instant, it came to her. Suggesting this diagnosis for a patient unable to relay his history, experience, and internal state of mind was blasphemy by therapeutic standards. She would never be able to justify her thinking. Nonetheless, as if someone were controlling her voice, moving her jaw up and down like a marionette's, she heard herself say, "PTSD. If a trauma occurred at age two, that could explain some of Geary's subsequent development. Or C-PTSD—the *c* stands for *complex*, and it means that personal relationships are involved."

Louise was frowning. "But—nothing traumatized Geary." She let out a little laugh. "If anything, he traumatized us, me and Michael!" A pause. "What would've traumatized him?"

Arles shook her head mutely. "I don't know."

Something was trying to scale the wall in her mind, fingers scrabbling at its rough surface. Arles kicked it back down, left it writhing in the dirt at the bottom. She shut her eyes for a second, summoned back by the sound of Louise's voice.

"How can you treat him if you don't know what he has or what caused it?"

Here was a question Arles could answer. "Look, I don't want to call out my whole profession, but to a large extent, we clinicians have got it all wrong. You've run into limitations over the years as you sought help for Geary, haven't you?"

Louise nodded vigorously.

"We treat symptoms instead of people." Arles counted fingers. "Look for disorders, diseases, diagnoses when we should identify dynamics. We also see clients in isolation, as if they don't exist every minute in an interconnected web, which is one reason I've turned to FIT."

"I love it so far. That girl with the eating disorder. It was just amazing."

Louise's comment posed only a distant murmur. Because of that thing in the dirt. Arles stamped on it till it went still. "Perhaps most damning of all, we turn to medication as if mental health is found in a capsule. And don't get me wrong; pharmaceuticals can be essential and life changing. But not as often as we'd like to believe they are—or Big Pharma would like us to."

"None of the pills Geary has ever been prescribed helped him."

Arles glanced at the boy in his shaft of dust-dotted light. "He may never have been given the correct medication. Or he might not need meds at all."

Louise gazed at Arles. Now was the time to tell her. It wasn't ethical to put this off, withhold crucial info from a juvenile client's mother. What information did Arles really possess, though? The details to which she had access were pieces, fragments, not a cohesive whole.

"Louise," she began, trying not to speak haltingly, "Geary has interests—well, more abilities—both, really—that I don't think you're aware of—"

A thud of footsteps came from out in the hall. "Anybody here? M'I in the right place?"

"That sounds like my ex," said Louise.

After a delayed beat, Arles followed her out of the room.

Louise made introductions while Geary wandered in at a slow pace.

"Hiya, son." Michael's eyes lit up in a way that was heartwarming to witness. "Faraway high-five." He held his palm in the air.

Arles led the small group into the parlor where Michael scooted his seat toward the one Louise had dropped into as simultaneously she chair-walked hers closer to his. A family unit coalescing, like a multi-cellular organism forming. Even Geary wiggled on his bottom over to a window nearer his parents.

Louise got going right away. "So, the really good news is Geary's doing super well here."

"Wow," said Michael. "That's wonderful."

Wow, that's great, Arles heard Dan say earlier in her bedroom. She didn't mind the echo; it crowded out the other voices clamoring for attention in her head.

Louise nodded enthusiastically. "In fact, just before you got here, Dr. Shepherd was about to describe some behaviors that even *I* don't know about. It sounds as if Geary's diagnosis might be different from what we thought, or at least more complicated—" She broke off for a reason it didn't take a skilled clinician to pick up on.

Her ex sat there, forearms resting on his thighs with his hands balled, a glower visible on his face despite his hunched-over position.

Arles spoke up, gentling her tone in contrast to his demeanor. "Michael, you look as if you're feeling something that perhaps Louise wouldn't have expected."

He lifted his head. "I'm sorry, Doc. I'm grateful for whatever you're doing for my son." He shifted in his seat. "And Lou, I owe you an apology too. I love you, I guess I've realized that I'll always love you—"

Louise's expression switched from faint perplexment to complete and total shock.

"But you know what? I also love our son. He's cool in a lot of ways, and he's Autistic, and what's wrong with that? Not a thing. Sometimes he's a massive pain in the ass, but hell, what kid isn't? Which is why I can't stand watching you go through life like this. It's the reason we're over, you and me—and always will be—even if Terra and I did break up—"

"You and Terra broke up?" Louise interjected.

Michael gave her a distracted nod.

"Go through life like what, Michael?" Arles asked, steering them back.

He turned in her direction. "Louise acts like there's some other explanation for Geary being the way he is. Something that everybody else is missing—"

"But there *is*!" Louise cried. "I'm telling you, especially lately, I've seen—"

He twisted back toward her. "Which only raises false hope, and twists a knife in my gut every time, like I don't know my own kid. But even worse than that . . ." He ground to a halt.

Louise stared at him, a glassy sheen on her eyes.

"What's worse than that, Michael?" Arles asked quietly.

He opened and closed his mouth a few times before answering. "It isn't fair, Lou. What you do isn't fair to us. And most of all, it isn't fair to Geary."

Louise looked as if a pail of ice water had been thrown in her face.

Michael got up from his seat. "I've got a helluva long drive ahead before I have to be back at work. Bye, Lou, I'll see you at home. Thanks again, Doc." He took in a breath that sounded hard won, strangled, then looked down at his son on the floor. "Goodbye, Geary."

It was too soon for a new family member to leave, especially after coming so far. But Arles let him go without an offer of a wrap-up, or even some food, because she could see the effect he had on Louise. He'd discounted her parental instinct from the start in favor of his own.

She turned toward her two remaining patients, trying to gather some words.

Louise shook her head with a smile as tears fell. "Don't worry, Dr. Shepherd. Michael is right. I've spent eight years looking for something that isn't there. When Geary was okay—more than okay—all along. Come on, Gear. Twenty minutes of dust time later if you get right to lessons."

The boy stood up, and Arles watched him exit just after his mom.

Knowing it was true.

There were unique glories to being neurodivergent and to life as an Autistic person. It was just that in this particular instance, Arles had the sense that she and Louise and Michael, along with other key people in Geary's life, were all failing to learn something about him. Something so crucial, it could make a difference not only to the boy's therapy, but to his entire future.

CHAPTER TWENTY-FOUR

The front door felt heavy and resistant to Louise's pull. Stephanie had said morning classes were to take place on the porch, and as the door finally gave up just before Louise was about to, Geary stepped outside. Lissa instantly began jumping up and down, clapping both hands.

"Guess what, Geary? We're going to the lake!"

The little girl's obvious delight at seeing him put some life back into Louise.

Stephanie got up from a porch chair. "Oh, hey, Louise, I have a couple of things to ask you. Easy one first."

Louise felt a pinch in her stomach. She didn't know if she could handle *difficult*, whatever that might mean coming from Stephanie. Today had been hard enough so far already.

"So, Lissa says Geary can swim? Because they're going to do some specimen collecting."

Louise nodded, wondering how Lissa knew. How did the two children communicate?

"It's not like I want them in the lake on the first warm day, but in case of an accidental dunking, I could have Geary put on a life jacket?"

Louise flapped a hand. "No need. He's really good in the water."

"Yeah, so Lissa told me," Stephanie said.

Again, Louise wondered. "What's the not-easy thing?"

Stephanie smiled. "Right, so, the kids will have instructions and be able to self-direct. That's part of my protocol, letting them guide themselves and each other. But I don't want them alone near the water, so I wondered if you'd mind supervising? I've got dinner to prepare."

It was the perfect ask, an antidote to Michael's gut-punching accusation. Now she'd be able to watch her son—she could take any punch, so long as he was okay—learn, interact, and function in his Geary way. "Sure. And I can't wait for dinner, by the way. You make PB&J taste gourmet."

As soon as Stephanie set them loose, Lissa ran down to the sandy soil by the lake, with Geary crossing it gingerly, high on his tiptoes. They carried pails and shovels and what looked like sifters for flour; Louise had never used one, but she'd seen them on baking shows. The children squatted at the water's edge, Lissa scooping up shovelfuls of heavy, wet sand to drop into her sifter, Geary tracing lines in the slick muck and watching them fill in with water.

Lissa chattered aloud the whole time. "It's a freshwater lake fed by a stream, so the aquatic life is mixed. Not brackish, 'cause there's no salt water, but the extra oxygenation means more species can thrive—" Her narration cut off suddenly. "Ooh, I got one!"

Geary continued digging a series of finger-wide trenches while Lissa jumped to her feet and ran to place something beside Louise on the slats of the dock.

Louise looked down. A tiny miniature lobster. "Hey, that's pretty cool," she told Lissa. "But doesn't it need to stay in the water?"

Lissa looked at her. "Well, it's dead. So I don't think it does need to anymore."

Louise let out a laugh. The little thing lay so still. Of course it wasn't alive. "I've never seen a lobster before except for just its tail in a restaurant once."

Lissa studied her. "That's a crayfish. I guess it's like a lobster. A really small one."

Louise laughed at herself again. "I haven't been to the country since I was really young. Like your age, at summer camp. Geary and I live near the city."

"I know that," Lissa told her.

That niggle she'd had before, burrowing into her brain like a parasite. "Lissa? Can I ask you something before you get back to your schoolwork?"

The little girl looked in Geary's direction before turning to face Louise. "Okay."

"This is going to sound silly, but has Geary ever talked to you? I mean, you know so much about him. Do the two of you have conversations, like maybe in secret, when no one else can hear? Not very long ones, of course. But a word, or even two?"

Lissa's brows drew down. "No, because Geary doesn't know how to talk."

Louise gave her head a jog. "Right. I know that." Still, despite being prepared, her vision went watery, lake and sky blurring into one.

"Please don't look sad, Ms. Drake. Geary still can tell me stuff."

Louise sniffled in raggedly. "Oh yeah? Like what?"

"Like, if I'm talking about something and he listens for a long time without doing anything else, then I know he's interested. And sometimes that's because he's never done the same thing, so then I show him something about it, and then he gets even *more* interested. See?"

Louise didn't, but she smiled at Lissa.

"We know how to talk without talking, Ms. Drake. Geary shows me other ways."

Louise couldn't make out the little girl standing in front of her anymore, although she heard water chuckling around Lissa's feet, sending up small splashes. How wonderful to grow up during a generational shift, a new crop of people viewing things like this child did. Everybody different. Each of them unique, unusual, impossible to compare. And all, at heart, the same.

A heavy drum of footsteps overtook the lapping of the lake.

Louise lifted her head, her vision clearing.

A man walked in their direction, coming up from the woods.

He had an easy grin on his face and wore jeans slung low with a T-shirt that looked like he'd painted it on his chest. Louise blinked away any final evidence of tears, angling her head to smile a hello as she got to her feet.

"That's my father," Lissa said in her high, sweet voice. "He's not supposed to be here."

Girls were so cute. For a second, Louise wondered what it'd be like to have a daughter. The idea of a second child wasn't a place she'd ever allowed herself to go, but Geary was doing so amazingly, and then there was Michael's revelation about still loving her . . . Whoa, she'd better bring this line of thought in for a landing. She could feel color seeping into her cheeks.

Lissa's dad was regarding Louise with the kind of open, appreciative man-stare she'd missed out on for so long. He and Stephanie must be divorced, separated, something, right? She lived here on her own with Lissa. Maybe the two had never been a couple.

She made herself switch focus to Lissa. "Oh, you mean 'cause he's not a patient?" Her gaze rose, and she and the man traded adult smiles. "I think Dr. Shepherd would understand." She tinkled a laugh. "This place is all about families!"

"That's right, Lissie," he said. "It's all about family here."

"I'm Louise," she told him. "A patient along with my son. That's him by the lake."

The man turned his head. "Cute kid. How old?"

"Ms. Drake?" Lissa said. "I have to tell you something important."

"Thanks," Louise said to the man. "Just one sec, sweetie." She never got the chance to engage in parental chitchat and found she was enjoying it. "Um, Geary's ten."

The man gave Lissa's braid a playful tweak. "You like it here, Lissie? You having fun?"

Lissa reached up and rubbed her scalp. She took a step into the lake, submerging her shoes, the water level rising to her ankles.

"Oh my God, so much," Louise answered for her. "Right now, they're doing a lesson on fish, I think. Is that right, Lissa? And yesterday, they had a sleepover!"

"A sleepover!" her dad echoed. "How cool is that?"

This guy, plus Michael . . . Louise was reminded of the little girls who came into Glam & Go and stared at the wall of bottles for what seemed like hours before settling on a color. It was embarrassing to feel this way, but on the other hand, couldn't she be allowed something just for herself? She wondered how people hooked up when they didn't have access to their phones.

"I'm going up to the house," Lissa announced. "I have to tell my mom something. Um, it's about the lesson." And she sent her dad a look, a really nasty one, features all bunched up.

Louise would not have believed such a sweet girl capable of that kind of defiance, and the act awakened a flash of distrust. But the man appeared so hurt that she began to feel sorry for him instead. And then, thinking of how she was getting ready to welcome her own father to this place, an idea came to her. FIT taught that everybody had a role to play in helping families.

"Hey, Lissa?" she said, and the little girl turned. "How about spending some time with your dad at this awesome lake? Show him one of those things—you know, the little lobsters."

"Crayfish," the guy put in. "You find a crayfish in this mud puddle, Lissie?"

He had to be kidding. Being ironical or something. The lake was gorgeous.

Louise glanced in his direction. "Oh my God, I keep forgetting the word! A *crayfish*." She turned back to Lissa. "You and your dad are interested in the same stuff, huh?"

Point out how they were bonded. Dr. Shepherd might use that as an intervention.

The guy took a step closer to his daughter. "We sure are."

Down at the lake, Geary let out a hellish, howling screech. He got to his feet, rising like a stalk, but his long legs slid out from under him, and he fell.

Louise pitched forward instinctively. "You okay, Geary—"

He was back up with the sifter thrust out like a weapon, its contents raining down in a sand shower while he bent to rake up fistfuls of lakeshore. He began flinging muck while Lissa froze. Geary had darted into her orbit, and she seemed to know better than to risk brushing against him. Usually contact between Geary and another person was like two magnets repelling each other, but the way he spun and twirled brought him closer to Lissa, not farther away.

"Lissie, get over here," her dad said. "Come away from that brat."

Everything inside Louise turned red. Blood, heat, pulsing organs. "He's not a brat," she said deliberately. "He's Autistic—and maybe has another diagnosis—so he gets upset. The best thing to do now is leave him alone and let him calm down on his own—"

Geary wailed louder, kicking up water as he made loops and circles around Lissa. He looked like he was shielding the little girl, the carnival-ride whirl of his body creating a cyclone of motion that made her harder to get at. Just then, sideways movement caught Louise's attention, and she had to take her eyes off her son.

Stephanie was coming down from the house, alerted by the noise, surely, drawn by the screams. Her course arrow straight, running so fast, her body blurred. The kid-sister-with-braids type was gone, and in its place was a meteor shower, sparks of pure rage and fury.

Suddenly, Louise felt choked, starved of air. She'd gotten things wrong. Badly, terribly wrong. Lissa's father went from good-looking to a monster before she could blink.

"We'll leave your freak kid alone, all right." He growled the words, a harsh, ugly sound.

Then he scooped up his daughter, pushing past Geary's flailing limbs, jumping out of the way of the hands Louise suddenly stuck out, her desperately reaching body. He marched off with Lissa's small fists and feet hammering at him before Stephanie could even get close.

As her shower of rocks rained down, people started crawling out from under the tarp.

Soldiers in a zombie army.

She'd seen this before, one time at an old abandoned gas station outside town, and once behind the playground when she'd stayed late after school, before the police came and rounded everyone up. The people had a tense, jittery look to them, an urgency as if they were trapped underwater, trying to get up to air. Like their yucky, rotted-out teeth made it impossible to take in breath. Three, four, maybe more were now standing on the ledge, peering up at her, squinting.

"Hey there!" one called.

"Hey, little girl!" shouted another. "Pretty girl!"

"Got any money? In your pocket, maybe? Don't need a lot."

"Could you throw down a little cash? Hey! Give me some goddamn cash!"

Not one of these people would be able to save her. There were no saviors.

The man came and picked her up, his arms almost gentle.

"Hey, mister!" one of them screamed from below.

"It's not going to be that bad, you know," the man said as he carried her. "I don't want to hurt you—or touch you—or do any of the things you've read about or seen on the news."

The weird part was, she believed him.

"I'm not like those other kinds of men. All I want is for us to talk, for you to listen to me. And if you get too loud, I'll make you go to sleep. That's all."

A piercing yell. "You holding, mister? I could pay you something better than money!"

"Throw down your fucking wallet or I come shoot your kid!"

Howls filled the air, blotted out the sun, like a great swarm across the sky.

She would never have believed she'd be happy to get back in the van.

WHITE FLAG WAVING

Cass stood in Don's yard with Bea's sweater pressed to his face. Lest he'd still been stuck on his nonexistent fashion sense, doubting himself for even a second, the scent trapped in the downy soft fibers confirmed it. Here was his daughter, the smell that had belonged to her and so had become part of him since the day she was born.

Don came shuffling across the yard with Maggie at his heels.

"What's this all about, Cassius?" he asked. "I've known you a long time."

Cass thrust the sweater out, and Maggie emitted a high canine yelp, closing the distance between him and her to yank it out of his grasp.

"Why do you have Bea's sweater, Don?" Cass asked sorrowfully. Weighted with the certainty that his daughter had to be dead. There was no place Don could be keeping her. Cass or Maggie would've found her by now. Had Don buried her somewhere nearby?

Don peered at Maggie, who held the garment to her nose just as Cass had done.

"I don't know," Don said. "I didn't know that we did." He turned shakily, pointing in the direction of the gazebo. "Bea and Beth used to sit out here betimes. Maybe she left it behind?"

Cass shook his head. "This hasn't been outside that long, Don. Look at its condition."

The pure white of untouched snow. Not a streak of dirt on it. The gazebo was protected, though. Only screens and lattice for walls, but roofed. Could that have been enough to preserve the sweater? Hope jolted his heart like a defibrillator.

"Where is she?" Maggie wailed. "What did you do to our baby?"

"What did I—" Don clapped a hand to his chest, an old-man gesture Cass recognized. From his father in his later years. From himself. "Do to Bea? That's what you think? That I'm the maniac who took your daughter?" A pause. "Is that why you folks are here?"

Maggie sank onto her knees, still clutching the sweater. "Call the police, Cass!"

"Ayuh," Don said. "You call Abe right now. That matter, I'll go call him myself."

And he turned in the direction of his house.

"No!" Maggie shrieked. "You're not going anywhere! Cass, don't let him get away!"

She lunged at Don from her position on the ground, and the old man was walking uncertainly enough, bowed by the death of his wife, the events of that morning, and their awful supposition, that she was able to grab hold of his arm.

Don went down in a slick of mud and lay there.

Cass shook his phone to life.

Two patrol cars and an ambulance came screaming up to the house, the sheriff and everyone who accompanied him crossing the yard at a run.

Don rose unsteadily to his feet. "Let your men take a look around," he said to Brawley. "Search anywhere you like."

A deputy approached him. "I'm afraid I'm going to have to cuff you, Mr. Parker. It's protocol. Seeing as what Mr. and Mrs. Monroe have to say."

"You do what you have to, son," Don said, and extended his arms.

Brawley was instructing an EMT to attend to Maggie. Cass dropped beside his wife, attempting to cradle her, but she resisted. She twisted her head in Don's direction, notching her neck at so sharp an angle that it looked like it would crack.

"We trusted him! We gave him our baby!" Her voice spiraled shriller and higher, drowning out birdsong and the soughing of trees, until it finally broke.

An EMT crouched beside her, sinking a needle into her upper arm, and whatever it contained was so powerful and of such sufficient quantity that her eyelids fluttered, her words cut out, and she went slack on the ground.

The deputies raided Don's house, his property, his life.

Tore everything apart into pieces, left it like the remains of a city after a bombing, but found no sign of Bea. Cass couldn't see how Don would ever live there again. Even if he—or a team of professionals—could make the place whole, it still stank of disbelief and distrust, of his hometown's willingness to consider what Cass and Maggie thought he had done. Could Don even stay in Cheleo?

He was a gentleman the one time they'd approached him.

"You gotta do anything when it comes to getting your child home safe," he'd said. "There can't be any limits on that."

But he'd spoken from inside the wreckage, keeping Cass and Maggie on the porch, and closed his front door before either of them had a chance to respond to his grace.

"Who are we now?" Maggie asked that night in bed. "What do we do?"

He shook his head.

"There're no more dividers," she said, and he knew what she meant.

"What happens tomorrow?" she went on. "Next year? For the rest of our lives?"

He didn't know. He suspected no one did, or really, that there was no answer.

The following day—or it might've been the one after that, or the next one—they drove to the region of Vermont where Brit Warren had spotted the van. They combed the whole area, not knowing what they were looking for or what they would do if they found it. What if they did pass a vehicle matching Brit's description? The two of them weren't qualified to take on some action-movie car chase. Call the cops? They'd burned all their credibility with Brawley. The sheriff wouldn't phone in any favors from a police force two states over.

But even though it was pointless—and if there *had* been a van containing Bea, it'd be long gone by now, maybe in a whole other part of the country—Cass and Maggie still spent that night in the car so they could put more time into looking the next day. The weather was finally warm enough that they wouldn't freeze, although such a fate might've been preferable to the one they did face. By dawn, they were putting more miles on the aging engine of their car.

Without intending it, they wound up at Brit's house; she'd given them her address. It was past midnight, according to the clock on the dashboard, but she opened her door and welcomed them inside. She was crying.

Back home without knowing how they'd gotten there. When had they left Brit's?

Cass woke in the night with a giant fist clutching his chest. Was this how it happened? Painfully, with a violence to it? *Did you feel like this, Dad?* he asked in his head. Or did a man just slip away soundlessly? There one moment, gone the next, crossing some invisible threshold like a car sliding over an embankment?

Maggie stirred fitfully beside him, like a feverish child.

Had he been a good father? Given Bea what she needed in the cruelly short time he'd had with her? For that matter, was he a good husband? His wife and daughter were the only people he'd ever loved in the world. And he did love them, to distraction. He put them on pedestals.

But did that mean that he knew them, in all their faults and flaws and complexity? Allow them to be full, rounded human beings? Or did he just expect them to be a queen and a princess, there for him to adore, appreciate, admire? It made a difference, of course, that what he showered on Maggie and Bea was positive. Wonder and awe. He wasn't a monster like the men on the podcasts who used women in other ways, horrific ones.

But it might not change things as much as he would've liked to believe.

Cass fell back to sleep. He thought he did, anyway.

He thought that he woke up too, though he couldn't be sure. The days melted and pooled in a swamp of sameness, an insanity from which there was no escape.

CHAPTER TWENTY-FIVE

Arles was in her office, writing treatment plans and applying to be on insurance panels, when she heard the slap of sandals on stone—feet dashing down the hallway—and the sound of the heavy front door being thrown open and striking the wall behind it. She caught a glimpse of a woman in the doorway, her body adopting a stance made for pure speed.

"Stephanie?" she called out, but got no response.

Arles leaped up from her chair and raced outside.

Stephanie had a head start and was going at a pace that kept Arles from gaining on her. The best she could do was break into her own run, skidding down the hill and bisecting the dirt drive, then rounding a berm of soil by the lake. As she ran, she took in the scope of the situation, all five—no, six—of her senses firing.

Geary thrashing in a meltdown state; Louise paralyzed, standing with her palms open and pleading; Stephanie a missile headed straight for her daughter. Finally, Nick, back at Fir Cove—of course he was, needing no invitation, probably preferring to have one withheld.

He walked at a good clip, moving fast to get away, but leering, triumphant, as if he held all the cards. Which he did, given the burden he carried. In a second, Arles was going to catch up to the scrum of people, but what then? No time to go for the gun. This incident—loathsome word—was unfolding in micro-instants. And a firearm would do no good in this case, anyway. Having Lissa trapped in his arms meant that Nick could call anyone's bluff.

He held the girl as if he were a human straitjacket, managing to keep any of her limbs from gaining purchase. Stephanie lunged forward in one giant, unwieldy step.

"Another inch, Steph, and I break Lissie's neck," Nick said lightly.

Stephanie wobbled, halting her momentum. Lissa's torso had been twitching as she fought to free her arms, but she too went as still as if cast in cement. Geary's voice soared frantically skyward while Arles clapped mental hands over her ears. She needed to focus.

Louise whipped her face back and forth between Nick and Stephanie, gibbering, "I'm so sorry! Clearly I didn't know! I'm sorry!"

Arles reached her. "Louise!" she hissed. "Quiet! It's going to be okay!"

Louise clamped her lips shut.

"Nick!" Arles bellowed.

His head turned a notch, though he kept on going.

It tends to come to me, Arles had told Stephanie. *In the moment when I need it.*

Her mind reached, scrabbling for things Stephanie had shared that first day after Arles drove Nick off her land. His parents had been okay, absenteeism the most frequent of their sins, except that they overindulged Nick's older brother, let him get away with whatever he wanted.

Something in her brain pinpointed itself, like a rifle settling its sights.

She modulated her voice. "Your brother carry you like that when you were little?"

His lengthy strides didn't falter. So his brother probably hadn't. She'd missed the mark.

Course correct. "Didn't he used to take you along, make you hang out with him and his friends? At that park?"

A hitch in his step.

"Where his buddy liked to play with you alone. What was his name?" She pretended to ponder, watching as Nick slowed. "A weird name. A nickname, obviously. Rhymes with Doug."

Nick came to a stop, Lissa clamped to his hip.

"Tug," she said quietly. Abuse deserved deference, even if victim had become victimizer.

Stephanie jumped onto the dock in one silent maneuver, moving like a large cat.

Nick had gone momentarily motionless, standing with his back turned.

Arles watched to make sure she wasn't sending him into free fall, then went on with a veneer of empathy. "He must've been overpowering. He was big, right? That's how everyone described him. And you were younger."

Nick didn't slump to the ground, stricken by her use of his past, digging the sharpened tip of his childhood trauma into soft psychic tissue. But his muscles must've loosened their hold, because Lissa twisted as violently as a live wire and was able to free one of her hands, which she raked down his face. From where she stood, Arles saw four tracks open on Nick's cheek, blaring stoplight red. Pain wrenched his features, and in that split second, Lissa slid down.

She went racing along the water's edge, small feet kicking up splashes.

Arles parsed the nightmarish layout of the situation. Lissa a little ways down the shoreline. Her father, angered like any wounded apex creature, bleeding and still dreadfully close to his daughter. A stretch of land Stephanie had no chance of covering, but the dock offering the short leg of a triangle. If she could make it to the end, she'd be able to jump in and swim for her daughter, come out of the water at a spot Lissa would soon reach.

Mother and daughter working in tandem, one anticipating the other's moves before they had happened. Arles's heart lurched inside her at the thought of that bond.

Stephanie's sandaled feet were struggling with the slick boards of the dock, however. Nearly wiping out, she slowed down to right herself. From the shore, Nick waded into the lake, then set out swimming in large, ungainly strokes.

He cut Stephanie off, scaling the dock from the water, getting first one knee up, then the other. He was momentarily vulnerable, hoisting himself out and flopping onto the wood surface, and Arles went after him. She'd kick him if he was still down when she got there, present an obstacle in his path if he had risen to his feet. But before she could do either, Stephanie attempted to make her way around Nick's prone form, and he reached out and grabbed her ankle, his hand snapping shut like a vise.

He never laid a hand on me, Arles heard Stephanie say.

Well, now he had. Somehow, they always did.

Stephanie kicked out madly, the front of her shoe connecting with Nick's face hard enough that his fingers flew open. But the slippery surface of the dock got the better of her, and the force of her kick made her stumble.

She fought to remain upright, staggering backward in steps too big for her legs to support, before she finally fell. Her head hit the dock with a sickening thwack, two objects slammed together, and the softer one taking the brunt. She went over, disappearing beneath the surface of the lake without a sound or a splash.

"Mommy!" Lissa shrieked from the lakefront.

Nick was closest to the point where Stephanie had gone in, and not far from their daughter. But instead of going after either one, he covered the distance between dock and land, then reached the road and ran.

Arles dived into the lake. The water was unspeakably cold, not even its skin warmed up yet, and its depths felt like black ice. She fought to find the trail of bubbles Stephanie had to be leaving, but the water was murky with feathery fronds of lake growth and clouded by particles so tiny, they looked like swarms of gnats. She could hardly see a thing.

Sticking to the spot where Stephanie had fallen in, she scuba-kicked down as far as she could go before having to surface and heave in a breath. Scanning for signs of disruption, she swam first one way, then the other, until she was completely disoriented, only knew which way was up by exhaling her final store of oxygen and following the blooms.

From the end of the dock, there came a splash.

Her mind registered the plume of water before it gave her an image of what had caused it.

Geary had gone into the lake.

She swam in his direction until he dived cleanly under; then she followed him down. And first, there was a cloudy veil of pink in the water, almost pretty until she realized she was seeing blood, and then there was Stephanie, drifting in untroubled descent toward the bottom.

Geary clamped one hand around Stephanie's braid, arresting her motion, while Arles got her arms beneath both of Stephanie's. She kicked madly, hauling the two of them upward, to light, to air. Louise and Lissa stood on the dock; with Arles's help from below, they were able to lift Stephanie out and lay her on the boards.

Geary had begun swimming steadily and intently for shore, and Arles let him go. She heaved herself out and knelt beside Stephanie. Pinched her nose shut and administered two swift rescue breaths, then raised her head.

"Louise, I need you to go get your car. The signal cuts in at that first pullout on Brick Road. Call 911, and tell them Fir Cove." Another set of breaths. Stephanie's eyelids didn't even flutter. A stream of blood flowed from her head, mixing with the water on the dock to make that comely pink again. So much blood to produce that volume of fruit-punchy liquid. Then again, scalp wounds bled a great deal. The head injury might be superficial. If only Stephanie would begin breathing. Every second she didn't was one step closer to unrecoverable.

"Lissa, I'm asking you to be the way-beyond-your-years kid I know and practically love, and find Geary." She started chest compressions while continuing to issue instructions. "Go with him to his cabin. I know it feels warm out, but it isn't for Geary now that he's wet. Tell him he needs to get out of his clothes and dry off completely with a towel before wrapping himself in a blanket. Two blankets." And two more breaths. "Can you do all that?"

"Is my mom going to be okay?" Lissa asked, wobbly.

"I hope so," Arles said. It wouldn't do to answer the question facilely. Children sensed it when they were being lied to. "But Geary won't be if you don't get to him. Be careful while you're still on the dock—it's very slippery—then run as fast as you can. Do you understand?"

Lissa took off.

Tim Lurcquer was chief of police. He'd been first on scene at WCH last year, managing to bring Arles back from the brink she'd slipped over while at the same time keeping pressure on her patient's wound. He arrived first at Fir Cove today too, the bus getting there next, just like it used to when Arles had worked in the psychiatric ER early in her career. *Adirondacks Paramed* in glow-in-the-dark lettering on either side and across the twin doors at its rear, a big, awkward vehicle whose tires jounced along the dirt road. EMTs jumped out, swapping machinery for Arles's linked hands and straining lungs. Then the ambulance took off with a shriek of sirens and fireworks display of light, leaving Fir Cove different, subdued, a battleground after the war was over.

Louise had gone to look after the children. Tim needed to take a report, so Arles pointed him toward the house. Her adrenaline had ceased spiking, and she was feeling the cold.

As the two of them mounted the hill, Tim's radio squawked. His officer, a woman who might've been friend material if Arles ever made any friends, had picked Nick up, wet, shivering, and muddy in the woods. He could dry out—heh—in the tank, she joked.

Arles mustered a tight smile, shaking now, knees knocking, flesh moon white and goose-pebbled.

"Go warm up," Tim told her. "Any luck, we're looking at a charge of aggravated."

Assault, she filled in. Along with something else unsaid. *As opposed to manslaughter.*

She opened the front door for Tim, then indicated the dining room, where Stephanie—a painful jog in Arles's throat—had set up the fixings for a coffee bar.

The stairs to the second floor loomed like a mountain.

Arles dragged herself upward in molasses, dreamlike steps. When she finally reached her room, she almost passed right by, heading toward Stephanie's instead. With tears scalding her icy cheeks, not bothering to shed her clammy coat of clothing, she got into the shower, stood under the hot spray, and sobbed.

When she returned downstairs, wearing her heaviest sweater and flannel-lined jeans, Tim filled a cup with coffee for her, then went for a row of liquor bottles on an antique shelf.

Arles stopped him.

"I think I knew that," he said. "Apologies."

"Dry in more ways than one," she replied.

"You do look better," he said. "Feel okay? I can get a medic back here."

"I'm fine," she said. She sat down at the table with her cup and sipped.

Tim took a seat across from her, flipping open his notepad. "Stephanie Fletcher. Unmarried. Nicholas Rudd is our perp. Their daughter, Lissa Fletcher, is eight years old. Stephanie and Lissa have been living here."

Arles nodded. He'd put pieces together while she'd been upstairs, though the darkest matter leading to today's event still lurked in the depths.

"And Lissa is now with another—guest?" A glance at the pad. "Louise Drake."

"Not a guest, a patient," Arles replied. "Stephanie . . ." She looked down at her cup momentarily, letting steam warm her face. "She's been working in the facility I've set up here. She instructs the younger patients and her daughter as well."

"I didn't realize you'd left the hospital," Tim said.

"It was a bit—abrupt."

"They've lost a real resource," he said. "I'll miss working with you."

"Any word from the CCU?" she asked.

He shook his head. "Not yet."

Arles looked away. She knew Tim would be the first to hear from a nurse or doc in the critical care unit. And she also knew that in this kind of scenario, no news was bad news.

"I'll need to speak to the girl. Considering her mother's absence and your profession, it makes sense for you to be the accompanying adult as she gives her statement. Then, since Dad is out of the picture for the foreseeable future—"

Arles shuddered, thinking of the psych eval, custody investigation, and legal proceedings that would've been necessary to keep Lissa away from Nick if he weren't locked up right now.

"We'll have to make arrangements for her care," Tim said. "But let's start with that statement."

She rose effortfully to her feet, sliding back her seat like a piece of heavy equipment instead of a chair, as if it weighed a thousand pounds. Once Lissa finished talking to Tim, Arles came back in with a plate of Stephanie's cookies, which the girl politely pushed away.

Tim eyed Arles. "Lissa and I were just discussing plans for tonight."

Arles didn't know if Stephanie had family in town—as a longtime local, it seemed likely—or a close friend. But squatting at Fir Cove suggested her support system wasn't robust.

Tim bent down in front of Lissa. "You said you'd like to stay here for the night, honey?"

Lissa nodded furiously.

Something squeezed inside Arles, a painful, sweet sensation.

Tim straightened. He took a cookie from the plate. "Given your line of work, I can have CPS make you an emergency foster. Assuming this is okay with you."

Arles thought of all that was about to happen tomorrow. Louise's parents were due to arrive, and with them, hopefully—oh, please, let it be so—a long-withheld resolution to the provenance of the photo. Who better to know the circumstances surrounding a childhood picture than the mom or possibly the dad? How could Arles navigate everything that was going to entail while also being responsible for Stephanie's daughter? She looked down.

Lissa stared straight ahead. Her braids had come raggedly undone, and her mouth was pressed into a thin line that made her look more like an old woman than a young girl.

"All right," Arles said.

Lissa's shoulders dropped an inch or two. She ducked her head.

Tim beckoned Arles outside, opening the door to his police SUV. "I'm going to leave you with one of the department's sat phones. Messaging isn't enabled, but it'll work for calls. I want you to have connectivity in case we need you to get the little girl over to the hospital—"

He broke off, and Arles turned around. Lissa had come out to stand on the porch steps.

"So she can visit her mom," Arles said meaningfully. She took the satellite device.

Tim got in his car and drove off.

The refrigerator, with the plethora of goods it held, thanks to Stephanie, might as well have been an airport control tower for all Arles knew what to do with it. It was lucky she'd allowed Lissa to stay. "I'm guessing you'd be able to work up dinner from something in here?"

Lissa's face was tear-tracked and grimy, but a spontaneous smile flit across it. "I could cook about a bajillion dinners out of that stuff."

There were balls of pizza dough in the freezer—people made pizza from scratch; who knew?—and putting toppings together, heating sauce, and shredding cheese all worked to distract Lissa. She, Arles, Louise, and Geary ate a quiet meal, everyone matching Geary's customary level of silence. Afterward, Arles and Lissa made the trek upstairs.

"Dr. Arles?"

Arles stopped outside her bedroom door. "Yes?"

"Can I sleep in your room tonight?"

Responses pinged in her head. *What's the matter with yours? Wouldn't you be better off in a real bed? Why would you want to stay near me?* That last most of all.

But before she could decide how to reply, the girl went trotting down the hall to the pair of rooms at the end, then made the same trip in reverse with the sleeping bag dragging behind her like the train of a wedding gown. She laid it on the floor next to the high bed and burrowed into its depths. Although sleep seemed an unlikely prospect, Arles got into bed as well, stepping carefully over Lissa's softly snoring form.

It took a while for the sat phone to rouse her, an electronic intrusion so unexpected here that Arles had to fumble. The voice seemed to be traveling from a distant galaxy, stout walls impeding the satellite signal, but she got the gist. A mother would probably never have done this, but Arles reached down and touched the small bulb of Lissa's shoulder, shaking the child out of her slumber.

"Your mom's awake," she said when Lissa opened her eyes. "She's going to be fine."

Lissa appeared to fall back to sleep, or perhaps she'd never wakened at all, merely displayed some dream-state glitch. Except that a second later, Arles saw tears collect beneath the girl's lashes and slide silently down her cheeks while a smile took hold of her mouth.

Around dawn, Lissa bolted upright, fighting the constraints of the sleeping bag, punching and kicking. Arles climbed out of bed to shush her until the girl stopped flailing. Arles didn't know how much Lissa had taken in of the moments she'd spent in her father's arms, but this night terror suggested it hadn't been nothing. She smoothed the sleeping bag back over Lissa's legs.

"How'd you get that cut on your cheek, Dr. Arles?"

Arles reached up. It was nearly healed already, and her wrist no longer felt tender. Sometimes she thought of her body like one of those clown toys from the seventies. Knock it down, kick or punch or bash it—who cared? It could take anything. That must've been why her mother chose to serve up Arles on a platter instead of dealing with her own husband's advances.

"I hiked up a mountain in a very stupid way," she said, climbing back into bed.

"Don't call yourself stupid. Saying you're stupid is the only thing that's stupid."

"Clever," Arles said. "I had a teacher who used to talk about that."

"You're smart," Lissa said over a yawn. "You knew what to say to my father to get him not to break my neck." She spoke so matter-of-factly, it was heart-wrenching.

Arles answered slowly. "If it helps you to cope with that terrible memory, I don't think your father was going to hurt you." She was pretty sure that was true. Oh, how she hoped it was true. "I think he was using that extremely ugly threat to get your mom to do what he wanted."

"I know that," Lissa said, rolling back and forth. "He loves her so much, he can't stop."

"No," Arles responded. "That isn't right, Lissa. You're very smart, but you've got that part wrong. What your father feels for your mother—this is sad to say, but still true—isn't love. It's not any kind of love."

"Dr. Arles?" Lissa said, and this time her yawn was so wide that her jaw creaked.

"Hmm?" Arles had begun drifting off herself.

"How come you don't have any children?"

For a sliver of time, Arles let it take shape in her mind. The ghastly heft of being responsible for another human being. The effervescent joy of a child like Lissa or the acuity and spellbinding focus of one like Geary. Or someone she couldn't even imagine. "That's a question so complicated, I'm not sure I can answer it," she replied. "Even to myself."

"You said you loved me. Practically."

Even in her distress, Lissa had taken in what Arles had told her on the dock.

"I think you'd be a good mommy."

"Do you?" Arles asked, the question sounding wistful to her ears.

But Lissa had finally fallen back to sleep.

They both slept late. Upon wakening, Arles went to gather fresh clothes and Lissa's toothbrush from her room. She hadn't thought to have Lissa wash up or brush her teeth the night before, and this morning, Lissa had asked. Louise intersected Arles in the hallway.

"Dr. Shepherd!" she said, breathless, her cheeks pink. "I'm sorry. I looked downstairs, but couldn't find you."

"You're good, Louise. No worries." Arles worked up a smile. "How was your night? Is Geary doing all right after his unexpected swim?"

"Oh yes, he's fine!" she said. "That isn't why I came up. I wanted to let you know that my parents just got here."

CHAPTER TWENTY-SIX

Arles went back to her room to get herself ready for work and Lissa squared away. The girl would proceed with her curriculum on her own—which, apparently, she'd done in the past—while awaiting her mother's return that afternoon. After a belated beat, it occurred to Arles that children needed to eat; she should offer Lissa something, at least cold cereal. Then she realized that Lissa was capable of fixing herself a breakfast a lot better than Honey Flakes.

As Arles selected an outfit and dashed on a few touches of makeup, she sensed her surroundings hovering around her like a cloak. They seemed to exist in grayscale, creepiness clinging like cobwebs to the rooms and hallways, even to the sunny skies glimpsed outside, a second day promising to be warm. But despite the balminess in the air, a sense of cold seeped in.

She owed Dan a text, especially in light of yesterday's calamity—which, given the interconnected fungi that was a small town, he might've already heard about. She could contact him on the sat phone, but the intimacy of making a call out of the blue versus sending a few words not even freighted with capitalization or punctuation caused her stomach to lurch.

Without being aware of her brain commanding her fingers to move, she'd opened the contacts on her phone; now, she began striking the pad of the satellite device.

It took several rings before her call was answered. Unfamiliar number and all.

"Hello?"

It occurred to Arles how rarely she said her first name aloud. *It's me* seemed both presumptuous and like something that belonged in a rom-com as opposed to her life. She nearly resorted to her usual—*this is Dr. Shepherd*—before considering how ridiculous that would sound.

Dan saved her. "Arles?"

"I wanted to say I'm all right. Everyone is. There was some . . . activity here yesterday."

"Yeah, I heard. My brother has a police scanner, and he told me."

Dan had let his brother know about her?

"I'm really glad you got in touch," he said.

"Well, good, because I wanted to say . . ." This was even harder than figuring out how to identify herself. Dan kept quiet, as if sensing her struggle. "That we should connect again soon. I have something to take care of today, but tomorrow should work."

"Then I'll see you tomorrow," he said.

Louise's parents deserved an official welcome, and the day promised to be a truncated one, what with ducking out to check on Lissa. But she took another second to tell Dan goodbye.

No multigen family of four hung around downstairs, reuniting over their morning cuppa in the dining room or waiting in the parlor for group to begin. Louise had coffee pods in her cabin; she'd probably given Geary breakfast there, and if her parents had arrived this early, they must've overnighted somewhere nearby and caffeinated before completing the final leg of their journey. Arles walked out onto the porch but saw no new vehicle in the sickle of drive, just her own car with Louise's parked alongside.

She walked down the steps and over the hill, experiencing a queasy roll in her stomach when she caught sight of the dock, which surely needed a dousing, Stephanie's blood drying to flakes beneath the sun. Neither Louise nor Geary—and certainly no newcomers—appeared.

How much time had Arles spent in the house after Louise came to fetch her? Her mind dipping and swaying for some unclear reason, as it'd been doing ever since she'd left Stephanie's room so late the night before last. Ever since TaskMiner's alert, really, if not for most of her life. Minutes and more gobbled in unregistered, undigested chunks.

Just then, she saw a cluster of people walking up the path through the woods.

Louise must've decided to show her parents the grounds.

"Dr. Shepherd!" she called as the foursome emerged from the trees. "These are my parents!"

Arles lifted one arm in a wave.

"I brought them to my cabin to leave their things. I'm not sure if theirs is ready yet?"

Geary came to a stop, facing the site of his lifesaving swim.

"Dad, Mom, this is Dr. Shepherd, the therapist I told you about," said Louise.

Arles summoned a smile. "Now, we definitely don't have Uber way out here. Where did you leave your car?"

Louise laughed harder than Arles's remark merited. "They were more intimidated by the dirt road than I was! Parked off to the side where it starts to get twisty."

"We're city slickers," Louise's father acknowledged. He wore a ball cap, flannel shirt, jeans, and boots, appearing perfectly at home in Wedeskyull, despite his self-effacing comment. He extended a hand, taking Arles's in a warm, firm grasp. "Max Drake. And my wife, Tina."

Louise's mother tsked her tongue. "My husband is selling himself short. He could've made the drive easily—that's what he does for a living! But his vehicle is on the large side, and that road of yours is in some disrepair." She looked around. "This whole place is, come to say."

Arles took an instant dislike to the woman, and it tickled her therapist antenna. The rude remark notwithstanding, when a client or family member incited a reaction this strong, so-called countertransference, it meant there was content of her own for the psychologist to deal with.

Tina Drake was as tightly wrapped visually as she was in her manner. Gray hair raked back from her forehead, a plain skirt cinching her legs together, blouse buttoned up to her throat. At least Louise's father seemed pleasant enough. Arles beckoned the party up to the house, trying to hold at bay the feeling that she was calling them to their doom. Or to hers.

Everyone took seats in the parlor, except Geary, who dropped down in his preferred floor location and began staring fixedly out the window. Arles led the quartet in intros, contributing a condensed version of her own since Louise was the primary patient and had heard it before.

Then she launched in. "One of the methods we utilize in FIT is to pull back the curtain, take a peek at what's behind it."

Louise offered up an enthusiastic smile while her parents looked on.

Arles continued. "Louise, would you mind sharing a thought you have about your parents vis-à-vis Geary? Let's say, your father." He seemed to be the safer point of entry.

Louise's eyebrows shot up. "My dad? It's my mother who has a problem with Geary."

Tina's lips were pressed so tightly together, they disappeared into the white skin of her lower face. It looked as if she had no mouth.

"Well, just tell us a little about your dad, then. Not necessarily concerning Geary."

Louise gave a *Got it* kind of head bob. "Um, well, one thing is that he's not really used to being around other people. So I hope it's okay to have brought him here!" She giggled girlishly. "My father has this very solitary job. Works long hours. He was away a lot when I was young."

Max nodded in agreement. The thinning hair below his cap and deeply hewn lines around his eyes prompted a brain tug, like an actor you knew you'd seen recently in a role. Only men were allowed to age this naturally and still be considered pleasing to look at. But most appealing of all was the way Max seemed to keep a lid on his boiling wife, engaging her with eye contact, one hand laid gently on her skirt-clad knee.

"He and my mother don't go out very much. At all, really." Louise let out a small laugh again. "They keep to themselves. When I was young, my mother was never the Girl Scouts troop leader or PTA type, and my dad didn't coach sports. We hardly even know our neighbors! My parents don't socialize or have many friends." She paused as if to consider. "Any."

Arles nodded. "Is there more you'd like to say before I ask your parents about Geary?"

"Um, well, now that I've been in this program, I see things I didn't before. Or in a new light, is a better way to put it." Louise went on in a fierce rush. "Like, that my mother dominates my father. I don't know what he'd be like—how friendly or interactive—if it wasn't for her. My dad has always been a very loving person." She took in a rattly breath. "But my mother tells him how much he can love. And who. Which is where Geary enters into this."

Arles was about to make room for a pause when Max jumped in.

"Your mother is my biggest fan; it's true. She's got my back, as the kids say." He gave Arles a nod affirming his statement before turning to his daughter. "But you've always been the second biggest, Lulu." He tugged the bill of his cap lower, and Arles spied a glimmer of tears.

"Dad?" Louise said. "Are you okay?"

Max lifted a *Hold on one second* hand. "We've missed out on too much of your life, my girl. And our grandson's too. Don't you agree, Tina?"

Tina sat as rigidly as a length of barbed wire in her chair, but she gave a scant nod.

Even FIT didn't work this fast. Arles looked suspiciously from one elder Drake to the other, then decided to call a break. When she went to look in on Lissa, the girl asked whether Geary could join her for schoolwork, and Arles passed the suggestion along to Louise. She didn't know what was going to happen during the second half of group, but instinct told her it might be best not to have a child present for it.

She got started again by asking how Tina and Max felt about what their daughter had shared. Tina responded first, drawing her chair forward to shield her husband from view. Arles wondered if the maneuver was conscious.

"I suppose I do talk or even act for the two of us sometimes. I know Max so well, I can tell what he's thinking. What he wants and when he's going to need it." She gave an affectionate glance over her shoulder; the expression transformed her whole face.

"I guess I figure not talking is easier," Max put in. "Safer. You know, 'keep quiet and nobody has to get hurt,'" he said, putting on a cartoon bad guy kind of tone. "Seriously, though. Sometimes when you say stuff, folks get upset."

"Ah, but there's a din to silence," Arles remarked. "By not saying anything, you're actually communicating a great deal." She took her eyes off the small assemblage while the past came calling. "People think of silence as peaceful," she concluded from a distance. "In reality, it's anything but."

Louise stared at Arles while Tina remained twisted around, gaze pinned to her husband.

"I never thought of it like that," Max said, looking past his wife to give Arles a smile.

Something pitched inside her head as if she were standing on a foundering ship. Silence. The cost of silence. Its dreadfully high price. Her own mother had kept silent. And who else? She had to clamp the arms of her seat with both hands to remain upright.

The door to the parlor slammed against the wall behind it, and Arles jumped, bearing down with such force that it felt as if the wooden chair might splinter. She wrenched the top part of her body around to get a look at the doorway.

Lissa stood in the opening, bouncing up and down on sneakered feet.

Arles felt the rapid flutter of her pulse in her neck. "Yes, Lissa? What is it?"

A tone so sharp, it sliced her throat. But the girl didn't appear to notice, caught in the throes of some excitement.

"Dr. Arles! Ms. Drake! You have to come see what Geary is doing!"

CHAPTER TWENTY-SEVEN

Once, a shout like Lissa's would've triggered panic in Louise, knowing she was about to race off to find her son in one of his frantic, exposed states, upset and emotions laid bare like the muscles and veins on a body stripped of skin. She was relieved that her parents didn't trail along when she and Dr. Shepherd went upstairs, jogging to keep up with Lissa. She had also been glad that Geary left group to do lessons, aware of how he must appear to her parents, sitting silently, staring at sun bolts. Staring at nothing, her mother probably thought.

In her opinion, though, Geary was deserving of pride, like one of those kids whose video clips got a million views on YouTube. He was a hero! Her skin puckered with goose bumps, as if she'd been the one to enter the water, every time she thought about it. For as long as she could remember, people had acted like she had the lesser child, someone damaged and missing important parts, whose outbursts occurred just to annoy anyone around. But Geary had shown Dr. Shepherd where that lady went down in the lake! At age ten, he had helped save somebody's life. How many people could say that about their child?

Dr. Shepherd had looked a little funny when she started group this morning. At first, Louise had been worried she was mad at her; after all, Louise had nearly gotten Dr. Shepherd's employee killed. Geary's act of heroism couldn't offset that, and Louise had slept all night with guilt wrapped around her like a snake. Despite having learned that Lissa's mom was going to be okay, shame still had her in its grip. But it loosened at the sight of Lissa, who came to a stop at the end of the hallway where Geary stood, one skinny arm extended.

With two fingers and his thumb, he pinched a pair of dice.

The events of yesterday vanished. Her son was all she could see.

Before it became clear what kind of deficits—not Louise's word—Geary had, when he was roughly at age level except for his lack of speech (a big *except*, but still), and in early intervention with kids who would go on to be mainstreamed, the teachers spoke about parallel and cooperative play. *Cooperative* meant interacting. Sharing toys. Playing games with pieces and instructions and rules. Geary had never reached that milestone. Now he was standing in the doorway of his friend's bedroom—he had a friend!—holding dice.

Louise fought to come up with something to say, settling on the most basic of questions. "What're you guys doing, Lissa?"

"Hot and Cold!" The little girl could barely contain her excitement, bouncing on her toes, jumbling out words. "Watch this! Look!" She turned to Geary. "You get to choose where to put them this time. Okay? It's your turn. And I'll count."

She faced the wall with a hand over her eyes. "One . . ."

Geary began walking, and Louise and Dr. Shepherd followed. At the end of the hall, he lifted the top of a carved wooden bench to peek inside before lowering its lid. After that, he went down on hands and knees, poking between the spokes of the staircase railing.

From Lissa's room came the sound of numbers interspersed with *Mississippi*.

Geary got up and began walking in the opposite direction, one hand sliding along the wall, the other bunched in a fist around the dice. He paused at a window and patted its sill before moving on. Finally, he came to a door and pulled it open. A closet.

"Maybe not there," Dr. Shepherd said. "Can you look for a different spot—"

Louise interrupted. "Oh, please, let him! He's never done anything like this before!"

"I'm just afraid there could be something in there that you wouldn't want him to touch. I don't know what all is in that closet—"

"Oh, I'm sure it's fine! Probably just blankets and stuff." Or extra toilet paper, cleaning supplies—knives, for all Louise cared—because look at what Geary was doing!

Turning around with both hands open, empty, his arms hanging at his sides.

He'd found a hiding place.

"Forty-eight Mississippi, forty-nine Mississippi, fifty!" chorused Lissa.

She came running out of her room, spying them in front of the closet and hurrying over.

"This is the best part," she said.

Breath had collected in Louise's lungs, ballooning them to the point of pressure, as if she'd taken too deep a dive.

"I have to ask instead of him telling me 'cause, well, you know. He can't talk." Then she said, "Am I warm?"

And Geary nodded.

The breath Louise had been holding exploded out of her with a harsh, ragged gasp. Tears pricked her eyes, stinging her cheeks as they fell, and she spun around so fast, she nearly pitched over. She had the impulse to grab Dr. Shepherd's arm like a little kid, ask if she'd seen—and if not, well, Louise didn't want to be rude to someone she liked and admired basically more than anyone she'd ever met, but why *wouldn't* Geary's therapist have been watching what he just did?

Because she had her back turned. Dr. Shepherd faced the other way.

"Good choice," Lissa was muttering aloud. "Lots of places where the dice could be." She began feeling around on the closet shelves. "Warmer?"

Again, Geary nodded.

"Can I put these on the floor, Dr. Arles?"

It took a long time for Dr. Shepherd to respond; Louise couldn't imagine why. Lissa asking permission seemed a childish courtesy; she was pointing to a stack of new sheets, still in their packaging, which could easily be set down without harm.

Lissa bent over and deposited the plastic zippered cases on the floor, then went up on tiptoes to take a look at the emptied shelf. "Hot?"

Geary jerked his head up and down, but it was a different kind of nod from the ones he'd been giving. This motion looked frenzied, hysterical, Geary's chin hitting his chest hard enough to put a red flame on the flesh. His eyes were so wide, they looked ready to pop.

Despite the unprecedented event she was witnessing, fear shot through Louise's veins like an injection of ice water. But then the game took over again, carrying her away like a flood.

Lissa slid her hand to the right. "Hotter?"

A furious headshake. He'd shaken his head!

Lissa brought her hand left. "Now, hotter?"

Geary's chin bobbed so wildly, it left an indent on the skin above his T-shirt collar.

Louise was torn between wonder—her son communicating; what did this mean for him, for her, for the rest of their lives?—and worry over what might be getting him upset. Distressed without melting down; a smile tugged the corners of her mouth upward. She felt manic-depressive, thrown from one pole of emotion to the other, like standing on a storm-tossed boat.

Lissa pulled her hand free of the closet. It came out with the dice balanced on some sort of card. No, not a card. A glossy print photograph. Lissa tilted the photo to view its image, and the dice slid, dropped, went rattling across the floorboards, as if a gambler had given the pair a roll.

"Hey, that's—" Louise broke off. Still smiling, while also sniffling in a few last tears, but frowning now too. "Me. My dad used to have that picture clipped to the visor of his van."

CHAPTER TWENTY-EIGHT

The wall began to crumble in Arles's mind. First, a snow of gritty particles, then bigger bits of cement before chunks broke off, and finally boulders, all tumbling down until at last she could see what lay behind it. *Who* lay behind it. Her former best friend's father.

But Rory's dad hadn't been the worst one. How far he had been from the worst.

"Let us give you a ride the rest of the way," he'd said, buzzing down the window of his slick, sporty, midlife-crisis car, a choice of vehicle Arles understood because she'd had lots of exposure to men who used too-young girls to gratify themselves. "This isn't a great road to be walking home on. I was upset that my wife allowed you to leave."

His words carried an ominous cast, but that wasn't why Arles began backing away.

She hadn't been raised to be self-protective in that way, on guard, watching out for the kinds of criminals—whether strangers, or the man next door, or someone occupying an intimate corner of her life—who preyed on girls. The opposite. She'd been taught to hand herself over with a flourish. *You're welcome. To me.*

But her reason for refusing to heed Rory's dad's request had nothing to do with any of that. He was probably a perfectly decent guy who'd just been concerned for the safety of his daughter's friend. Arles's reticence came down to one thing: the sight of the girl who'd been her best friend till a couple of hours ago, sitting in the car and staring straight ahead, arms folded across the front of a cute shirt that she'd borrowed from Arles and probably didn't even recall wasn't hers. That's how much of a duo they were, their lives and their belongings merged.

Rory didn't make eye contact; she acted as if no one stood on the shoulder of the road. Arles was worse than invisible. She was so disgusting that she'd ceased to exist.

The thought of getting in that car, sharing a tight space with Rory, made Arles feel physically ill. For a moment, she thought she was going to throw up right there. She whipped around, ignoring a deep male shout, the grumble of the engine as Rory's dad got going again. Arles fled up the road, nearly colliding with a van stopped a little ways ahead.

Engine running, exhaust pluming from its tailpipe as the driver leaned across the front seat to push open the passenger door. "Climb on in," he said in a friendly sort of way. "I saw you back there a few minutes ago. Looks like you're trying to make some kind of getaway."

"I am," Arles replied, and got one foot up on the running board so she could jump inside.

After that, things went dark, still lost to the caved-in area of her mind. Except for one more part she could see now, a pinprick of light penetrating some minute hole in the bedrock.

Her arrival back home. With the photo wedged in the depths of her backpack, though she hadn't known that yet. How much time had passed since she'd gotten in the van? Nine hours, eleven at the max. She'd left Rory's house around ten that morning. It was midsummer, night coming on, her stepfather back from his weekly card game. Going on nine o'clock.

He'd opened the front door, letting out a possessive lion roar. "I was just about to call the police, little girl!"

Bullshit. Peter was best buddies with the chief of police in Wedeskyull at that time and would never have called ole Uncle Vern's attention to Arles. Peter guarded her from other men with a jealous ownership. Unconscious guilt was also at work, she came to understand, once she grew up and embarked on her career. Fear of capture, which was absurd, given his privilege.

He'd grabbed hold of her wrist, his hand hot and dry, reptilian against her skin.

Arles's mother was in the kitchen, stirring a pot of something murky on the stove.

"Arles decided to grace us with her presence at this late hour," he'd said, still holding on.

"She was at a sleepover," her mother had replied vaguely. "With Rory, I think."

Who else? Rory was the only friend Arles would ever have.

"Not all day. I called over there and was told she left early. It's gone nighttime."

Her mother had given a girlish giggle. "Uh-oh, we've got trouble, then. Teenagers are tough."

"She's twelve," Peter had said flatly.

Rubbing the tender flesh on the inside of her wrist with his thumb.

Arles had caught the stark look of satisfaction her mother gave him.

"Well. Arles has always been precocious. Hasn't she?" And she'd turned back to her stew.

A funereal hush, the quiet of a cathedral or a cave, had fallen over the upstairs hall while Arles and Louise stood without blinking, seemingly without breathing, regarding the photo that rested on Lissa's palm. Lissa didn't say anything, just let the grown-ups look, somehow intuiting that now was not the time to ask questions.

Louise broke the silence first. "Hey, how did my picture get here?"

Arles didn't reply. She couldn't.

"Did Geary bring it from home? But I keep photos in my bedroom. He never goes in there." Louise sounded as if she were talking to herself, thinking something through. "You didn't—you couldn't have known me, Dr. Shepherd. Did you? Before I came here?"

Arles was no more able to respond than she'd been a moment ago. So much that was necessary to answer Louise's question still hunched, toadlike, in shadows underground.

"Is that why you were able to tell me that stuff about Geary?" Louise went on. "Like, how his diagnosis isn't complete? He might also have PTSD?"

The last barrage of questions prompted a fiery explosion inside Arles.

Because what had severed her mind, cutting it as cleanly as a scalpel, that night in Stephanie's room? Geary's computer bulging with true-crime podcasts, specifically ones covering a series of crimes so ghastly, they'd sent Lissa into a stupor. Some guy had been at it for possibly decades. Dozens of the missing and the murdered—no, that was too impersonal—dozens of *girls*, strung like beads on a necklace. If nothing had stopped that man, limited his appetite, didn't that suggest he might still be going strong?

"What's the matter, Dr. Arles? Ms. Drake, something's wrong with Dr.—"

"Dr. Shepherd! Are you okay? Where are you going—"

What were the chances that Arles would finish descending these stairs and find Max Drake sitting docilely by his wife in the parlor, waiting for group to resume? There for the taking by the police she would summon to Fir Cove using the sat phone?

Zero. The parlor was empty.

Bad Max—that was what she'd called him, the sudden memory an arrow, a partial recollection, shot through her head—hadn't even bothered to close the front door. Sunshine streamed into Fir Cove, lighting up the whole place.

Arles would've bet Bad Max left his belongings behind, didn't so much as pause at Louise's cabin to get his things before making his escape. Coming here entailed taking a terrible chance, invited scrutiny of a kind he'd evaded in every aspect of his life: solitary job, no social support or contact with friends or neighbors. He must've deemed refusing his daughter's request the greater risk, resistance likely to cause Louise to up the urgency, wonder why her parents would present an obstacle to healing. Better to get it out of the way, dispense with the demand.

Or maybe Bad Max simply believed he was fireproof, impervious to getting caught. After all, he had gotten away with this for years. Gotten away with what, in her case? She still couldn't remember. And it didn't matter now. She couldn't *let* it matter, allow anything to slow her down.

Had he known to flee Fir Cove because he'd overheard the children's game, stood at the bottom of the stairs, and listened? If so, how much of a lead did he have?

Arles leaped for the heavy oak door, ready to run.

Then she remembered the charges in her care.

Louise had come down behind Arles, but the children weren't with her.

Arles parsed the parameters instantly, her previous snaillike, sluggish traces of memory wiped away by panic. There was nothing in the house to worry about. Mountain, lake, terrain—none of them posed any immediate danger. The most likely source of harm for Lissa and Geary would be if Bad Max got to either child, used them to guarantee his escape.

She grasped Louise by the arms. "Find the kids. Then keep them with you."

Louise looked like Arles so often felt, as if she'd come unbolted from her own existence and been sent hurtling through thin air.

"Get Geary and Lissa!" Arles commanded. "Do you hear me? Can you do that?"

The mention of her son's name appeared to snap Louise back, rejoin her mind to her body. Arles thought she also detected a brimming awareness, pieces of the past colliding in Louise's gaze. Because on some level, she must've known who her father was, right?

All the things women knew but didn't say, or pretended they didn't realize, or didn't allow themselves to recognize. And in this case, it was Louise's beloved father tacitly requiring her to keep the silence, which must have made the chains that much more constricting.

Arles and Louise faced each other, their eyes reflecting a dawning comprehension, if not entirely of who was whom and what had happened, then at least that something gruesome and long-unvoiced had placed that photograph in the closet at Fir Cove. While at the same time registering how much was and always would be impossible to understand in this world.

Arles's hands were still wrapped around Louise's wrists. She was holding Louise up and holding on to her for balance at the same time.

Louise gave Arles a quick squeeze in return, then wrested herself free, and ran.

Where did Bad Max leave his oversize van? Not due to any difficulty handling it on the dirt road, Arles realized, as she stood on the porch and looked out over the land. He must've stashed it close to the gates in case the need arose for a quick getaway. Or hid it because he couldn't allow anyone to observe the van among the other vehicles parked on the premises.

Suddenly, her heart gave a lurch; the bones in her legs turned to Silly Putty.

A thick, solid mass had begun to fill her throat, cutting off air. Did Bad Max have a victim with him right now? Arles wheezed in a strangled breath. Is that why he couldn't bring his van up to the house? If so, and he drove away, it would be the end for that girl.

According to the podcasters, he had killed before—multiple times—and now he must suspect he'd been identified. He would murder whomever he had and dispose of her body where it would never be found. Everything inside Arles turned icy cold, the temperature of some planet inhospitable to life. She had known this madman was out there and let herself forget. *Made* herself forget. Built a wall, and put the truth behind it. Her hands formed fists, nails digging pits in the skin on her palms. How many torturous, terrified ends was she responsible for?

None. Bad Max bore the responsibility, and she wouldn't impose on herself the blame for one more man's evil. No woman should ever do that.

But neither would Arles allow *this* man to get away with it again.

Off to the side where the road starts to get twisty, Louise had said. Was there any truth to that claim, or had it been a lie Louise's parents fed her, as they must've been making things up for decades to conceal their grotesque sham of a life from their offspring? How much awareness did Tina possess, and what did Max keep hidden from his wife? One thing Arles knew for sure was that there weren't many places along the road leading to Fir Cove big enough to conceal a vehicle, sufficiently out of sight that its sitting in one spot wouldn't draw attention.

In fact, she could only think of one.

Standing on the front porch, she took a last look up at the house, hoping Louise had located the children inside, that all three were sequestered. Then, taking the flight of stone steps at a run, she set off along the shortcut through the woods. It would meet up with the road not too far away from the site where she believed Bad Max to be headed.

And he didn't know this land like she did.

—

This whole time, for the majority of her life, Arles had been telling herself it was Louise she sought. She'd searched over the course of years, using whichever methods she had at her disposal, and ultimately enlisting TaskMiner. Whereas, in truth, she'd needed to find the father of the girl in the photograph. So he could be stopped.

That picture had been a beacon, a blinking indicator light to her subconscious, warning her that there was something she was going to forget, press into the thick muck of memory and bury too far down to recall. The photo made sure she knew something was missing and had to be excavated. But she still didn't know how she'd gotten a hold of it. Or the purpose it had served.

She wove through trees in a jagged run, protecting her face from the whiplash of twigs. One arm up to screen her eyes, then tripping, unseeing, into grooves in the ground. Flailing with her arms thrust out before straightening up. So deep in the woods that the sky was blotted out by a fretwork of branches, dark as dusk at 10:00 a.m., and she could only hope that her sense memory remained intact; she was staying oriented, and the road lay ahead.

Cursing herself as she ran because she had fallen prey to the oldest trap in the history of mankind—emphasis on the *man*. She'd aimed her lens at the bitchy female—the mean, angry wench—leaving the male blameless and unaccused. Hungry and given free rein to eat.

No wonder Bad Max had aped the fastest turnaround of any patient since Freud started asking people to lie down on his couch. Hoping to be pronounced cured and placate his daughter so that he could get out of here. Promise whatever so he wouldn't be compelled to stick around.

Be a family again.

Confess to having missed Louise.

Embrace the grandson he had shunned.

How much did Geary know, and how the *hell* had he figured it out? Did he visit his grandparents one day around age two, and see something there, some terrifying sign of his grandfather's sick pursuits, his grotesque predilections? Perhaps Bad Max had gotten sloppy with his daughter grown and out of the house, and his wife clearly complicit in at least some part of his crimes. Previously maintained barriers and restraints had been lifted, enabling Bad Max's toddler grandson to stumble upon something that literally and figuratively scared him speechless.

Too young to make sense of what he'd seen, let alone share it.

A different kind of brain than Geary's might not have picked up on whichever aspects he did. Bits and pieces that may've been invisible, or gone unnoticed by someone with another way of perceiving, had lived on in him. Geary's mind drew a map that no one could read or follow.

Except it had been followed, hadn't it? Because if Geary hadn't registered what he had, and filed it away in the way that he did, then he might not have been in therapy. Louise wouldn't have wound up in that Facebook group; she and her son would never have come to Fir Cove.

And Arles wouldn't have been given this chance to stop Max Drake for good.

She swerved out of the woods and onto the road, its flat surface a relief beneath her pounding feet. But still no van, no Bad Max, and that caused her legs to strain, calf muscles twanging as she put on a burst of speed. Breath coming hard, sweat stinging her eyes and making her face itch madly, heart like a herd of clopping hooves inside her.

Wondering as she ran how Geary discovered the photograph she had tucked high up in the linen closet. Old habits died hard. Historically, it was the place where she always kept the photo, whether at the house in town or at Fir Cove, because her stepfather had a penchant for going through her things. He never would've deigned to look in a place where sheets and towels were stored, however. He was a graduate of the women's work school of misogyny. A little wifey to cook and clean and tend to him. He only strayed from his 1950s duality of gender roles when it came to the childcare. That, Peter had seen to himself.

Geary might well have recognized the photo's subject if he accidentally came across it; he would've seen childhood pictures of his mom. Did that zip-smart brain of his put enough together to steer Lissa's game? Or was it a coincidence? To her eyes, it had looked as if Geary were trying to identify the perfect hiding spot for the dice, going for someplace specific.

Then again, on some level, Arles had known that the photograph needed to be found.

This road wasn't as smooth as it'd felt at first in comparison to the forest floor. Rubbly with stones, cratered with holes. Her knees jolted painfully, and her ankles kept turning as she raced over the uneven surface, attempting to ignore the bumps and dips. But willing away reality didn't feel as easy as it used to. Her knees hurt, and she winced with every throbbing footfall.

Every patient contained some part, however minute, that the therapist could relate to, see herself inside, if she were only brave enough to look. But Arles and Geary had more in common than most. Both with memories like graveyards, secrets to be exhumed. Young, vulnerable, and made victims by Bad Max's exploits in ways neither had been able to communicate.

At age twelve, Arles must've been such easy pickings, primed and ready to inhabit the role of prey. No clue where real danger lived because the threat she'd had to face resided in her very own home. And thanks to Peter, her mind knew how to slip in and out as automatically as she drew breath, allowing Bad Max to proceed.

Now, she recalled sitting beside him in the front of the van. The picture had been for distraction, a focal point. She'd stared at it until her eyes bled, filled with red tears upon observing a young girl whom this man probably never scared or hurt, her image kept lovingly with him when they were apart. Floating high above her younger form, Arles watched herself studying the photo as fiercely as if her life depended on it. Which perhaps it had.

The photo had been stuck to what looked like some form of identification slid inside a plastic film with elastic straps adhering the case to the sun visor. She'd been trying to get a name, a company title, maybe even an employee number. She must've been planning to turn in her abductor. Smart kid, she would've said if she'd been her own client. But the photograph covered the bulk of the ID card; all she could make out were the first three letters of a name.

She'd called him by it, not knowing whether it was his full name or a nickname, if he ever went by the shortened version. Max, Maxwell, Maximillian? It'd been a risk, but ultimately a turning point. He could've decided to drug or kill her right then, given the scrap of identifying information she possessed, but instead, he'd begun to talk. What had they spoken about? She couldn't hear their voices through the distant tunnel of the past. And she couldn't stay in the long ago anymore; she needed to lasso her mind, yank it back to the present.

She spied a late-model sedan pulled over on the road, and her heartbeat kicked up as she veered toward it. But the seats were empty—she pounded on the trunk and got nothing in return—and then her fevered brain made sense of things. This was Louise's mother's car. She'd driven separately—unable to ride in her husband's work vehicle for so many reasons—and left her sedan near the gates to rationalize the excuse she'd vocalized upon arrival. *I couldn't drive on that road even in my smaller car!* Or to help Bad Max flee, if need be. So many machinations and manipulations, conscious and unconscious, required for Tina Drake's sick life to work.

Arles set forth running again. She rounded a bend and found herself standing at the spot she'd had in mind, a clearing wide enough to house a large vehicle. Screened by a row of saplings so young and supple, they could be driven over and bounce back. As these had been, now standing upright, the damage they'd suffered detectable only to someone looking for signs. Splintered wood bleeding sap, bark as fragile as baby skin scraped away, thin trunks marred.

But the land behind them was vacant. No hulking, cumbersome van visible through the mesh of new leaves, no whiff of exhaust lingering in the air. Arles pushed into the thicket and felt something in her gullet make its way up as her feet sank into zippered veins, depressions in the soft spring soil. Tire tracks.

She had missed him by minutes, maybe less. Water oozed up from the ground, not yet having gotten a chance to soak in. Mud squelched around her shoes as she crept forward. The treads she was following led deeper into the woods. She was on a hunting trail that would soon widen into what used to be a logging road. Visible on a map, assuming Bad Max thought to check his surroundings before coming here, and a man who'd gotten away with what he had for as long as he had must be calculating like that, canny.

In the event of needing to escape, being cut off at some point along Fir Cove's winding private drive would pose a real threat. Bad Max must believe he could avoid that fate by taking this old cutaway through the woods to meet up with the paved road that would lead to freedom.

But the map didn't take into account the condition of this land.

Or how it had deteriorated around the ravine that lay ahead.

CHAPTER TWENTY-NINE

Geary wasn't in the house, and Lissa didn't turn up during Louise's search, either. She'd already gotten some sense of the size of this place, but she didn't grasp it fully until she had to peer into every room and each tiny inlet. The front door stood open and had since she'd come downstairs with Dr. Shepherd. Plenty of time for two kids to slip out unnoticed. The grown-ups hadn't just been distracted; they'd been brain-dead, zombified by Geary's discovery.

A high, toneless note played in her ears; it was hard to hear anything over it. Something clanged in the pit of her belly, and her throat wasn't working right; she couldn't swallow. How did Dr. Shepherd come to have a picture of her, and why did it make Louise dry-mouthed with terror that her son and an innocent little girl were outside unaccounted for? Louise didn't know in what way her school photo had wound up inside a closet in a castle half a state away, each step it must've taken to get there. But deep down, she sensed the trip meant something horrifying.

Her father traveled long distances for work. His routes brought him this far.

Louise had seen moms discuss the topic online, how much information to give their daughters versus what was too scary to say, about men who had jobs like that, drove vehicles like those, stopped by the sides of roads on the lookout for little girls.

She forced herself to take a step onto the porch, calling in a shaky voice, "Geary! Lissa! Come back here right away! I mean it—right this second!"

Geary could follow instructions, even better than she'd realized. And Lissa didn't seem like the type of kid who made trouble. If they didn't appear, then they were either too far away to hear—which would present its own reason for worry—or else something had happened to them.

Her heart thrummed. Where to look? This place was massive. A light, lilting voice in her head suggested she go back inside. There were pieces of furniture she hadn't checked behind; maybe the kids were playing a different hiding game. Her feet felt drawn to the hallway as if by a magnetic force. She did not want to stay outside. Something was very wrong out here.

But her son was out here, and so was another woman's child. Which left Louise no choice but to venture off the porch. At the edge of the woods, as still as one of the trees, stood a shape.

Slowly, it resolved into a human form. Her mother.

Louise took the final step so fast, she twisted her ankle. It gave with an agonizing twinge, which she ignored because she had to cross the dirt road before her mother reached it from the opposite side and blocked her. Louise needed to look for the kids without interference.

She wasn't sure why she suddenly saw her mother as not just rejecting, even cruel, but someone who would actively stop her from trying to track down two children lost in an area far too big and wild for them to wander around in. But she did.

Back to the photo. The change in her thinking had to do with that. In the shot, Louise had been the age Geary was now. At first, she'd thought—hoped, prayed—that Geary might've brought it from home, like he did his puffy coat and computer. Went into her room, even though he never did that, found her class picture, then stuck it in Dr.

Shepherd's hall closet for some unknowable Geary reason. Louise cherished her copy of that photo, had recently uploaded it for a prompt in a Facebook group she belonged to. She'd been sad when it disappeared from her father's delivery van; she'd liked that he kept her with him during the periods when he was far away from home.

"Louise!" somebody called.

There was only one other person outside, but no way did that voice belong to her mother.

"Where is that son of yours?" The same warm, sweet cry.

Impossibly, it did come from her mom, words that grew more distinct the closer she got.

"What your father said in therapy was right," it said.

She said. Her mother said. But whoever this was seemed like an *it*.

A bot that knew how to act like the mother Louise had always wanted.

"We didn't know what this Autism thing was, and it scared us. Fear makes ignorant people mean. I'm sorry we let it drive us away." Her tone softened another degree. "From you."

There was some lack of awareness in there, but still, how long had Louise yearned to hear words like these? Her heart pulsed with need. Her mother stood just a few yards away, on the slope in front of the porch. Impossible to get past her now. But maybe that wasn't necessary.

Her mother held out her arms, and she looked just like any normal mom who gave hugs.

Normal. Not a word you were supposed to use.

"Come," her mother said. "We can do better. Let your father and me do better."

The land and trees and faraway glint of lake all wobbled as Louise blinked back tears.

"Let's go find my grandson," her mom said. Just steps away now. "I've waited so long."

Geary appeared behind his grandmother, standing in the long, slanted shadow she threw across the grass, while Lissa followed more hesitantly, taking looks around.

Relief gushed through Louise. She hurried forward, about to suggest they all go inside and have something to eat. Never mind for now where her father might be. Why think about that? He'd roamed and rambled all her life, and who was she to put up a fuss? Lissa knew how to fix the yummiest food, and what with all the progress Geary had been making, he'd probably stay put at the table for the longest stretch ever, a real meal with grown-ups! Her mother could eat with her grandson for the first time since he'd graduated from basically jarred baby goop.

But just then, Lissa kicked out a foot, sending a gritty roll of rocks down the hill, and Louise's mother wheeled around. Louise watched as her eyes lit, and she lunged, one of her arms shooting out in Geary's direction like a snake about to strike.

Geary leaped messily backward, and Lissa staggered, in a vain attempt to keep him from falling. Louise's mother stood by emotionlessly, observing her grandson as he hit the ground. She didn't love Geary and never would. But Louise finally had an inkling of why she must hate him.

Her mother had been telling the truth moments ago about one thing at least.

Fear made people mean.

"Oh my God." Louise fought for a cut-off, whistling breath. "When you asked me if Geary's new therapist was going to be able to help him talk, you weren't hoping she would." A gulp of air that seemed to contain no oxygen. "You were terrified."

If something traumatized him, Dr. Shepherd had said.

On that day eight years ago, her mother got physical with her grandson, as she had a habit of doing. Life took such a nosedive afterward that Louise hadn't paused to reflect on the circumstances. She'd been consumed with trying to keep everyone from crashing: Geary, Michael, herself. She'd never stopped to think about what had happened beforehand. Nothing stood out as unusual; they'd visited her parents plenty of times, and sometimes her mother got nasty. Par for the course. Louise didn't have the time or wherewithal for further consideration, and nobody had asked. Not one of the therapists they'd seen until Dr. Shepherd. The others all listened to Louise recite Geary's symptoms and then put him in their diagnostic box. Mothers who claimed their children's behaviors dropped off or changed all of a sudden tended to be dismissed as hysterics. She could remember one doctor saying, "There's no precipitating incident with Autism." But there had been an incident, whether related to Geary being Autistic or not.

She'd just never had any reason to see it as such.

Over coffee in her parents' kitchen, the back door open to let in soft breaths of summer air, Louise became aware that Geary was no longer playing his Tupperware stacking game underfoot. She'd taken her eyes off him for a moment, and he'd gone outside. He used to do that then, enjoy the outdoors. Her father realized it at the same second she did. He and Louise were always in sync.

He put down his cup and got up, aiming a look in her mother's direction. The recollection made Louise's skin go slimy with sweat, though she'd thought nothing of it at the time. Her father and mother had always been one for intense, romantic looks. Or what passed for romance.

Her dad strode into the backyard with Louise beside him. She took a look around before spotting Geary by the garden shed. When Louise had been a child, that shed was off-limits. It was always bolted, locked up tight. Her mother's gardening supplies were kept there, plus a lawn mower and some dangerous tools. But on that day, one of its doors hung partially open.

The metallic *screech* of hinges could be heard, more of an echo than an actual sound, as if the door had recently been pushed or otherwise disturbed, then swung slowly to a stop.

Louise hadn't put that together at the time; now, the sound grated rustily in her ears.

Her mother came flying across the lawn and grabbed Geary, securing his pudgy little wrist in her fist. His wobbly legs gave out, and he fell, a yowl soaring skyward, the likes of which would wreck Louise's life during the months and years to come. Her father calmly plucked the small boy up by the strap of his overalls, walked over, and deposited him in her arms.

"Two-year-olds," he'd said with a smile and shake of his head. "It's all about independence, right? *I do it*," he had added, quoting Louise as a little kid, an oft-told family anecdote, his tone adoring. Then he'd turned back to seal up the shed, his tall form looming outside the door for a second before he closed it snugly against a hazy shaft of sunshine.

Nothing to think about. Certainly not a little dust scattered by light. And her mother being controlling? What else was new? Same for her father, stepping in to restore peace.

Louise had been preoccupied, anyway. "Sweetie!" she remembered saying, trying to keep from showing alarm now that any danger was safely past. *Seemed* to be past. "You can't wander off like that! You have to get Mommy, okay? Next time, ask me, and I'll come with you."

But there hadn't been a next time. Geary wasn't the same by the next day.

She had left her childhood home, carrying her son, and plopped him into his booster seat, not knowing he would refuse to ride in anything else after that point. His brain veering and darting from that moment forward in the ways that it did, coming back to a day she hadn't even known was important.

How did the shed door come open? Who messed with it? Geary, while out in the yard—or—oh God, she was going to be sick—somebody else from within? And what had served to lure Geary over to the structure? What did he hear or see when he got there? *Who* did he hear or see?

Her mother had always been an episodic gardener; she went through spells when she didn't go near the shed. She hung see-through, gauzy curtains on the windows in the house, refusing shades when Louise asked for them. So the yard could be viewed at all times, a watchful eye kept out? Louise had to recast everything in her mind now, all of it, down to her mother's relentless push for curb appeal, not one flake of paint or overgrown grass blade to draw attention.

Geary had been trying to make sense of an atrocity for most of his life, confused and overwhelmed and attempting to reveal it. And she'd let him down. Hideously, grotesquely failed to hear. Because she herself had been confused and unseeing her whole life, even if she hadn't known it. She'd kept a silence, and it had silenced her son.

Suddenly, she pitched forward and retched, everything she'd eaten that morning—no, for forever, for always—coming up in a raging stream, burning her throat, and landing like lava on the ground. Incinerating the earth. She went down on her knees, tears mixing with the puddle of undigested solids. Secrets. What secrets had lived inside her home, the family growing around them, accommodating but distorted, forced to take on a bloated, tumorous shape? And how many of the pieces slamming into place for Louise now had Geary been able to put together?

Something as insubstantial as memory had a terrible weight, like lead in the mind.

From the ground, Louise blinked to try and clear her vision. The two children stood side by side, Geary upright and pinned, one wrist clamped by his grandmother's hand.

"Lissa!" Louise screamed. "Run up to the house! Hurry!"

There was a phone thing, some kind of clunky device, in the parlor; Louise had seen Dr. Shepherd holding it before she started group this morning. Louise wondered how likely it was that Lissa would find the thing and figure out how to use it to call 911.

Even from her prone position, she could see her mother tightening her grip on Geary. Pain seized his face, and he looked around wildly, his eyes meeting Louise's for the first time since he was two, a current of the pure and brightest blue. The impact so strong, it entered her body like voltage, and she shot to her feet. Geary yanked his arm roughly enough that his grandmother struck the ground, bony knees first, then her belly. In no time at all, she was back on her feet and bounding in his direction, but Geary raced off before she could reach him.

His path looked sure and certain. Louise had no idea where he intended to go.

Dear God, what had happened in the car at the supermarket that day? Talking to the director of Elward, it had occurred to her that Geary might've heard something on the radio. Could it have been a news story? And when he went out to the parking lot at the rest stop—was that because of the visit he and Louise had just paid to his grandparents, where Geary learned they would soon be making their way up here? He might've been searching for a van.

That Louise now needed to find before her father drove off.

She was the only person who could stop him from leaving.

CHAPTER THIRTY

Arles left the row of saplings downtrodden to signal anyone who might come this way, then kept walking along the old logging trail, ducking low so as not to be visible to a driver scouring his rearview mirror. She could hear the growl of a motor now, smell fumes in the fresh spring air. She'd been right about Bad Max's plan. He was a quarter mile ahead, driving slug-slowly in deference to the conditions. The way he was going ran perpendicular to the main road, eventually leading to pavement. But something else came first.

The woods were growing thicker. She could no longer walk a straight course, and the tire marks she was following began to weave, zigzagging around trees, backing up, then angling. Soon, this route would become all but impassable, but that wasn't the issue. Bad Max was about to face a problem of topography.

In this section of forest, just to the left of this road, a shelf of earth gave way to a chasm, and the feature was eroding. Pieces of it routinely broke off; trees downed in winter would feel the ground where they'd been rooted disappear, crumbling into the depths. If the van strayed too close, it would plummet. A great way to take out Bad Max. But not if he wasn't alone.

When Arles finally caught sight of the van, the temperature changed, a few hellish degrees of heat added to the woods. Not due to the mechanics of a combustion engine; this was a supernatural phenomenon. Because of what this van held, and who steered it.

The devil at its wheel.

It wasn't the same vehicle, of course. Twenty-five years had seen a few replacements. This one was slightly more compact, slanted sides, a model called a Transit. But a close enough match that Arles's final sequence of memory slammed into place, like a cartridge in a rifle.

Victory Vendors was the name of his company. *Pro solutions for all your vending needs.* Painted letters, ever so slightly faded, in a font just a tad out of date. In a few years, would Victory Vendors be gone, Bad Max put out of business? People—some of them at least—had drifted away from candy and chips, or even granola bars, now known to contain as much sugar as a Snickers, with sugar being the real evil these days, the current demon at your door. Far less soda and garishly colored drinks—horrors! Parents—again, some of them, the ones who didn't know from true devilry—no longer chose to feed their kids shelf-stable snacks.

The moment after Arles climbed into Bad Max's van twenty-five years ago, the locks had engaged with a clunk. An uneasy chill had crept up the backs of her legs.

"You locked the doors?"

"You bet," he'd said casually. "You can't believe how many people lean against a door and fall out. For that matter"—his gaze sidled in her direction—"put on your seat belt, okay?"

Something told Arles not to, but she followed his instruction.

She was used to obeying instructions.

He began driving faster, the van screeching around bends, taking turns with a shriek of tires. Laying waste to empty country roads, as if headed somewhere specific.

"Don't you want to know where you're supposed to be taking me?" she'd asked, not liking how small her voice sounded. Her throat felt raw and ragged; perhaps she had screamed for a while. "Don't you need to know where to go?"

"Sure do," he replied, still in that casual tone.

But he was slowing down now, and he gave the wheel a spin with one lazy-looking forearm. They were on the access ramp to the Northway. A four-lane highway that most people drove at eighty miles an hour or faster. No escape from a moving vehicle.

She was about to tell him this wasn't the right way. But she knew there was no point.

He eyed her shrewdly. "You seem like a very smart girl."

Arles gave a faint nod. She was.

"I get lonely out here on the road," he went on. "I like to pick someone up to take with me. For a little company, you know? I'll get you where you need to go eventually, don't worry. Let's just spend some time together first."

And Arles said: "Okay."

Late in the day, he had stopped, pulling over at a highway lookout, views as far north as Canada, or maybe they were even *in* Canada by then—who knew? Bad Max offered her snacks from the cartons sitting on shelves in the back of his van.

"One thing you gotta say about what I do for a living," he'd said, chuckle-y and jovial. "Makes for great road food. What would your mom do if she knew you were eating as much junk as you liked?"

She wouldn't give a shit, twelve-year-old Arles had thought.

But instead of answering, she eased herself across the bench seat and squiggled onto Bad Max's lap. Chocolate coated her tongue with sticky sweetness, and she gagged. This was why she barely ate at home. You couldn't get within a hundred miles of her stepfather and contain any sustenance. Thick walls, enormous swaths of land, nothing provided sufficient protection. Vampiric, he would absorb every ounce of nourishment she possessed, lap it up for his own.

From the passenger seat, she'd had to contort her body to keep the photograph in sight; here on Bad Max's lap, she could study it head-on. But he was jolting as if he'd touched a live outlet, and the motion dumped her off his legs. She scooted sideways, then sat there, unmoving.

He turned a wounded expression on her.

"Don't do that." His voice strangled, not casual anymore. "I said I didn't want that."

Arles didn't answer.

"What would make you think I'd want something like that?" Still so hurt-sounding.

Uh, because you snatched a strange girl off the street?

But he hadn't, had he? She'd climbed in of her own volition. Did that change things? What other purpose could he have taken her for? Was it possible he didn't want the same thing as Peter? Her mind zigged and zagged, trying to home in on something that would save her.

"You just looked so lost." He tore off a block of candy bar with ragged incisors and chewed. Following her inner thoughts—no one had ever done that before. Usually, it was Arles who knew what other people were thinking. "And I'm lost too. So I stopped."

She kept quiet, and it led him to speak. Years later, in her career, she would put this tactic to use under much less dire circumstances.

"I like to think I can help you find what you need. Or at least we can be lost together."

Even at twelve, the blatant duplicity had astounded her. This man had locked her in, taken her speeding down a highway, foiled all her escape attempts, nearly drugged her, and was now parked at a desolate location, just one other car in the lot. The rear of his van was padlocked—she'd seen a silver-linked chain twisted around the handles when he'd gone back to get their snacks. He'd prepared for contingencies, the likely event that she would try to get away.

"Have you ever done this before?" she'd asked. Leaning to look at the photograph.

"Sure," he replied, sucking traces of chocolate off his fingers. "A time or two, maybe more, to be honest. There're lots of lost girls like you out there. And I enjoy having a high, sweet voice in my ear as I drive. I miss that when I'm not home."

"That's your daughter," Arles had said, following the snaking line he was laying. She gestured to the picture. "It's her that you miss."

"So much," he'd replied thickly. "She's the sweetest girl you could ever hope to meet."

Arles studied the child's clear blue gaze, shining out from the photo. "What would she say if she knew what you were doing to me?"

His deadened eyes changed minutely. "Little girls don't understand a man's needs."

This one does, Arles thought brutally.

"I remind you of her, don't I?" she asked. "I look a little like her."

She didn't at all—Arles was older, a ginger with startlingly green eyes, while the girl in the photo was blonde with summer-sky blue ones—but something went gauzy in the man's gaze, her words mesmerizing him, as if she were a snake charmer conjuring a cobra from a basket.

"You know what? You really do," he said. "Especially around the mouth."

Yuck, she thought. "Does she like being outdoors? Would she want to see that view?"

"She sure would," he said. "We'd walk all the way up and look at it together."

"Let's!" Arles said, making her voice a little younger than it was—Peter liked to say she had the pipes of a woman—and applying a thick coating of eagerness. "Can we take candy?"

He gave her an affectionate glance. "*More* candy, young lady?"

She nodded. "Please? Just one piece?"

He heaved a sigh that sounded pleased rather than annoyed, and bent low, inching his way into the rear cargo space. He returned with two chocolate bars, and she held out her hand.

"Nuh-uh," he said, his tone teasing. "Not yet. It'll be your reward for reaching the top."

"Okay," she said, pretend sulky.

"I'll come around and let you out," he said, waggling a ring of keys.

Keeping the laser light of her eyes and a fake grin on him as he made his way over to the passenger side, she snatched the photo by feel; it came free with a chewing-gum snap of Blu Tack.

When she shot out of the van, her brain seizing on the best route, legs already covering ground, the friendly guy who'd offered her salvation from her sixth-grade daymare, the wounded soul who couldn't imagine why the girls he took might raise a fuss, vanished in a poof of blackened soot. His features folded into an ugly leer, those uneven teeth transformed into fangs, and he sprang in the direction she was running with a snarl of sheer rage.

But there was that other car in the lot with potential witnesses in it, and then Arles decided to swerve, go racing the wrong way down the highway to prevent him from pursuing her in his van. On foot, he would've attracted attention, and by that point, a minivan was veering into the breakdown lane, anyway, the concerned mom inside offering her a lift. *Just buckle yourself in next to the baby's booster, sweetie. You look too young to ride up front.*

Arles had always been told she looked old for her age. Mostly by Peter.

In years to come, the Blu Tack on the back of the photograph would turn dry and crusty, crumbling away to dust gone gray with grime, so frequently did she take the picture out to thumb and peer at it, rotate and examine it from every angle, the memory of how she'd come by the thing evaporating even as she climbed into that minivan, no idea why a photo like that would've entered her possession.

Or that the girl it depicted had saved her life.

"What happened to you, honey?" asked the woman who stopped to pick her up.

So there were a few saviors in the world after all.

This van—of the mini variety, doors on runners, three rows of seats—felt safe and cool, the AC running, even though it wasn't that hot out. A big, comfy vehicle for a big, close family. Nothing like the man's evil chariot, fire-breathing horses at the reins.

The toddler started crying in his booster seat. She picked up the toy he'd dropped, held it out, and the little boy took it. He gave her a smile, his tears drying already.

Little short-lived woes. She wanted some of those.

"How did you come to be out here?" the woman asked her. "Where do you live?"

She couldn't talk. Couldn't say a word.

The toddler began crying again, even though he had his toy. She patted him on the cheek, and he stopped. So simple for a girl to make a boy feel better.

"We have to get you home," the woman said. "Or no, I should bring you to the police."

That finally compelled her to answer.

"Same difference," she replied. "My stepfather plays poker with the chief on Sundays."

CHAPTER THIRTY-ONE

Arles was close enough now that she began clawing up rocks. They clanked like rifle fire when she hurled them at the van's metal flanks. Bad Max started driving in fits and starts; he'd have to get out soon to investigate. She continued pelting the vehicle, bending back fingernails, grating the skin on her hands. The disturbance would hopefully also alert the girl if Bad Max did have someone imprisoned. Unless she had sipped from his deadly cup, was difficult to rouse.

That was how he kept his victims contained, Arles now knew. When he made deliveries, peddled his poison wares, or in this case, stopped at his grandson's treatment center.

She threw another furious shower of stones, and the van bucked to a halt.

Arles dodged left, concealing herself behind a protective sweep of branches.

Bad Max shoved open the driver's-side door, then climbed out, taking a look around before bending down to check the tires.

He'd removed his cap—Arles could see it lying on the dash, and also spied a purple-brown rut high on his forehead, a scabbing-over slice of flesh previously shielded from view.

She needed those double doors at the rear of the van open so that whoever was inside had a chance to flee while Arles dealt with her captor. But if Bad Max still did things the way he had twenty-five years ago, the doors would be chained from the inside. No reason in hell for him to unlock them. Potential moves cycled through her head, from unlikely to work, to foolish, to death-wish dumb. None that would afford Bad Max's latest victim anything like sure safety.

He came stomping around to the back of the van and pulled the doors open.

Arles went weak-kneed with surprise, followed by a great gust of relief. There was no current victim, because if there were, he'd be granting her egress by opening her tomb. Perhaps his appetite had finally been slaked, or else she'd caught him between rounds. Why open the rear doors, then? Who the fuck knew? Easiest means of access to his favorite snack.

Now all she had to do was wait for Bad Max to drive on, presuming himself undetected. Sic the cops on him if he made it out to the road; she had memorized his license plate as she followed his trail. Tim would be on the guy faster than you could say Cheez Doodles.

But more likely, given the terrain, was that in a matter of seconds, Bad Max would come too close to that rotten rim of earth. Be sent hurtling to his death, no Victory for this particular Vendor. This place was a serious liability. Arles would have to do something about it before she welcomed the next batch of patients.

Then Bad Max took a step to one side, and she caught a glimpse inside the van.

With a little wishful thinking, the silver gleams almost resembled foil. But she knew with sick certainty that she wasn't looking at snack packaging. Sunbeams bounced off a mummifying amount of duct tape, securing the ankles, wrists, and jaw of a young girl. She lay in a curl, chest rising and falling, nostrils emitting air with enough force that it stirred her lank strands of hair. Her eyes were shut, the artificial sleep of an artificial princess.

"I thought that was you," Bad Max said, keeping his back turned.

Arles's whole body cemented. She hadn't strayed from her cover, nor made a single sound. He had the acuity of a nocturnal predator, the heightened senses of some creature that dwelled underground. Maybe that was how he'd evaded capture for so long.

"You hardly look any older than the day that we met." Bad Max gave the girl inside the van a shake, as if checking her condition. Her body didn't so much as twitch.

Arles stooped down, affording herself a denser screen of leaves.

Then he swiveled around with his gun aimed, as casually as someone might wave a fork in the air. The weapon was sighted pretty damn close to where she hid, his stance one with which she was all too familiar. That of a man who knew his way around firearms.

"Come on out," he said in that tender tone from days of yore, as if time had ceased working, were stuck twenty-five years in the past. "I gave this one I've got with me right now a good hit before all of you woke up this morning. She won't feel it if I have to shoot her."

He was bluffing. Didn't know Arles was here. How could he, images of predator fish lurking in lightless caverns aside? And she couldn't believe, refused to believe, that he would blithely kill his precious cargo, just like that, especially if he thought a witness was present.

"I can always get another one," he said, keeping his gun aimed at Arles.

Still with that eerie ability to follow her thoughts. Her spine rigidified; she bore down to keep from making a move.

"There are plenty more," he added, deliberately provocative.

Girls like bushels of fruit to be picked.

He switched the position of his gun, using it to caress the smooth, unblemished crescent of his latest victim's throat, and a yelp escaped Arles. Threatening her with her own death didn't carry much weight. But factor a child into the equation and things changed.

"That hair," he murmured when she emerged from her bower of branches.

Arles stilled in place.

His words wafted over birdsong and a brief breeze. "I've never forgotten that hair."

Not even *your* hair. She was completely depersonalized, a nonperson to him. They all were. All of the girls, just berries in a bucket. A ripe crop, there for his plucking.

"I could hardly believe it when I saw you. How long has it been?"

As if they were at a family reunion.

"Come close so I can get a better look."

Sickening, his tone. Cloying, like the candy he'd fed her.

He beckoned with his free hand, pistol still trained on the interior of the van.

Arles stayed where she was until he flicked off the safety, its light click a thunderclap in the suddenly still air. Barely registering her own motion, she took a few steps.

"Good girl," he said softly. "I never got the chance to tell you, but you were always my favorite. Even though you escaped." As if the thought had just occurred to him: "Maybe *because* you escaped. None of the others were that clever."

"You killed them?" she asked faintly. She should've known better than to refuse to believe anything. She never would've encouraged a client to dwell in denial.

He sent her the wounded look she remembered. "I would've given all those girls back. Every single one of them."

How many? Arles wondered, so weak that she swayed on her feet.

"It's the truth!" he said, sounding less imploring than entitled. To mercy, exoneration, being let off the hook. "I just didn't know how. To return them, I mean. How could I let them go back to their parents, or homes, or lives without sacrificing myself? Without getting caught?"

Sounds like a you problem, Arles thought, her gaze shifting to the shelf of dirt she sought. Although, of course, it hadn't been. Bad Max made his sickness everyone else's disease, the ruination and devastation of families whose total hadn't yet been tallied.

She shuddered, then set forth again. Surely Bad Max would choose to maneuver her away from his stolen wares, an instinct cultivated over decades. *Don't let anyone get close to the van.* He would've learned to take precautions. Except in this instance, he'd be missing the real danger. Because by guiding her away, he would draw perilously near that unsound rim of soil.

Indeed, he gave his vehicle a wide berth as he edged past it, and she followed, letting him think he was controlling her movements instead of vice versa.

"We could leave here together," he noted in a bright-idea kind of tone. "I only took this one a little while ago. She hasn't had much time with me yet. You and I could take care of her on our own. Best of both worlds."

Whose world? Yours. Not mine. And definitely not hers, the one she deserves to inhabit.

Rage shook Arles, and she let it drive her forward, coming for him.

She had learned about this section of the forest during those hunting trips with Peter. He'd warned her to stay clear, which of course, she'd chosen not to do. Someplace dangerous enough to frighten her fearsome stepfather? What a resource; what a boon. The perfect location to seek shelter. Peter was so stupid. Never understanding that he posed the greater risk. An accidental misstep, even one that resulted in her death? Nothing compared to the time left in her sentence with her stepfather. Or the memories from which she'd never be granted pardon.

Bad Max seemed suddenly aware of Arles's fierce focus, some aspect of her intent.

"Not one step closer," he stated. "I don't want to kill you. Don't make me."

As if she'd be responsible for his crime.

"My daughter seems to like you. If you stop now, you can continue to help her."

Arles huffed a breath. "Don't go up against me in the psych-a-person-out game, Max."

She had no need of manipulation or mind fucks this time, though.

Just the brute physics of nature.

She took another few steps, welcoming the faint give beneath her feet. Just the slightest sloshing; you wouldn't know the earth was rotting here like a brown apple unless you felt for it.

Or maybe you would. Bad Max had reached a point in the soil where something caused him alarm, his dead eyes going wide, his trigger finger jerking in a seemingly involuntary spasm.

She didn't hear the noise when he shot, or feel his bullet enter her, but she knew that both had happened. Her body had always been a dartboard men pierced for their entertainment. And in reality, this particular man killed her a quarter century ago. All the others he'd taken had died; why should she be different? She had been within his sights, within reach, this whole time.

He was about to arrive at that last lip of soil, however. She quickened her pace, lunging at him with a furious roar, leaving him no choice except to back up. He clearly didn't have a clue how to handle it when someone charged him instead of the reverse. In an instant, he transformed, displaying not the fright of a little girl—as schoolyard bullies might taunt—but the terrified panic of a man being opposed for the very first time. Once, she had run from him; now, she was at war. When he fired again, his shot went wild, missing her by yards. She surged forward, ignoring a twinge in her belly, until Peter's—no, Bad Max's—arms windmilled, and the ground disappeared beneath his boots, solid one moment, nothing but air and a torrent of earthen debris the next.

Dirt fell with a sound like a thunderous rainstorm.

The gun dropped; then Bad Max plummeted.

His weapon clattered through a webbed canopy of leaves, a split second ahead of him landing with a series of sharp, wood-dry cracks. The breaking of tree limbs or bones or both. She kept a semi-safe distance away, lighter in weight than Bad Max and also knowing how to maintain her footing, so often had she done it with her stepfather in pursuit. She peered down.

One long branch impaled Bad Max through the belly like a piece of meat on a skewer. But a slimmer stick had done the worst damage, sticking up like a knitting needle through his neck. He scrabbled wildly, trying to pull the length of wood out of his throat. But he was losing blood too fast to take any kind of meticulous action, red fluid jettisoning out in gushes and splashes that coated his hands until both went limp, and the madness finally cooled in his eyes.

His body flopped once around its prison of treetops, then went still, leaving him staring blankly up at a blue blanket of sky.

Arles switched focus to see her own share of blood leaking from her midriff. She'd been acquainted with field medicine from a young age, so knew she'd already lost more than a person could spare and reliably survive. The bottom of her shirt was soaked with enough dark liquid that the material couldn't contain it. Her pants dripped; there was a puddle around her feet.

It didn't even hurt.

It did hurt.

The time when she could pretend it didn't—truly *feel* that it didn't, the sensation simply absent from her consciousness—was gone. There was no way she could go get help for the child inside the van. And they were so deep in the woods, with Dead Max having concealed his tracks from the road. Arles had left the saplings disturbed, and the noise of gunfire should carry. Still, it was possible that nobody would stumble upon this location until it was too late for the girl.

Nonetheless, Arles had to sit down. She had to stay very still now.

The ground was uneven and unbearably hard. She leaned against a tree for support, and its bark felt rough, abrading the knobs of her spine. Every part of her hurt, organs deep within her body, cells too microscopic to see. All the pain she'd blocked out her entire life came for her in one agonizing wave, and she passed out in the face of its wrath.

When she next stirred, the season had changed, winter come round again, because her whole body was racked with shivers. She heard herself from somewhere far off repeating one word over and over, a tremble on her lips. *Dan.*

She blinked, and a great gathering of people had arrived.

Lissa, like an angel, only very much terrestrial, of this time and place, because the sat phone was pressed to her ear. Louise, marching up from behind. Geary, a little ways off, stopping abruptly at the van's rear doors, which still hung ajar.

"Who's Dan?" one of them asked.

Probably Louise. The fuzzy outline of her form—Arles could scarcely see anything anymore—was taller than the person who stood beside her, shaking her head because of course she didn't know the answer, had no idea who Arles might've been talking about.

Lissa, that smaller figure. Had to be, because Geary remained by the van.

Arles rested while a red stream coursed out of some hidden coil of guts.

Other things began to be cleansed as her wound washed clean her body. All the men who'd hurt her gone, Bad Max, and Peter, dying wretched in some care facility in the not-too-distant future, along with nameless others, whole armies of them, legions driven over that ledge. Dying, flailing, on a bristling pincushion of branches, like so many kebabs. Arles could live with this fate—live with dying—if it meant more children of the world stood in safety and strength.

Their voices a chorus rising.

Whose voice was she hearing?

A silver bright sound issued forth. Notes like the purest spring water, clear and bright and precise, each tympanic vibration audible where Arles lay, sure and certain, even though this particular noise had never before been made. Nothing nascent about it, although it was a first, a sunburst, a new planet exploding into being, taking on the shape it was always meant to assume.

A glorious sound to hear for her last.

"That's Bea," said Geary.

THE FIRST TO BE FOUND

Cass had been in Room 211 of the Cardiac Care Unit when the news came in.

He wasn't allowed out of bed yet, so Maggie bent down to hold the phone between their ears, his right, her left. As if they were one person.

"Let us talk to her." That was the first thing Maggie had said to Brawley. "I need to hear her voice." Cass could sense the way his wife was both instantly sure and at the same time didn't believe it was true when their daughter came on the line, whispering a weak *Hello*. He felt divided the same way, a body that had been cut into pieces soldering itself back together.

The heart attack—or cardiac event, as Cass now knew to call it—had gotten him in the middle of the night right before Bea had been found. He hadn't known anything happened, just woke up at UMaine Institute of Medicine at daybreak. He hoped it'd gone the same way for his father. The not-knowing-a-thing part, since his dad hadn't gotten the chance to wake up.

According to Maggie, Don had come running down the road, summoned by her screams, which carried between the open windows of their houses. Luckily, the weather had finally warmed up enough to allow in the nighttime air; also lucky was that Don's hearing didn't turn out to be as far gone as he had thought.

He'd administered CPR while Maggie stayed on the line with 911. Emergency services could take a while to reach their neck of the woods, and apparently, Don had kept Cass alive.

"Knock, knock," a voice called, and the door to his hospital room swung open.

Cass had to be the first patient to inhabit this particular unit with an irrepressible grin on his face. "Hiya, Doc."

This one was young and liked to wear scrubs in cool colors. She pulled a chair over to his bed and took a seat. "We've got you set for discharge tomorrow, Mr. Monroe."

If his smile got any wider, it would crack his face.

The doctor lowered a pair of glasses from her head to her eyes and studied a sheaf of papers. "I'm ordering ten weeks of cardiac rehab and six psychotherapy sessions, Mr. Monroe. Six to start—you're of course free to continue, if it's helping. As I hope that it will."

Cass gave a nod. "You mean because of all the stress I've been under? That's why you think I had the heart attack?"

The doctor pushed her glasses back up on her head. "I don't think it helped, clearly. And let me say again how thrilled I am—as is everyone on the unit—by how things turned out."

Surely, his cheeks were going to split.

"But I don't think this event was triggered only by that," she went on. "Based on our tests, something like this has been coming for a while. And your self-report indicates things you haven't worked through from your past. We cardiologists are learning how that impacts health and longevity. Emotional damage damages the heart. You *feel* hurt, and your heart *gets* hurt."

"That makes sense," Cass said. And smiled.

The doctor smiled back at him as she stood up to leave the room. "Enjoy the rest of your life, Mr. Monroe. No reason it shouldn't be a nice long one."

After they'd been given the wondrous news, and Maggie had fled his side, Cass finally broke down and got comfortable with texting.

Stuck in the hospital, it was the only way to keep up with everything that was happening, the restoration and resurrection of his life.

And earlier today, he and Maggie had an exchange, *talked*, as Bea would put it, though no matter how used to texting Cass got, he didn't suppose it'd ever feel like conversation.

He'd asked after the therapist who'd saved their little girl, and Maggie had told him they'd had to medevac her out, and last she'd heard, it didn't look good. Guilt and gratitude both weighed him, but even the tragedy of that therapist dying failed to suppress his smile. The skin on his cheeks was stretched so far, it felt like it might snap. Better than a facelift. He was years younger. Hell, he could text just like the kiddos, toss off a question without thinking about it.

everything ok? you all set to leave as planned tomorrow?

Look at him; no capitals.

Three blips and bubbles, indicating a response in the works. Normally, there would be a delay of at least a few minutes, if not hours. Maggie had a lot to attend to and focus on out there.

His phone dinged, and a photo appeared.

A woman lying in a hospital bed with an IV bag on a stand at her shoulder, fluid slowly dripping into her arm. Head raised just an inch or so, hair a flash of red flame against a pillow as white as her skin, one hand lifted as if she were trying to give a small wave.

wait, is that the therapist? you mean she's going to be all right?

full recovery her doctor says

that's fantastic!

He heard an instantaneous chime but didn't receive another text. No blips or bubbles, either. The sound hadn't been made by his phone; it'd come from one right outside his room.

His mind had begun working quicker, along with his body. Due to increased blood flow, the doctors all said. Maybe Maggie and Bea weren't leaving as planned. Maybe they were ahead of schedule, and the text he'd just heard arriving had been received by his wife.

He launched himself off the bed as if taking a leap from a high perch, the wings of his hospital gown flapping. But he didn't care how silly he looked, just went flying across the room in bare feet. Faster and stronger than he'd been for as long as he could remember, and not because of his new stent, but due to what he thought he was going to find on the other side of the door. He pulled it open at the same time as it was being pushed.

"Daddy!" cried Bea.

He caught her when she jumped into his arms.

And for a while, there was silence. But it was the good kind, an illusion, Bea would probably tell him as she grew up and got even smarter, during one of the conversations they were going to have. At the moment, Cass chose to believe in it, though.

That a kind of lull could settle after the very last note has faded, the final word has been said, and all of the once-quieted voices have been heard.

AUTHOR'S NOTE

Every book is a journey, but this one took me to places darker than I've ever written about before.

Readers of my past work will know, and new ones will come to understand, that while the topics that haunt me as a writer are all deeply troubling, they progress to points of triumph.

This is especially true for the character you've just met, Arles Shepherd. Arles is a person who feels she's been put on earth in order to save children, and sadly, many of them need saving. In this country, one in four children will experience abuse or neglect, and of these, 9 percent will be abused sexually. These figures may well be underreported. Arles is herself a survivor, and in the book you've just read, in addition to grappling with her past, she also puts a stop to a far rarer form of predator.

It was very important to me to keep these horrors off the page, for the shadows of the story to be evocative but not explicit. I believe this is necessary both in order to do right by readers for whom these issues might be triggering and because monsters are unleashed in secrecy and silence.

Thank you for coming with Arles on this journey. I hope that her battle lends hope to the idea that if a fight must be had, it is at least sometimes winnable.

Jenny Milchman
Catskill Mountains, New York
March 2024

RESOURCES

If you or a child you know is experiencing abuse or neglect, or if you or someone you know is an adult survivor of child abuse, these resources are here to help:

Childhelp National Child Abuse Hotline
https://www.childhelphotline.org/
Hotline: 800.422.4453

RAINN
https://www.rainn.org/
Hotline: 800.656.HOPE

National Center for Missing & Exploited Children
https://www.missingkids.org/home
Hotline: 800.843.5678

ACKNOWLEDGMENTS

Looking back, I believe there will be a divide to my career, with this novel representing what kicks off the next chapter. (See what I did there? Book metaphor.)

The opportunity to write this came about when I least expected it—and most longed for it. Thanks are owed to my new agent-in-arms, the legendary Victoria Sanders, along with Bernadette Baker-Baughman and Christine Kelder—the whole fabulous VSA team. I appreciate your taking me into the fold and helping to launch the most exciting creative unfolding a writer could hope for. Thanks doubly for your wisdom, steering, expertise, and reach when the chance arose.

Finding your wish list editor takes luck and timing in addition to a meeting of the minds.

To Gracie Doyle, deep thanks for an inspiring (and delicious) breakfast—then kicking off the most thrilling phase of my career thus far. I am beyond grateful that Jessica Tribble Wells tapped into exactly the book I needed to write. One of the biggest twists in this novel is 100 percent down to her. Jessica said, "What if you did *X*?"—What? You didn't think I was gonna spoil it, did you?—and then I *did X*, after which I had one of those shivery, gooseflesh-y author moments. If Jessica hadn't conceived of her idea, this book would not have become what it was meant to be.

Charlotte Herscher has an acuity and exacting eye that allowed me to grow and shape and breathe life into this novel in ways I never anticipated.

She was willing to bat around everything from macro plot points to micro literary allusions and diction choices as if every single word in a forest of more than a hundred thousand of them matters—as of course they do. Charlotte + Jessica = editorial dream team.

Miranda Gardner in production steered a process the likes of which I've not gotten to experience before. Valerie and Kellie probed everything from the origins of words—*gibe* stands out as one fascinating example—to a sensitivity catch concerning one inadvertently and blithely used adverb. Then Jill came on board—and wow. She alerted me to differences and distinctions I'd never considered before (and I'm an overthinker when it comes to diction). Jill could probably spot a chipmunk from an airplane. The eagle-eyed gaze of this team deserves a less cliché description of their prowess—as no one would catch better than they!

In a slew of happy surprises I've encountered since signing with Thomas & Mercer, one of the biggest was having the first-ever culture read done of my work. I wish every writer could experience this unique kind of attention. I remember raising the prospect with my editor only to have her say something like, "It's already been arranged." (See above re: the meeting of minds and dream editors.) Huge thanks go to Emily for reading with such depth and sensitivity that I jotted off a midnight email from my couch, in a state of something close to shock, saying, "Mind blown." Emily helped me to find uniqueness and nuance in a character I already loved but hadn't layered fully on the page.

If you've read this novel, you probably noticed its glorious cover. The cover process is a fascinating thing to be part of as an author—how to encapsulate a hundred thousand words into one intricate and holistic image? To art director Michael Jantze at Thomas & Mercer, and designer Amanda Hudson at Faceout Studio, thank you for blending conceptual with artistic in a way that speaks to thriller fans—and even beyond. Thanks are also owed to Darci, who steered the after-the-book-was-in-print process. When I opened the shipment of ARCs Darci sent me, the box glowed as if it held rubies. Sinister rubies.

To everyone at Amazon Amazing, thank you—it's been an incredible ride so far.

Benee Knauer read an entire draft of a different novel whose germ grew into the one you're looking at. At which you're looking? Benee would know. She is responsible for much more than that in my life as a writer, and there will hopefully be another set of acknowledgments in the future where I can expand on this. For now, let me thank her for studying a seed and assuring me it could grow into a beanstalk.

Writers need other writers. To share with, moan at, and entrust their work to. I owe tremendous thanks to two authors and friends who served as trusty readers. Carla Buckley and Karyne Corum, you helped make this book stronger in its earliest incarnation—and beyond. Turn to the former to find a great list of reads, and keep the latter on your radar for the same in the future. Others of the posse include Holly Brown and Stefanie Pintoff. Another great list of reads for you between these two, both people I am lucky to have in my writing life and life-life. Are those two separate for people like us? Only sometimes.

A book like this takes a fair amount of research, and two resources in particular stand out: *10 Things Every Child with Autism Wishes You Knew* by Ellen Notbohm and the film *The Reason I Jump*, based on the book of the same name by Naoki Higashida, were invaluable. Emily—whom you met above—pointed me to several sources that proved instrumental, including Medium writer Rebecca Cokley; an article titled "I Am Not Ashamed: Disability Advocates, Experts Implore You to Stop Saying 'Special Needs'" by David Oliver in *USA Today*; a site called NeuroClastic; and Amethyst's Tumblr, *neurowonderful*.

Madelyn Simring Milchman, PhD, specialist in childhood trauma and traumatic memory, helped me work through several thorny points. It's great when your mom is your expert because you can do things like call her on nights and weekends and implore her to come up with a way *X* plot point or *Y* character trait can be made to ring true because *no way are you letting that go*.

Which brings me to my family, whom some of you know from the road—husband, daughter, son. My kids came of age during this birth of a new series. It took a level of support neither I nor my husband was prepared for, and he's built of supportive stock (which is how some of you know us from the road—we lived there on tour as a family during the release of my first three novels). My hubby is one of my best early (and late) readers—I think he read like eight full drafts of this book, improving it every single time. My older is an editor as an intern and college student, and my younger fills this role on his high school newspaper—their catches were illuminating and transformative. And their vision and perspectives from the other side of the Gen Z divide helped make this book something I hope will speak across age groups. I couldn't have done this without the faith, optimism, and unwavering devotion of all three. Thanks for pretend-doing my Wiki till it really exists.

Enormous thanks are due to librarians, booksellers, book bloggers, reviewers, and critics—everybody in the whole wonderful bookish ecosystem of which I am so grateful to be a part.

Most of all, thanks go to readers. First, I tell the story to myself. Then I tell it for all of you.

ABOUT THE AUTHOR

Photo © 2024 Franco Vogt

Jenny Milchman is the Mary Higgins Clark Award–winning and *USA Today* bestselling author of the psychological thrillers *Cover of Snow*, *Ruin Falls*, *As Night Falls*, *Wicked River*, and *The Second Mother*. Her work has received praise from media ranging from the *New York Times* to the *San Francisco Journal of Books*; earned spots on Top 10 lists from *Suspense Magazine* to the *Strand Magazine*; made Best Of lists from PopSugar to PureWow; and garnered starred reviews from *Publishers Weekly*, *Booklist*, *Library Journal*, and *Shelf Awareness*, in addition to numerous other mentions. Before turning to fiction, Jenny earned a graduate degree in clinical psychology and practiced at a rural community mental health center for more than a decade. She lives in the Catskill Mountains with her family. For more information, visit www.jennymilchman.com.